CAPITAL RUN

Two men, both in Russian military uniforms, one armed with a holstered pistol, the other with an AK-47, appeared at the end of the corridor. They reacted to Hickok by one grabbing for his holster and the other soldier sweeping his AK-47 up.

Hickok was 30 feet from them. He never broke his stride as he leveled the Colts and fired.

The one with the pistol simply fell forward, but the trooper with the AK-47 tottered backwards, crashed into the left-hand wall, and dropped.

Hickok slowed as he neared the soldiers. He holstered the Colts and leaned over the soldier with the AK-47. ''I need this more than you do.''

NEW YORK RUN

Geronimo backpedaled as more Zombies poured from the abandoned vehicles. Something collided with his back.

Geronimo whirled, and found Blade alongside him. ''What do we do?'' he asked.

The Technics opened up with their Dakon IIs, their fragmentation bullets tearing into the hissing Zombies and ripping them apart, blowing their chests and skulls to shreds and spraying greenish fluid everywhere.

The Zombies never wavered. Their grisly arms extended, their yellow fingernails glinting in the sunlight, their thin lips quivering in anticipation of their next meal. . . .

Other books in the Endworld series:

ENDWORLD

DOUBLE

CAPITAL RUN/
NEW YORK RUN

DAVID ROBBINS

LEISURE BOOKS   NEW YORK CITY

A LEISURE BOOK®

September 1991

Published by

Dorchester Publishing Co., Inc.
276 Fifth Avenue
New York, NY 10001

CAPITAL RUN

1

The two women were fleeing for their lives.

They raced over the crest of a low hill, the statuesque redhead and the petite brunette, their legs churning, sweat caking their skin, their breathing labored as their straining lungs gasped for air. The redhead was in the lead, a few feet in front of her companion. Both women wore similar black-leather outfits consisting of a tight vest and skimpy shorts, appropriate attire considering the heat of the June day and their strenuous exertion.

"We'll never make it!" the brunette cried, wheezing.

The redhead glanced over her right shoulder and scowled. "We'll make it, damnit! Don't give up on me now!"

"I'm doing the best I can, Lexine," the brunette stated.

Lexine smiled encouragingly. "Hang in there, Mira," she said, her tone reflecting her concern for her friend. "Another mile and we'll take to the trees."

The duo jogged onward, sticking to the center of the highway, carefully avoiding the dozens of potholes and deep ruts pockmarking the ancient asphalt surface.

Mira stumbled and almost fell.

Lexine slowed and grabbed Mira's right hand, supporting her. "Lean on me," she offered.

Mira shook her head, her short hair bobbing. "I'd

only slow you down."

"Don't worry about it," Lexine said.

"Maybe we should take to the trees now," Mira suggested.

Both sides of the highway were lined with dense vegetation, affording ample hiding space and shelter from the sweltering temperature.

"We've got to put as much distance between them and us as we can," Lexine declared. "This way is faster."

Mira panted as she struggled to stay abreast of Lexine. "I don't like being out in the open like this!" she remarked. "At least in the woods they wouldn't find us."

"Don't forget the dogs," Lexine reminded the brunette.

Mira blanched and increased her speed.

Minutes passed in relative quiet, broken by the pounding of their leather sandals on the roadway and the ragged sound of their breathing.

"You know this is crazy, don't you?" Mira asked.

"Save your energy," Lexine said.

"We'll never make it₁" Mira reiterated.

From behind them, in the distance, came a peculiar buzzing.

Mira slowed, cocking her head. "Do you hear it?" she wailed.

Lexine stopped and turned, her shoulder-length hair whipping around her neck. "I hear them," she confirmed.

"Dear God! What do we do?" Mira almost screamed, panic contorting her narrow features.

Lexine glared at her friend, her green eyes blazing. "Get a grip on yourself!" she commanded.

The strange buzzing was becoming louder and louder.

"They're going to catch up!" Mira whined.

Lexine pointed to their left. "Into the trees. Move!"

Mira shuffled toward the woods, her brown eyes wide, staring at the hill to their rear.

Lexine moved to the left, her right hand gripping the handle of the 15-inch survival knife attached by its brown sheath to her black belt, just above her right hip. If they were caught, she told herself, she would give a good accounting for her life! She wouldn't be wasted without a fight! But maybe they wouldn't be caught. If they could only reach the trees and take cover, there was a good chance Cardew and the others would pass them by.

If they could only reach those trees!

Lexine was a yard from the edge of the highway when she heard a sharp screech followed by the dull thud of a body slamming to the pavement. She whirled, knowing what she would see.

Mira had tripped in a pothole and fallen onto her stomach, scraping her knees and elbows in the process.

Lexine hurried to her friend and took hold of her left elbow. "On your feet!" she snapped. "We've got to reach the woods!"

Mira, moaning, rose to a crouching position. "My right leg feels like it's broken!" she wailed.

"It's not broken!" Lexine disputed, well aware of Mira's propensity for exaggeration. "Now move your ass!"

Mira abruptly straightened, forgetting all about her "broken" leg. "Look!" she screamed. "It's them!"

Lexine spun.

There were four of them poised on the crown of the hill, their cycles idling, their black-leather jackets and pants lending an ominous aspect to their appearance.

"Damn!" Lexine fumed. Why the hell had she ever agreed to bring Mira along? Mira wasn't up to this. She had slowed them down, and now they were as good as dead.

"Here they come!" Mira shrieked.

The four riders gunned their motorcycles and roared down the hill, zooming toward the two women.

Lexine drew her knife and stepped in front of Mira, her countenance grim, her determination revealed in the compressed line of her red lips and the jutting set of her pointed chin.

The motorcycles closed in. Three of the riders were women, the fourth a tall man. His dark hair, dyed blue, was shaped in a Mohawk, the exposed skin on either side of his mane of hair tanned a deep brown by the scorching sun. A chain belt secured his leather pants. Attached to the belt above his right hip was a brown holster containing a Browning Hi-Power 9-mm Auto Pistol.

Lexine warily watched the approaching bikers, wishing she had a gun of her own.

The three women bikers all wore black leather, and only one of them was armed with a handgun, a Charter Arms Bulldog in a shoulder holster under her left arm. The other two women were each packing a knife and a sword. One of them, a blonde, wore her knife on her left hip, while the other wore the knife on her right. Both women carried their swords in leather scabbards strapped to their backs.

"What do we do?" Mira wanted to know.

Lexine didn't answer. There was nothing they could do.

The man with the Mohawk braked his big Harley to a stop not ten feet in front of them. The woman with the Bulldog slid to a halt six feet to their right, the blonde did likewise to their left, and the final woman circled and stopped about eight feet behind them.

Lexine frowned. They were surrounded.

All four switched off their bikes at the same moment. The resultant silence, after the rumbling clamor of the cycles, seemed unnatural.

Lexine detected a slight ringing in her ears.

Mohawk grinned, displaying a gap where two of his

upper front teeth had once been, and leaned back on his Harley. "Well, well, well," he said sarcarstically, winking at the blonde. "What do we have here?"

The blonde snickered. "It's big, bad Lex and her shadow, Mira the wimp."

"Who are you calling a wimp?" Mira demanded defensively.

The blonde glanced at Mohawk. "Mira is all mine," she told him.

"Whatever you want, Pat," Mohawk said.

Lexine snorted. "How do you stand it, Cardew?" she asked the male biker.

"Stand what?" Cardew responded.

"That brown stain coating your nose," Lexine stated.

Cardew laughed at her insult. "I always did like your sense of humor, Lex. I'm going to miss it."

"Just like that, huh?" Lexine said.

"Yep. Just like that. I have my orders," Cardew informed her. "Terza was real clear on what she wants done with you."

"I'll bet she was," Lexine snapped.

Cardew sighed and shook his head. "You knew this was coming, Lex. No one defies Terza. You know that."

"Let's get this over with!" Pat interjected. "Let's waste these dumb bitches and head back."

Lexine faced the blonde. "You talk real brave when the odds are four to two. But how are you when it's one on one?"

Pat scowled. "You think you can take me?"

Lexine nodded, her green eyes twinkling. "I know I can take you."

"We'll see about that!" Pat slammed her kickstand down and climbed from her Triumph.

"What are you doing?" Cardew asked her.

"What does it look like I'm doing?" Pat retorted.

"Terza said we're to make it quick," Cardew said.

"I'll make it quick," Pat promised. She smiled and
slowly drew her sword.

"Cut Lex to ribbons!" urged the woman with the
Bulldog.

"Don't worry," Pat said. "I will."

Lexine moved to her right, keeping her eyes on that
sword. It had a 30-inch double-edged blade and a
large hilt, and it had been especially crafted for Pat by
one of the blacksmiths.

Pat, confident in her ability and the superior reach
of her weapon, walked directly toward the redhead.
"I'm going to take your head back to Terza as a gift."

"Come and get it," Lexine said, baiting her
adversary.

Pat charged, swinging her sword in a wide arc.

Lexine quickly ducked and dodged to her right,
avoiding the gleaming sword.

Pat swung again, drawing nearer, aiming an overhead swipe at Lexine's head.

Lexine parried the sword with her survival knife,
the blades clanging as they struck.

The blonde brought her sword around again.

Lexine managed to deflect the blade with her knife
as she deftly slide aside, darting to the left.

"Lexine!" Mira cried in alarm.

Without warning, before Lexine could fathom her
intent, Pat turned and took three steps, her arms
upraised, the sword clasped with the blade upright,
only a foot from Mira.

"No!" Lexine shouted.

Mira, too terrified to react, flinched as the sword
flashed downward.

Lexine, shocked to her core, saw the sword cleave
Mira's face, splitting it from the forehead to the chin.

Mira stiffened and gurgled as Pat withdrew her
blade. A crimson flood poured from the wound as
Mira sagged to the ground.

"*No!*" Enraged, Lexine leaped at the blonde. She

stabbed and slashed in a frenzied fury, but Pat was able to block or counter every blow. Heedless of her safety, Lexine pressed her attack. She forced the blonde to retreat several paces. Eager to bury her knife in Pat's chest, she gambled on a desperate lunge.

Pat easily sidestepped.

Lexine felt her right foot catch in one of the deep cracks in the road and she stumbled forward, unable to regain her balance. Her left knee smashed onto the asphalt. She frantically struggled to rise, to confront her foe, fearing Pat would plunge the sword into her exposed back.

But nothing happened.

Lexine rose and turned, her knife at the ready.

Pat was only three feet away, but she wasn't looking at Lexine. Neither were Cardew or the other two women.

What in the world? Astonished, Lexine glanced in the direction they were staring, to the west. That's when she saw him.

The stranger. Calmly standing in the middle of the road, not ten feet away, he was a wiry, diminutive man dressed in black. His features were handsomely Oriental, his eyes and hair dark. A long, black scabbard was clutched in his left hand.

Lexine had never seen a man like this newcomer. There was an unusual quality about the man, a visible air of supreme self-confidence combined with a palpable aura of inner strength. His expression exhibited an inherent honesty and fearlessness. Lexine experienced a stirring deep within her, a reaction to the stranger's mere presence. Unlike the servile men in the Leather Knights, she intuitively sensed that here, at last, was a *real* man.

Cardew was the first to recover his voice. "Who the hell are you?" he demanded, his right hand inching toward his Browning Auto Pistol.

"I am called Rikki," the newcomer replied in a soft, low voice.

"Where did you come from?" Cardew angrily demanded, scanning the vegetation on both sides of the road.

"My body came from my mother's womb," the stranger said quietly. "My spirit came from the Eternal Source of all life."

Lexine almost laughed at the ludicrous contours on Cardew's face as his mouth dropped open in amazement.

Pat walked toward the newcomer, cautiously extending her sword. "Cut the crap, jerk! We want some answers and we want them now!"

"I have supplied the proper answers," the stranger stated.

"Maybe we should take this bozo back to Terza," Cardew suggested nervously.

"I am not going anywhere?" the man in black said.

"Wanna bet?" Pat countered.

"I do not gamble," the newcomer told her.

"Is this guy for real?" asked the woman with the Bulldog. Her right hand was resting on the revolver.

Pat stopped a yard from the stranger. "We want to know where you came from," she reiterated, "and we want to know right now."

Lexine saw the man in black gaze at Pat. Surprisingly, Pat backed up a step—surprising because Lexine had never seen Pat back down from anyone or anything.

The newcomer shifted his attention to Lexine. "I do not understand the reason for your conflict, but I do not believe four against one are honorable odds. Would you care for my assistance?"

Pat moved forward again before Lexine could respond. "Who the hell do you think you are? This is a private matter."

The man in black locked his dark eyes on Pat. "Not

any more," he said, accenting each word.

Something seemed to snap inside of Pat. "Damn you!" she bellowed, and aimed a swipe at the stranger.

Lexine could scarcely believe what transpired next. In her 23 years she had participated in dozens of fights and witnessed dozens more, savage engagements, life-or-death exchanges conducted by men and women skilled in the many arts of combat. She had seen swordsmen and swordswomen of consummate proficiency. But not one of them had come close to matching the lightning speed of the man in black.

The stranger called Rikki twisted slightly, and his right hand was a streak as he drew his sword. The stroke was impossible to see; one moment he was drawing his sword, and in the next instant Pat had frozen in her tracks, her head flopping backward, nearly decapitated, a shred of skin and her upper spinal column all that remained of her neck.

Cardew and the other two women went for their weapons.

Lexine saw the man in black drop his scabbard, his left hand reaching behind his back and emerging with an odd metal star clasped in his fingers. His left arm swept up and out.

The biker on Lexine's right was drawing the Bulldog, the revolver clear of its shoulder holster and leveling when the metal star arced across the intervening space and imbedded itself in her forehead. The woman with the Bulldog jerked in her seat, her eyes widening in disbelief. She gasped and began to slide to the ground.

The third woman biker was drawing her sword when the man in black took two rapid steps and plunged his blade into her throat.

Lexine abruptly realized they were still in danger and spun to confront Cardew.

The Harley roared to life even as Lexine turned,

and before she could reach him Cardew gunned his bike and executed a tight U-turn, heading east, his motorcycle accelerating rapidly. Within seconds, he passed over the crest of the low hill and vanished.

"Now we know who the real wimp is," Lexine said aloud. She stared sadly at Mira, then looked at the three other dead women lying sprawled on the highway.

The man in black wiped his sword clean on Pat's vest, then crossed to the woman with the Bulldog. He leaned over and extracted his metal star from her forehead, wiping it on the woman's leather pants.

"What is that thing?" Lexine asked. "I've never seen anything like it."

The stranger slid the star into a brown pouch attached to his belt, positioned in the small of his back. "It is called a shuriken," he informed her.

"You're real good with that shuriken," Lexine said, complimenting him.

He retrieved his scabbard and carefully slid the sword inside.

"I've never seen a sword like yours either," Lexine commented.

The man hefted his weapon. "This is my katana. It was constructed centuries ago by a master metalsmith in Japan."

"Where's Japan?" Lexine inquired.

The man in black studied her.

"What did you say your name was again?" Lexine probed when he continued to scrutinize her. His examination made her feel uncomfortable; she entertained the ridiculous notion he could see into her inner being.

"I am Rikki-Tikki-Tavi," he stated.

Lexine chuckled. "That's a weird name. Where'd your parents ever get a name like that?"

"My parents did not bestow it on me," Rikki said. "I selected it at my Naming."

"Let me get this straight," Lexine remarked. "You picked your own name?"

Rikki nodded. "It is a common practice where I come from. The man responsible for starting our Family wanted us to go through our vast library and select whatever name we liked for our own."

"Why?"

Rikki glanced at the four bodies. "We can discuss this in depth later. I must report this incident immediately. You are welcome to come with me if you desire."

Lexine gazed at Mira. "Don't mind if I do. Nothing's holding me here."

"Do you want your friend buried?" Rikki queried her.

Lexine frowned and shook her head. "Nope. Let the buzzards have her. We'd best make tracks."

"What is your name?" Rikki asked.

Lexine tore her eyes from Mira. "Oh. I didn't tell you, did I? I'm Lexine. But all my friends call me Lex."

"Tell me, Lexine—" Rikki began.

"It's Lex," she quickly corrected him.

The corners of his thin lips twisted upward. "Tell me, Lex, will the one who escaped return with others?"

Lex looked at the hill to the east. "Most likely. Terza will want your hide after what you did to three of her Knights. And they want me for trying to skip."

Rikki pointed to the west. "Are you up to some running?"

"Try me," Lex said gamely.

They began jogging westward down the middle of the highway, side by side. Lex found herself surreptitiously admiring Rikki's firm features and his lithe, easy stride.

"Are we far from St. Louis?" he unexpectedly asked her.

"Nope," Lex responded. "St. Louis is about seven miles to the east. That's where I came from."

"Why were you leaving?"

Lex glowered. "I want to live my own life. There has to be something better than the Leather Knights."

"What are the Leather Knights?"

Lex glanced down at him. "You sure aren't from around these parts. Everybody knows about the Leather Knights. They run St. Louis."

"You mean they control the city?" Rikki asked.

"They own the turf," she clarified for him.

"Are you a Leather Knight?"

"I was," Lex admitted. "But not any more. Now I'm just a traitor to them. They'll waste me if they get their paws on me again."

Rikki looked up into her green eyes. She was at least ten inches taller than him. "We'll have to see to it they don't."

Lex, for one of the few times in her life, blushed, a pink tinge capping her rounded cheeks.

"Tell me about these Leather Knights," Rikki urged her.

"What's to tell?" Lex replied. "There's about four hundred Leather Knights. And there's about two hundred studs. That—"

"Studs?" Rikki interrupted.

"Yeah. The auxiliaries. Each one takes the oath before they get their bike, same as the regular Leather Knights, but of course they don't have the same privileges."

"You take an oath?"

"Of course. That's why my life is on the line. We take an oath, a blood oath, to always obey the code of the Leather Knights." Lex sighed. "Anyone who betrays it is automatically sentenced to death."

"They won't even permit you to leave?" Rikki inquired.

Lex shook her head, her red hair flying. "Not on

your life. When you take the Leather Knight oath, you're a Knight forever."

"And every Leather Knight receives a motor-cycle?"

"Yep. They . . ." Lex abruptly stopped. "Damn! What an idiot I am!"

Rikki halted and faced her. "What's the matter?"

Lex pointed at the bodies and the three abandoned bikes, now 50 yards distant. "Why didn't we take one of their bikes?" she demanded.

Rikki shrugged. "It never occurred to me. I don't know how to drive one."

"Well I do!" Lex exclaimed, annoyed at her stupidity. Why hadn't she thought of it? Probably because she was too busy thinking of him.

Rikki gazed westward. "I have some friends about a mile down the road. Perhaps we should use one of those cycles. We would reach them faster."

"The faster, the better," Lex agreed.

They started running back toward the cycles.

"You say you've never ridden a bike before?" Lex asked.

"No. I've seen photographs of them in books in the Family library, but I've never ridden one," Rikki stated.

"Then you're in for a treat," Lex said. "Riding a bike is the second best feeling I know."

"What's the first?" Rikki innocently queried.

Lex shot him a puzzled look. "You're putting me on, right?"

Now it was Rikki's turn to appear perplexed. "No," he assured her.

Lex laughed. "You really are weird, aren't you?"

They ran in silence for several moments.

"Did you hear that?" Rikki asked.

"Hear what?"

"That."

From the east, from the other side of the hill, rose

an eerie howling.

"Son of a bitch!" Lex blurted.

"What is it?"

"The dogs," Lex answered anxiously. "The three you wasted and the dummy who got away were probably the advance riders from a hunting party. That dummy, Cardew, must have reached them and they've sicced the dogs on us!"

The howling grew in volume and intensity.

"There must be at least a dozen," Rikki speculated.

"They'll tear us apart," Lex said.

"Not if I can help it," Rikki vowed.

They were 20 yards from the bikes when the dog pack appeared on the hill to the east. At the sight of the two people below, their intended quarry, the pack burst into a refrain of baying and barking. Galvanized by the sight of their prey, the dogs loped down the hill and raced toward the man and woman.

Rikki counted 16 dogs, all of them large and mean, the pack consisting mainly of German shepherds and Dobermans.

Lexine, her long legs flying toward the cycles, was mentally berating herself for her dumb behavior. Not only had she completely overlooked the possibility of using one of the bikes, but she'd also neglected to retrieve the Charter Arms Bulldog from the biker Rikki had killed with the shuriken. She had to get a grip on her emotions. Sure, she found the little guy exceptionally attractive, but that didn't excuse her mistakes, not when those mistakes could wind up costing her life.

The dogs were covering the ground in a feral rush. Two of them, a dusky shepherd and an ebony Doberman, were 15 feet in front of the pack and closing at an astonishing clip.

We'll never make it! Lexine told herself. She reached the first cycle and grabbed the handlebars even as Rikki swept past her, his katana drawn and held in his right hand, his scabbard in his left.

The dogs never hesitated. The German shepherd and the Doberman ignored the bodies on the road and bounded toward the man in black.

Rikki took out the Doberman, the closest one, first, his katana a gleaming blur as he sliced the canine open from its chin to its sternum. He twisted, avoiding the hurtling Doberman and concentrating on the shepherd. Several seconds were required before the Doberman realized the gravity of its wound. It twirled, preparing for another attack, when its front paws slipped on a moist substance coating the highway and it fell. Vertigo overwhelmed it, and the Doberman watched helplessly as the man in black hacked off the top of the shepherd's head with his flashing sword.

"Look out!" Lex screamed.

Rikki barely had time to brace himself before the rest of the pack was on them. He dropped his scabbard and assumed chudan-no-kumae.

2

"He should have been back by now, pard."

"We'll give him a little while yet."

"Whatever you want. I've just got a bad feeling, is all," said the first speaker, a lean, blond man with long hair and a drooping mustache dressed in buckskins and moccasins. Strapped around his narrow waist were twin holsters containing a pair of pearl-handled Colt Python revolvers. The fringe on his buckskin shirt stirred in the afternoon breeze as he glanced at his traveling companion. "I reckon we should check on him, Blade."

The other man slowly nodded. He was a towering giant, a powerhouse with an awesome physique and bulging muscles. His wardrobe consisted of a black-leather vest, green fatigue pants, and black boots. On each huge hip, snug in its respective sheath, was a Bowie knife. Slung over his left shoulder was a Commando Arms Carbine with a 90-shot magazine, modified to full automatic by the Family Gunsmiths. His dark hair and eyes lent a grim, somber aspect to his appearance. "Maybe you're right, Hickok," Blade said to the gunman. "Rikki was only supposed to scout ahead for a mile or two. According to the maps, we're almost to the outskirts of St. Louis. Whether he saw any sign of the city or not, he should have been back by now."

"I just hope he didn't go and get into a fix," Hickok griped. "I want to get this assignment over with and return to the Home.''

''You didn't need to come along,'' Blade reminded him. ''This was a volunteer mission. You knew that.''

''Yeah,'' Hickok said wistfully. ''When Plato first announced it, I figured I could use the break. Get out of the cabin for a spell. Break the monotony. You know what I mean?''

Blade nodded.

''But I miss 'em,'' Hickok said sadly. ''I miss Sherry and my son. Little Ringo,'' he stated proudly. ''I want to see 'em both so bad.''

''I know how you feel,'' Blade assured the gun-fighter. ''I miss my wife and boy too.''

''Where the blazes is Rikki?'' Hickok snapped impatiently.

Blade gazed to the east, reflecting, recalling the day only three months before when the Leader of the Family, Plato, had called all of them together in the walled compound designated their Home, located in the extreme northwest of Minnesota. ''We require volunteers from the Warrior ranks,'' Plato had informed them. ''As you know, we have established peaceful relations with the Flathead Indians in Montana, with the horsemen known as the Cavalry in the Dakota Territory, and with what's left of the U.S. Government to the west and south, in the Civilized Zone. We're also friendly with the refugees from the Twin Cities now living near us, and with the Moles to our east. But we are ignorant of what exists west of the Rocky Mountains and east of the Mississippi River. Consequently, the leaders of the various groups I've mentioned, which we now collectively refer to as the Freedom Federation, have decided to send an expedition into uncharted land, to venture where none of us have gone in one hundred years. We've heard many terrifying rumors about the country east of the Mississippi. We must determine if the rumors are true or mere fabrications. It is imperative we learn if there is any danger to our Family and the Freedom Federation as a whole. We now have fifteen Warriors safeguarding our Home and preserving us from harm. I propose to have the Warriors draw lots, and the three drawing the shortest straws will make the journey. Do you agree?'' Plato had asked.

Blade frowned at the memory. The Family had concurred with their leader, and Plato had held a conference with the head of the Warriors. Blade, despite his better judgment, had offered to lead the expedition, to forgo drawing a lot. Plato had gladly accepted his offer. The rest of the Warriors drew lots, and Rikki-Tikki-Tavi and Geronimo had drawn the shortest straws. But Geronimo's wife, Cynthia Morning Dove, had given birth only a week before the drawing. Hickok had therefore stepped forward and volunteered to go in Geronimo's place, and Plato had accepted the proposition after Geronimo had reluctantly acquiesced.

So here I am, Blade told himself. Almost to St. Louis and wishing I was anywhere but here. What a jerk I was to agree to go! And all because I think I can drive the SEAL better than anyone else in the Family, and certainly better than any of the other Warriors.

The SEAL. The pride and joy of the Founder of the Home, a man named Kurt Carpenter.

Carpenter had wisely anticipated the advent of World War III. A wealthy filmmaker, he had devoted his millions to constructing a survivalist retreat he had dubbed the Home. Shortly before the outbreak of hostilities, he had invited a carefully selected group to the Home. Because the retreat was located hundreds of miles from any primary, secondary, or even tertiary targets, it was spared a direct hit. Thanks to the prevailing high-altitude winds at the time of the war, the Home received only minimal dosages of radiation. Carpenter had planned for practically every contingency. He'd stocked ample supplies of every conceivable type.

His crowning achievement was the vehicle he bestowed on his followers, a vehicle he'd spent a fortune having developed. Carpenter had christened it the Solar Energized Amphibious or Land Recreational Vehicle—SEAL for short. The SEAL was a van-like transport, green in color, with an impervious body composed of an indestructible plastic. The plastic was tinted, allowing those within to see out but preventing anyone outside from viewing the interior. Four enormous tires allowed the transport to navigate virtually any terrain. The SEAL received its power from a pair of solar panels attached to the roof, which in turn supplied converted energy to six revolutionary batteries mounted under the vehicle. As if all of this weren't enough, Carpenter had then hired skilled mercenaries to install special armaments in the SEAL. As far as Blade knew, there wasn't another vehicle like it on the entire planet. He abruptly became aware of Hickok speaking.

"—listening to me or am I flappin' my gums for the fun of it?" the gunman demanded.

"Sorry," Blade apologized. "What were you saying?"

Hickok chuckled. "I never realized how much you and my missus have in common," he quipped.

"What's that supposed to mean?" Blade inquired.

"It means you're both pretty darn good at ignoring me at times," Hickok said. "It must be my introverted personality."

"Yeah, right," Blade responded. "You're about as introverted as a bull elk during rutting season. What were you—"

Hickok suddenly held up his right hand for silence. "Shush, pard! Give a listen!"

Blade complied, his ears straining. "I don't hear

anything," he declared after several seconds.

"You'd best clean your ears out," Hickok cracked, then paused. "Now do you hear it?"

Blade did. A faint sound coming from the east. An odd noise. Sort of a soft whump-whump-whump. What could it be?

"There!" Hickok exclaimed, pointing. "See it?"

Blade saw it. About a mile off to the east, hovering in the air, a huge dragonfly-shaped object.

"What the blazes is it?" Hickok asked.

"I don't know," Blade admitted. He racked his brain, recalling all the hours spent in the huge Family library personally stocked by Kurt Carpenter. Hundreds of thousands of books on every conceivable subject: dozens upon dozens of how-to books for everything from woodworking to herbal remedies; history books; literature books; religion and philosophy books; photographic books depicting the state of civilization before World War III one hundred years ago; and many, many more. Several of the books were devoted to aviation, and one of the photographs came to mind as Blade watched the aircraft. "I think that thing is called a helicopter," he remarked.

"A helicopter?" Hickok repeated doubtfully. "Who would have a functional helicopter? Where did it come from?"

From far off, from the vicinity of the helicopter, came the sharp retort of gunfire.

Blade and Hickok exchanged worried glances.

"Rikki!" Hickok said apprehensively.

"We'd better check it out," Blade declared. He turned toward the SEAL, parked behind them in the center of the highway.

"Look!" Hickok cried. "That contraption is comin' our way!"

The helicopter was rapidly approaching them, apparently flying directly over the road, following the course of the highway.

Blade's hands dropped to his Bowies. As the craft neared, he could distinguish its features. The helicopter was a dull brown in color with some sort of glass or plastic bubble in the front section and a long metallic tail behind. There was a spinning rotor on top of the craft and another one attached to the rear. Long, metal legs were affixed horizontally to the underbelly of the helicopter.

"Orders?" Hickok asked.

The bubble on the helicopter was tinted, just like the body of the SEAL, preventing Blade from viewing the interior of the craft. He debated the wisdom of remaining in the open, of attempting to persuade the occupants to land, hoping they would be friendly.

"They're almost on us," Hickok said, stating the obvious.

What to do? Blade hesitated.

Without any warning, the helicopter abruptly opened up with its machine guns, belching death and destruction from a pair of 45-caliber guns mounted on the front of the craft.

"Look out!" Hickok shouted, diving to the right as the highway in front of them erupted in a violent spray of asphalt and dirt.

Blade leaped aside, sprawling onto the ground. Damn his idiocy! How could he forget his favorite motto! Better safe than sorry!

Several of the rounds struck the SEAL, whining as they ricocheted from its steely structure.

Blade rolled to his feet.

Hickok was already on, his Pythons out and angled. As the helicopter passed overhead he fired four times in swift succession.

The helicopter kept going, circling around for another strafing run.

"In the SEAL!" Blade commanded. He ran to the driver's door, yanked it open, and vaulted into the driver's seat.

Hickok holstered his Colts and clambered into the passenger side. "Dangblasted varmints!" he muttered as he slammed his door. "Do you reckon they got Rikki?"

"We'll check on Rikki after we take care of these bastards!" Blade promised.

The SEAL was hit again, the screeching of the heavy slugs as they were deflected by the bulletproof body almost painful to the ears.

The helicopter streaked overhead, swinging for another try.

"Let's take 'em!" Hickok said.

Blade turned the key in the ignition and the engine purred to life.

The interior of the SEAL had been designed with economy of space in mind. Two bucket seats were in the front, one for the driver and another for a passenger, separated by a console between them. Behind the bucket seats was a wide seat for additional passengers, while the rear section, embracing at least a third of the transport, was devoted to storage space. The Warriors had their food, spare ammunition, and other provisions stacked in the rear section.

Blade shifted into drive and plastered the accelerator to the floor. The SEAL surged forward.

"They're comin' straight at us!" Hickok yelled.

The helicopter gunner fired again.

Blade swerved to the left as the windshield was rocked by a sustained burst.

"Are those bozos in for a surprise!" Hickok predicted, his right hand resting on the dashboard next to four silver toggle switches.

The mercenaries Kurt Carpenter had employed were proficient at their craft. The SEAL incorporated four offensive armaments into its framework: a pair of 50-caliber machine guns mounted underneath each front headlight; a flamethrower positioned behind the front fender; a rocket launcher in the center of the front grill; and even a miniaturized surface-to-air missile secreted in the roof above the driver's seat.

Hickok's hand touched the toggle switch marked S. "Ready when you are, big guy."

Blade had lost sight of the helicopter. Keeping the SEAL at 50 miles an hour, he leaned down and craned his neck in an effort to locate their antagonist. "I can't see them," he said.

"So what?" Hickok replied. "This surface-to-air dingus is heat-seeking, isn't it? Just say the word and it will take care of the rest."

"I don't want to waste it," Blade stated. "I want to be sure."

Hickok peered out his side of the transport. "I see a starling up there. Do you want me to practice on it?"

"Find the copter!" Blade ordered.

A minute passed without another attack.

"Maybe they headed for the hills," Hickok said.

"We've got to be sure," Blade told the gunfighter.

The SEAL was heading east, toward St. Louis.

"Where do you think it came from?" Hickok absently queried.

"How would I know?" Blade retorted.

Hickok grinned. "Boy! Somebody tries to kill you and you go to pieces! It doesn't take much to put you in a bad mood, does it?"

Blade braked the transport. "Get the binoculars."

Hickok climbed over the console and the wide seat into the rear section. "Where the blazes did we put them?" he asked.

"They've got to be there somewhere," Blade said, still searching for the helicopter.

Hickok unexpectedly started coughing. "Oh no!" he cried in mock horror.

"What is it?" Blade demanded, turning in his seat.

Hickok was pinching his nose shut with his right hand while he held a pair of black socks aloft in his left. "I found your dirty socks!" He wheezed.

"Whew! How does Jenny stand it?" he asked, referring to Blade's wife.

Blade glared at this friend. "Forget the socks and find those binoculars!"

"We don't need them," Hickok said, dropping the smelly socks.

"Why not?"

"Look!" Hickok pointed out the passenger side of the SEAL.

Blade turned.

The helicopter was coming in from the south, angling for a broadside run.

In the fraction of a second before Blade reacted, he spotted a bright red star painted on the tail of the copter. He buried the accelerator and slewed the SEAL to the left, off the highway and into the trees, barreling through the brush and snapping limbs and small saplings as the transport plowed onward.

To their rear, a large portion of the road exploded skyward as a deafening blast rocked the countryside.

"They must have rockets!" Hickok exclaimed as he climbed over the center seat and the console and reached his bucket seat.

Blade stopped the SEAL under the spreading branches of a large maple tree. The vehicle's green color, he reasoned, would serve as excellent camouflage in the midst of the forest.

"Do you reckon those hombres lost us?" Hickok queried.

"Let's hope so," Blade answered.

"I still think we should have used the surface-to-air gizmo on those suckers!" Hickok said.

"If they come back we will," Blade pledged.

But the helicopter didn't return. The two Warriors waited and waited, their windows lowered, listening for the whirlybird.

"They must have skedaddled," Hickok speculated after a while.

"Maybe they were low on fuel," Blade guessed. He

had left the SEAL's engine idle while they waited, knowing there was no way the occupants of the aircraft could have heard its barely audible motor. Besides, he realized, he might need to make a hasty getaway.

"We'd best check on Rikki, pard," Hickok suggested.

"Yes, we'd better," Blade agreed. He carefully wheeled the transport between the trees and other vegetation as he executed a wide circle back to the highway. "He shouldn't be too far ahead."

"What if he heard the fireworks and came a-runnin'?" Hickok inquired. "That helicopter might have went after him."

"We would have heard it," Blade said. "What I want to know," he added thoughtfully, "is what was all that shooting we heard when we first saw the copter?"

The SEAL broke though the final row of trees and reached the highway, coming out into the open about 20 yards from the point where they entered.

"Did you see that red star?" Hickok asked.

"I saw it," Blade confirmed, driving east.

"What's it mean?" Hickok questioned.

"Beats me," Blade responded. "We'll have to study up on insignias after we return to the Home."

"If we return to our Home," Hickok mumbled.

"Nothing's going to prevent us from returning to our loved ones," Blade vowed.

As if on cue, the helicopter zipped into sight from the north. It hovered stationary for a moment directly in front of the SEAL. There was a puff of white smoke from the underbelly of the craft.

"They've fired a rocket!" Hickok shouted.

Blade could see the black rocket or missile hurtling toward the transport. There wasn't time to reach the safety of the woods again! And they certainly couldn't outrun it!

What else could they do?

3

Rikki-Tikki-Tavi's skills as a martial artist was
renowned, the tales of his exploits matched or sur-
passed by only a few of the Warriors: Blade,
Geronimo, Yama, and definitely Hickok. For years
his deadly expertise as the consummate lethal per-
fectionist in hand-to-hand combat or with Oriental
weaponry had been common knowledge among the
Family in northwestern Minnesota. Later, when the
Family and the other members of the Freedom
Federation fought the demented Doktor in a battle
dubbed Armageddon, and again when the Freedom
Federation launched an assault on Denver, Rikki had
demonstrated his prowess against human and bestial
foes. True, the stories told about him had not attained
the epic proportions of those told about Hickok, but
in an age devoid of mass entertainment, when tele-
vision and movies no longer fabricated false heroes
for the populace, when the lost art of storytelling had
regained its deserved prominence around countless
campfires and dinner tables, the name of Rikki-Tikki-
Tavi was one to be reckoned with. From northwestern Minnesota south to Texas, from Denver east to
Kansas City, whenever people talked about the
monumental clash between the Freedom Federation
and the Civilized Zone, whenever the principles in
that bloody, brutal conflict were mentioned, his name
was high among them. And on this day Rikki lived up
to his reputation.

Lexine drew her survival knife as the dog pack closed in. She backed against the motorcycle, hoping the bike would protect her flank while she concentrated on the dogs in front of her.

None of them reached her.

Rikki's katana was an invisible blur as he waded into the ferocious mass of canines. The first dog lost its front legs, the second half of its head, and the third was gutted in the twinkling of an eye. Rikki spun and slashed, twisted and sliced, constantly moving, his sharp-edged sword cleaving a foreleg here, a stomach there, or splitting a skull as easily as an overripe melon. The bravest dogs and the fleetest of foot were the first to die; eight went down in as many seconds, some gushing blood and howling in torment. Rikki's custom-made black clothing, especially sewn together by the Family Weavers, was spattered with crimson splotches and chunks of furry flesh.

The six dogs remaining hesitated, deterred by the swift demise of their leaders. They warily circled their prey, growling and snapping, searching for a weakness, any opening they could exploit. A large Doberman, overeager, crouched and sprang.

Rikki was ready. He dropped to his right knee, below the hurtling dog, and swung his katana with all of his considerable strength.

The Doberman yipped as it lost three of its legs.

A shepherd attempted to reach the man while he was down on one knee, but its throat was neatly cut open before it could sink its fangs in its intended victim, and it withdrew, gurgling and whining, blood pumping everywhere.

The last three dogs were reluctant to engage the man. The sight of their dead or dying comrades, many writhing in sheer agony and uttering pitiable cries, was too much for them. They broke and ran, heading for the hill to the east.

Rikki slowly straightened, his alert eyes scanning

his fallen foes for any capable of jumping him.

All of them were out of commission.

Lexine, a silent, stupefied witness to the fierce fight, shook her head in disbelief.

Rikki glanced at her. "Are you all right?" he asked.

"Never been better," Lexine responded in a daze.

Rikki walked toward one of the crippled dogs, intending to dispatch the lot of them and put them out of their misery.

A burst of gunfire erupted from the direction of the other side of the hill, followed by a peculiar noise from above.

Rikki looked up, startled.

A strange flying contraption was almost overhead, bearing to the west, powered by a spinning blade on its top and a smaller one located at its rear.

"A red copter!" Lex shouted. "Slave hunters!"

A what? Rikki looked at her, puzzled.

"Did you hear those shots?" Lex inquired nervously.

Rikki nodded. "Was it the . . . Red copter?"

Lexine's green eyes widened as she stared over Rikki's left shoulder. "No," she replied, pointing. "It was them!"

Rikki turned and was surprised to discover the crest of the hill crammed with bikers. Where had they come from? Why hadn't he heard them approach? The answer to both questions was self-evident: they had approached from the east while he was battling the dog pack, and he'd been so intent on dispatching the dogs he'd failed to note the bikers. Until now.

The one called Cardew was with them.

"We've got to get out of here!" Lex exclaimed, starting to climb onto one of the abandoned motor-cycles.

The riders on the crest gunned their bikes and roared down toward the pair below.

Lex, straddling the cycle, was futilely striving to start the machine. "What the hell is the matter with this thing!'' she fumed. ''Why won't it kick over?''

Rikki ignored her rhetorical question and faced the bikers. He noticed all of them wore black-leather apparel and all were armed. Two women were in the lead. One was a tall brunette, the other a hefty blonde.

Lexine jumped from the useless cycle and ran to another of the bikes. ''We've got to get out of here!'' she repeated.

Rikki knew it was too late. Departure was out of the question. Already 20 bikers appeared, and more were rumbling over the hill every second.

The tall bunette motioned with her right arm and the bikers fanned out, some veering to the left, others to the right, surrounding the man in black and Lexine.

Lexine, finally realizing escape was impossible, crossed to Rikki's side, standing to his left, her survival knife at the ready. ''Looks like we blew it, handsome!'' she shouted to make herself heard over the thundering cycles. ''Sorry!''

Over 40 bikers had encircled the pair. At a signal from the brunette all of the riders killed their engines.

Rikki studied the brunette, the apparent leader. She wore a leather jacket and pants. A pair of revolvers were strapped around her lean waist, and Rikki recognized the handguns as Llama Super Comanche V's. Her facial features were angular and hard, her mouth set in a tight frown. Pale blue eyes regarded him with calculating intent. Under her right eye, in a ragged line from the eye to the tip of her chin, was an old scar, as if one side of her face had once been torn apart.

''So, Lex,'' said the brunette in a mocking, strident tone, ''who's your boyfriend?'' She smirked at Rikki.

''Leave him out of this,'' Lex stated. ''It's me you want, Terza.''

The woman named Terza glared at Lexine. ''I want you, all right, sweetheart. You'll pay for trying to desert us! And so will lover boy here!''

"Leave him go!" Lex urged.

"No can do," Terza said, shaking her head. She looked at the bodies of Pat and the other two women. "Cardew told me what he did. This bastard is going to pay!"

"Listen!" one of the other bikers yelled.

From the west, distinctly audible, came the harsh chatter of machine guns.

"Look!" Cardew pointed westward.

Rikki shifted his stance. The red copter was perhaps a mile off, swooping above the highway. He instantly perceived the reason for the machine-gun fire: that thing was attacking the SEAL, was going after his friends. He had to reach them! But how? He was completely hemmed in by a wall of motorcycles.

"Do you think they're after one of us?" Cardew queried.

"None of our people are out that far," Terza said. "They must be after somebody else."

"Should we go check?" Cardew asked her.

"No," Terza answered. "We're going to take these two back before that copter returns." She paused, absently biting her lower lip, reflecting. "Whoever the copter is after is doing us a favor. I was sure the Reds would strafe us after we shot at them. Our rifles and hanguns ain't much use against their firepower."

The portly blonde, a squat woman with a perpetually mean expression, nodded at Lexine. "Climb up behind me," she ordered.

"Get bent, Erika!" Lex retorted.

Terza raised her left arm and over two dozen firearms were trained on Rikki and Lexine. "What's it gonna be?" she asked Lex. "If you and lover boy don't mount up, right now, we'll blow you away!"

Rikki, despite his calm exterior, was in a profound turmoil. There was no way he could hope to prevail against so many opponents. If he resisted, they would simply kill him. But if he allowed them to take him into St. Louis, he would be unable to aid Blade and

Hickok. He scanned the rifles, revolvers, and pistols pointed in his direction and knew he had no choice. He would be of no benefit to his friends dead.

"Drop the sword!" Terza commanded.

Rikki reluctantly obeyed.

"And the knife!" Terza snapped at Lexine.

Lex angrily tossed her weapon aside.

"Now get behind Erika," Terza told Lexine.

The redhead glanced into Rikki's eyes for a moment, wanting to let him know how sorry she was to have involved him in this mess.

"Move it!" Terza barked.

Lexine mounted Erika's bike.

Terza grinned and winked at Rikki. "And you, lover boy, can get behind me."

Rikki dutifully slid his small frame behind the brunette. He stared at his bloody katana, averse to leaving it. His katana was an extension of himself, his most prized possession, a symbol of his Warrior nature, an essential component for a true samurai. Ordinarily, he would not relinquish the weapon under any circumstances. But this was an exception, and it just might save the lives of his companions.

Terza led the cyclists to the east.

As they crossed the low hill, Rikki caught his first glimpse of St. Louis. He saw many towering buildings miles off, the skyline of the inner city. What had they called those tremendous structures in the days before World War III, before the Big Blast—as the Family referred to the war? After a minute he remembered. Skyscrapers. He'd seen such buildings once before, in Denver, Colorado, and after his return to the Home had researched them in the Family library. Prewar architecture fascinated him, as it did a majority of the Family. Many of the photographic books contained stunning pictures of incredible buildings: edifices reaching into the heavens, bizarre spherical structures and glistening domes, individual residences of every shape and size—some too fantastic to comprehend. Rikki had received the impression each city was a veritable concrete and metal labyrinth. How could people have lived in such an unhealthy environment? Deprived of rejuvenating contact with the earth, denied the pleasure of experiencing the joys of nature, of strolling through a verdant forest pulsing with the vibrant rhythms of animal life? It was no wonder the cities reputedly festered with asocial, deviate, and criminal behavior. And here he was, heading into a sweltering city.

The cyclists passed a small group of six bikers, parked at the side of the road. Rikki spotted a small trailer hitched to one of the bikes. On the blue trailer was a cage, and in the cage were the three dogs from the pack. Two other trailers, both empty, were connected to stout bars to other cycles. So now he knew how the Leather Knights transported their hunting dogs.

Small buildings appeared on both sides of the highway. Frame homes, brick houses, and others, comprising the outskirts of St. Louis, the suburbs. Some were occupied, as evidenced by their well-preserved state, their clean sidings, intact windows, and neatly trimmed lawns. One man was cutting his grass with an ancient rotary mower. Other homes were obviously vacant, their windows broken, their roofs and porches sagging or collapsed. Some of the residents waved at the Leather Knights.

"The people seem to like you," Rikki commented in Terza's right ear.

Terza glanced over her right shoulder. "Why shouldn't they, lover boy? We keep the peace, don't we? We protect 'em from the lousy Reds. The streets are safe at night. Why shouldn't they like us?" she demanded indignantly.

Indeed. Why shouldn't they? Had he erred in siding with Lex against the others? Rikki looked to his left and found Lexine watching him. She grinned sheepishly and averted her eyes, her long tresses whipping in the wind as Erika's bike paced Terza's. The sight of Lexine's features was enough to confirm his decision; there was an air of truthful sincerity about the woman.

The Leather Knights continued into the inner city area. The further they went, the more indications of habitation they encountered. Bikers seemed to be everywhere, but there was a singular lack of other vehicles. No cars or trucks or jeeps.

Rikki searched for a landmark and tried to read every street sign they passed. Many of the signs were missing or illegible, the letters having faded with the passing of a century. The bikers made a number of turns, some to the east, some to the south, ever bearing inward, deeper into the grimy bowels of the metropolis.

A large sign appeared. From it, Rikki learned they were traveling east on Market Street. Huge buildings lined the south side of Market Street, while there was a park bordering the northern edge. Something ahead, something gleaming in the sunlight, arrested Rikki's attention. He couldn't see it clearly at first, but after a minute it became visible, rearing skyward to the east.

Rikki gawked, amazed. What was it? What purpose did it serve? The structure was gigantic, some sort of tremendous, glistening arc or arch. The bikers wheeled their cycles to the left, driving north on Broadway. As they turned, Rikki gazed to his right and saw a mysterious, gargantuan building, a circular affair. He caught only a glimpse of it out of the corner of his eye.

A city of marvels!

The street ahead became crowded with Leather Knights, most of them parked on the sidewalks and involved in idle conversations. They turned to stare as Terza's cavalcade rode past.

Where were they going?

A dingy edifice appeared to the left. Two faint but readable words were painted on one wall: Bus

Terminal. The street and lot to the south of the
terminal were filled with Leather Knights. They
gathered around as Terza angled her cycle up to a
cracked curb and killed her motor. The other riders
did the same.

"Who's the runt?" a bearded biker inquired.

"Lex is back!" shouted a woman.

Terza slid from her bike and motioned for Rikki to
do likewise. "Gather round!" she yelled to the
throng.

Rikki saw Erika yank Lex from her bike. Lexine
clenched her fists in frustration, and Erika shoved her
toward Rikki.

"We caught the traitor!" Terza announced. "Just
like I said we would!"

"Where's Mira?" asked a husky woman.

"Wasted," Terza responded. "And she isn't the
only one. This sucker," and she nodded at Rikki,
"wasted three of our sisters!"

There was a detectable stir in the assembled
Leather Knights as each and every one fixed a baleful
glare on the man in black.

"We know what we do with traitors!" Terza
bellowed. "And we know what to do to anyone who
wastes one of our own!"

"Let Slither have 'em!" cried a furious woman.

"Slither!" echoed another woman.

Dozens of voices rose in unison, almost as if they
were chanting. "Slither! Slither! Slither!"

"I demand a trial!" Lexine said to Terza.

Terza smirked. "Traitors don't deserve trials!" She
stood aside, waving her left hand toward Rikki and
Lexine.

The Leather Knights swarmed in, enclosing Rikki
and Lexine in a sea of black leather and sweaty flesh.
Hands brutally grabbed the duo and propelled them
along the street.

Rikki mentally debated the wisdom of resisting.
There was a possibility he might be able to fight his

way free of the mob, but he would have to leave
Lexine behind to succeed and he would not abandon
her under any circumstances. He noted her cool
composure, her defiant demeanor, and admired her
calculated courage. Here was a woman after his own
heart!

The Leather Knights pulled, pushed, and shoved
their captives to the east, in the direction of a wide
body of water.

Rikki recognized the river ahead. They were being
led toward the Missouri River. Why? What connec-
tion did the river have with the one called Slither?

Terza, walking alongside the prisoners, followed
Rikki's glance. "It's the Mississippi River," she told
him.

"I know," Rikki replied.

"Are you in the mood for a bath?" Terza asked.

"Not really," Rikki said.

"Too bad, turkey!" Terza laughed. "You're gonna
get one whether you like it or not!"

Rikki tried to see the scenery on either side of the
street, to serve as a reference for later use, but the
mass of bikers prevented him from accomplishing his
aim.

The Leather Knights bore to the right, leaving the
road and marching down to the river. Trees lined the
bank. Below a spreading maple tree was an old
wooden dock, dilapidated beyond hope of
redemption. One of the maple's thick lower branches
extended over the dock and the murky water beyond.

The crowd halted.

"I'm sorry I got you into this," Lex said to Rikki.

"Ahhh. How sweet!" Erika cuffed Lexine across the
mouth. "You bitch!"

Two ropes were produced and a pair of leather-
garbed women carried them to the end of the dock.
With practiced ease they tossed each rope over the
lower branch in the maple tree, then turned and
leered at the prisoners.

"Get moving!" Terza ordered, and shoved Lexine.

Rikki walked along the dock, the wood swaying under his feet. He was surprised by the rampant stupidity the Leather Knights displayed. Why hadn't they thought to frisk him for additional weapons? Why hadn't they interrogated him? They were enraged by the deaths of their fellow Knights, but unrestrained emotion was a pitiful substitute for seasoned leadership and responsible judgment.

Lexine reached the two women at the end of the dock first. One of them secured her rope to Lexine's wrists, using one end of the rope for each arm. The woman gleefully tied the knots as tightly as she could.

The second woman hauled Rikki to her side and performed a similar binding operation on him.

Lexine was watching the surface of the water, her green eyes darting to the left and the right.

"What's down there?" Rikki queried her.

"Find out for yourself," said the woman who had tied him, and she grunted as she abruptly shoved him from the dock.

Rikki's arms were wrenched upward by the force of the rope tugging on his arms. He dropped a few feet before the rope brought him up short with a jarring snap. The pain was intense but fleeting. He grit his teeth and looked to his right.

Lexine was also dangling above the river. Her eyes were closed, her mouth twisted in agony.

Rikki appraised their situation. Both of them were about a yard from the dock, Rikki being slightly further away because his rope had been placed beyond Lexine's on the limb. His custom-made black shoes, constructed from dyed deer hide and cougar sinew, were only a foot above the Mississippi.

The Leather Knights gathered along the west bank, collectively surveying the expanse of water beyond the dock, eagerly waiting.

But for what?

4

The rocket was almost on them!

Blade instinctively executed the only maneuver possible; he wrenched the steering wheel to the right, causing the transport to lurch sideways, angling the passenger side of the vehicle, Hickok's side, away from the hurtling rocket.

With an ear-splitting roar the rocket struck the highway about seven feet in front of the SEAL. Massive chunks of asphalt, dirt, and rocks were blasted upward. A jolting concussion, an irresistible shock wave of puissant force, slammed broadside into the transport like an unstoppable tidal wave onto a beach. The synthetic body withstood the shattering explosion intact, but the SEAL was flipped onto its passenger side and propelled several feet along the highway before it came to a rest.

Inside the SEAL, the two Warriors were tossed and buffeted by the tumbling vehicle. Blade struggled to maintain his grip on the steering wheel to prevent himself from falling onto the gunman. Hickok crashed against the passenger door, the handle digging into his ribs. The provisions in the rear section spilled over the central seat. One box of ammunition flew forward and narrowly missed Blade's head.

Blade leaped into action as soon as the SEAL stopped moving. He lunged for the driver's door and threw it open. Using the steering wheel for support, he vaulted outside onto the upturned body.

The helicopter was still hovering to the east of the transport.

Hickok was trying to untangle his contorted form from the bottom of the SEAL. "Dangblasted varmints! I'll fix their wagon!"

"Stay put!" Blade ordered. "I'll try to lead them off." He jumped to the ground and ran toward the trees on the south side of the highway.

The helicopter, as if it were a metallic bird of prey, swooped down for the coup de grace.

Blade weaved as he ran, knowing the copter would open up again with its machine guns.

A crackling spray of lead from the whirlybird confirmed his expectation.

Blade flinched as the earth around him was stitched by a pattern of lethal slugs. He was only five feet from cover and safety when he risked a hasty glance over his left shoulder.

The helicopter wasn't more than ten feet above the SEAL, swiveling for a clearer shot at its intended victim.

Blade dodged to the left, and as he did his right foot caught in something and he went down, sprawling onto his hands and knees, vulnerable and helpless.

The helicopter pilot instantly took advantage of the situation by edging his copter nearer to the trees and his rising target.

Blade, only two feet from the trees, braced for the impact of the machine-gun bullets, realizing it would be impossible for the copter gunner to miss at such close range.

Gunshots boomed to the Warrior's rear, but they weren't the sound of .45-caliber machine guns; they were the welcome bang-bang-bang of a pair of pearl-handled Colt Python .357 Magnum revolvers.

Blade spun around.

The gunman was only partially visible, with his

shoulders and arms protruding from the open door on the driver's side of the SEAL.

What did Hickok hope to accomplish? Blade wondered. The Pythons against an armed helicopter were seemingly insurmountable odds. But then he saw the gunman's intent and grinned.

Hickok was going for the tail blade. The Colts bucked in his hands as he fired six shots in swift succession. He had to distract the copter gunner's attention from Blade, and he succeeded.

On the gunman's sixth shot, the helicopter suddenly lurched to one side, then began swerving back and forth. It darted upward, its flight uneven, the pilot evidently experiencing difficulty in keeping the craft level.

"Got ya'!" Hickok said, elated.

The helicopter continued to ascend until it was 100 feet above the highway. Its front end dipped as the craft proceeded to speed to the east. Within less than a minute the helicopter was a dark dot on the eastern horizon.

Blade walked to the transport. "Thanks," he said, smiling at Hickok. "You saved my life."

Hickok adopted the air of casual nonchalance. "It was a piece of cake," he declared, then smiled. "Besides, I didn't want your missus bawling her brains out on my buckskins."

Blade's brow furrowed as he studied the SEAL. "We have a major problem on our hands."

"When don't we?" Hickok said. He slid to the ground and immediately set about reloading his Pythons.

Blade slowly made an inspection of the transport, searching for structural damage. He conducted a complete circuit of the vehicle.

"What did you find, pard?" Hickok asked as Blade rounded the front end.

"It looks okay," Blade replied.

Hickok's left Colt was already in its holster. He ejected the last spent shell from his right Python, removed a bullet from his gunbelt, and dropped it into the cylinder. Satisfied, he swung the cylinder closed and twirled the Colt into his right holster.

"We won't really know how it is until we try to start it," Blade said, pondering their dilemma, "and we can't try starting it until we have it upright again."

Hickok frowned. "How the blazes are we gonna do that?"

"I wish I knew." Blade stared at the east. This mission, like all the others, had devolved into a typical fiasco. Why was it events never went as you planned? Why did things always have to go wrong? Here they were, not more than ten miles from their destination, and now their transport was inoperational and one of them was missing. What next?

"What are we gonna do about Rikki?" Hickok inquired.

Blade stroked his square chin. "There is no way we can right the SEAL on our own," he said, reasoning aloud. "We could do it if we had enough people or another vehicle and a lot of rope—"

"Which we don't have," Hickok interrupted.

"—so we'll have to go look for what we need," Blade stated. "And since we have to find Rikki, we'll kill two birds with one stone. One of us will head for St. Louis."

"One of us?" Hickok repeated.

"Just one of us," Blade confirmed.

"Why not both of us?" Hickok wanted to know.

"We can't leave the SEAL unprotected," Blade explained.

"We've done it before," Hickok protested. "All we have to do is lock this contraption up tight as a drum and it'll be safe and sound until we get back."

Blade pointed at the exposed undercarriage. "And what about that?"

"What about it?" Hickok asked, puzzled.

"The bottom of the SEAL might not be as impervious as the special body," Blade said. "Someone could come along and damage it, render it totally useless. I can't allow that to happen. The SEAL is invaluable to our Family. You know that."

Hickok looped his thumbs in his gunbelt near the buckle. "And which one of us gets to waltz into St. Louis?"

"I'm going," Blade said.

"Why can't I go?" Hickok demanded.

"Because I said so," Blade stated, settling the matter. Since he was the head of the Warriors, his decisions were final.

"What am I supposed to do while you're gone?" Hickok groused. "Twiddle my thumbs?"

"You can check our supplies," Blade instructed the pouting gunman. "Make sure they're okay and clean up the mess inside."

"What if something happens to you?" Hickok queried. "How long should I wait?"

Blade considered a moment. "Give me three days. I should find Rikki and be back by then."

"Fine," Hickok said. "Three days it is. But if you're not back here by then, I'm comin' after you, SEAL or no SEAL."

Blade chuckled. "Keep an eye peeled while I collect the provisions I'll need." So saying, he hoisted himself up and climbed into the transport. The interior of the vehicle was a mess, but he found the items he wanted without much difficulty: a canteen, a canvas backpack confiscated from soldiers in Wyoming, strips of venison jerky, extra magazines for his Commando, and the Commando itself. He stuffed the canteen, jerky, and magazines into the backpack and clambered to the open driver's door. "Here," he said to the gunman, and tossed the backpack.

Hickok caught it with a deft flick of his left wrist.

Blade used his powerful arms to haul his body from

the SEAL. Holding the Commando in his left hand, he
leaped to the highway.

"You sure ain't takin' much, pard," Hickok
observed, hefting the light backpack.

"I won't be gone that long," Blade said. He took the
backpack and handed the Commando to the gunman.

"I hope Rikki is okay," Hickok remarked, gazing
eastward.

"Rikki can take care of himself," Blade commented. He placed his brawny arms through the
backpack straps. "You make certain that you stay out
of trouble while I'm gone."

"Who? Me?" Hickok quipped. He gave the
Commando to the Alpha Triad leader. "You're the
one who'd best take care."

"May the Spirit watch over you," Blade said. He
started walking due east. About 50 yards ahead was a
turn in the road, the highway evidently bearing
slightly to the southeast. Blade could feel the heat
from the sun on his broad back and legs as he
marched along. He stopped when he reached the turn
and glanced at the SEAL. Hickok was still standing
exactly where he had left him, the gunman's thumbs
hooked in his gunbelt. Blade couldn't discern
Hickok's face clearly, but he received the impression
the gunman was frowning. Blade knew Hickok didn't
like the idea of staying behind one bit, but the
gunman was too loyal a Warrior to lodge more than a
minor protest.

Blade waved.

Hickok began jumping up and down and flapping
his arms like crazy. After a minute he ceased and
made a show of blowing a farewell kiss in Blade's
direction.

Blade shook his head as the gunman started
laughing. Thank the Spirit the gunman was on this
mission! Rikki was naturally rather taciturn, and the
lengthy ride would have been monotonous without
the loquacious gunfighter. Blade resumed his

journey, following the highway, sticking to the middle of the road. If anything came at him, he'd have the time to see it coming and respond accordingly. He raked his eyes across the forest to the right and left of the crumbling asphalt, alert for any sign of a mutate or other horror.

Time passed.

Blade was less than a mile from the SEAL when he spied the corpses on the road ahead. And three—what were they?—motorcyles!

What was this?

He slowed, advancing cautiously, his finger on the trigger of the Commando.

Bodies. Lots and lots of bodies.

Was Rikki's one of them?

Blade paused 15 feet from the prone forms. He could see 3 dead women and counted 13 dogs, a few of which were alive, whining and whimpering in torment.

What had happened? Had the helicopter done this?

Blade walked up to the first corpse and examined the area. Why would anyone leave three motorcycles, apparently functional, out here in the middle of nowhere? Could he ride one? he wondered. If he could manage to figure out how it was done, he'd find Rikki that much faster. He'd never ridden one before, but that didn't—

No!

Blade froze as his gaze rested on a bloody sword lying amidst the slain canines. It was a katana! Rikki's katana! Blade would recognize the sword anywhere! And there was the scabbard! But Rikki would never cast aside his cherished weapon. Or would he? There was no sign of Rikki's body, and it was doubtful anyone would bother to cart it off but leave the three women behind. So Rikki must be alive, and he must have deliberately left the kantana as a warning to his fellow Warriors. The katana's presence conclusively proved Rikki *had* been here, but was gone now.

To where?

St. Louis?

Blade retrieved the sword and the scabbard. He wiped the blade clean on a dead dog and slid the katana into its scabbard.

A low rumbling sounded from beyond a hill to the east.

Blade quickly eased the scabbard under his belt, aligning it in front of the Bowie knife on his left hip. He crouched and darted across the road and into the trees on the right side of the highway. He was barely out of sight before more motorcycles appeared at the top of the hill. Without hesitating, they descended toward the bodies.

Would Rikki be with them?

Blade peered around the trunk of an oak tree, watching the approaching riders.

There were three motorcyles, each hauling a trailer with a cage on top. In one of the cages were three dogs. Two men were on each motorcycle: the driver and a passenger, each man straddling his narrow seat with accomplished ease, despite the numerous ruts and bumps the bikes struck as they sped nearer.

They reminded Blade of the Cavalry, the superb horsemen occupying the Dakota territory. These bikers displayed the same casual mastery of their cycles shown by the Cavalry toward their horses. Whether it was man and machine or man and faithful steed, both seemed as one.

What was going on?

The three cycles braked and halted near the bodies. One after the other the drivers shut off their motors.

One of the passengers, a skinny man with baggy leather pants and a bushy brown beard, sighed as he eased to the ground. "I don't see why we had to be the ones," he said bitterly. "She could have sent somebody else."

"Oh, yeah?" countered one of the drivers. "Who? We were the closest."

"Besides," added another, "I think Terza was pissed at us over what happened to the dogs."

The bearded biker stared at the dogs littering the highway. "It wasn't our fault," he said sadly.

"It was that damn guy in black," commented another.

Guy in black? That had to be Rikki! Blade inched a bit further around the tree, not wanting to miss a word.

"Who was that joker?" asked a portly biker as he climbed from his cycle.

"Beats me," answered the bearded one. "The messenger from Terza didn't know. He told me she wanted us to get these bikes and take care of the dogs. That was all."

"Damn!" fumed the third driver as he walked up to the slain dogs. "Look at this! How the hell did the guy do it?"

The bearded biker shook his head. "I don't know. But he must be one mean son of a bitch."

One of the other men snorted. "Not for long, he won't be. You can bet Terza will rack his ass for what he did to Pat and the others."

"And we'll probably miss out on the fun," complained the third driver.

"I wouldn't say that," interjected a deep voice from the edge of the highway.

Startled, the bikers spun, shocked to behold a towering man with dark hair and simmering eyes pointing a machine gun in their general direction.

"Who the hell are you?" demanded the bearded biker.

"Would you believe the tooth fairy?" replied the big man.

The bikers exchanged confused, worried glances.

"Drop your weapons," Blade commanded.

All of the bikers were armed, four with revolvers and two with knives. A Winchester was strapped to one of their motorcycles.

Blade waited, sensing one of them would make a play, watching their eyes for the telltale hint of an impending violent attack. Very few fighters could disguise this instinctive reaction, a slight tightening of the eyes, a shifting of the pupils, prior to galvanizing their body into action. Almost every fighter telegraphed his assault in one way or another, whether it was a movement of the eyes or a contracting of the shoulder muscles right before he threw a punch. Only an extremely skilled and accomplished fighter was capable of perfectly masking his intent. Such a fighter didn't reveal his maneuver or foreshadow his blow beforehand; he simply executed it with lightning speed and devastating results. While all the Family's Warriors were trained in hand-to-hand combat, only a few demonstrated this exceptional ability of concealment, and Blade knew of only one who was the acme of perfection: Rikki-Tikki-Tavi.

One of the bikers, a hefty, unkempt individual with pink hair and an earring in his left lobe, was cautiously moving his right hand toward the revolver tucked under his belt.

"I don't want to kill you if I don't have to," Blade said, hoping they would wisely avoid a clash.

They weren't that wise.

Pink Hair clutched at his revolver, and that was the signal for the rest of them to go for their respective weapons.

Blade was left with no other option. He swung the Commando in an arc as he pulled the trigger, holding the barrel at chest height.

Pink Hair was the first to drop, his torso racked by the Commando's heavy slugs, his body spurting crimson geysers as he was flung backwards onto the highway. The three other bikers with guns were likewise decimated. One of the bikers with a knife managed to whip his weapon from its sheath and lunge at the giant with the machine gun, but a veritable hail of lead knocked him for a loop. Only one biker was left standing, untouched, with his knife partially drawn; it was the skinny man with the baggy leather pants and the bushy brown beard.

"Drop it or die!" Blade snapped.

Bushy Beard promptly discarded his knife. "Don't k-kill me, m-mister!" he wailed, stuttering, in fear for his life.

Blade strolled up to the biker. "Whether you die or not will depend on you. I'm going to ask some questions and I want truthful answers." He rammed the Commando barrel into the biker's abdomen. "One answer I don't like and you're going to develop a split personality. Understand?"

The biker nodded vigorously.

"What's your name?" Blade asked.

"Jeff," the biker replied.

"What are you?"

Jeff's eyes narrowed and his brow furrowed, as if he was puzzled. "How do you mean?"

"Are you part of a gang?" Blade queried. He nodded at the bodies around him. "All of you wear black leather. Why?"

"That's our color, man," Jeff said.

"Color?"

"Yeah. Where are you from? Don't they have colors where you come from?" Jeff inquired.

Blade pressed on the Commando and Jeff blanched. "I'll ask the questions," Blade reminded him.

"Sure thing," Jeff promptly responded.

"What is the name of your gang?"

"We're called the Leather Knights," Jeff said proudly.

"And do the Leather Knights have their . . ." Blade paused, trying to recall the words he wanted. Once before, during Alpha Triad's run to the Twin Cities, he had dealt with street gangs. What was the name they used for their territory? Something to do with grass or sod or—" . . . turf in St. Louis?" he said as the word came to him.

"St Louis is our turf," Jeff boasted.

"The Leather Knights control the entire city?" Blade interrogated the biker.

"Yep." Jeff beamed. "Have for years."

"Detail the history of the Leather Knights," Blade instructed.

"What?" Jeff almost laughed. "Are you kidding?"

Blade leaned forward, his raging eyes burning into Jeff's. "Do I look like I'm kidding?"

Jeff gulped. "No, sir. You sure don't."

"Then start talking."

"There's not much to tell," Jeff said in a frightened tone. "I don't know a lot about it, honest!"

"You must know something."

"All I know is what I've heard," Jeff explained, "what some of the old-timers have told me."

"I'm waiting."

Jeff reflected a moment. "The Leather Knights got started way back before the war," he detailed. "When the war broke out, most of the people in St. Louis took off. I think they were evacuated by the Government, or something like that. Anyway, the Knights stayed put and got involved in some fights with two or three other gangs over who was going to claim the turf. The Knights came out on top."

"Are there any other people in St. Louis besides the Leather Knights?" Blade asked.

"Yep. Bunches. A lot of people strayed back after the war was over. I don't know how many there are now, but there's got to be at least a couple of thousand," Jeff said.

"How many Leather Knights are there?" Blade questioned him.

"Six hundred, if you count the studs," Jeff answered.

"Studs?"

"Yeah. I'm a stud. The guys you just wasted were studs. You'd be a stud, too, if you were a Knight."

Now it was Blade's turn to be confused. "I don't understand," he admitted.

"You've got balls, don't you?"

"Balls?"

"Nuts. Coconuts, man. Gonads," Jeff said, accenting the last word.

Blade was more bewildered than before. "What do my sexual organs have to do with it?"

"Everything. If you ain't got nuts and a pecker, you can't hardly be a stud," Jeff explained.

Blade's eyes widened in comprehension. "You mean all of the men are studs?"

Jeff snickered. "The foxes ain't got the hardware, if you get my drift."

"And the studs control the Leather Knights?" Blade speculated.

Jeff snorted again. "Where'd you ever get a dumb idea like that?" He hesitated, appalled at his own stupidity. "I didn't mean anything by that crack," he quickly blurted out. "Honest!"

"If the men . . . the studs . . . don't control the Leather Knights, then who does?" Blade demanded.

"Who else? The foxes."

"The women?"

"Why do you look so surprised? Ain't it the same where you come from?" Jeff inquired.

Blade shook his head. "Our men and women share responsibility. You can't really say one dominates the other."

"You're putting me on!"

"I'm serious," Blade stated. "How did the women assume control of the Leather Knights?"

"It's always been that way," Jeff replied.

"Always?"

Jeff frowned. "I did hear a story once, but I thought the old guy who told me was wacko. He said that long ago, way back about the time of the war, the men ran the show. But all the fighting over our turf killed off most of the men. The Leather Knights became top dog in St. Louis, but few of the men survived. So the foxes, the mamas, sort of took over."

"And the women have been running the show ever since," Blade concluded.

"They do now," Jeff affirmed.

"How many of the Knights are studs?"

"Oh, about two hundred," Jeff answered.

"But you said there are six hundred Knights?"

"That's right," Jeff said.

"And the other four hundred are all women?" Blade asked.

"Yep."

"That doesn't make sense," Blade said. "How can you have so many women and so few men?"

"We've got more men," Jeff responded. "Lots more. But the women don't let every man into the Leather Knights. Only enough to handle their dirty work."

"Dirty work?"

"Yeah. Things like the cleaning and the laundry and stuff like that. It's a real drag! I wouldn't of joined up, but it was the only way I could get me a bike," Jeff elaborated.

"Only the Knights are entitled to motorcycles?"

"Of course."

Blade stepped back, studying the biker, debating. He believed the man. But where did it leave him? What good did the knowledge do? In the final analysis, what did it matter whether the women or the men ran the Leather Knights and controlled St. Louis? Either way, getting Rikki out of there promised to be no easy task. "You mentioned a guy in black earlier."

"The one who wasted our dogs," Jeff said. "We were after Lex and Mira, when Cardew came hauling ass and told Terza about this guy in black who racked three sisters. That's what the women all call themselves. The sisters. Anyhow, Terza got real ticked off

and ordered us to send the dogs out." Jeff paused.
"I've been on the dog detail for six months. I'm so
damn sick of dog shit I could scream."

"Back up a bit," Blade directed him. "Who are Lex
and Mira? And Cardew and Terza?"

"Lex is one of the sisters," Jeff said. "She got tired
of the Knights and was trying to split. But the sisters
ain't allowed to split once they take the oath. As for
Mira," he said, shifting to his right and pointing at a
woman lying among the dogs, "she got racked."

"And Cardew and Terza?"

"Cardew is one of the studs. He was riding point
when they caught up with Lex and Mira. He's the one
who told us about the man in black."

"That leaves Terza," Blade reminded him.

"Terza is our head, man," Jeff revealed. "She runs
the whole show."

"Terza rules the Leather Knights?"

"You got it."

"What kind of a woman is she?" Blade asked.

"She's one mean mother!" Jeff said. "She don't take
any crap from anybody. Sort of like you."

Blade grinned. "Where are they holding the man in
black?"

"Is he a friend of yours?"

"Yes. Where is he?"

"I don't know," Jeff answered.

Blade took a step forward.

"Hey!" Jeff held up his hands. "Really, man! I don't
know where they've got him! He's in St. Louis, but
that's all I know."

"What will they do? Hold him prisoner?" Blade
inquired.

"The Leather Knights don't take no prisoners," Jeff
said. "He may be dead by now. Terza don't like it
when one of the sisters gets wasted, and your friend
racked three. One of them, that one there," and he
pointed at another corpse, "was called Pat, a real

good buddy of Terza's. I imagine Terza will rack your
friend first thing. Maybe take him out herself, or
stake him out for Grotto, or even feed him to Slither.''

Blade wanted to pose additonal questions, but he
realized time was of the essence. He had to reach
Rikki as swiftly as feasible. ''You're taking me to St.
Louis,'' he announced.

''You're crazy!'' Jeff responded.

Blade hefted the Commando. ''Pick a cycle. I'll ride
behind you. Don't try anything funny,'' he warned.

Jeff glanced at the Bowies and the sword. ''I'll take
you, but there's no way you're gonna get your friend
out in one piece.''

''You let me worry about that. Start a bike.'' Blade
waited while Jeff climbed on one of the cycles and
kicked it over. He straddled the seat behind the
Leather Knight and tapped Jeff's head with the Commando barrel. ''Let's go.''

Jeff gunned the bike, executed a U-turn, and
headed toward the east. ''This just isn't my day,'' he
muttered to himself.

5

An hour must have elapsed, possibly longer.

Rikki's arms were aching, hurting from the sustained strain of being suspended from the coarse rope. Periodically he glanced at Lex, and although she never complained or uttered a moan or other sound it was obvious that she was in extreme agony.

The crowd on the bank had grown until over 200 men and women were now gathered for the event.

But what were they waiting for? Rikki scanned the river for the umpteenth time. What was down there? He had asked Lex once, but all she said in reply was "Slither." What was this Slither? It must be some sort of creature lurking in the river's depths. Rikki twisted and gazed at the watchers on the west bank. None of them was anywhere near the dock, which was good. But firearms were in abundant evidence, which was bad. How could he free himself and Lex and escape before Slither arrived and avoid being shot? "When will Slither show up?" he asked Lexine.

She shook her head, gritting her teeth as a spasm lanced her shoulders. "Any time," she said after the pain subsided. "It comes when it feels like it, when it's hungry."

"Is it a large animal? Reptile, amphibian, mammal, what?" Rikki inquired.

"I don't know," Lex said softly. "It's not like any other animal I know."

"A mutant," Rikki stated. Ever since the war a

century before, since the environment had been
ravaged by massive dosages of radiation and deadly
chemicals and other toxins, the animal life had
altered drastically. The genetic constitution of many
forms of wildlife had been radically affected by the
radiation and chemicals; mutations had become
commonplace. Bizarre carnivorous strains had
developed. Giantism had appeared in some species.
Although in some areas, such as the inhabited major
cities still standing and in the Civilized Zone, the
mutants had been ruthlessly exterminated over the
years, there wasn't a solitary place on the continent
completely safe from the biological deviates. Or so it
was believed. One could crop up anywhere, anytime.

Like now.

There was a rustling and murmuring along the west
bank.

Rikki glanced at the assembled mob, noting they
were all staring upriver, to the north. He looked in the
same direction and spotted a commotion in the water
approximately 50 yards away.

"It's Slither!" Lex cried.

Nothing was visible on the surface of the
Mississippi except for an eight-foot wake, a rippling
of tiny waves expanding outward as a massive form
swam under the water.

"Rikki . . ." Lex said.

Rikki faced her.

"I'm sorry. So sorry. I wanted to get to know you
better," Lex told him sadly.

"We're not dead yet," Rikki reminded her.

Lex looked at the approaching monster. "Not yet,"
she said halfheartedly.

"And I'm not quite ready for the higher mansions,"
Rikki wryly declared. "So brace yourself."

"For what?"

"For this," Rikki said. As surreptitiously as
possible, he had been striving to extricate his wrists

from the ropes. After an hour of strenuous effort, constantly working his wrists back and forth, back and forth, while pulling downward at the same time, he had succeeded in loosening his right wrist. His arm wasn't free yet, but the coil of rope around his slim wrist had developed sufficient slack to enable him to escape. His exertion had torn the skin on both his wrists, and there was a crimson coating between the surface of his wrist and the rope. With the sweat from the heat and his prolonged effort, all it would take was one mighty tug and his right wrist would be free, one wrench at the right moment.

That moment was now.

The wake generated by the underwater creature was 40 yards off and closing.

The Leather Knights and others on the west bank were concentrating on the wake.

Rikki bunched his sinewy shoulder muscles and strained, adding his considerable strength to his body weight and the force of gravity. His right wrist slipped clear of the rope, leaving him dangling by his left arm. Instantly, his lean frame coiled into action. He swung his leg outward, forcing the rope to move, to carry his body out over the water. Even as the swinging motion began, his right hand reached behind his back to the brown pouch in the small of his back, the pouch containing his shuriken and other items. One of those items was his personalized kyoketsu-shogei, a double-edged five-inch knife attached to a lengthy, leather cord. At the other end of the cord was a metal ring. When still a child of ten, Rikki had become an expert with the weapon. The kyoketsu-shogei could be used in several ways: the knife alone could be wielded offensively or defensively; or, while he held the knife, the cord could be whipped around an opponent's arms or legs, rendering the enemy vulnerable to a slash from the knife; or the ring could be held in one hand and the cord whirled until the precise angle and trajectory were attained and with a flick of the wrist, a straightening of the arm, the knife flashed into an adversary's body.

The wake was 30 yards from the dock.

Rikki's sensitive fingers found the kyoketsu-shogei just as he attained the apex of his swing. He whisked it from the pouch, and as he began to sweep downward toward Lexine he slid the two-inch metal ring over his index finger while retaining a precarious grip on the knife with his thumb.

Someone on the west bank spotted the man in black's maneuver and gave a shout. "Look! What's he doing?"

The creature was only 20 yards from the dock, and a large, green hump had appeared at the center of the spreading wake.

Rikki tensed as he swung toward Lexine. The next several seconds were critical. If anyone on the west bank thought to open fire, Lex and he would be riddled before he could complete what he had in mind.

The huge thing in the Mississippi River had increased its speed, as if it sensed its prey was making a determined bid for freedom.

Lexine's green eyes widened in wonder as Rikki closed on her.

Rikki opened his legs and swiveled slightly to the left, wrapping his legs around Lexine's waist, the impact of his form against hers driving them inward, toward the bank and well clear of the dock.

The creature known as Slither was ten yards from the dock.

Rikki reached up, slashing at Lexine's rope with his knife. He freed her right wrist in one quick slash, but only partially succeeded in severing the rope on the left wrist before the people clustered on the bank went absolutely wild, cheering and screaming encouragement to the thing in the river.

Rikki glanced over his right shoulder.

A ten-foot-long serpentine neck had emerged from the murky depths. The face of the mutant was hideous, repulsive beyond belief. Two horny appendages protruded from the head, one on each side. The shape of the head was circular, with a sloping forehead and a slender, bony jaw. Its eyes were smoldering pools of ferocity. A hissing sound filled the humid air as the creature opened its wide mouth, displaying neat rows of tapered teeth. The face also had a bumpy or lumpy appearance, lending a hellish aspect to the monstrosity. The perpetually ravenous abomination closed on its targets with astonishing speed for something so gigantic.

Rikki sliced at the rope securing Lexine's left wrist again, and this time he was successful. Lexine sagged as the rope parted, and Rikki clamped his legs around her to prevent her from falling into the river. The toll on his own left arm was terrible; her added weight made it seem as if his arm would be torn from its socket. Undaunted by the torment, he looked at the creature.

Slither was almost upon them, the head not more than seven feet away and closing.

Now!

Rikki released Lexine, spreading his legs wide and dropping her into the Mississippi.

Slither, focused on the suspended man, ignored the plummeting woman.

Rikki, expecting to feel those razor fangs imbedded in his back any second, reached up and cut the rope holding his left arm. As he fell, he turned, knowing Slither had to be but inches from him.

It was. The creature was poised with open mouth, about to lunge and bite.

Rikki's feet were entering the river as he drove his right arm up and in, plunging the knife into Slither's left eye. Hot, fetid breath was on his face as the knife sank home to the hilt, and he released the ring as his body sank beneath the water. He bent at the waist and swam toward the bank, away from the mutant, heading downstream, to the south.

Something was breaking the surface of the water ahead of him. He glanced up and distinguished the outline of Lex's body. She was treading water, apparently searching for him.

There was a tremendous commotion in the river to his rear.

Rikki swam upward and reached Lexine, emerging a foot to her right.

"Thank God!" Lex exclaimed.

Rikki gulped in fresh air and gazed back at the dock.

Slither was in a blind rage, thrashing and convulsing, splashing water in every direction and driving mini-waves onto the west bank. Transfixed by the sight, the people on the bank were gaping at its death throes in amazement.

"We've got to keep moving," Rikki said to Lex. "They'll recover in a bit and be looking for us."

Lexine reached over and tenderly stroked his left cheek. "That's twice I owe you for saving my life."

"You'd do the same for me," Rikki stated, and began swimming southward.

Lexine paced him to his right, between him and the bank.

About 40 yards south of the dock, cloaking the west bank, was a thick stand of brush and trees.

"There!" Rikki said, pointing. "Hurry!"

They swam for all they were worth, and Rikki found himself admiring her endurance and ability. Not once during Slither's attack had she screamed or otherwise betrayed any hint of panic. The woman was brave, there was no doubt about that. And as a dedicated Warrior, Rikki appreciated courage the most.

Loud voices swelled from the vicinity of the dock.

Rikki and Lexine were only ten yards from the bank when a shot rang out, followed by another and another.

The water to Rikki's left was smacked by a slug, spraying water in his eyes.

Lexine reached the bank first and slid under the overhanging growth of a large bush.

Rikki joined her.

"Which way?" she asked.

Rikki continued swimming, hugging the bank. After 20 feet he spied a narrow strip of barren earth and swam toward it.

The shooting had ceased.

"They'll be after us," Lex predicted.

"I know," Rikki agreed. He climbed from the Mississippi and assisted Lex in joining him on the bank.

"What now?" Lex asked.

"Stay close," Rikki advised. He hurried to the south, hugging the river bank, sticking to the thickest undergrowth despite the difficulty in negotiating passage. Sharp thorns tore at their limbs and ripped their clothing. Pointed branches gouged them mercilessly when they weren't careful. The ground underfoot was often damp and slick. Flies and mosquitoes were everywhere, buzzing about their ears and alighting on any exposed skin. The mosquitoes, in particular, descended on them in bloodthirsty droves.

Clamorous voices could be heard well to their rear.

A stand of trees loomed ahead, and beyond the trees a field.

Rikki stopped behind one of the tall maples and peered around the trunk.

On the far side of the field was an enormous, ramshackle building.

"Do you know what that is?" Rikki asked.

Lex stood to his left. "An old warehouse, I think. Nobody uses it anymore."

"Let's go." Rikki ran across the field, dodging rocks and rusted pieces of discarded junk, Lexine on his heels.

The warehouse ran the length of two city blocks. All of the windows were broken or missing. Dust and dirt caked the exterior. A large opening beckoned on the northern side. A shattered door hung by its top hinge to the right of the opening.

Rikki darted into the dim interior and crouched to the right of the doorway, waiting for his eyes to adjust to the gloom.

Lex did likewise to the left of the door.

The floor was covered with broken crates and crumpled boxes of all shapes and sizes. Evidently, years ago, the warehouse had been systematically looted. At the west end of the structure was a glimmer of light.

Another doorway? Rikki stood and nodded, then took off, cautiously advancing between the crates and boxes and circumventing any debris in his path.

There was a faint scratching sound to their left.

"Did you hear that?" Lex asked.

Rikki nodded. He kept going, his ears alert for additional noises.

An audible patter of padded feet came from behind a wall of crates to their left.

"Something's pacing us," Lex said, stating the obvious.

Rikki hastened toward the western doorway. If it was an animal, then the light might discourage it.

The pit-pat of the mysterious feet increased their tempo.

Rikki reached behind his back and into his brown pouch. His fingers closed on empty space.

No!

Rikki's fingers probed the bottom of the pouch to be sure. It was definitely empty. But how? The answer came to him in a rush. He had neglected to properly close the pouch after removing the kyoketsu-shogei!

Undoubtedly, sometime during his swing on the rope, his plunge into the river, or his swim to the bank, the contents of his pouch had spilled out.

The stealthy pad of the feet was now coming from the top of the wall of crates.

Rikki scanned the cement floor for a possible weapon. He spotted a smashed crate on the floor ahead and ran to the pile of splintered wood. One spear-like piece drew his attention. He knelt and picked it up. About four feet long and the width of his wrist, it was flat on one end but tapered on the other.

"Rikki!" Lex shouted suddenly.

Rikki rose and spun.

A hairy visage was studying them from atop the crate wall. An extended black snout, capped with whiskers several inches long, was quivering as it sought their scent. Fiery reddish eyes fixed on them with baleful intent.

"It's a river rat," Lex said.

Rikki held his makeshift spear in his right hand. He'd been told about the rats in Thief River Falls and the Twin Cities, rats encountered by Blade, Hickok, and Geronimo. But he'd never seen them himself, and he'd never expected them to be this large. The head of the one on the crate wall was at least 12 inches in length. "Make for the west door," Rikki instructed her.

Lexine slowly edged past him and started running.

Rikki, his gaze on the rat, followed.

The river rat disappeared.

Rikki tensed. Where had the rodent gone? To summon others?

Lexine was ten feet ahead, weaving between the boxes and crates littering the aisle.

Something scraped to Rikki's left, and the slight sound saved his life.

Rikki whirled.

The rat was already in motion, leaping from the top of the wall of crates, its body as big and solid as a

Doberman's, its pronounced yellow incisors exposed as it snarled and hurtled downward.

"Rikki!" Lexine screamed.

Rikki angled his spear, the tapered tip elevated in his left hand, the flat end held in his right.

The river rat crashed toward its prey, its bulky body carrying it onto the point of the spear, the shaft tearing into its neck at the base of its hairy throat and exiting at the top of the head just behind the ears.

Rikki was slammed to the cement by the stunning impact. He ducked his head to one side as the rat's nasty teeth snapped at his eyes. His arms bulged as he struggled to retain his hold on the spear.

The rat was squealing and jerking back and forth, attempting to wrench free of the shaft.

A raking paw narrowly missed Rikki's face.

And then Lex was there, standing behind the rat, a heavy metal pipe in her hands, and she crashed her club onto the rat's skull. Once. Twice. Three times.

The rat abruptly gurgled and stiffened, vomit bursting from its vile mouth.

Rikki kicked clear of the rat and rolled to his right, his own stomach inadvertently heaving as the rat's vomit spattered onto his chest. He jumped to his feet, forcing his stomach to subside, his nose assailed by the nauseating stench of the rat's puke.

The front of his black shirt was liberally sprinkled with the disgorged matter.

Rikki quickly stripped the shirt from his chest and flung it to the floor.

"Rikki!"

Rikki glanced up at Lexine's warning.

Two more rats were perched on the crate wall.

"The west door!" Rikki yelled.

Lex took off.

Rikki raced on her heels, watching the rats over his left shoulder.

One of the rats vanished, but the other bounded along the top of the crates, pursuing the humans.

The west doorway was visible now, not more than 15 yards distant.

Rikki was beginning to think they would reach the doorway without further trouble, but he was wrong.

Lexine unexpectedly stopped, holding her club in front of her.

A rat was on the floor ahead, blocking their path to the door.

Rikki reached Lex.

The second rat was still on top of the crate wall.

Rikki grabbed the metal pipe from Lexine. "When I make my move," he said, "go for the door."

"I won't leave you," Lex declared.

"You must leave—" Rikki began.

The river rat on top of the crates abruptly screeched and launched itself into the air.

The rat blocking the exit tittered and charged.

They were working in unison!

Rikki shoved Lexine to one side. He glanced up, bracing himself, as the rat from the crates dived downward. The second rat was ten feet off, squealing as it surged forward. He clenched the heavy pipe, relying on his superb reflexes, knowing one misstep would prove fatal.

The rat from the crates reached the Warrior first.

Rikki's body was a blur as he swung the pipe and twisted aside, his blow smacking onto the rat's head, and he was already turning to confront the second rat, the pipe arching around and up and catching the second rat on the tip of its twitching nose.

There was a resounding racket as the rat from the crates struck a pile of boxes and tumbled to the hard floor, while the second rat was jarred backward by the force of Rikki's blow. It retreated several steps, shaking its head, stunned.

"Stay close!" Rikki cried, and ran toward the rat still blocking the west door.

The rat skittered to the left, snapping at the pipe as Rikki aimed another blow at its face.

Rikki swung three times, each time missing as the odious rodent skipped out of range, but he succeeded in driving the rat away from the aisle, clearing the path to the doorway.

The rat from the crate wall had recovered and was cautiously stalking them.

Lexine was searching for anything she could utilize as a weapon.

Rikki grabbed her right hand. Keeping his eyes on the rat from the wall and constantly waving the metal pipe at the other rat, he began backing toward the doorway.

Neither rodent showed any inclination to pursue them too closely.

Rikki and Lex hastily withdrew, their backs to the doorway, watching the rats.

"They don't like the light," Lex commented.

Rikki was relieved when they finally emerged from the dim warehouse. The brilliant light of the scorching sun temporarily dazzled them as they turned away from the warehouse.

"Going somewhere?" a female voice asked.

In the instant his vision cleared, Rikki perceived their predicament.

"No!" Lex exclaimed.

Terza, the blonde named Erika, Cardew, and 25 other Leather Knights were standing not eight feet away, ringing the west door, all of them pointing guns at the man in black and the redhead.

"Having fun?" Erika cracked sarcastically, her jowly jaw trembling as she snickered at the pair.

"We heard your yelling over by the trees and came to investigate," Terza said coldly. "Did the rats give you a hard time?"

Rikki didn't answer.

"So what now?" Lex demanded.

"What do you think?" Terza angrily retorted. She looked at Rikki and grinned. "You're one tough son of a bitch, you know that, dude? You've wasted three of our sisters, butchered our dogs, and even managed to escape from Slither. And now this! Now you get away from the rats! You're incredible, bastard!"

Rikki's features were like granite.

"I've decided I shouldn't be in such a rush to kill you off," Terza said.

"Should we thank you now or later?" Lex asked.

Terza glanced at Lexine. "Not you, sweetheart. I was talking to lover boy here. We can waste you anytime."

Cardew took a step toward the duo, his Browning Auto Pistol in his right hand. "Let me do it, Terza!"

Rikki moved in front of Lexine.

Terza's blue eyes narrowed. "What have we here? Don't tell me lover boy really cares about you, Lex?"

Lex didn't answer.

"Ain't this interesting," Terza remarked thoughtfully.

"Can I blow her away now?" Cardew inquired hopefully.

"No, dipshit," Terza replied. "I've got a better idea."

"Like what?" Erika queried.

"You'll see soon enough," Terza said. She nodded at Rikki. "Drop the pipe."

Rikki hesitated.

"Drop the pipe or I let Cardew blow Lex away," Terza warned him.

Rikki dropped the pipe.

Terza started laughing.

"What's so funny?" Erika asked.

"I've got 'em right where I want 'em," Terza said.

"What do you mean?" Erika inquired, perplexed.

"You'll see," Terza promised. She faced Cardew. "Listen up, airhead! Erika and I are going to split. I want you to bring those two to the library—"

"You mean the book place?" Cardew interrupted.

Terza sighed. "Yeah, mush-for-brains! The book place. Hold 'em there until I arrive."

"Will do," Cardew said.

"And Cardew," Terza added.

"Yes?"

"If they get away from you I'll have your balls hacked off and force you to eat 'em. Got it?"

Cardew swallowed hard. "I got it," he guaranteed.

"That's a good boy," Terza said. She winked at Erika and they walked off to the north across the field.

"Okay, asshole!" Cardew snapped, stepping up to Rikki and gripping his right arm. "Let's get in gear!"

Rikki hardly seemed to move other than a rippling roll of his right shoulder, but Cardew lost his hold and stumbled backward two yards before he could recover his footing.

"Damn you!" Cardew waved his Browning at Rikki. "One more fancy move out of you—"

"And what?" Lex interjected. "Terza said you're to take us to the library. You can't kill us."

"Maybe I can't kill you," Cardew said, leering maliciously at her, "but there's nothing to stop me from roughing you up a bit. Terza didn't say I had to get you there in one piece."

Lex glared at Cardew.

"So what's it gonna be, buster?" Cardew asked Rikki. "We can do this the easy way or the hard way. It's up to you."

Rikki stared at Lex for a moment, his expression unreadable. Finally he turned to Cardew. "I will not resist the trip to the library," he said.

"You're not as dumb as you look," Cardew quipped. He waved at a tall black biker and a burly one with Hispanic features. "Willy! Pedro! Get some ropes. I want these two tied up real tight!" He chuckled gleefully. "Are we gonna have some fun with you!"

"That's what I'm afraid of," Lex said under her breath.

6

"But I told you before!" Jeff whined, his beard quivering. "I don't know where they'd take your friend!"

"You must have some idea," Blade said. They were parked next to the curb on Clayton Boulevard, the cycle's motor idling. Several children were playing 40 yards to the east. A man and a woman were leaning against a building 20 yards from the children. None of them paid any attention to Blade and the biker. Why should they? Blade reasoned. With his leather vest, he must appear to be another Leather Knight. He had forced Jeff to stick to the side streets after they'd entered St. Louis. Once a pack of seven bikers had passed, but they'd only waved and continued riding. Blade had beamed at them and returned their wave.

"There are a bunch of places they could've taken him," Jeff said. "I wouldn't know where to start."

Blade, seated behind the biker on the cycle, placed his right hand on the Leather Knight's right shoulder and squeezed.

Jeff flinched and cringed.

Blade allowed his steely fingers to relax. "I'm losing my patience," he informed Jeff. "I don't care where you start looking, but you had better start right now!"

Jeff nodded and quickly accelerated from the curb. He traveled east on Clayton Boulevard, then made a left on Hanley Road, and shortly thereafter took a right on Delmar Boulevard.

Blade saw more and more people as they drew
closer to the inner city. Most of them did not wear the
distinctive black leather of the Leather Knights. He
was surprised to discover St. Louis inhabited by
thousands of residents, and he wondered why St.
Louis had been spared a direct hit during World War
III. Weren't there any primary or secondary military
targets in the St. Louis area at the time of the war? He
couldn't remember.

They passed four Leather Knights heading in the
opposite direction.

And what about the Leather Knights? Blade asked
himself. How was it the people of St. Louis allowed
themselves to be dominated by the Knights? Was it
the protection the Knights afforded? Or simply the
fact that, according to Jeff, the Leather Knights
possessed almost all of the functional firearms and an
armory of other weapons?

Up ahead loomed an intersection. Jefferson
Avenue, said a sign.

Blade's reverie deepened. He mentally compared
the Leather Knights to his Family. In the Family, men
and women equally shared the responsibilities and
duties of preserving the Home and rearing children.
Women were even accorded Warrior status. But here
in St. Louis it was different. The women evidently
lorded it over the men. Why did the men permit it? By
Jeff's own admission, the men were no longer
numerically inferior, as they had been immediately
after the "turf wars." So why didn't the men, if they
resented the treatment they were receiving, rectify
the situation? Was it because, after a century of
female control, the men were conditioned to accept it
as an indisputable fact?

Lost in thought, Blade failed to notice the three
Leather Knights parked at the side of the road, in a
small grassy stretch behind a ruined truck, just past
the intersection with Jefferson Avenue.

But Jeff did see them. One of them glanced in his direction, and Jeff silently formed the word "Help!" with his lips.

The Knights' eyes narrowed.

Jeff repeated his action, twisting the left corner of his mouth backwards after he mouthed the word.

Where did the Leather Knights obtain their motorcycles? Blade speculated silently. How were they able to maintain the bikes? Where did they find the spare parts and the fuel? Why didn't—

There was a loud rumble from the rear.

Blade looked over his left shoulder.

Three Leather Knights were rapidly bearing down on them.

Blade shifted in his seat. Why was the trio coming so fast? Were they on urgent business of some nature? Or did they suspect he was an imposter? Blade leaned forward. "Faster," he ordered. He peered over his shoulder again, expecting his command to be obeyed. Blade knew Jeff was intimidated by him, and he confidently disregarded the possibility of the craven biker resisting. Complacency, one of the cardinal errors a Warrior could commit, inevitably precipitated adversity. And this time was no exception.

Jeff gunned the motor and the cycle streaked forward from 40 to 50 miles an hour. When he reached 50, Jeff unexpectedly rammed his left elbow around, slamming it into Blade's side. At the same instant he jerked the cycle to the left, adding the momentum of the bike to his blow.

Caught completely unaware, Blade, one hand holding the Commando and the other loosely on Jeff's shoulder, was knocked from the bike. It happened so quickly he scarcely realized what occurred; one second he was riding the motorcycle, and the next he was on the road, his body rolling end over end to the south side of the highway. His body crashed into a hard object, his right side bearing the brunt of the impact. Stunned, he shook his head to clear the cobwebs, then urged to his feet as the true magnitude of his dilemma hit home.

The three Leather Nights, guns drawn, were 30 yards off and roaring toward him.

Jeff had accelerated after dumping Blade, and was now hightailing it to the east.

Damn!

Blade realized the Commando was still in his hands. He'd instinctively clasped it to his chest as he tumbled from the cycle. Thank the Spirit his stupidity wasn't total!

The three Leather Knights began firing. Two of them had revolvers, the third a rifle.

Blade crouched and fired a burst from the Commando.

One of the Knights screamed as his chest was cut to ribbons and he was flipped from his cycle. The bike crashed to the road and slid for 20 feet, sparks flying from underneath, before it came to a rest.

The two remaining bikers veered to the other side of the road, vanishing behind an overgrown hedge.

Doubledamn!

Blade rose and turned, scanning the nearby buildings for the best cover. His left foot caught on something and he sprawled to the ground.

What the—?

It was a peculiar object, sort of a metallic reddish mushroom, with caps of some sort on both sides and a curved top. The red paint was peeled and faded. The lower end of the object was imbedded in the concrete curb. It was the thing he'd hit after falling from the bike. What in the world was it?

A shot cracked from behind the hedge and the sidewalk near Blade's eyes was chipped by a bullet, fragments spraying outwards.

Blade felt a cement chip strike his left cheek,

drawing blood and he leaped up and ran for a large
tree ten feet away.

The two Leather Knights opened up at random.

Blade reached the tree and ducked from sight. What
now? He was afoot, in enemy territory, and he had no
idea where Rikki was being held—if Rikki was still
alive—in St. Louis, an immense city impossible for
one man to adequately cover.

The Leather Knights had stopped shooting.

Maybe Hickok had been right. Maybe both of them
should have ventured into the city.

Far off, to the east, appeared more bikers.

Terrific!

It was probably Jeff with reinforcements. So now he
had Knights behind him and Knights in front of him.

What to do?

Blade peeked around the trunk of the tree. All was
quiet in the vicinity of the hedge. He darted from the
tree and raced to the corner of the street. A weather-
ravaged sign indicated this was the junction of
Delmar and 23rd. He jogged to his right, staying on
the worn sidewalk, seeking a hiding place or somewhere he could make a stand. He lost track of the
distance he ran as he took one side street after
another, first in one direction, then in another, hoping
to lose the Leather Knights. He could hear their bikes
to his rear and to his left. They were probably
conducting a sweep.

Over a dozen residents saw him run by, but none of
them displayed any inclination to interfere with a
bronzed giant carting a machine gun.

An alley appeared on his right, its entrance filled
with rusted trash cans and other debris.

Blade paused and surveyed the street he was on. He
was alone. Perfect! He hurried into the alley and slid
behind a pile of moldy boxes and piled garbage.

None too soon.

Two Leather Knights thundered into view, slowly

cruising the street, each biker concentrating on one side.

Blade flattened against the west wall of the alley and tensed. Would they stop and investigate the alley?

The pair of Knights, a woman and a man, a "sister" and a "stud," drew abreast of the alley.

The woman braked.

Blade could see them through a crack between the boxes.

The woman was eyeing the alley speculatively, apparently considering whether to check it out.

The man stopped and glanced at the woman. "Come on," he said. "No one would hide in that crap."

"You never know," the woman stated. She turned off her bike and dismounted.

Blade placed his finger on the Commando's trigger.

The male Knight sighed and did the same.

Blade focused on the slim opening dividing the boxes and garbage at the mouth of the alley.

The sister drew an automatic pistol in her left hand and cautiously advanced.

The stud was ten feet behind her, his revolver still in its holster on his right hip, certain they were wasting their time.

Blade made a calculated decision. If the women ruled the Leather Knights, then one of them was his best bet for supplying the information he required.

This woman was of average height, about five feet six, and in the neighborhood of 115 pounds. She wore a black vest and black shorts, revealing an ample cleavage and very shapely legs. Her hair was a dusty blonde, her facial features lean but attractive. The automatic was aimed straight ahead and her brown eyes alertly probed the alley as she neared it.

Blade held his breath and clutched the Commando. The woman reached the mouth of the alley. She took a tentative step forward and glanced to the east.

Blade sprang, sweeping the Commando stock around and in, catching the Leather Knight in the abdomen.

The woman doubled over as the stock plowed into her stomach. She gasped and dropped the pistol, dazed, out of breath.

The stud's face had betrayed his astonishment as the sister was struck, and now he went for his revolver, clawing at his holster, frantically attempting to draw.

Blade, thankful his opponent lacked even a third of Hickok's speed, raised the Commando and fired over the woman's back.

His hand still striving to draw his gun, the Knight was hit in the head by the burst. His eyes and nose caved inward in a spray of red and he toppled to the street.

No time to lose!

Blade clipped the woman on her jaw as she took a step backwards. She moaned and sagged to the ground, unconscious.

If only he knew how to ride a motorcycle!

Blade knelt and lifted the woman in his brawny left arm. He effortlessly draped her over his broad shoulders and wheeled, making for the gloomy interior of the alley. His nose was assailed by absolutely revolting odors, almost prompting him to gag. Avoiding soggy mounds of garbage, his boots squishing with every step, he reached a low wall at the end of the alley. The top of the wall was six feet from the ground.

The Leather Knight groaned.

Blade slung his Commando over his right shoulder, then leaped, his arms clearing the top of the wall up to his elbows. He easily pulled himself over the brick wall, with the woman over his shoulder, and dropped to the ground on the other side.

A vacant parking lot fronted the alley wall.

Blade unslung his Commando and began walking across the lot. Tumble-down buildings bordered the parking lot on three sides, possibly former apartment dwellings now in a state of terminal decay. The north side of the lot was adjacent to a street.

Would the Leather Knights be hunting for him in this area? Or had they already done so and departed?

Blade glanced in both directions when he reached the street. Good! No one was in sight. On the other side of the street rose a three-story brick building, obviously uninhabited to judge by the number of broken windows and its grubby appearance. He jogged across the street and up a flight of cement steps to the landing. The door was slightly ajar, and he eased it open with his right foot. The hinges creaked as the door swayed outward. He crept inside, keeping his back to the wall, listening for sounds.

All was quiet.

Blade resisted an urge to sneeze. There was a lot of dust in the air and a musty scent about the place. He was in a wide hallway leading into the dim recesses of the building. A flight of stairs to the right led to the floors above.

The woman was moaning.

Blade opted for the stairs. He took three at a stride as he climbed to the third floor. This floor received considerable light through its missing or cracked windows, illuminating the rooms with a diluted, dusty haze. He entered a room providing a vista of the street below and deposited his prisoner on the floor, near the one window, propping her against the wall to the left of the sill. He took a step back and aimed the Commando at her head.

She woke up.

Blade had to admire her reaction. There wasn't a hint of fear in her brown eyes, just a trace of surprise and unconcealed defiance.

"Who the hell are you?" the blonde demanded angrily.

Blade grinned and wagged the barrel of the Commando. "I'll ask the questions, if you don't mind," he said.

The blonde shrugged. "Suit yourself, slime! You've got the upper hand, for now anyway."

"How are you feeling?" Blade asked.

She gingerly rubbed her sore chin. "I'll live, no thanks to you."

"What's your name?"

"Mel," she answered, examining him from head to toe.

"Mel? That's a strange name for a woman," Blade said.

"It's short for Melissa," Mel revealed.

"I'll get right to the point, Mel," Blade said. "I'm looking for a friend of mine, a short man dressed in black with what you might describe as Oriental features. Have you seen him?"

Mel's face tightened. "No," she responded defensively.

Blade moved the Commando closer to her facee. "You're lying. I don't have time to play games with you. Either you cooperate, or I'll take this gun and smash your teeth in."

Mel studied him a moment. "I believe you would at that," she said. "And I sure don't want to call your bluff. My teeth are important to me." She smirked and moved her mouth back and forth. "I'm lucky I have any left after that sock you gave me."

"So where is the man in black?" Blade pressed her. "Have you seen him?"

"Yep. Just a short while ago. Terza hung him and Lex out for Slither, but they escaped." Mel laughed at the memory. "No one's ever got away from Slither before! Terza was ready to shit bricks!"

"You say they escaped?" Blade inquired hopefully.

"Yes and no," Mel said.

"How do you mean?"

"They got away from Slither, but then they were caught again nearby," Mel elaborated.

"Where are they now?"

"Terza is holding them at the library. I don't know why. She probably has something special in store for your friend. Maybe she'll feed him to Grotto," Mel disclosed.

"What is this Grotto I keep hearing about?" Blade inquired.

Mel seemed to shiver. "Grotto is one of the things— you know, like Slither—those mutant things we've got all over the place."

Blade pondered for a minute. "How far are we from the library?"

"Not far," Mel said.

"How long would it take us to get there?" Blade asked.

"Not long."

"Be specific," Blade instructed her. "Fifteen minutes? A half an hour? What?"

Mel appeared to be confused. "What's a minute?" she questioned him.

Blade chuckled. He kept forgetting! People living outside the Home or the Civilized Zone existed, for the most part, in profound ignorance. Public education was a thing of the past. Few books survived because most had been destroyed in the century since World War III, many used as kindling for fires during the frigid winters. Here and there, isolated pockets of humanity retained minimal knowledge of the cultural and scientific achievements extant at the outbreak of the war. "A minute is a measure of time," Blade told her. "Don't any of the Leather Knights own a watch?"

Mel shook her head. "Nope. Should we?"

"No," Blade stated. "I guess not. It's hard to imagine a watch lasting a hundred years." A puzzling thought occurred to him. If most of the Leather Knights were as ignorant as Melissa, then how were they able to maintain their motorcycles? "About your bikes," he said.

"What about them?"

"Where do you obtain them?" Blade queried. "Where do you get them from?"

"We get them from our head when we take the oath," Mel answered.

"Your leader gives them to you when you take your oath of admittance?"

"That's what I said," Mel declared.

"But where does your leader get them from? Do you have your own mechanics?" Blade asked.

Mel nodded. "A lot of the Knights can fix their own bikes."

"Where do they learn to do it? Where do they get the parts?" Blade inquired.

"As far as fixing the bikes goes," Mel said, "we sort of pick it up from each other. The parts we get from the Technics."

"The Technics?"

"Yeah. They live up north, in a city called . . ." She paused, trying to recall the name she wanted.

"Is it a big city?" Blade goaded her. "A small city? What?"

"I've never been there," Melissa said. "But I heard it's real big. I remember something about wind . . ."

"The Windy City? Chicago?" Blade ventured.

"That's it! Chicago," Mel confirmed.

"Who are these Technics?"

"I don't know much about them," Mel said. "Except that they control a lot of turf north of us and they're very powerful."

"Why do they supply you with parts for your cycles?" Blade asked.

"Because of the pact."

"What pact?"

"There's a pact between us Knights and the Technics. They've agreed to help us out with our bikes, and we help them by controlling this territory and making sure the Reds don't get past us."

"I had a run-in with the Reds," Blade disclosed. "Who are they?"

"The Reds? They're the Commies," Mel said matter-of-factly.

"Communists? These Reds are Communists? Are they Russians?" Blade inquired in an excited tone.

"I don't know nothing about no Russians," Mel responded. "I only know we've been calling them Reds or Commies since I was a little girl. They're our enemies. They spy on us a lot with those copters of theirs, and we take potshots at them whenever we get the chance. Mostly they stay on their side of the river and we stay on ours."

"So the Communists control the land east of the Mississippi?" Blade probed.

"They control a lot of it, I hear," Mel affirmed. "The Technics control some too. And there are other groups." Her voice lowered. "The Dragons are the ones you want to avoid. I've been told stories about them you wouldn't believe!" She trembled.

"Where are these Dragons located?"

"Way to the east of here," Mel replied. " But south of the Reds."

Blade contemplated her revelations. He'd never heard of the Dragons or the Technics before. But the Communists were another matter. The Family's leaders had often wondered what happened to the Russians after the war. Why hadn't the U.S.S.R. taken over the U.S.? After the devastating nuclear exchange, not to mention all of the chemical and conventional weapons employed during the war, the remnants of the U.S. Government had evacuated the populace and reorganized their forces in the Midwest and Rocky Mountain region, locating the new capital at Denver, Colorado. They had braced for a Russian invasion, an eventuality which had never transpired. Except for vague rumors, the Russians had never materialized. The U.S. Government had devolved into a dictatorship known as the Civilized Zone, and only recently had the people of the Civilized Zone reclaimed their heritage and asserted their independence. During the intervening century, as the years rolled on and the Russians never attacked, the people in the Civilized Zone had forgotten about their former adversaries. But if, as Melissa asserted, the Russians did control a section of the U.S., then the Civilized Zone and all of the other members of the Freedom Federation must be warned! The Family, the Cavalry in the Dakota territory, the Flathead Indians in Montana and the Moles in their subterranean city in northern Minnesota must all be alerted to the Soviet presence.

Melissa was waiting for Blade to speak.

"Has anyone ever gone into Red territory?" Blade asked.

"Years ago some tried," Mel answered.

"What did they discover?"

"Nothing. They never came back," she said.

Blade stared out the window, noting the light was fading. "I want you to take me to the library where my friend is being held."

Mel started to rise.

"Not now!" Blade said. "After it's dark we'll leave."

She resettled herself on the floor. "Fine by me. But you'd be doing yourself a favor if you took off. There's no way you're going to save him."

"I've got to try."

"Any last words you want me to say when we plant you?"

7

So what the blazes was he supposed to do? Count the stars?

Still smarting at being left behind to babysit the SEAL, Hickok was seated on the highway, his back resting against the undercarriage of the transport, a canteen on the ground near his left knee. His rifle, a Navy Arms Henry Carbine in 44-40 caliber, was propped against the vehicle to his right.

Talk about boring!

The night sky was rich with stars, a fantastic display of the mightiness of creation, splendid galaxies traversing their ordained course much like the prescribed circuits of electrons on the subatomic level of reality. Hickok experienced a rare sense of awe as he admired the spectacular heavens. He recollected his schooling days at the Home, the survivalist compound in northwestern Minnesota constructed by Kurt Carpenter immediately prior to World War III. Carpenter's close-knit descendants— the Family, as they called themselves—were dedicated to insuring every child in the Home received a quality education. With the Family Elders as Teachers, the school developed self-reliant personalities with noble, moral character. Many times, Hickok remembered, he'd been told there was a grand design to the scheme of things. The Elders wisely taught there was a distinct purpose to every element of creation. Now, as he gazed at the sea of stars and was impressed by the immensity of the cosmos, Hickok began to wonder what his purpose was in life. How did he fit into the scheme of things? The only special talent he possessed was in handling firearms, especially handguns. The others might label him as too cocky, but he positively believed that nobody, but *nobody*, could match him with a revolver. His expertise was inherent, a totally unconscious aptitude on his part. The Family Elders taught thankfulness for the gifts bestowed by the Maker. Was it possible, he asked himself, his gift was his ambidextrous ability with revolvers? Was it conceivable the Maker had placed him on this planet to be exactly what he was: one of the Family's preeminent Warriors, devoted to safeguarding the Home and protecting his loved ones?

Was it likely?

Hickok shook his head, clearing his mind, bemused by his train of thought. He'd never really considered the issue much before, and now was hardly the time to start. The only reason he gave it any attention at all was because of the sermon given by the Family's spiritual sage, Joshua, shortly before his departure to St. Louis. Why was it, Hickok wondered, folks like Josh always had to analyze everything to death? Why couldn't they just accept things for what they were and leave it go at that?

The gunman chuckled. It was way over his head, that was for sure! Oh, he could recollect a few details from his Family science courses about the formation of galaxies and the formation of matter and stuff like that, but what good did it do him? All he ever wanted out of life was a cool breeze, his Colts in his hands, and his wife and son by his side.

What else mattered?

Hickok relaxed, listening to the sound of the insects and nocturnal critters emanating from the forest on both sides of the highway. There were crickets by the thousands, tree frogs, an occasional owl, and others. Once, far off in the dark depths of the woods, arose the challenging roar of some large carnivore.

Maybe this waiting wasn't so bad after all.

At least he'd catch up on his shut-eye.

The forest suddenly became quiet, absolutely silent, not a creature so much as fluttering its wings.

Hickok was instantly alert. He grabbed the Henry and rose, staring into the gloomy vegetation on his side of the highway.

The silence could only mean one thing.

Something was prowling through the woods, something deadly, something the other animals were deathly afraid of.

But what? A cougar? Was this neck of the woods part of their range? How about a bear? Or worse? One of the ravenous, mutated horrors proliferating since the Big Blast? Or the deadliest killer of all?

Man.

Hickok crouched and moved to the edge of the road, his head cocked to one side.

An unnerving hush enveloped the forest.

Was something stalking him?

The gunman flattened, knowing the lower he was, the less of an outline he presented, the less of a target he was. At night, the surest way to detect someone or something in your vicinity was to drop to the ground and scan the near horizon for the fluid movement of a figure silhouetted by the backdrop of the sky.

Nothing.

Which meant whatever was out there was lurking in the trees.

So!

Sneaky bunch of varmints!

Hickok crawled toward the treeline, his knees and elbows propelling him forward. He reached the base of a mighty oak and stood, flattening against the tree.

So far, so good!

The next move was up to whatever was out there.

A branch snapped off to his left.

Something crackled to the right.

There was definitely more than one of them!

Hickok could feel the rough bark of the tree through his buckskin shirt. A stub or a broken section of a branch was gouging his lower back.

Another twig crunched to the left.

No doubt about it! They were making too much noise to be critters. No self-respecting animal would be so klutzy sneaking up on a meal.

Had to be humans.

Or something similar.

A black form detached itself from the wall of vegetation not ten feet to Hickok's left.

A second later, a second shape did likewise on the gunman's right.

Upright.

Bipeds, as Plato would say.

Men. Or women.

Lugging lengthy sticks in their hands. Sticks . . . or guns.

Time for a surprise party!

Hickok raised the Henry and aimed at the figure to his left. The 44.40 boomed, and the shadow disappeared. He spun, sighting on the middle of the form to his right and pulling the trigger. The Henry's stock slammed into his shoulder, and the silhouette screamed as it was brutally flung backward to the turf.

Two down!

Hickok dodged behind the sheltering oak, and not a moment too soon.

A machine gun opened up from the other side of the highway, its heavy slugs biting into the tree in the exact spot the gunman had vacated.

Someone out there was a darn good shot!

Hickok darted into the brush, avoiding trees and

tangled bushes, treading carefully to avoid tripping on
a rock or limb on the ground, heading deeper into the
forest. The SEAL was locked up tight as the
proverbial drum, and there was no way these dudes
would be able to bust inside. So his best bet was to
lead them on a merry chase, a chase away from
the transport. Considering he was obviously outnumbered, it was the sensible thing to do. The
murky forest would reduce their mobility and limit
their effectiveness.

Someone was crashing through the undergrowth to
his right.

Hickok fell to his knees, peering through the
vegetation.

A bulky form was foolishly plowing through a
thicket eight yards away.

What a cowchip!

Hickok aimed at the advancing figure and fired, the
44-40 thundering in his ears.

Cowchip screeched and dropped, uttering an awful
gurgling sound as he thrashed on the ground.

Hickok kept going.

From the rear, from the direction of the SEAL, a
man began barking orders.

Hickok stopped, perplexed. What language was the
rascal using? It sure wasn't English. Or Spanish. It
was like no language he'd ever heard before.

The underbrush was alive with the passage of black
figures seeking the Warrior.

So much for catching up on his shut-eye!

Hickok reached a rocky knoll and quickly climbed
to the top. A ring of small boulders furnished
excellent concealment and an ideal spot to defend
himself.

Let them come!

They did. Four, five, six forms slowly moving
toward the knoll.

How the blazes did they know where he was?

The figures stopped and abruptly vanished.

Hickok realized they had gone to ground or were hiding behind trees or other cover.

More orders were shouted in the strange tongue.

There was a rustling and a series of metallic clicks from the woods below the knoll.

Now what?

A shadow appeared for an instant from behind the trees, and there was a loud whooshing sound.

Hickok sighted the Henry, but the form receded behind the tree before he could fire.

There was a muffled thump followed by a strange hissing noise as something struck the top of the knoll five feet below the rim.

What the blazes was going on?

Wispy smoke tendrils began filling the night air, spiraling upward, assuming the proportions of a hovering gray cloud.

More distinct whooshing sounds came from the forest below the knoll, one after the other, nine in all.

More thumping noises ringed the knoll.

The mysterious gray cloud grew bigger and bigger, completely enshrouding the knoll.

Confounded by the odd sounds and wary of the clouds, Hickok eased over the boulders and crawled toward the woods. The gray cloud descended to ground level. Caught by the smoky substance, the gunman almost gagged as he breathed in his first mouthful. An intense burning sensation erupted in his throat and chest and his eyes started watering. He coughed and held his breath, rolling down the knoll, trying to get well out of the cloud before he would need to take another breath.

Was it a poison gas of some kind?

Hickok resisted an impulse to gag, his lungs heaving. He rolled into a boulder and was jarred by the impact. Unable to control himself, he accidentally inhaled.

It was as if he had swallowed a handful of red hot coals.

Hickok doubled over as his body was rocked with painful spasms, his breathing impaired, his breaths coming in great, ragged gasps. The burning sensation in his chest increased, becoming acute, nearly unbearable.

Poison gas! It had to be!

The Warrior staggered to his feet and stumbled toward the trees. Fortunately, the lower he went the thinner the cloud became, until he reached the bottom of the knoll and clear, fresh air.

Hickok inhaled the cool, crisp air, endeavoring to pump the poison from his system.

Black figures were advancing toward him from the woods.

The lousy varmints! They couldn't take him fair and square! They had to resort to their poison gas! They may have succeeded in killing him, but they had horse patties for brains if they expected him to lie down and die without so much as a whimper of protest! By the Spirit! He'd show them what it meant to tangle with a Warrior! Despite the reluctance of his limbs to comply with his mental commands, he managed to raise the Henry.

Someone was yelling in the unfamiliar language.

Hickok squeezed the trigger, his effort rewarded by the collapse of one of the approaching forms.

That'd show the curs!

His eyes moist from his copious tears, his arms feeling leaden and burdened by the heavy Henry, Hickok opted for a change in tactics.

If it was his time to buy the farm, he might as well go in style!

Hickok dropped the Henry and drew his Pythons, his arms sluggish, his draw a mere fraction of its normal speed. His feet shuffled forward, directly at his foes.

There were more of them than he'd imagined. Ten or more, closing in from all sides.

Why weren't they shooting?

Hickok swiveled the Colts, going dead center on one of the figures. The Pythongs cracked and bucked in his unsteady hands.

Another opponent bit the dust.

Why weren't they returning his fire?

Hickok turned, wobbly, and fired his right Python. Yet another form screamed and fell.

What was going on? Why didn't they fight back?

Hickok's ears detected a slight rustling behind him, and he tried to swing around to confront the source.

He never made it.

The gunman felt a hard object slam into his head, and he was knocked forward onto his hands and knees. He wheezed as he struggled to stand, but before he could rise someone leaped onto his back and strong hands gripped his blonde locks and yanked.

Hickok grunted as his head was snapped backwards.

What were they trying to do? Break his neck?

Something soft and reeking of an obnoxious odor was pressed over the gunman's nostrils and mouth.

What the—!

Hickok knew they were expecting him to try and stand, to toss the attacker from his back. Instead, he did the opposite, allowing his body to pitch forward, hoping the unexpected motion would dislodge or disorient the person on his back.

He was right.

The man on the gunman's back lost his hold and toppled to the left.

Hickok rolled to the right, extending his Colts.

There was more shouting in the weird lingo.

A bulky form reared above the Warrior.

Hickok let the vermin have it. Both Pythons from

point-blank range.

The blurry figure was hurtled backward by the impact.

Hickok rose to his knees, relieved because his vision was beginning to return.

They converged on the gunman in a rushing mass, piling on him from everywhere. Powerful hands grabbed his arms and legs. Someone had him by the hair again.

Hickok was knocked onto his back. A knee rammed into his stomach. Fingers were tugging on the Colts, striving to strip them from his hands. The obnoxious odor penetrated his nostrils as the soft material was again pressed over his mouth and nose.

What were they doing?

Hickok thrashed and heaved for all he was worth, knowing he was dead if he didn't break free.

There were simply too many of them.

The gunman's last thoughts were of his wife and son.

8

"On your feet. It's time to leave."

"You'll never make it."

"You let me worry about that," Blade said. He gazed out the window at the night sky. Darkness had enveloped the city long ago. Lacking public utilities, St. Louis was plunged into an inky abyss. The towering skyscrapers seemed like brooding monoliths. Streets and alleys resembled lighter ribbons in a tapestry of black fabric. All outside activity ceased as residents took to their dwellings, families to their homes and singles, for the most part, to their apartments. After he had questioned Mel, Blade had learned more concerning the Leather Knights and their domination of St. Louis. Because structurally sound houses were at a premium, the Knights had ruled only families could reside in individual homes. The single men and women tended to live in clusters, in apartment buildings relatively unscathed by the ravages of time and the elements.

Blade glanced down at the woman. "Take me directly to the library where they are holding my friend. One false move and I'll slit your throat."

"You sure have a way with the ladies," Melissa quipped.

Blade stepped away from the window and motioned with the Commando. "Let's go."

Melissa slowly stood, her legs cramped from her prolonged sitting.

"Do the Knights patrol the streets at night?" Blade asked.

"Yeah," Mel replied. "But the patrols are few and far between."

"I would think you'd want to insure the Reds don't sneak into the city after dark," Blade said. "You must have a lot of patrols."

Mel snickered. "After dark? Are you nuts? The . . . things . . . come out after dark. The Reds aren't any more likely than we are to run around at night. It's bad enough having to look out for the mutants in the daytime. At night it's worse because you can't see them coming."

"Haven't you cleared them out of the city?" Blade inquired.

"We've tried," Mel answered. "But it's not that easy. The giant rats are impossible to control. There are too many of them. Some of the things, like Slither and Grotto, are too big to handle. And although we can keep many of the monsters out during the day, some of them sneak back into the city at night looking for food. Most people stay inside at night with their doors locked. And one of the first rules you learn as a child is this: never go outside at night alone." She paused. "No, you don't have to worry about running into anybody this late at night."

"Good. Then we should reach the library without any problem," Blade said.

"Yeah," Mel cracked. "Unless we run into one of the . . . things."

"I'll protect you," Blade assured her.

"I hope so," Melissa stated. "Being eaten alive by one of those ugly suckers isn't high on my list of things to do."

Blade nodded toward the doorway. "Walk slowly. And remember what I told you. Don't try anything funny."

Mel moved to the doorway, stopped, peered into

the hallway, then walked from the room.

Blade stayed glued to her heels.

They descended the stairs to the ground floor and reached the front door.

Melissa hesitated, her right hand on the doorknob.

"Let's go," Blade goaded her.

Mel took a deep breath, squared her shoulders, and opened the door.

The night air was cool and crisp.

Blade followed the Leather Knight as she hurried down the cement steps to the street and took a left. She kept to the middle of the streets as she proceeded into the murky bowels of St. Louis, constantly scanning the surrounding buildings for any hint of movement or the slightest sound. He lost track of the route they took. The few remaining street signs were vague markers impossible to read in the eerie gloom. Ominous rustling noises and scratching sounds emanated from gutted structures and darker alleys.

Melissa drew up short as a loud hissing issued from the mouth of a gaping alley.

Blade prodded her with the Commando barrel. "Keep going."

"I don't like this," Melissa muttered nervously. "I don't like this one bit!"

Blade nudged her again. "I'm right behind you."

Mel glanced over her left shoulder. "I hope Terza feeds you to Grotto!" she snapped. She resumed their journey.

Blade stared into the impenetrable alley as he passed, but he couldn't see a thing.

The sooner they reached the library, the better!

Mel increased her pace, evidently equally anxious to reach their destination.

Headlights appeared at the far end of the street they were on.

Blade gripped Melissa's right shoulder and shoved her toward the left sidewalk. "Take cover!" he ordered.

Melissa blinked.

Blade pushed her, causing her to stumble and almost fall. "Take cover!" he repeated, his tone a threatening growl.

Melissa crossed to the sidewalk and crouched in a dim doorway.

Blade joined her, flattening his powerful frame against the right jamb. "Don't make a sound!" he warned her.

Blade ran his finger along the Commando trigger.

It was a Leather Knight patrol, five riders moving at a leisurely pace, packed close together, every one of them armed to the teeth.

Blade watched Melissa, wondering if she would betray him.

The patrol passed without incident.

Blade waited until the five bikers were out of sight to the west. "Thanks for not giving me away," he said.

Melissa rose. "Don't thank me," she said angrily. "I just didn't want to get caught in a crossfire."

Blade stepped into the street. "Okay. Lead out."

Mel frowned and took to the street again.

Blade's mind drifted. Even after he freed Rikki, he was still facing a major problem—namely, how to raise the SEAL to an upright position. If the transport weren't flat on its side, he might be able to use leverage by inserting a huge board or limb between the SEAL and the ground. But as it was, leverage was impractical. Then how could they manage it? Without the vehicle, none of the Warriors would be able to return to the Home. The distance was too great and the dangers insurmountable.

There must be a way!

Melissa led the Warrior ever inward, block after circuitous block. The gigantic skyscrapers blotted out the stars overhead. Instead of being freshly invigorating, the night air became dank and foul. The residents of St. Louis were not meticulous about their personal or civic hygiene; piles of rotting garbage and rodent-infested trash filled most of the alleys.

Just when Blade began to doubt the Leather Knight was really leading him to the library, she stopped and coughed.

"There it is," Mel said, pointing across the street.

Blade could distinguish a huge building about 20 yards off, utterly devoid of life and light. "There aren't any guards," he whispered suspiciously.

"Why should there be?" Mel countered. "Who'd want to break into the library? There's nothing there but a few moldy books."

"But what about keeping your prisoners from breaking out?" Blade asked.

Melissa laughed. "No way."

"You're that confident?"

"No one busts out,' Mel assured him.

"You don't know Rikki-Tikki-Tavi," Blade said.

Melissa took a step away. "Well, you won't be needing me any longer."

Blade covered her with the Commando. "Yes, I will."

"But I brought you here like you wanted," she protested.

"Now you'll take me to where they're holding my friend," Blade told her.

"And what if I don't?" Mel challenged him. "What are you gonna do. Shoot me? The noise will attract the others."

Blade patted his left Bowie. "I could always use this," he said. "Or this," he added, touching Rikki's katana.

Melissa got the message. She turned and headed for the library, moving cautiously, manifestly nervous.

Blade sensed something was wrong. She had been antsy on the way here, true, but not like this. She was acting . . . different. Had she lied? Were there guards posted outside the library? Was she attempting to lead him into an ambush? Was it likely to—

A machine gun opened up from the direction of the library.

"No!" Melissa screamed, throwing her arms up. "It's me! Mel! Don't shoot!"

Her cry came too late.

The street around them was struck by a zigzag pattern of slugs.

Blade heard Mel grunt as she was hit. She doubled over and fell forward, and in that instant he spotted the flash of the gunner hiding at the top of the library steps.

So! She had tried to trap him!

Blade was caught in the open. If he endeavored to reach cover, the guard would have ample opportunity to fill him with lead. In the microsecond it took him to perceive the threat and evaluate his position, Blade decided on the timeworn couse of action proven in innumerable conflicts: the best defense is invariably a good offense. He charged the library, weaving back and forth, firing from the hip, going for the gunflash on the library steps.

A bullet nicked his left thigh.

Blade executed a diving leap for the tarmac, scraping his elbows and the katana's scabbard as he rolled to the left and came up on his knees, the Commando pointed at the library stairs. He fired a burst in a sweeping arc.

Someone shrieked, and a moment later a woman toppled from the deeper shadows at the top of the steps and tumbled to the sidewalk.

Damn!

They'd probably aroused every Leather Knight in St. Louis!

Blade rose and ran to the prone form on the sidewalk. The woman had been shot in the chest and was oozing blood from a cavity where her right breast had once been. He turned and raced up the stairs to the glass doors.

Please let them be open!

He gripped one of the handles and yanked, and was rewarded by the door flinging outward.

The interior of the library was, if anything, even darker than the outside.

Where the hell would Rikki be?

Blade ran down a wide corridor, his footsteps creating a hollow echo as he pounded from door to door, his boots smacking on the tiles, searching for his fellow Warrior. Four doors opened into stark offices. The fifth revealed a massive chamber filled with bookshelves. Most of the shelves were empty.

Where could he be? Had Melissa lied about Rikki being here? He didn't have much time! The other Knights were certain to investigate the gunfire and discover Melissa and the dead guard.

Where?

Blade reached a stairwell and, on a hunch, darted into it and began descending to the lower levels of the library. If the Leather Knights had converted a portion of the library into a dungeon or jail, logic dictated the holding cells might be located in the basement.

If the library even had a basement!

Blade reached a landing and paused, listening.

The night was deathly quiet.

Strange.

They should have found the bodies by now. Why wasn't there an uproar, or at least the sounds of pursuit?

Very strange.

Blade opened the landing door and found himself in a dingy hallway. It branched to the left and the right.

Terrific!

Which branch should he take?

Blade opted for the right branch and jogged along the hallway until he reached a closed door. He grabbed the doorknob, tensed, and pushed the door open.

Another damn office!

Annoyed, Blade continued his hunt. He ran another 15 yards and spied a door to his left. The doors, constructed of wood and painted or stained a pale yellow, stood out against the gloomy hallway walls.

Here goes nothing!

Blade shoved the door open.

Bingo!

This room gave every indication of being a recent fabrication. The walls were made from brick, and the floor was barren dirt. A musty scent permeated the chamber. The room was circular, perhaps 30 feet in diameter. And secured to the far wall across from the doorway, their arms locked in chains, were a man and a woman.

Rikki and another.

Blade easily recognized his small companion, despite the lack of light.

"Rikki!" Blade called. "Are you all right?"

There was a muffled noise from the other side of the chamber.

Blade took a step forward. He could see Rikki and the woman thrashing, striving to slip free from their chains, and he could hear the chains clanking against the brick wall. There was black patches over Rikki's and the woman's mouths.

They were gagged!

"Hang on!" Blade yelled. "I'll have you out of there in no time."

The huge Warrior started toward the hapless pair. He reached the center of the room.

Rikki-Tikki-Tavi was surging against his chains like a madman.

"Calm down!" Blade said. "I'm almost there! I'll get you out."

"No, you won't," said a harsh feminine voice from above.

Even as Blade glanced upward, something heavy fell onto his broad shoulders and covered his arms and torso, pinning his arms to his sides, rendering the Commando useless.

Light flooded the chamber.

A net! He was snared in a net!

Blade caught a glimpse of a balcony encircling the room, a balcony swarming with Leather Knights. He strained his arms, attempting to loosen the net, to bring the Commando into play.

His effort was wasted.

Leather Knights, men and women, poured into the chamber through three recessed doorways. They rushed to the middle of the chamber and tackled the Warrior, tightening the net until movement was impossible.

Blade, mentally berating his stupidity, wound up flat on his back staring through the strands of the nylon net at a dozen hostile faces. Now he knew what Rikki had been trying to do: warn him about the trap.

The Leather Knights parted and a brunette bearing a scar under her right eye appeared, standing over the Warrior's head. She was grinning in triumph. "Ain't you the big one?" she asked playfully.

Blade refused to respond.

"The name is Terza," she said. "And you must be the friend of Lex's hunk! Am I right?"

Lex's hunk?

Terza chuckled. "The strong, silent type, huh? Fine. There's no need to talk right now. You'll do enough talking later. I can promise you that!" She paused, then kicked the net with her right foot. "Not bad, eh? Jeff told us all about you. We knew you were coming in to save your buddy. Did you think we'd let you walk right in here and take him?"

Blade didn't answer. He was feeling monumentally dumb.

"If so," Terza continued, "you ain't as bright as you look." She laughed. "Why don't you get a good night's sleep, and we'll get down to cases in the morning." She glanced at a man with a blue Mohawk. "Cardew, why don't you tuck him in?"

"My pleasure" Cardew replied.

Blade saw the biker named Cardew walk beyond his line of vision. What was the Knight planning to do?

"Nighty-night!" Cardew said, from just beyond Blade's head.

What the—

Something crashed into Blade's face, something hard, smashing his right cheek and jarring his jaw.

Blade heaved, his arms bulging, vainly attempting to remove the net.

"One more time," Cardew stated.

The bastard must be using a club! Blade tried to roll to the left, away from Cardew's blow.

They mustn't knock him out! If they succeeded, they'd disarm him! He'd be at their mercy! They'd be . . .

9

He thought he was going to puke!

The gunman felt as if he were bobbing on the surface of a lake. Nausea engulfed him. His stomach was contracting, threatening to expel the venison jerky he'd consumed earlier.

Where the blazes was he?

What was that weird noise?

His eyelids fluttered open, and he glimpsed men in uniform seated on both sides of him. Brown uniforms with red stars on the collars. Who were they? He couldn't seem to focus, to concentrate. Why? He closed his eyes and drifted into dreamland.

10

Dear Spirit! How he hurt!

Blade's senses responded sluggishly as he struggled to regain consciousness. He vividly recalled being clobbered by the Leather Knight called Cardew, and as his eyes opened and a wave of agony washed over his head he inadvertently flinched, expecting to be struck again.

But Cardew was gone. And so were the others. The circular chamber was empty except for the nylon net in the middle of the dirt floor.

"Welcome back to the land of the living," said someone to his left.

Blade slowly turned, discovering his arms in chains.

Rikki-Tikki-Tavi was shackled to the brick wall not four feet away. He had succeeded in slipping the gag from his mouth. Beyond him hung a redheaded woman with her gag still in place.

Was she the woman named Lex?

Rikki scanned the balcony to insure it was unoccupied. "Is Hickok with you?" he asked in a low voice.

Blade shook his head and immediately regretted the movement. The right side of his face was lanced by an acute pain. "I came alone," he mumbled through swollen lips.

"I noticed you found my katana," Rikki stated.

Blade looked down. The Leather Knights had stripped all of his weapons: the Bowies, the

Commando, the katana, everything.

"They took them last night," Rikki revealed, accurately deducing Blade's train of thought, "after Cardew knocked you out. I saw them carry my sword away." He paused, his jaw muscles taut. "I intend to retrieve it."

Blade tried to speak, but his throbbing mouth balked at the effort. What had that bastard Cardew done to him? He licked his puffy lips and mustered his resolve. "Do you . . ." He said haltingly, "have . . . any idea what they plan to do with us?"

Rikki nodded. "Their leader, Terza, wants to know who we are and where we come from. She wants to question us."

"She'll be wasting her breath," Blade muttered.

Rikki glanced at the closed doors. "Why did you come in alone?" he inquired. "Why didn't you use the SEAL?"

"It's out of commission," Blade said.

"What?" Rikki asked in surprise. "How?"

"A Red copter," Blade explained.

"Can the SEAL be salvaged?" Rikki queried.

"I think so," Blade said. "It's lying on its side, but otherwise seems to be in working order. I left Hickok behind to watch over it."

"At least *he's* out of danger," Rikki commented.

"Now all we have to do is get our butts out of here," Blade remarked.

Rikki rattled the chains secured to his wrists. "Easier said than done."

One of the recessed doors abruptly opened, and in walked Terza, Cardew, and six other Knights, four of them women. All of them bore handguns.

"Morning, Turkey!" Terza greeted Blade, her attitude cheerful, her bearing haughty.

Blade glared at his captors.

Terza walked up to the strapping Warrior and grinned. "My! My! Didn't you wake up on the wrong side of the sack!'' She cackled. ''Didn't you sleep well?'' She reached up and slapped his right cheek.

Blade recoiled in anguish.

''What a wimp!'' Cardew said disdainfully.

Blade lunged at the biker with the blue Mohawk, but his chains prevented him from moving more than a few inches.

Cardew retreated a step and reached for his Browning.

''Cardew!'' Terza barked. ''I want him alive.''

Cardew's mouth curled back from his teeth. ''Okay,'' he hissed. ''But I want the honor of wasting this creep when the time comes.''

''You'll have it,'' Terza assured him.

Cardew snickered maliciously.

Terza moved over to Rikki. ''So? Are you ready to spill the beans yet?''

''What kind of beans did you have in mind?'' Rikki countered. ''Lima or string beans?''

''Funny boy, ain't you?'' Terza said. ''Okay. I tried to be nice about this. But if you won't tell me where you come from, then I'll have to persuade you to talk.''

''I will not answer your questions,'' Rikki assured her.

''We'll see about that, lover boy.'' Terza turned and nodded at two of the women. They crossed to Lex, and one of them unlocked her shackles while the second kept her covered with a revolver.

Lexine rubbed her sore wrists, then removed the gag from her mouth. ''You bitch!'' she snapped at Terza.

Terza motioned toward the center of the chamber. ''Set her up.''

The two women grabbed Lex by the arms and hauled her from the room.

''What are you going to do to her?'' Rikki asked.

''You'll see,'' Terza replied.

Blade surveyed the chamber, lit by a dozen lanterns positioned at regular intervals along the balcony, affixed to metal brackets. Where did the Knights obtain the fuel for the lanterns? From the Technics? The ceiling was vaulted, constructed of polished wood. Evidently this chamber had been under construction at the outset of World War III and never finished.

Lex and the pair of Knights appeared on the balcony on the far side of the room. One of the women was carrying a coiled rope.

"You sure you don't wanna tell me everything I want to know?" Terza asked Rikki.

Rikki remained silent.

Terza shrugged. "Suit yourself. But I think you're about to change your mind."

One of the Knights on the balcony tied the rope to the balcony railing, then turned and said something to Lexine.

Rikki saw Lex shake her head

The second Knight shoved her revolver into Lexine's stomach.

Lex walked to the edge of the balcony. She held her arms straight out.

The Knight with the rope used it to bind lex's wrists.

"Last chance," Terza said, mocking Rikki.

Rikki resembled a granite statue.

"Do it!" Terza shouted to the two women on the balcony.

The Knights seized Lex and forced her to the edge of the balcony. Lex fought them, striving to wrest her arms free, but she was unable to avert their intended design; she was rudely jerked off her feet and pushed over the balcony railing. She dropped like the proverbial rock, her descent brutally terminated when she reached the end of the rope, her feet dangling five feet above the earthen floor. She gasped in torment as her arms were wrenched upwards, her head snapping back, whiplashed, and her teeth jarring together.

"The fun's just getting started," Terza said to Rikki. "You can put a stop to it by telling me where you come from. What do you say?"

Rikki looked Terza in the eyes. "If it's the last act I live to perform on this planet," he said calmly, "I am going to eliminate you."

"Tough talk!" Terza said, chuckling. She slowly drew the Llama Super Comanche V's belted around her slim waist. "You know what to do!" she yelled to the Knights on the balcony.

The pair of Knights leaned over the railing, gripped the rope, and started moving the rope in wide arcs, back and forth, causing Lex to swing like a human pendulum.

Terza aimed her left Comanche and fired.

The brick wall beyond Lex sprayed chipped mortar and brick onto the floor.

"Damn!" Terza said, laughing. "I missed." She stared at Rikki. "One more time. Where do you come from?"

Rikki frowned and lowered his gaze.

Terza pointed the Comanches in the direction of Lex. "I thought you had the hots for Lex, lover boy," she said. The Comanches boomed, the twin shots narrowly missing Lex's swaying form. "I guess I was wrong."

Rikki stared at the dirt floor, struggling to restrain his seething emotions. Maintaining his self-control was of paramount importance: self-control was the essence of a Warrior's character, and exhibiting self-control during a crisis was the critical test of anyone dedicated to the martial arts. He quivered from the intensity of his fury, but his inner discipline was superlative.

"Sooner or later," Terza said, baiting him, "one of

my shots is bound to hit her. Won't it bother you knowing you're responsible for her death?''

Rikki's fists were clenched so tightly his nails were digging into his palms.

Terza's right Comanche thundered, but again Lex was spared any injury.

"Let me try," Cardew interjected eagerly.

"What do you say, lover boy?" Terza asked Rikki. "Should I let Cardew have a go at it? He's not as good a shot as I am. He'll probably put a bullet right between her eyes."

Rikki glared at Cardew.

"Still the tough guy?" Terza said to Rikki. "Well, don't say I didn't warn you." She looked at Cardew. "Have some fun."

"Thanks!" Cardew drew his Browning.

"Enough of this!" declared a deep voice.

All eyes focused on the muscular giant.

"Did you say something?" Terza asked.

"Enough of this," Blade reiterated. "I'll answer your questions."

Terza studied him quizzically. "You will, huh?"

"I will answer whatever I can," Blade said.

"Just like that?" Terza remarked skeptically.

Blade nodded toward Lex. "Release her first."

Terza snickered. "Don't tell me that you've got the hots for Lex too? What's she got that I ain't got?"

Blade straightened. "I do not have the . . . hots . . . for her. I already have selected my mate for eternity."

"Eternity?" Terza laughed. "Who said anything about eternity? I figure you want to jump her buns for a one-nighter."

Blade's mouth curled downward disdainfully. "I also have no desire to jump her . . . buns. I have pledged loyalty to my wife, and I will not violate my vow."

"Yeah. Sure." Terza tittered. "Big words, mister. But they don't mean crap! Are you tryin' to tell me you would say no if a fox wanted some fun in the sack with you?''

Blade nodded. ''The only fox I want to have fun with is my wife. We are loyal to one another because we love each other.''

''Loyalty?'' Terza said angrily. ''Who the hell cares about loyalty?''

''Loyal couples are growing couples,'' Blade stated. ''Without loyalty, love withers and dies.''

''What the hell are you? Some kind of poet?'' Terza shook her head in wonder.

''Sounds like a real wimp to me,'' Cardew commented.

''What's it going to be?'' Blade demanded. ''Will you release Lex?''

Terza holstered her Comanches. ''Sure. But remember one thing. I can have her strung up again if you give me any grief.''

''I have given my word,'' Blade reminded her.

''Your word don't mean diddly to me,'' Terza said. She raised her face to the two Knights on the balcony. ''Cut her down! Then chain her on the wall next to lover boy!'' She grinned at Blade. ''Satisfied?''

''Ask your questions,'' Blade said.

''Not here,'' Terza said. She glanced at Cardew. ''I want you to bring him to my room after Lex is chained. I'll be waiting.'' She wheeled and stalked from the chamber.

Cardew walked up to Blade and winked conspiratorially. ''Ain't you the lucky one!''

''What do you mean?'' Blade inquired.

''Don't play innocent with me!'' Cardew nudged the Warrior in the ribs. ''I think Terza wants you for herself. You should be flattered.''

''Wants me?'' Blade repeated, puzzled. ''But I just told her I already have a mate.''

''Terza could care less about your mate,'' Cardew disclosed. ''If she decides she wants a man, she ups and takes him.''

"And the man doesn't have any say in the matter?"
Blade queried.

"A man can't refuse a woman," Cardew said.
"That's the law."

"Not where I come from," Blade informed him.

"You ain't there now, are you?" Cardew teased the
Warrior. "You're here. And what Terza says, goes. If
you give her any lip, you'll never see your wife again.
No man has ever refused her. Am I getting through to
you yet, asshole?"

"Loud and clear," Blade responded. He watched
the Knights lowering Lex to the ground. How were
they going to get out of this fix? Would Terza want to
be alone with him? If so, would it be to his advantage
to escape while Rikki and Lex were still being held?
Terza might execute them out of sheer spite. He
closed his eyes and sighed. At least Hickok was free.
He hoped he could rely on the gunman's customary
impatience. Let's see. Hickok had agreed to stay with
the SEAL for three days. But would the gunfighter
wait that long? Highly unlikely. One day, definitely.
Two, possibly. But never for three. Hickok would
come looking for them, but not for another day and a
half, minimum.

A lot could happen in a day and a half.

Blade opened his eyes and stared at Cardew's
leering expression.

Yes, sir.

A whole lot.

And none of it good.

11

"Not now, honey," Hickok mumbled. "I'm plumb tuckered out." He rolled over and started to fall asleep again, but Sherry wouldn't leave him alone. She was insistently shaking his right shoulder. Funny thing about wives. Before the marriage, they were all over your body and coudn't seem to get enough. Then it was "I do," and "Whoa, there, buckaroo!" "Not tonight! I've got a headache!" Except when *they* were in the mood. Then the man had best be able to get it up, or it was cold stares and leftovers until the woman decided the man had repented enough for another go. Contrary critters, those females! Sherry was shaking harder now.

Hickok eased onto his back and opened his eyes.

Uh-oh.

It wasn't Sherry standing over him. It was three men, all wearing brown uniforms with red stars on their collars and other insignia.

Hickok suddenly remembered everything in a rush, and he automatically reached for his Colts. But his fingers closed on empty holsters.

They'd taken his Pythons!

One of the men, a burly man with sagging cheeks, a protruding chin, and bright blue eyes, held the Pythons aloft in his right hand. "Are these what you are looking for?" he asked in clipped, precise English.

Hickok started to rise, but the other two men had already drawn automatics from holsters on their right hips.

"Please," said the first man, evidently an officer, "don't do anything foolish. We have no intention of harming you."

"Then what am I doin' here?" Hickock demanded. "And where the blazes am I?" He rose on his elbows and scanned his surroundings, finding himself on a metal table in a well-lit room. Four overhead lights provided ample illumination. A row of equipment— medical equipment, if he guessed right—was lined up along one of the walls.

"We will ask the questions," said the burly officer. "What is your name?"

"Annie Oakley."

The officer's blue eyes narrowed. "That is a woman's name."

"Would you believe Calamity Jane?"

"Another woman's name," the burly officer remarked. "What kind of game are you playing?"

"Poker," Hickock said.

One of the other men began speaking to the burly officer in a foreign tongue.

Hickok listened intently, but couldn't make hide nor hair of their babble.

"Ahhh. I see," the burly officer said in English. "Lieutenant Voroshilov informs me you refer to a period in American history hundreds of years ago. Is this not true?"

Hickock glanced at Lieutenant Voroshilov, a youthful officer, in his 30s, with green eyes and crew-cut blond hair. "Don't tell me. Voroshilov is partial to readin' about the Old West!"

The burly officer shook his head. "Not exactly. But Lieutenant Voroshilov does have what you call a . . ." He paused for a moment. "Photographic memory. He read a book once about the history of cowboys and Indians, or some such silliness, and never forgot what he read."

"Photographic memory, huh?" Hickok said. "Then he should have smarts enough to know who you jokers are and where the dickens I am."

Burly Butt smiled. "Please forgive my rudeness. I should have introduced myself. I am General Malenkov."

"Malenkov. Voroshilov. With names like that, it's a cinch I ain't in the Civilized Zone," Hickok quipped, alluding to the area in the Midwest and Rocky Moutain region occupied by the remnant of the U.S. Government after World War III.

"Are you from the Civilized Zone?" General Malenkov asked.

"Didn't you ever hear about what curiosity did to the cat?" Hickok countered.

General Malenkov's facial muscles tightened. "I have tried to be polite, but you will not cooperate. If you will not supply the information I need willingly, then I will use other methods."

"Give it your best shot," Hickok taunted him.

General Malenkov smiled. "I will." He barked a series of orders at Lieutenant Voroshilov. That worthy wheeled and stalked to the row of medical equipment. The third, unnamed, soldier kept his pistol trained on the man in buckskins.

"What are you aimin' to do?" Hickok inquired nonchalantly.

"We will inject you with a substance our chemists developed for recalictrant subjects," General Malenkov answered.

"What's it do?"

"It is a truth serum," General Malenkov explained. "Once injected, you will divulge everything we want to know."

Hickok watched Voroshilov remove a hypodermic needle from a glass cabinet. He didn't like this one bit. It didn't take a genius to figure out who these bozos were. He'd attended the history classes in the

Family school, and he knew about the Russians and the part they'd played in the Big Blast. Who else could these clowns be?

Voroshilov was filling the hypodermic from a small vial.

Hickock calculated the risks. If they injected him with the truth serum, he'd probably spill the beans about the Family and the Home and the whole shebang. But if he went along with them for a spell, he might be able to withhold information crucial to the safety of the Family and essential to the Freedom Federation.

Lieutenant Voroshilov had finished filling the hypodermic needle. He turned and returned to the metal table.

"You don't need to go to all this trouble on my account," Hickok said.

"It's no trouble," General Malenkov assured him.

"I'll answer your questions," Hickok declared.

"Why have you changed your mind so quickly?" General Malenkov inquired.

"I'm fickle," Hickok responded. "Ask anybody. They'll tell you I never know if I'm comin' or goin'."

General Malenkov smiled, but the smile lacked any trace of genuine friendliness. His eyes were impassive pools of indeterminate intent. He said something in what Hickock assumed was Russian to Voroshilov. The lieutenant retraced his steps to the glass cabinet and replaced the hypodermic.

Hickok trusted the general about as far as he could toss a black bear. He instinctively sensed the general was up to something, but he didn't have the slightest idea what it might be. General Malenkov had acceded too readily to not using the truth serum. Why? What did the tricky bastard have up his sleeve?

"Tell us your name," General Malenkov demanded.

"Hickok." He abruptly realized Malenkov wasn't

holding his Colts.

Lieutenant Voroshilov interjected several sentences in Russian.

General Malenkov frowned. "Why do you persist in these games?"

"I told you the truth," Hickok said. "My name is Hickok. I know it's a name from the Old West. That's why I took it. It's the name of an old gunfighter I admire a lot."

General Malenkov reflected for a minute. "All right. I will give you the benefit of the doubt. For now. Where are you from, Hickok?"

"Montana," Hickok lied. Actually, the Family resided in northwestern Minnesota.

"You are far from home," General Malenkov observed.

"We were on our way to St. Louis when your men jumped me," Hickok detailed.

"Why St. Louis?"

Hickok hesitated. The general had to know about the Civilized Zone. How much more did the Russians know? Were they aware of the existence of the Cavalry in the Dakota Territory? What about the Flathead Indians or the Moles? "We were sent to see if it's inhabited," he said.

"Who sent you?"

"The Government of the Civilized Zone," Hickok fibbed again.

"I have heard of the Civilized Zone," General Malenkov said slowly. "What do you know about it?"

"Not a bunch," Hickok replied. "I know the Government of the United States reorganized in Denver after the war, and they evacuated thousands of folks from all across the country into the Midwest and Rocky Mountain area. Later it became known as the Civilized Zone."

"And you do not live there?"

"I told you," Hickok said, enjoying their verbal

sparring, their game of cat and mouse. "I live in Montana."

"Why would someone from Montana be on a mission for the Government of the Civilized Zone?" General Malenkov asked.

"My people have a treaty with 'em," Hickok revealed. "They sent us because we have the best vehicle."

"I was told about your vehicle," General Malenkov stated with interest. "A most unusual vehicle too, I might add. Where did you obtain it?"

"It was left for us by the man who founded our Home," Hickok replied. "He spent millions building the contraption, then had it secreted in a special vault until we decided we needed it."

"I intend to retrieve your vehicle," General Malenkov declared.

"It won't be easy," Hickok said. "Didn't your men tell you about the fight we had with your helicopter?"

"One of our helicopters," the general corrected the gunman. "Another of our helicopters transported our commando unit to the site and captured you, a larger version than the one you saw. I am having one of our bigger helicopters outfitted to bring your vehicle here."

"What are you aimin' to do?" Hickok joked. "Take it apart, fly the pieces here, then put it back together again?"

"No," General Malenkov said. "Our helicopter will use a winch and a sling and fly it here."

"Fly the SEAL?" Hickok laughed. "You're crazy! It weighs tons."

"The SEAL? Is that what you call it?" General Malenkov inquired.

Hickok wanted to sew his lips shut. Of all the green-horn mistakes! He'd gone and blurted out the name of the SEAL without realizing what in tarnation he was doing! What an idiot! "Yeah," he had to agree. "We call our buggy the SEAL."

"Interesting," General Malenkov remarked. "And I am not crazy. Our tandem helicopters can transport over fifteen tons. By tomorrow morning, my crew will be at the site. Believe me, our helicopters can easily bear the load of conveying your SEAL. You don't seem to know much about helicopters."

"I don't," Hickok admitted. "I never even saw one before the fight we had with that copter of yours."

"Odd. Don't they utilize helicopters in the Civilized Zone?" General Malenkov innocently inquired.

What was the general up to? Probing for secrets concerning the Civilized Zone's military capabilities? "I wouldn't know," Hickok answered "I haven't spent a lot of time in the Civilized Zone. But I did see a flying contraption of theirs once," he added. "Something called a jet."

General Malenkov's interest heightened. "A jet? What type of jet?"

Hickok shrugged. "Beats me. I don't know jets from turnips. It flew real fast, and it could fire machine guns and rockets." He didn't bother to mention the jet had been destroyed, downed in a battle with the SEAL.

General Malenkov and Lieutenant Voroshilov exchanged looks. The obviously considered the news of the jet important.

"Did you see other military hardware in the Civilized Zone?" General Malenkov queried.

Hickok repressed an impulse to laugh. The general was totally transparent; he was milking the gunman for critical tactical information. But why? Were the Russians planning to invade the Civilized Zone? If so, why now? Why had they waited so long after the war? "I saw a heap of trucks and jeeps and a tank," Hickok stated.

"Do you know any more?" General Malenkov goaded him. "How large a standing Army they maintain, for instance? What shape their weapons and equipment are in? Where their outposts are situated?''

''Nope,'' Hickok replied. ''Like I told you, I haven't spent much time in the Civilized Zone.''

General Malenkov studied the gunman for a moment. ''You said your people live in Montana?''

''Yep,'' Hickok said, confirming his lie.

''Do they have a name?''

''No,'' Hickok fibbed again.

''What about the name of the town you live in?'' General Malenkov pressed the issue.

''We don't live in a town,'' Hickok said, telling the truth for once. ''We have our own compound and we keep pretty much to ourselves.''

''Could you pinpoint its location on a map?'' General Malenkov asked.

''Sure,'' Hickok responded.

''We will bring one here later,'' General Malenkov informed him.

''Do you mind if I ask a question?'' Hickok politely inquired.

''What is it?'' General Malenkov asked.

''Who are you guys? Where do you come from? And where am I?'' Hickok swept the medical room with his right hand. ''Where is this place?''

General Malenkov nodded. ''Fair is fair,'' he said. ''You have answered me, so I will answer you. Perhaps you will the better understand the nature of your dilemma, and you will realize why resistance is futile. You must continue to cooperate with us. You have no other choice.''

Hickok sat up on the metal table.

''As you have undoubtedly guessed,'' General Malenkov declared, ''we are professional soldiers in the Army of the Union of Soviet Socialist Republics.''

''You're a long ways from home too,'' Hickok quipped.

General Malenkov paused. "True," he said sadly. "We are far from the Motherland." He sighed and stared at red drapes covering one of the walls. "As to your location," he said slowly, "a demonstration will be far more eloquent than mere words."

Lieutenant Voroshilov and the third soldier moved aside, clearing a path between the metal table and the drapes.

General Malenkov beckoned toward the drapes. "Go ahead. Take a look."

Hickok slid from the metal table. He noticed the general had placed his Colt Pythons on a wooden stand about four feet from the table.

"Open the drapes," General Malenkov directed the gunman.

Hickok walked to the right side of the drapes and found several cords descending from the traverse rods. He gripped the first cord and pulled.

Nothing happened.

Hickok tried the second of the three cords.

The drapes didn't budge.

What the heck was going on here? Some of the cabins at the Home were outfitted with drapes, and he knew how to work them. He pulled on the final cord.

With a swish, the red drapes parted, opening wide, revealing a picture window and a spectacular view.

It took a minute to register. Hickok had seen pictures of the scene in the photographic books in the Family library. But he'd never expected to actually *be* there.

It was impossible!

It just couldn't be!

But there it was!

General Malenkov noted the astonishment on the gunman's features. "Your eyes do not deceive you," he said.

"It can't be!" Hickok exclaimed. "It can't!"

"But it is," General Malenkov said, beaming. "It's the White House."

12

"What kept you?" Terza demanded.

Blade gaped at her, scarcely aware he was responding. "Cardew took a potty break," he wise-cracked. "Must of read *War and Peace* while he was in the bathroom."

"I don't know nothin' about no *War and Peace*," Terza said. "But I do know Cardew can't read."

Blade scanned her room, which was located on the top floor of the library. Plush green carpet covered the floor, in excellent condition despite the passing of a century. The walls were covered with mahogany paneling. An easy chair and a couch were positioned directly in front of the Warrior. Beyond them, reached by climbing two small steps, was an elevated section incorporating a huge bed as its centerpiece. Terza, attired in a skimpy white-lace garment, reclined in the middle of the bed, her legs spread out, resting her head on her left hand.

"Do you like it?" Terza asked.

"I had no idea libraries in the old days were so extravagant," Blade commented.

Terza laughed. "Stupid. This was an office once. I had some of the men fix it up for me, scavenging from the abandoned stores. You'd be surprised what you can find."

"I guess I would," Blade admitted. He was perplexed by Terza's behavior. She was exhibiting none of the habitual hostility he'd observed earlier. In fact, she was going out of her way to be nice, to be friendly.

To be attractive.

Blade walked to the steps leading up to the bed. "We must talk," he told her.

Terza grinned, reached out her right hand, and patted the brown bedspread. "I didn't have you brought here to talk."

"We must talk," Blade stated.

Terza sat up. "What's the matter with you? Can't you see I have the hots for you? I don't get a craving for a man very often. You should be flattered."

"I don't seem to be getting through to you," Blade said. "I already have a wife."

"So?" Terza giggled and patted the bed again. "I'll never tell!"

Blade pondered his next move. He saw her eyes raking his body from head to toe. Something was inconsistent here. This wasn't the tough-as-nails woman he'd met. The way she was staring at him, with her nostrils flared and her eyes dilated . . .

Her eyes dilated?

Blade moved to the edge of the bed.

"Come on!" Terza urged him. "I ain't waitin' all day!"

Blade leaned over and peered into her pale blue eyes. Her pupils were expanded and unfocused, and her entire demeanor verged on inane giddiness. What was she on? Alcohol? He doubted it. Her breath lacked the telltale odor. What then? Drugs? He straightened, frowning. The Family deplored the use of drugs. For the Warriors, any addicting substance was strictly taboo. With their lives on the line daily, only a moronic jerk would distort the senses and inhibit the reflexes. Survival was frequently a matter of split-second decision-making and timing; no one on drugs would last more than a minute if confronted by a mutate, one of the monstrous giants, or any other

124   David Robbins

deviate.

Drugs were plain stupid.

"Come on, handsome!" Terza said, eyeing him lecherously. She slid her left hand between her thighs. "I want it!"

"You want it?"

"Ohhhh! How I want it!" Terza cooed.

"Are you sure you want it?" Blade asked.

Terza sat up, smiling, weaving slightly. "I'm sure! Give it to me!"

Blade grinned. "If you insist."

"Do it, damnit!"

Blade hauled off and slugged her on the jaw.

Terza collapsed onto the bed, unconscious, her mouth slack, blood dribbling from her lower gum.

"Sorry about that," Blade remarked. "But I tried to warn you. Marriage without loyalty is nothing more than disguised prostitution, as our spiritual mentor, Joshua, would say. And I will never violate my oath to my mate." He shook his head, feeling foolish conducting a conversation with an unconscious woman.

Time to get the hell out of here!

Blade crossed to the door and paused. There should be a pair of guards outside the door to Terza's room. They had escorted him to the room from the basement cell. He would need to catch them by surprise. Putting a broad smirk on his face, he slowly opened the door.

There they were. Cardew and one other.

Blade glanced over his right shoulder and laughed. "Okay," he said to Terza's unresponsive form. "I'll tell them." He smiled at Cardew and the other man. "Terza wants to see you."

Cardew chuckled. "What's the matter? Can't you find where it goes without help?" He snickered and motioned for the other man to follow.

Blade, beaming, stepped aside.

Cardew and the other man had taken several steps into the room before Cardew awoke to the danger. He saw the blood on Terza's chin and grabbed for his Browning. ''Damn!''

Blade pounced. He kicked with his right leg, connecting on Cardew's left knee, and heard a distinct popping sound as Cardew screeched and dropped to the floor.

The second Leather Knight, a tall, lean black, went for the knife he wore in a sheath on his right hip.

Blade drove his right fist around and in, catching the black on the nose, crushing the cartilage and driving fragments into the Knight's forehead. He swung his left fist, boxing the Knight on the ear.

The stud started to drop.

Blade rammed his elbow into the man's jaw, then turned his attention to Cardew.

Still on the floor, wobbling on his right knee, Cardew was drawing his Browning.

Blade lashed out with his right foot, his toes smashing into Cardew's chin.

Cardew's head snapped backward. His teeth crunched together, and crimson spurted from his mouth.

''This is for last night!'' Blade said, and hammered his left fist down on the right side of Cardew's face. Once. Twice.

Cardew groaned and sprawled onto the carpet.

Blade took the knife from the black and Cardew's Browning and hurried to the door.

The hallway was empty.

Blade closed the door behind him as he took a left. Reaching Rikki and Lex quickly was imperative. There was no telling how soon Terza and the others would be found.

Every moment counted.

The hulking Warrior reached a flight of stairs and hastily descended. Surprisingly, he reached the bottom level undetected. Maybe it wasn't so surprising, he told himself. Except for Terza, Cardew, and the guards, why would any of the Leather Knights be hanging around the library? From what he'd gathered, very few of them could even read. He cautiously opened the stairwell door and peeked outside.

The hallway leading to the holding chamber passed by the door. No one was in sight.

Blade took a right and ran down the hall. If all went well, he would reach—

A door up ahead opened and two Leather Knights, one man and one woman, emerged.

No!

"You!" the woman bellowed, clutching at the pistol she carried on her left side.

Blade shot her in the chest.

The woman twisted and fell to the floor.

Undaunted, the stud was trying to clear his revolver.

Blade planted a slug in the stud's head.

There was no use trying to conceal his movements now! Every Leather Knight in the building had heard the gunfire and would come running! Blade ran faster. He reached the door he'd used last night and flung it open.

Rikki and Lex were hanging from the far wall, still in chains. Both were gagged.

Blade raced across the dirt floor. He tore the gag from Rikki's mouth. "Where are the keys to your shackles?" he asked.

"The one called Cardew has them," Rikki replied.

Damn! Blade glared at the chains. Why hadn't he thought to search Cardew for the keys? After all, Cardew had unlocked *his* chains!

"We heard shooting," Rikki said.

"Hostile natives," Blade said, examining the antiquated chains.

"Take off," Rikki advised him. "You can come back and free us later."

"We're leaving here together," Blade stated.

"Without the keys?" Rikki asked.

"Who needs keys?" Blade tucked the Browning under his belt and handed the knife to Rikki. "Hold this."

"What do you have in mind?" Rikki inquired.

"This." Blade took hold of the chain attached to Rikki's right wrist. Removing the shackle encircing Rikki's wrist wasn't feasible; he could do it, but he might hurt Rikki in the bargain. No, his best bet was to concentrate on the link joining the chain to the shackle. He gripped the chain in his right hand and held the shackle with his left. "This might smart," he warned his companion.

Rikki's arm tensed. "Go for it."

Blade strained, exerting his herculean strength to its limit, pulling on the chain, his massive muscles bulging, his arms rippling with raw power.

Rikki had adopted the horse stance, striving to facilitate Blade's effort by staying as immobile as possible.

Blade was gritting his teeth, his neck pulsing, the veins protruding.

Lexine was watching the operation in wide-eyed astonishment.

Blade could feel the chain biting into his right hand. He igored the discomfort and heaved, thankful the chain was old and the links on the rusty side. If only they were weak enough! Sweat beaded his brow as he continued to apply pressure. Every muscle on his arms stood out in sharp relief. He closed his eyes, concentrating, channeling every iota of power into his brawny hands.

Rikki was striving to maintain his balance. Despite his horse stance, a normally immovable posture, Blade's awesome strength threatened to propel him from his feet.

Blade's sinews were at their utmost, his face a beet red, when the link affixed to the shackle on Rikki's right wrist snapped, parting with a loud crack.

Rikki relaxed. "You did it!" he said, elated.

Blade wiped his perspiring brow. "One down and three to go."

"You should rest a bit," Rikki advised.

"No time for that," Blade said. He moved sideways and applied himself to the shackle on Rikki's left wrist. This chain was more stubborn. The perspiration was pouring from his pores, his arms trembling from his exertion, when the connecting link finally broke.

Rikki rubbed his tender wrists, massaging the skin under the metal shackles. "Thank you," he said to his friend.

Blade nodded and crossed to Lex. He pulled the gag from her mouth.

"I don't believe it!" Lex declared. "How did you do it?"

"They don't make chains like they used to," Blade remarked.

Rikki joined them.

"You'll need to steady her arms," Blade directed Rikki. He looked at Lex. "If this hurts, say the word. If I'm not careful, I could tear your arms from their sockets."

"Don't worry none about me," Lex stated. "Just get me out of here!"

"I don't believe you two have been formally intro-duced," Rikki said as Blade took hold of the chain attached to Lexine's right wrist. "Blade, this is Lexine. Lex, this is Blade."

"Pleased to meet you," Lex mentioned.

Blade nodded and began applying himself to the chain.

Rikki gripped Lex's right wrist, adding support,

struggling to keep Lex's arm steady.

Lex grimaced as Blade started straining against the chain. The edge of the metal shackle bit into her flesh, drawing a thin line of blood. Even with Rikki holding her arm, she felt as if it really would be ripped from its socket any second.

Blade stared at the last link on the chain. He could see the rusted metal giving way and stretching. With a grunt, he wrenched the chain and was rewarded by a sharp, popping noise.

"Only one to do," Rikki said.

From off in the distance, from upstairs, came the din of upraised voices.

"They're after us!" Lex cried. "Hurry!"

Blade paused, gathering his energy. The clamor upstairs was growing louder. If the chain fastened to her left shackle was as sturdy as the others, it would require minutes to break.

He didn't have minutes to spare.

"Hold her left arm tightly," Blade said to Rikki, then he grinned at Lexine. "Close your eyes and count to three."

Lex did as he requested.

On the count of three, Blade tightened his arms and huge chest, took a deep breath, and savagely tugged on the chain.

Lex gasped as her left arm was jerked outward. Her left shoulder lanced with agony.

Blade uttered a growling sound and yanked his arms in opposite directions.

Lex groaned.

The link abruptly burst asunder, causing Blade to stumble backwards two feet.

"You're free!" Rikki said to Lex.

Lex leaned on the brick wall, holding her left arm pressed across her stomach. "Am I in one piece?" she asked, her eyes still shut.

Rikki rubbed her sore shoulder. "How bad is it?"

Lex opened her eyes and chuckled. "I'll live. We'd best get the hell out of here."

The approaching racket was much, much closer.

"Where are our weapons?" Blade queried Rikki.

"I don't know," Rikki replied.

"Then we'll have to make do with the Browning and the kife," Blade said. He glanced at Lex. "Which way?"

Lex scanned the chamber. "I'm not sure. I haven't been down here very often. One of these doors leads to an alley. But I can't remember which one."

"Lead the way," Blade instructed her.

"What if I pick the wrong door?" Lex responded.

"We'll have to take that risk," Blade said. "Let's go." He drew the Browning and motioned for them to precede him.

Lex headed for the nearest door, Rikki by her side with the knife held in his right hand.

Blade backed from the room, keeping his eyes on the door to the far hallway.

The Leather Knights were pounding down the hall.

Blade reached the door used by Lex and Rikki, turned, and darted into its dim interior.

Not a moment too soon.

Dozens of Leather Knights surged into the brick chamber. A great shout went up at the sight of the dangling chains.

"They're gone!" a man yelled above the rest. "But how?"

"We didn't pass 'em!" a woman bellowed. "They must have used one of the other doors!"

Immediately the Leather Knights divided up, some taking the first recessed door, others the second, and the smallest group the last door. In a minute, the chamber was vacant.

Far along the murky hallway and racing like the wind, Blade detected a swelling in the voices behind him as leather garbed bikers filled the narrow corridor.

Where did this lead?

Blade hoped the hall wasn't a dead end. He doubted the Leather Knights would bother to take them prisoner a second time, not after what he had done to Terza and Cardew. He locked his gaze on the shadowy forms of Rikki and Lex 30 feet ahead. If they could reach the alley Lex had mentioned, they might be able to hide in a nearby building. He wished he were outdoors instead of deep under the earth. A troubling sensation of claustrophobia enveloped him.

Spirit preserve him!

Blade glanced over his right shoulder, but couldn't perceive any movement to his rear.

Good.

They were losing the SOBs!

Blade faced front again and pounded after Rikki and Lex—

Rikki and Lex!

They were gone!

Blade stopped and peered into the gloom beyond. Had they outdistanced him? What could have happened?

"Blade!" came a subdued cry from Rikki. "Blade! Where are you?"

Blade twisted. Rikki's voice was coming from his left and behind him.

"Blade!" Rikki called once more.

"I'm here!" Blade yelled. "Where are you?"

"Did you miss the turn?" Rikki asked.

What turn? Blade realized he'd probably overlooked it when he had turned his head and scanned the tunnel! Now they were separated! "I must have missed it!" Blade confirmed.

"I'll keep talking," Rikki shouted. "Follow my voice."

Blade backtracked, running full speed, searching for a fork in the hallway.

''There's light ahead!'' Rikki was saying. ''It might be the alley!''

Blade reached a darkened bend in the hallway and discovered another branch bearing to the left. He was about to enter, but a sudden commotion rearward drew his attention.

Leather Knights were charging toward him from the direction of the brick chamber!

Blade hesitated. If he followed Rikki and Lex, the Leather Knights would chase after them to the alley and beyond. But if he stayed where he was, if he didn't take the left branch, Rikki and Lex could escape unmolested.

''There's one of 'em!'' screamed a tall woman.

He'd been spotted! Blade turned his back on the left branch and took off, the Browning in his right hand.

With gleeful cries, the Leather Knights ran after the giant Warrior, ignoring the left branch in their eagerness to capture Blade.

As he raced deeper into the winding labyrinth below the library, with many of the tunnels and hallways bearing evidence of recent excavation, Blade wondered if he'd made the right move. Lit lanterns were few and far between. Often he would cover over a hundred yards in nearly complete darkness.

Some of the Leather Knights were carrying torches or lanterns, and the swiftest of them kept their quarry in sight as they doggedly pursued him, his fleeing form always visible, but barely, at the periphery of their flickering light.

Blade was beginning to think he might outdistance them. A grim smile touched his lips at the prospect. After he eluded them, he intended to scour the library for his weapns. Leaving St. Louis without his Bowies was unthinkable; the big knives were as much a part of him as his arms or legs.

The Leather Knights were determinedly sticking to his heels.

A lantern appeared directly ahead, suspended from a hook in the wall.

A junction, Blade thought.

But he was wrong.

Blade slowed, expecting to find a branch or fork in the hallway. Instead, he discovered a solid brick wall.

It was a dead end!

Furious, he whirled, facing the converging Leather Knights. They had him right where they wanted him! Outnumbered, with nowhere to turn! He raised the Browning and sighted on the nearest figure, now approximately 20 yards away.

Let them come!

They were about to learn why the Warriors were respected and feared far and wide.

Blade sighted and squeezed the trigger.

13

Hickok's amazement was plainly written all over his face. He gawked at the edifice before him, feeling as if he had stepped back through the pages of history to a prior era, to another day and age. He'd seen aged photographs of the White House in several of the books in the Family library, but the reality of actually observing the historically significant structure dwarfed the perceptions derived from viewing a picture. He could see six massive columns, formerly white but now faded and tarnished, in the middle of the building. On either side of the columns the walls were in fairly good shape, although all of the windows were broken or missing. A section of roof above the columns had caved in, littering the base of the columns with debris. "I'm in Washington, D.C.," the dazed gunman said to himself.

"Indeed you are," General Malenkov confirmed.

"But I can't be!" Hickok declared. "How'd I get here?"

"You were transported via helicopter," General Malenkov explained.

"All the way from St. Louis?" Hickok was boggled by the news. "That must be a thousand miles!"

"About eight hundred and sixty," General Malenkov stated. "You were unconscious the entire trip."

Hickok forced his mind to buckle down, to get a grip on his dilemma. How in the world was he going to get back to St. Louis? Eight hundred miles through hostile territory would be well-nigh unachievable. He needed time to think, to formulate a plan of action.

"Washington is the last place you expected to be, eh?" General Malenkov said.

Hickok nodded. "I don't understand. I'd heard Washington suffered a direct hit during World War III."

"It did," General Malenkov affirmed.

Hickok pointed at the White House. "Then what's that doin' there? A direct hit would've leveled the city."

General Malenkov leaned on the metal table. "A direct strike by a conventional thermonuclear device would destroy the city, yes. But we did not use a conventional device."

Hickok glanced at the general. "What did you use?"

"A neutron bomb."

Hickok's brow furrowed. "A neutron bomb?"

"Do you know what they are?" General Malenkov inquired.

"I think I read something about 'em years ago," Hickok said. "But I can't recollect what it was I read."

"I will enlighten you," General Malenkov offered. "To understand what happened, you must appreciate our strategy during the war. You see, Americans back then were really quite stupid. Only half of the population really believed a war was inevitable. The other half was either too absorbed in their own lives to even reflect on the likelihood of a conflict, or else they were gullible liberal fanatics who ignored our conquests worldwide and discounted all of our literature and policy statements clearly stating our goal of global domination. And even when the subject of a nuclear exchange was considered, the fools panicked. To them, a nuclear war was a worst-case scenario. Total annihilation. Radiation contaminating the environment for thousands of years to come." The general chuckled. "Of course, the American military leaders knew better, but they could not overcome the bias and ignorance of the media elite. The American leaders knew we entertained no intention of destroying the country. Why should we? Soviet leaders knew how rich this land is in natural resources. At a time when we were barely able to feed our own people, why would we ruin the breadbasket of the Western Hemisphere? Our military leaders did use typical thermonuclear devices on carefully selected targets, but where possible we used other weapons like the neutron bomb."

"So what's a neutron bomb?" Hickok queried.

"A neutron bomb is a lot like an ordinary H-bomb, but it is not as destructive. It doesn't have the same explosive power and produces far less fallout. Some years before the war, there was a controversy in America over the deployment of the neutron bomb in Europe. The idiotic press campaigned against the idea. Their inconsistency was incredible. They preferred to use the terribly destructive hydrogen warheads instead of the smaller, cleaner neutron variety." General Malenkov paused. "I have dilligently studied the prewar era, and I was constantly shocked by the ignorance displayed by the predominantly liberal media in America. I think their unrestrained freedom gave them an illusion of power. They believed they knew how the country should be run better than the officials elected to run it. In the U.S.S.R.," he boasted, "we had no such problem."

"So Washington, D.C., is still standin'," Hickok said, gazing at the White House.

"We knew how important this city was to the American public," General Malenkov revealed. "What a monumental psychological victory to occupy the capital of our hated enemy! The neutron bomb inflicted damage to many of the buildings, but otherwise Washington emerged from the war much as it was before our invasion began." He nodded toward the White House. "No one is permited to live there now. It stands as a symbol of American decadence and capitalistic corruption. This room we are in is located in our North American Headquarters. It was constructed on the south lawn of the White House, both as a symbol of our victory and a reminder to the American people of our superiority."

"Don't you Russians believe in modesty?" Hickok cracked.

General Malenkov frowned. "What do we have to be modest about? We won, didn't we?"

"Did you?" Hickok countered.

"What do you mean?" General Malenkov demanded.

"I've been doin' some thinkin'," Hickok said. "And some things don't add up. For instance, why didn't you take over the whole country? Where'd you stop—at the Mississippi? How much of the country do you control anyway?"

General Malenkov straightened. "You ask too many questions, Hickok. I can't answer them all now. Why don't you rest, and we will continue our conversation later?"

"Whatever you say," Hickok stated, and stared out the window.

General Malenkov took a step toward the door, positioned at the opposite end of the room from the window.

"Pardon me, my general," Lieutenant Voroshilov made bold to speak, resorting to Russian so the fool in the buckskins could not understand.

General Malenkov stopped. "What is it?" he responded in kind.

Lieutenant Voroshilov indicated Hickok with a nod of his head. "I don't trust him," he said. "Why don't we subject the idiot to proper interrogation and be done with this nonsense? Why do you treat him so politely? You know he must be an enemy of the people?"

"Of course I know it," General Malenkov said with a trace of annoyance, irritated his subordinate would presume to challenge his judgment.

"Then why not inject him with our serum?" Lieutenant Voroshilov suggested. "Or hand him over to the Committee for State Security? They will make him tell the truth."

"Certainly they would," General Malenkov agreed, "but he might not survive the interrogation. The KGB are not gentle in their work." He sighed and draped his right arm over Voroshilov's shoulders. "My dear Nikolai," he said paternally, "how do you expect to advance in rank if you will not exercise the discretion required of a senior-grade officer? Yes, I could have permitted the KGB to take him. But what if he didn't survive their cross-examination? Where would that leave us? I receive the impression he is very strong, very disciplined. He would undoubtedly resist our efforts, force our interrogators to apply harsher measures. Many prisoners have died before they could be compelled to tell all they know. Even the serum has drawbacks. It is not infallible, and has adverse side effects. You say I am treating him politely. Hasn't it occurred to you there is a reason for this? I am judging the man, evaluating his character. By pretending to be friendly, I might win his confidence. I could learn his weaknesses. He might unwittingly reveal an exploitable factor we can use to our advantage. Didn't you see the look on his face when he mentioned the name of his vehicle? He didn't intend to tell us, but it slipped out. Do you comprehend?"

Lieutenant Voroshilov nodded sheepishly.

"I can turn him over to the KGB at any time," General Malenkov went on. "What's the rush? This is a most extraordinary case. I recognized its importance the moment I saw the report on this SEAL. Why do you think I took personal charge of the case? Why did I order this man to be brought here? We must proceed slowly. This calls for finesse, not brute force." He thoughtfully stared at the tiled floor. "Our own vehicles are in disrepair. We don't have enough spare parts to go around. Our helicopter fleet has been greatly reduced, and we dare not use our jets because they are too old and unreliable. Yet this SEAL appears to be in perfect shape. We must learn more about it and the people who own it. Do they have any more? Where did it really come from? I don't believe Hickok's story for a second. We must be patient, lieutenant. Haste only breeds incompetence."

Unnoticed by the picture window, Hickok surreptitiously peered at his captors. The general and the lieutenant were having a heart-to-heart about something, and they both had their backs to him. The third soldier, the one with the pistol, had relaxed his guard and was listening to the two officers.

This might be his big chance!

The wooden stand with his Pythons was to the left of the officers. The armed soldier was to their right.

How could he get to his Colts without being shot?

Hickok scanned the room. To his right was the row of medical equipment. He spotted a shelf near the edge of the window. On the shelf were shiny instruments: a forked object, one with a small circular mirror on its tip, a metal disk, and others. One of them appeared to be a thin knife.

The general and the lieutenant were talking away.

Hickok casually ambled toward the shelf, his hands clasped in front of him, his back to the room, feigning interest in the White House.

The Russians didn't seem to notice.

Hickok reached the end of the window and calmly glanced behind him, a smile on his lips.

General Malenkov and Lieutenant Voroshilov were still jabbering. The third soldier idly glanced at the gunman, then back at the officers.

Hickok nonchalantly leaned his right hand on the shelf while gazing out the window. Slowly, expecting to be challenged at any moment, he inched his fingers to the handle of the silver knife. He covered the handle with his palm, then slowly closed his hand around the knife.

Malenkov was expounding on some subject to Voroshilov.

Hickok mentally counted to ten, and then eased his right hand from the shelf and lowered it by his side.

None of the Russians had noticed.

Hickok held the knife close to his leg.

"I must leave now," General Malenkov said in English to the gunman. "I will return in an hour and escort you to the commissary."

"The what?" Hickok asked.

"The commissary," General Malenkov said. "You will be able to eat."

"Thanks," Hickok stated. "I'm so hungry I could eat a horse."

"I will treat you to some borscht," General Malenkov commented. "It's a traditional Russian dish."

"What's in it?"

The general licked his lips. "It's delicious. Borscht contains beets and sour cream."

"I can hardly wait," Hickok said deadpan.

General Malenkov smiled. "See you in an hour." He walked to the door with Lieutenant Voroshilov in tow. At the door he halted and looked at the soldier with the pistol. "If he tries to escape," the general ordered in Russian, "shoot him in the groin. I want him alive."

The soldier nodded and saluted.

Hickok waved as the general and the lieutenant left

the room. He grinned at the soldier and pointed at the White House. "They sure don't make 'em like that anymore, do they?"

The soldier didn't respond. He was a stocky man with dark hair and a square chin. The pistol was held steady in his right hand, aimed at the gunman.

"Don't you savvy English?" Hickok inquired.

The soldier remained immobile.

"What's the matter? Can't you palaver without permission?" Hickok asked.

The soldier's face creased in perplexity.

"So you can speak English," Hickok said.

"Please," the soldier remarked, "what is 'palaver'?"

"It means to shoot the breeze," Hickok explained. "Sling the bull. You know. Idle chitchat."

The soldier seemed even more confused. "I know English, yes. But I do not know many of the words you use."

Hickok took a few steps toward the soldier, acting innocent. He grinned. "That's because I'm partial to Old West lingo I picked up in books in our library."

"Does everyone where you are from talk like you do?" the soldier asked.

"Nope," Hickok acknowledged. "I'm the only one."

"Most strange," the soldier commented.

Hickok nodded in agreement and moved several feet closer to the soldier. "That's what my friends say too."

"Then why do you do it?" the soldier queried.

"I reckon my momma must of dropped me on my noggin when I was six months old," Hickok said. He took two more steps nearer to the soldier.

"You will stay where you are," the guard warned.

Hickok shrugged. "Whatever you say, pard. But I've got a question for you."

"A question?"

"Yeah. Do you mind if I ask it?" Hickok inquired.

"What is your question?" the soldier wanted to know.

"I don't reckon there's any chance of you letting me walk out that door, is there?" Hickok ventured to request.

The soldier laughed. "You are not serious, yes?"

"Deadly serious," Hickok gravely informed him.

The soldier shook his head. "Nyet. I can not allow you to leave this room."

"What would you do if I tried?" Hickok asked.

"I would shoot you," the soldier soberly responded.

Hickok sighed. "And I don't suppose there's nothin' I could say or do that would change your mind?"

"I will shoot you," the soldier reiterated.

"Well, you can't say I didn't try," Hickok said. He half turned, looking at the White House. "I can always spend my time counting the cracks in the walls."

The soldier shifted his attention to the decaying structure. "A most fitting fate for the decadent warmongers," he stated, quoting from a course he'd taken in Imperialist Practices and Fallacies.

"Speaking of fate," Hickok said slowly. He suddenly whipped his lean body around, his right hand flashing up and out.

The silver knife streaked across the intervening space and sliced into the soldier's right eye. He shrieked and clutched at the hilt, but the blood spurting from his ravaged eyeball made the handle too slippery to clasp. His trigger finger tightened on the trigger of his pistol, but before he could pull it he started to tremble uncontrollably. Spasms racked his body. His facial muscles quivered as he arched his back and staggered into the metal table.

Hickok knew the man was in his death throes.

The soldier's fingers involuntarily relaxed,

straightening, and the pistol dropped to the floor. He gasped and sprawled onto the table, on his stomach, blood dribbling from the corners of his mouth, his nostrils, and his punctured eye. His good eye locked on the gunman, and with a whining wheeze he expired.

Hickok walked to the wooden stand and retrieved his Pythons. He stared at the gleaming pearl-handled Colts, feeling complete again. What had they done with his Henry? he wondered. He hoped they'd overlooked it in the dark and it was still in the woods near the SEAL.

The SEAL.

How the blazes was he going to return to St. Louis? He needed to come up with one humdinger of an idea.

Voices, speaking in Russian, came through the closed wooden door.

It was time to hit the road.

Hickok quickly checked the pythons, and it was well he did. Someone had unloaded them while he was unconscious. He slipped the necessary cartridges from his gunbelt and reloaded both Colts.

Now let them try and stop him!

The gunman eased to the door and cautiously opened it. He found an amply lit corridor with brown floor tiles and white walls.

None of the varmints were in sight.

Hickok took a deep breath and stepped out of the medical room. He closed the door behind him and hurried to the left, searching for a place of concealment, somewhere he could get his bearings.

A door directly ahead abruptly opened and a tall woman in a white smock emerged.

Blast!

The woman spotted the gunman, her face registering utter bewilderment. She recovered and said something in Russian.

Hickok bounded forward.

The woman was opening her mouth to scream when the gunman slammed the barrel of his right Colt across her jaw.

The woman stumbled backard, bumping into the wall.

Hickok slugged her again for good measure.

She sagged to the floor in a disjointed heap.

Hickok ran now, knowing he had to get out of the building before the alarm was given. He hated being cooped up inside. Once outdoors, the odds of eluding his captors were infinitely better. He reached a fork in the corridor and bore to the left again. He was thankful he was on the ground floor; at least he wouldn't need to contend with finding the right stairs.

Two men, both in military uniforms, one armed with a holstered pistol, another with a machine gun— an AK-47, if Hickok remembered the gun manuals in the Family library correctly—appeared at the end of the corridor. They reacted to the gunman's presence instantly, the one with the pistol grabbing for his holster and the other soldier sweeping his AK-47 up.

Hickok was 30 feet from them. He never broke his stride as he leveled the Colts and fired, both Pythons booming simultaneously.

The two soldiers each took a slug between the eyes. The one with the pistol simply fell forward, but the trooper with the AK-47 tottered backwards, crashed into the left-hand wall, and dropped.

Hickok slowed as he neared the soldiers. He holstered the Colts and leaned over the soldier with the AK-47. "I need this more than you," he commented, scooping the gun into his arms and continuing to the end of the hallway.

Bingo!

Wide glass doors were on the other side of a spacious reception area. A woman at an oaken desk was frantically punching buttons on an instrument of some kind.

Hickok was abreast of her desk before he recalled the name of the contraption she was using: a telephone. They had used them before the Big Blast for communications purposes.

The woman started yelling into the receiver.

Hickok gripped the barrel of the AK-47 and swung it like a club, striking the receptionist on the left side of her head.

She slid from her chair to the floor, the telephone plopping alongside her.

Move!

Hickok ran to the glass doors. He paused, confused. The dang things didn't have any doorknobs! How was he supposed to—

The doors unexpectedly parted with a pronounced hiss.

What the—

Hickok raced outside. Never look a gift horse in the mouth! he always said. He scanned the scenery before him. From the position of the sun, he knew he was heading due south. In front, a park with trees and grass and couples strolling arm-in-arm and kids playing with puppies. To the right, a parking lot filled with vehicles. To the left, a sidewalk and a hedgerow.

Which way?

Hickok bore to the left, making for the hedge. He could hide and take a breather while he—

Four soldiers pounded into view, coming his way, jogging around the hedgerow on the sidewalk.

Someone in the park had seen the gunman and was shouting at the top of his lungs.

In the parking lot, three troopers hopped from a jeep and raced toward him.

Behind him, the glass doors hissed open, disgorging three more soldiers in hot pursuit.

Hickok crouched and raised the AK-47.

So much for subterfuge!

14

The blast of the Browning was practically deafening in the narrow confines of the hallway.

The leading Leather Knight toppled forward, shot through the chest.

Blade aimed at a second target, his finger tightening on the trigger.

A hard object rammed into the small of the Warrior's back.

"Drop it!" a stern voice commanded. "Or you can kiss your navel good-bye!"

Blade hesitated. How had one of them managed to get behind him?

"I ain't kidding, sucker!" snapped the speaker, a woman by the sound of her voice. "Drop it or I'll blow you away for what you did to Terza!"

Blade released the Browning and it clattered to the ground.

The onrushing Leather Knights had slowed and were cautiously advancing toward the prisoner, their weapons trained and cocked.

"Turn around, you son of a bitch!" ordered the woman behind the Warrior.

Blade turned, his hands held over his head.

She was a heavyset blonde with a scowl on her face. "The name's Erika, prick! And I'm gonna make sure you never forget it!"

"With a face like yours," Blade told her, "I doubt I ever will."

Erika's fleshy features reddened. "I'm gonna enjoy wasting you!" She held a Ruger Security-Six revolver in her left hand.

Blade studied the "dead end." The central portion of the wall was actually a concealed door. Beyond Erika's squat form was a spacious chamber basking in the light from ten lanterns. Other Knights were in the chamber, standing, staring at the doorway.

Erika glanced at the mob in the corridor. "You did a good job. We'll take him now." She paused. "What about the other two? Lex and her lover boy?"

"We didn't see them," admitted a stud.

"Go look for them," Erika said. "Search every nook and cranny. We want them found! They have to pay for what they did!"

The Leather Knights wheeled and ran down the hall. Two of them stopped and knelt alongside the man Blade had shot.

Erika poked Blade in the ribs with the Ruger Security-Six. "One false move and you're history!" she warned. She backed through the doorway, beckoning with the revolver for him to follow.

Blade entered the chamber, his arms in the air.

There were 11 Leather Knights in the room. Like the other sections displaying evidence of recent construction, this chamber was built of brick and the floor was mere dirt. Unlike the holding chamber with the balcony, this one had a large pit in the middle of the room. The Leather Knights ringed the pit, all of them armed. Two of them stood ten feet from the door, and they riveted baleful glares on the Warrior as he appeared.

"So happy you could join us," said Terza dryly. She wore her black leather jacket and pants. Her Llama Super Comanche V's were belted around her waist. "We're havin' a little party and you're the guest of honor." She seemed to experience difficulty in speaking, and her jaw was slightly swollen. Her pale blue eyes glittered as she gazed at Blade.

Next to her, Cardew's face reflected his sheer hatred. His right cheek was puffy and his right eye a narrow slit covered by a discolored, distended eyelid. Both of his lips were split and twice their normal size. A wooden splint had been applied to his left knee, and he had improvised a wooden crutch to support himself.

"I didn't expect to see you up and around so soon," Blade said to the stud. "I guess you have more guts than I gave you credit for. Too bad they're all between your ears."

Cardew went livid.

Terza motioned for the Warrior to come closer.

Blade lowered his arms and advanced to within a foot of the Leather Knight leader.

"You're a fine one to talk about Cardew," Terza said. "You aren't exactly the brightest man I ever met." She snickered. "But then, what else can you expect from a lousy man?"

"Not much," Erika chimed in.

Terza sneered at Blade. "You blew it, handsome. You had your big chance and you plain blew it." She lowered her voice so only Blade, Cardew, and Erika could overhear her remarks. "I wanted you, tiger. And like I told you before, I don't get the hots for a man all that often. Who knows? If you'd been any good, I might have spared your ass. But as it is—"

Blade snickered. "I don't think I missed much."

Terza's right hand gripped her right Comanche.

"You're the vainest woman I've ever met," Blade went on. "You think all you have to do is snap your fingers and any man in the world will do anything for the . . . honor . . . of bedding you." He paused. "You're wrong, Terza. You don't have the right to force a man to have sex with you. Sex isn't some mechanical function we perform for fleeting physical gratification. Sex should be an expression of our deepest love, our tenderest feelings. You denigrate it to an animalistic level. To you, sex is on the same par with eating or sleeping or any other purely physical sensation. Why don't you try exalting sex for once? Why don't you find someone to love, and express your love as meaningfully sexually as you know how. You never know," he concluded. "You might learn something."

"You dare talk to me like this?" Terza demanded.

"I'll talk to you any way I please," Blade countered. "I'm not one of your lackeys, your cowardly studs."

Cardew made a growling noise.

Blade glanced at Cardew's pulverized face. "What's the matter with you? Does the truth hurt? When was the last time the men around here had the balls to stand up to the women? Why do you let them push you around, to control your lives the way they do? Men and women should be equal partners in adjusting to life's responsibilities. Neither gender has the right to subjugate the other." He raised his voice so the others in the chamber could hear. "When are the Leather Knight men going to reclaim their proper place as equals with the women? When are the men going to stand on their own two feet and refuse to be little better than slaves? When will the men—"

Terza abruptly lunged upward, slapping Blade across the mouth. "Shut up! That's enough out of you! Who the hell do you think you are, coming in here and telling us how to live our lives? We've lived this way for a hundred years—"

"Does that make it right?" Blade interrupted.

"Yes!" Terza replied. "It's no worse than the way it was before the war."

"Before the war?"

"I'm not all *that* stupid," Terza declared angrily. "I can read some, and I know how it was before the war. The men ran everything. The government they had, all the businesses, the military, everything. Oh, there

were a few women at the top, but they were far out
numbered by the men. The men controlled things,
but they pretended the women had an equal say. The
damn hypocrites! At least we're honest about it!''

"Does that make it right?" Blade reiterated.

Terza was obviously flustered. She'd been taken off
guard by Blade's unexpected behavior. She'd
expected him to either beg for his life or else clam up
and take what was coming as stoically as possible. She
considered him to be the "macho" type, the "strong,
silent type," the kind who habitually lorded it over
women. She'd encountered outsiders before, and the
men were all pretty much the same. The last reaction
she'd anticipated was a verbal assault on her morals.

Blade sensed her emotional upheaval and
determined to press his advantage. "Terza, we don't
need to be enemies. We can be friends instead. My
people would welcome a treaty with yours. We could
work together, helping you to rebuild your city and
oppose the Reds. I came here on a peaceful mission.
I'd like to leave in peace."

"Peace!" Terza snorted. "Where is there peace in
this world? You tell me that, Mister High-and-Mighty!
If you want to survive in this rotten world, you've got
to be tough. It's survival of the fittest." She shook her
head. "Do you think we'd be dumb enough to trust
you? For all we know, your people are waiting for the
chance to jump us, to attack St. Louis the moment we
let down our guard. But I've got news for you! The
Leather Knights will never be beaten. Not even the
Reds have beaten us! Look around you. Why do you
think we've gone to all the trouble to build all these
new tunnels and rooms under the library? And we've
also done it under some of the other buildings.
Because we know the Reds are gonna come after us
someday, and we're gonna be ready for 'em! These
tunnels will be the last retreat for those who can't
make it out of the city. We have food stockpiled and

plenty of guns and ammo. We've thought of everything!'' she boasted.

"Except how the women and men can live in
harmony,'' Blade responded.

"Who the hell cares about that?'' Terza gruffly
demanded.

"The men do,'' Blade said. "And I bet some of the
women as well. I understand Lex was leaving the
Leather Knights because she doesn't agree with the
way you run things. Do you think she's the only
one?''

"No one leaves the Leather Knights,'' Terza said.
"And as for the men, they'll do what the hell we tell
them, when we tell them, or they'll get what you're
gonna get.''

Blade scanned the chamber, noting the pensive,
troubled faces of the men. He knew he'd touched a
raw nerve. "With an attitude like yours,'' he told
Terza, "it's only a question of time before the women
have a full-scale rebellion on their hands. It's
inevitable. Sooner or later, the men will have had
enough, they'll have taken all they will take. And
what will happen? You'll have a bloody civil war on
your hands, the studs against the sisters. After it's
over, one side or the other will assume control. What
if the men win?''

"They never will!'' Terza vowed.

"What if neither side wins?'' Blade continued.
"What if both sides are so depleted there aren't
enough remaining to rule St. Louis? And all because
the women believe they're better than the men. What
a waste!''

"We *are* better than the men!'' Terza stated
irritably. She saw the expressions on the six men in
the room and realized the giant stranger was right: the
studs did resent the sisters' domination.

"Women aren't better than men,'' Blade was
saying. "And men aren't better than women. They're

just different from one another. The secret is to recognize the differences and complement each other, whether in a marriage or in society as a whole."

"This bozo is so full of bullshit it's coming out of his ears," Erika interrupted.

Cardew took a tentative step toward Blade. He tried to speak, but couldn't form the worlds. At last, after licking his busted lips, he managed to croak a question. "Do you . . . believe . . . all that stuff?"

"Of course," Blade confirmed.

"Enough of this!" Terza barked. "You're just stallin'! We aren't here to shoot the shit!"

"Let's get down to cases!" Erika said eagerly.

"Do you have any idea where you are?" Terza asked.

"How should I?" Blade replied.

"This is a special room," Terza mentioned. "We built it for just one reason."

Blade stared at the gaping pit. The sight of it stirred memories of the last pit he'd seen, the one he'd been tossed into by a madman on the run to Denver, Colorado. He repressed an impulse to shudder.

"This hole is real unique," Terza explained. "It connects to the city's sewers. Ever seen a sewer?"

Blade shook his head.

"The sewers don't get used much anymore," Terza said. "Before the war, they pumped all the shit and the piss and the garbage through 'em. There's a lot of passages under the city, in all different shapes and sizes. Some of the sewer tunnels are real big, so big a person can walk in 'em. Others are so small even the rats can't use 'em. Do you know what else is down there, besides the rats?"

Blade simply stared at her.

Terza averted his gaze, facing the pit. "We don't know what caused them, but there are a lot of . . . things . . . in the sewers. Maybe it was the radiation in the water, or something was pumped into the sewer system. We found some old barrels once in one of the tunnels, and some chemical gook had seeped out of 'em. Whatever the reason, there are a lot of creepy, crawly things down there."

"So?" Blade finally said.

"So this hole leads to the sewers where the things live. One of the things . . ." she grinned, "is called Grotto. You have to see it to believe it."

"Grotto craves flesh," Erika commented, grinning wickedly.

"And Grotto hasn't eaten for a while," Terza declared. "Three guesses who its next meal is gonna be."

Blade frowned, calculating the odds of escaping from the chamber. There weren't any. The Leather Knights would gun him down before he traveled three feet.

Terza glanced at the Warrior. "Any last words?"

"I feel sorry for you," Blade said.

"Sorry for me?" Terza retorted in disbelief. "*You're* the one who's gonna be mutant bait, dimwit!"

"You may succeed in killing me," Blade said, "but in doing so you'll destroy yourselves."

"What are you babbling about?" Terza demanded.

"I have friends," Blade told her. "They'll come after me. One of them, in particular, won't rest until he finds out what happened to me. And when he does find out, one way or another he'll guarantee the Leather Knights are wiped out."

"Should we tremble now or later?" Erika joked.

Blade shrugged. "I knew you wouldn't believe me."

"What is this joker?" Terza queried. "Some kind of superman?"

"No," Blade said. "He's not a superman. But he's the most lethal person I know. You might say he's sort of a living leathal weapon."

"Oh! I'm scared!" Erika said in mock panic, and

laughed.

"Suit yourself," Blade said.

Terza walked to the edge of the pit. "Let's get this over with! Summon Grotto."

One of the Knights on the other side of the pit, a tall, bearded stud, sank to his knees. He grasped a board lying near the edge and raised it over his head.

"I can hardly wait!" Erika said, elated.

The stud proceeded to slam the flat board against the side of the pit, again and again, filling the chamber with a regular cadence of thuds.

Blade inched nearer to the hole, examining it. The sides were 20 feet deep and solid earth. The floor was littered with white bones: thigh bones, ribs, skulls, and more, all distinctly human.

Cardew was staring thoughtfully at Blade. "Say," he was able to croak, "I never did get your name."

"It's Blade," the Warrior said.

"Too bad we couldn't have met under different circumstances," Cardew stated wistfully.

Blade looked at the Knight, surprised. Cardew seemed to be sincere. Maybe he wasn't a total degenerate after all.

The bearded stud maintained his constant pounding.

"It won't be long!" Erika cried.

Terza glanced at Blade. "What a waste."

"I'm not dead yet," Blade reminded her.

"You will be," Terza said.

"Don't I receive a fighting chance?" Blade asked her.

"A fighting chance?"

"Yeah. Like my Bowies."

Terza laughed. "Are you wacko? Do you really expect me to hand your knives back to you? No way, turkey. They're upstairs. I may take one of them for myself after this is over."

"No weapons then?" Blade inquired, knowing how

she would respond.

"No weapons," Terza affirmed. "Just you and Grotto. You two should become real cozy down there."

The bearded stud was beginning to tire. His pounding was losing some of its force.

"Where the hell is it?" Erika snapped.

"It takes a while sometimes," Terza said. "You know that."

A loud hissing suddenly emanated from the pit.

"Grotto!" Erika cried happily.

They all craned their necks for a good view of the bottom of the pit.

For the first time, Blade noticed a subterranean entrance to the pit. Located on the north side, it was a black hole about ten feet in height and eight feet wide.

The Leather Knights were collectively watching that hole.

The hissing had ceased.

"We've been doing this for near thirty years," Terza said to Blade. "Not in this room, because it wasn't built at the time, but in the sewers. Some of the Knights had seen Grotto prowling the sewers, and someone once had the bright idea of feedin' outsiders to it. Grotto loves fresh meat," Terza said, grinning.

"What do you have against outsiders?" Blade asked.

"We don't need any more people in St. Louis," Terza answered. "We already have about as many as the Knights can handle. Besides, outsiders always want to change things. They're just like you. Know-it-all bastards who stick their noses in where they don't belong! So when we were constructing our underground retreat, we built this hidden room next to one of the sewer tunnels. Now we can call Grotto directly from here."

"How convenient," Blade said. "A walk-in

restaurant for a mutant.''

"What's a restaurant?" Terza inquired.

"A place where you can eat fine food," Blade replied. "They had a lot of them before the war."

"Then that's what this is," Terza said. "Grotto's restaurant."

Another stud had taken over the pounding chores, but there was still no sign of the mysterious monster.

"Maybe it doesn't like your service," Blade quipped. "Do you supply napkins and tableware?"

"I don't know what you're talkin' about," Terza said. "Grotto will show up. Sometimes it takes a while, but it always shows up."

"Once it took most of the day," Erika commented. "Damn! I hope it doesn't take that long this time!"

"I can wait," Blade informed them.

Terza laughed lightly. "I bet you can."

15

"What do you think happened to him?" Lex asked.

"I don't know," Rikki-Tikki-Tavi responded.

The Warrior was concerned for the safety of his friend. He'd heard the hubbub caused by the Leather Knights in the adjacent hallway, and it was easy to figure out Blade's selfless sacrifice in diverting the Knights away from the passage leading to the alley.

"What are we going to do?" Lex questioned him.

"Wait," Rikki told her.

"For what?"

"Until Blade returns," Rikki said.

"What if he doesn't?"

"Then we go looking for him," Rikki stated.

They were crouched along the hallway wall not ten feet from the exit to the alley. The Knights hadn't bothered to install a door at the end of the hallway. The opening permitted brilliant sunlight to flood the hall for over 20 yards.

Lex glanced at the exit: so inviting, so tempting, so close! One quick dash and she would gain her freedom. She looked at the lean man beside her, his face in profile as he gazed down the hallway hoping to see the big one called Blade. She remembered the pained look on his face when Terza had been using her for target practice. Her feminine intuition sensed he cared, and she found herself delighted at the prospect. "You're really worried about him, aren't you?" she asked.

Rikki nodded.

"How long have you know him?"

"All of my life," Rikki stated. "He's only a year older than I am. We were childhood friends and we grew to manhood together. We even selected the same path."

"The same path?" Lex repeated.

"Yes. The path of the Warrior," Rikki said. "Blade is the head of the Warriors. I will not depart St. Louis without him."

Lex could detect the undisguised affection in Rikki's tone. "Are there many of you Warriors?" she asked, keeping her voice low.

"Fifteen," Rikki disclosed.

"Why are you called Warriors?"

Rikki glanced at her. "My people are known as the Family. We live in a walled compound far away. The man responsible for constructing the compound and gathering the subsequent survivors of the war together knew they would require protection. He knew civilization would crumble after World War III. He predicted society would revert to primitive levels, and he was right. To safeguard the Family from the scavengers, the marauding bands of killers, and mutates, and others, he formed a special corps of fighters and designated them as the Warriors. For over one hundred years the Warriors have defended the Family from all attackers. We take a solemn oath, and any one of us would give our life in the performance of our duty."

"Why did you want to be a Warrior?" Lex asked.

"It is my nature," Rikki responded simply.

"I don't understand."

"No two individuals are alike," Rikki elaborated. "No two of us have the same personality, the same characteristics, or the same abilities. Our natures are essentially different. My Family is an excellent example. Some of us prefer to be Tillers of the soil.

Others choose to be Weavers, or Healers, or Empaths, or Blacksmiths. Each according to his or her nature. I wanted to become a Warrior because it was inherent in my personality. The Family Elders don't force anyone into a vocation against his or her will. They encourage each of us to find our particular calling and devote our talents to it." He paused. "It wasn't always this way. I've read some history books detailing life before the Big Blast—"

"The Big Blast?"

"That's what the Family calls World War III," Rikki explained. "Before the war, society tried to mold every individual into a set pattern. Every aspect of their lives was strictly regulated by countless laws. Amazingly, the people back then considered themselves to be free. The irony is, it took a nuclear war to actually liberate them."

"You don't sound like you would have been too happy back then," Lex remarked.

"I wouldn't have been," Rikki admitted. "I would have resented every intrusion on my freedom. Why, they even passed laws making it illegal to carry a weapon in public! Can you imagine that?"

"Why would they do such a thing?"

"Because they wanted the populace as docile as cattle," Rikki said bitterly. "Their society was overrun by criminals and degenerates, but the so-called leaders wouldn't allow the people to carry weapons to defend themselves. The leaders claimed it would promote vigilantism."

"What's that?"

"That's where the average person stands up to someone who is threatening them in some way."

"And the leaders didn't want that?" Lex asked, perplexed.

"Not according to my teacher, Plato," Rikki said. "You see, such an attitude promotes independence. If people can supply their own needs and defend them-

selves from the violent defectives, then they don't
have any need for anyone else to tell them how to
live, what they should wear and eat and think. No,
the leaders were afraid of vigilantism. They were
frightened by self-reliant individualism. So they
stifled intiative and suppressed creativity." He
frowned. "No, I would never have fit in back then.
Don't get me wrong. I'm not anti-social by any
standard. I believe in peaceful relations with all men
and women. But a lot of degenerates don't feel the
same way. They'd slit your throat as soon as look at
you." He smiled at her. "And I would never permit
that."

Lex recognized the compliment. "You've given this
a lot of thought," she noted.

"What use is a mind if you don't use it?" Rikki
rejoined.

"What's it like?" Lex inquired. "This place you're
from."

Rikki sighed. "You'd enjoy it. We all believe in the
ideal of loving our neighbor and serving the Spirit.
We may argue about various issues, but overall our
relations are harmonious. Far better than anything
I've seen anywhere else."

"It sounds like a dream come true," Lex said.

"Would you like to go there?" Rikki asked her.

Lex brightened. "Would they let me come?"

"They would welcome you with open arms," Rikki
confirmed. "Especially if you had a sponsor in the
Family."

"What's a sponsor?"

"Someone in the Family who vouches for your
integrity."

"Who—" Lex began.

"I would," Rikki said quickly.

"You'd do that for me?"

Rikki nodded and stared down the hallway.

Now the exit to the alley was even more appealing.

Lex wanted to flee the library, the leave St. Louis far behind. Rikki's home seemed too good to be true. She wanted to live to find out for herself. "What's this place where you're from called?"

"The Home."

"The Home?" Lex giggled. "Where else would the Family live, right?"

Rikki grinned.

"You must have a lot of friends there," Lex stated.

"Many close friends," Rikki affirmed.

"Tell me about them," she urged him.

"Most of my closest friends are Warriors like myself," Rikki said. "You'll meet them. There's Geronimo, who took his name after an Indian chief of long, long ago. One of them is named Hickok, the Family's supreme gunfighter."

"Is he better with guns than you?" Lex interjected.

"Much better," Rikki acknowledged. "His expertise with guns, particularly handguns, is sensational. We have a Warrior called Yama, and he's good with every weapon. Teucer specializes in the bow. Others excel with different weapons."

"What are you best with?"

"A katana," Rikki said. "My instructors felt I was the best martial artist in the family. Consequently, I qualified to possess the katana."

"What's a martial artist?"

Rikki stared at her. "Someone skilled in hand-to-hand combat and with Oriental weaponry."

"What's hand-to-hand combat? Punching somebody's lights out?"

Rikki chuckled. "My answer was rather simplistic. A martial artist is adept in the science of unarmed and armed combat. It's more than just knowing how to punch somebody's lights out. It's a way of life, a discipline in which you become the ultimate master of yourself. A perfected martial artist is at one with his Maker, with the universe, and with himself.

Sublime control enables you to live without fear. You achieve an inner peace, and this is reflected in your relations with others."

"This is all a little over my head," Lex admitted.

"I can teach you if you want," Rikki offered.

Their eyes met, and a mutual tenderness was silently shared.

"You never did tell me," Lex said after a bit, "why you picked such a strange name?"

"It was the logical choice," Rikki said. "The Founder of our Home encouraged all of his followers to learn from the mistakes humankind had perpetuated in the past. He was afraid we would lose sight of the stupidity behind the war. So he started the Naming at age sixteen. All Family members, when they turn sixteen, are allowed to pick any name they want from any of the books in our vast library. This way, the Founder hoped, we wouldn't forget our roots. At first, they used only the history books. But now any book is okay. I took my name from a story concerning an animal known as a mongoose."

"A mongoose?"

"Small animals," Rikki said. "They were used in a country called India to protect their families from deadly snakes known as cobras."

"So that's why you took the name!"

"Yes. It fits my chosen profession," Rikki stated.

They lapsed into a short silence.

"What about you?" Rikki finally asked. "I've told you a lot about myself. Tell me something about your life."

Lex shrugged, her green eyes betraying a hint of sadness. "What's to tell? I was raised by my mom and dad in the northwest part of the city. When I was fifteen, one of the sisters nominated me to become a Knight. I was thrilled. I thought it was the biggest honor there was."

"Now you don't think so?"

"No!" Lex said, her voice hardening. "They fed me all that garbage about women being superior to men when I was young, and I believed it. I ran roughshod over the studs like all of the other sisters. But something happened."

"What?"

"The older I got," Lex said bitterly, "the more I realized how sick the situation was. I mean, here we have all of these women bossing the men around like the males are the scum of the earth. No love. No deep feelings. No caring. Just the sisters and their sex toys. I knew the studs didn't respect us. In fact, I suspect they downright hate us. And I grew real tired of the whole trip."

"Is that why you wanted to leave the Leather Knights?" Rikki inquired.

Lex nodded, her red hair bobbing. "I just knew there must be a better place somewhere else. I planned to sneak out of the city, and my friend Mira agreed to come along. But you saw how far we got."

"How do the other residents of St. Louis feel about the Knights?" Rikki probed.

"They have to tolerate it because the Leather Knights protect them from outsiders," Lex detailed. "A lot of the people have what you might call normal families, but the sisters look down their noses at any woman who shares her life with a man. And the sisters never miss a chance to feed their lies to the little girls. Believe me, if a girl is told year after year that all men are scuzz, that men only want one thing from a woman and the only way to keep them in line is to make them into slaves, then the girl starts to accept all of this as true. I know. It happened to me."

"Do any of the other sisters feel the way you do?"

"Lots," Lex replied. "But they're too scared to defy Terza. They know what happens to traitors."

"Why is it," Rikki asked, "one sex is always trying to dominate the other? Why can't men and women learn to live in a state of mutual cooperation instead of antagonistic bickering?''

''How do the men and women get along at your Home?'' Lex asked.

''We have our problems,'' Rikki said. ''But from what I've seen, we relate much better than many men and women elsewhere. I don't think either side views the other as some sort of sex object. We're taught in the Family school to always seek for the inner beauty in every person. Having big breasts or a handsome face isn't a social advantage in the Family.''

''I can't wait to see this Home of yours,'' Lex declared longingly.

''You will,'' Rikki promised. He stood and stretched his legs. ''It's time to go.''

''Where are we going?''

Rikki pointed down the hallway. ''After Blade.''

''Can't we give him more time?''

''No,'' Rikki said. ''I've waited too long as it is. We'll search this building from top to bottom, every square inch. Do you have any idea where he could be?''

''You mean if they caught him?'' Lex pondered a moment. ''He might be in the holding cell, or maybe they're going to feed him to Grotto. Or Terza could be playing fun and games with him.''

''We'll try the holding cell first,'' Rikki advised.

Lex took a deep breath and straightened. ''I'm right behind you,'' she said, although she silently wished she were far away at Rikki's Home, where it was safe, where the men and women weren't constantly at each other's throats, where everyone tried to love one another.

Funny.

She'd assumed she was too mature to believe in fairy tales.

Lex shrugged her shoulders and stuck to Rikki's heels as he retraced their steps into the gloomy interior of the structure.

16

The gunfighter was in his element.

Hickok had been reared in the placid environment of the Home. He'd attended the Family school as required of all youngsters and teenagers, and been taught all of the profound spiritual truths the wise Elders knew. Although he perceived the validity of a doctrine such as "Love thy neighbor" intellectually, he found the practical applications left something to be desired. How was it possible, he often asked himself, to love your neighbor when that neighbor might be a scavenger intending to kill you and rob you, or a mutate bent on tearing you to shreds? He discreetly distinguished a flaw in such a philosophy. To him, it never made any sense for the spiritual people to allow themselves to be wiped out by their benighted brethren. There was only one viable alternative: the spiritual types, such as the Family, had to protect themselves from the manifold dangers proliferating after the unleashing of the nuclear and chemical holocaust. Early on, Hickok discovered his niche in life. He didn't think he was qualified to become a teacher or a preacher, but he knew he was more than competent to defend those who were spiritual from those who weren't.

Warrior status fit him like the proverbial glove.

Because he devoted his entire personality to whatever interested him, Hickok rapidly became one of the Family's top Warriors. His ambidextrous ability

with handguns insured his prominence. And because
he never fretted over the fate of the foes he downed
in a gunfight, because he sincerely believed the Elders
when they instructed him to accept the fact of
survival beyond this initial life for anyone with the
slightest shred of spiritual faith, he entertained few
compunctions about pulling the trigger. In short,
Hickok was one of the most proficient, and most
deadly, Warriors in the Family. Some, such as Blade,
insisted Hickok was *the* most deadly.

The Russians might have been inclined to agree.

Hickok spun and fired at the three soldiers coming
through the glass doors. The AK-47 bucked and
chattered, and the trio of troopers were struck before
they could bring their own weapons to bear. They
were catapulted backward by the impact of the heavy
slugs tearing through their chests. The glass doors
were hit too, and they shattered and crumbled with a
loud crash.

There was no time to lose!

Four soldiers were still advancing from the
direction of the hedgerow, and three were sprinting
toward the gunman from the parking lot.

Hickok darted into the building, dodging the prone
bodies blocking the doorway. He ran to the
receptionist's desk and ducked behind it, straddling
her unconscious form.

Footsteps pounded outside, and a moment later the
seven soldiers raced into the receptionist's area.

Someone shouted orders in Russian.

Hickok tensed, wondering if they would look
behind the desk or mistakenly suppose he had taken
one of the corridors.

The footsteps tramped past the desk.

Hickok counted to three and rose, the AK-47
cradled at waist level.

The seven troopers were ten feet off and heading
down one of the corridors.

"Peek-a-boo!" Hickok shouted.

To their credit, they tried to turn and shoot instead of diving for cover.

Hickok squeezed the trigger and swept the AK-47 in an arc. The soldiers were rocked and racked by the devastating hail of lead. Only one of them managed to return the gunman's fire, and he missed, his pistol plowing a shot into the desk in front of the Warrior.

Two of them screamed as they died.

All seven were sprawled on the tiled floor when the AK-47 went empty. Hickok tossed the gun aside and vaulted the desk. He ran to the glass doors and leaped over the three dead soldiers.

About a dozen people from the park, civilians by their attire, were tentatively congregating outside the Headquarters building.

Hickok charged them, drawing his Colts, hoping none of them was armed. They frantically parted as he jogged past, and then he was crossing a paved road and entering a large natural area with high, unkempt grass and a row of tall trees. He bypassed two children flying a kite and reached the safety of the trees.

No one was after him. Yet.

Hickok kept going, and once beyond the row of trees he paused to get his bearings.

That was when he saw it.

Whatever "it" was.

Off to his left, towering over the surrounding landscape, was a gigantic obelisk. The top portion was missing, apparently destroyed during the war, leaving a jagged crown at the crest.

What the blazes was it?

Hickok headed to the right. He spied a stand of trees 40 yards distant and made for them. He knew the soldiers would be after him in force, and he had to find a refuge quickly. But where? He didn't know the layout of the city. Were there any safe areas, sections

of the city inhabited only by descendants of the
original Americans? Or had the Russians imported
their own people to populate the city? And what
about the ones he saw in the park? Were they
Americans or Russians? For all he knew, he could be
alone in a city where every person was an enemy.

The gunman reached the trees.

Hickok dropped to his knees, holstering his
Pythons, gathering his breath. He saw a road yonder,
past the trees, and beyond the road a long lake or
pool.

Where the heck was he?

Frustrated, he slowly stood and walked to the edge
of the road. Directly ahead was the pool. To his right
was a wide, cleared space filled with pedestrians. To
his left, the road seemed to branch out and encircle
another pool. The air had a misty quality about it, and
he wondered if he was near a large body of water.

Which way should he go?

The Red Army would be sweeping the area any
minute. He decided to gamble, to mingle with the
masses, hoping he could lose himself in the crowd. He
walked from the trees and ambled parallel with the
long pool.

A young man and an attractive woman, seated on a
blue blanket with a wicker picnic basket by their side,
glanced up as he approached.

''Hi,'' the youth said.

''Howdy,'' Hickok greeted them.

The woman gawked at the gunman's waist and
nudged her companion. She whispered to him and his
brow knitted in consternation.

Hickok was five feet from them.

''Nice guns you have there,'' the youth commented
nervously.

''I like 'em,'' Hickok said.

''I thought guns were illegal,'' the youth stated.

''Not mine,'' Hickok assured him.

The youth and his lady friend exchanged hurried whispers.

Hickok passed them, his thumbs hooked in his gunbelt.

"Say, mister," the youth ventured.

Hickok stopped and looked over his left shoulder.

"We just heard some shooting," the youth said. "Was that you?"

Hickok scrutinized them, debating whether he could trust them.

"I've never seen anyone dressed like you before," the youth remarked, rubbing his hands on his jeans as he spoke. "You stand out like a sore thumb. It's none of my business, you understand, but if you're looking for somewhere you won't stick out, go around the west end of the Reflecting Pool, past the Lincoln Memorial, and go south. You'll come to Independence Avenue, and on the other side is West Potomac Park. They don't bother to cut the grass or trim the trees there and it's a real jungle."

"Why are you tellin' me this?" Hickok demanded.

"I can put two and two together," the youth said. "Gunshots. A stranger with a pair of revolvers." The youth lowered his voice. "I may not be with the Resistance, but that doesn't mean I like the Reds."

Hickok grinned. "Thanks, pard." He waved and walked toward the far end of the Reflecting Pool. What a stroke of luck! If he could reach West Potomac Park, he could lay over for a spell and figure out how to return to St. Louis. *That* was going to be the tough part. Evidently, they'd flown him from St. Louis to Washington, D.C., in just one night. The feat sounded impossible, but then he didn't know how fast one of those Red copters could fly. What was it General Malenkov had said? St. Louis was 860 miles from Washington? Did the Red Copters need to refuel en route? Seemed likely to him.

More people were in the vicinity of the Reflecting

Pool, enjoying the sunshine, idly strolling or chatting with friends. Several kids were floating wooden boats in the water.

Hickok realized he was attracting a lot of attention; nearly everyone was staring at him, a few going so far as to stop and gape. The residents he saw wore cheaply constructed clothing of an indeterminate fashion. None wore bucksins. And none packed hardware. That youth had been right on the money. He *did* stand out like a sore thumb.

The gunman reached the west end of the Reflecting Pool and paused, gazing at the edifice before him. The Lincoln Memorial, the youth had said. The structure was immense and impressive, with a massive dome and elaborate columns. Unlike the obelisk, the Lincoln Memorial hadn't been damaged during the war. A red banner with white lettering was suspended above the portal. The sign was in English: "Lincoln, Champion of the Proletariat."

Hickok absently scratched his chin.

What the blazes was a proletariat?

"Excuse me, comrade," intruded an insistent voice.

Hickok swiveled to his right.

A stocky man in a blue uniform and carrying a nightstick was approaching.

"Howdy," Hickok said to him.

"What play are you with?" the man asked.

Play? Hickok casually placed his right hand on the right Python.

"I'm Dimitri, Capitol Police," the man said, smiling, revealing even spaced teeth. "I saw a play last year at the People's Center. You know, the old Kennedy Center. It was about the reign of Napoleon, and the costumes were fabulous. What play are you with?"

"*Scouts of the Prairie,*" Hickok replied.

"When did it open?" the man asked, excited. "What is it about? I just love the plays!" he gushed. "There are so few anymore."

"It opens tonight," Hickok told him,. "At the . . . People's Center!"

"What is it about?" the policeman reiterated.

A flash of inspiration motivated the gunman. "It's all about how the Old West capitalists exploited the Indians and stole their land."

"Ahhhh, yes," the policeman stated. "We studied it in school. What part do you play? Your costume is most excellent."

"I play a man named Hickok," Hickok said. "He was what they called a gunfighter, or some such. It's a real exciting play."

"I can't wait to see it!" the policeman declared enthusiastically.

"Tell you what," Hickok said, leaning closer to the policeman. "I'm not supposed to do this, but I'll leave a message with the head honcho. Why don't you come and tell them Hickok sent you. I can promise you a time you won't forget. Bring the missus too."

"Free seats?" The policeman laughed, elated at his good fortune. "I can't thank you enough, comrade!"

Hickok shrugged, feigning humility. "That's what comrades are for, right?"

"Thank you just the same." The policeman continued on his rounds, whistling, content with the world.

Hickok turned from the Lincoln Memorial, bearing south. Yes, sir. There's no idiot like a happy idiot! He glanced behind him and detected a commotion at the eastern end of the Reflecting Pool.

Uh-oh.

Time to make tracks.

Hickok hurried, cutting across a lawn until he reached an avenue. Was it the one he wanted? Independence Avenue? There was no way of telling. But on the other side of the avenue was a veritable wall of vegetation, dense underbrush, and abundant trees.

The racket had reached the steps of the Lincoln Memorial.

Hickok looked both ways; nobody was nearby. Perfect! He ran across the avenue and into the bushes on the far side. The vegetation was thick, but negotiable. He pressed onward, keeping low, crawling under low limbs and protruding foliage or skirting them where possible. After 30 yards he stopped and listened.

Nothing behind him.

Maybe he had the breather he needed.

Hickok crept to the base of a spreading maple and leaned against the trunk.

So what was next?

The gunman thought of Blade and Rikki, and speculated on how they were faring in St. Louis. He certainly hoped they were doing better than he was. How would Sherry take it if he never returned to the Home? And what about little Ringo . . .

Hickok shook his head, annoyed at himself. Sure, he was in a tight scrape, but that was no reason to get all negative. He must look at the positive side of things.

There *had* to be a way out of this mess!

The air above abruptly became agitated by a stiff wind, and the tops of the trees started whipping from side to side as a funny "thupping" sound drew nearer and nearer.

Hickok drew his left Colt, craning his neck for a clear view through the tree limbs.

An enormous helicopter appeared, flying slowly to the southeast. It dwarfed the other helicopter Hickok had seen, the one responsible for flipping the SEAL on its side. This one was easily ten times as big. For a moment, the gunman believed the copter was searching for him, but it maintained a steady course to the southeast without deviating. A helicopter seeking him would be zigzagging all over the woods.

Where was it heading?

Hickok holstered his Python and rose. He hastened

after the copter, striving to keep it in sight, flinching as thorns bit into his legs and arms. He felt the helicopter might be landing close by. Why else would it be so low? He reached a small glade and stared upward.

The helicopter was descending toward the southeast.

He was right!

Hickok resumed running, ignoring the jabs and stabs from the sundry branches and twigs he passed. If he could reach that helicopter, and if he could force the pilot to fly him, he might be able to escape from Washington and head for St. Louis.

If.

If.

If.

Whoever invented that word should have been shot!

17

"The holding cell should be just ahead," Lex said.

Rikki nodded, a barely perceptible movement in the darkened hallway.

"I can't understand why we haven't seen any of the Knights," Lex whispered. "I doubt they gave up looking for us."

Rikki was bothered by the same consideration. Where *were* the Leather Knights? Even if Blade had been caught, it was doubtful the Knights would abandon their hunt for Lex and her "lover boy."

"I wish we were packing," Lex commented.

Rikki brandished the knife Blade had given him. "We're not defenseless," he reminded her.

"Oh, great," Lex said. "One lousy knife against all of their guns!"

A lantern hanging from a metal hook illuminated one of the recessed doors into the holding cell.

Rikki reached the door and gripped the doorknob. He listened, but all was quiet on the other side. Fully realizing he might be waltzing into a trap, he threw the door open. And there it was: the dirt floor, the balcony, the brick wall, and the chains.

But nothing else.

"We could try Terza's quarters," Lex recommended.

"Lead the way," Rikki said, stepping aside.

Lex crossed the holding cell to the far door. After ascertaining the hallway was unoccupied, she led

Rikki to the nearest stairs and up to the top floor of the library. ''There might be guards,'' she whispered.

''I'll go first,'' Rikki offered. He cautiously opened the stairwell door and peered around the jamb.

A solitary Knight, a lean man with a crooked nose and armed with a holstered revolver, was leaning against the wall about ten feet from the stairwell. He appeared to be bored to death.

The knife in his right hand, Rikki eased from the stairwell and silently advanced toward the unsuspecting guard.

The Leather Knight raised his right hand and began examining his fingernails.

Rikki was eight feet from the guard.

The Knight coughed.

Six feet.

The Knight sensed another presence. Not anticipating trouble, he glanced to his right, his eyes widening in alarm at the sight of the small man in black.

''What the hell!'' the Knight blurted out, and went for his gun.

Rikki was already in motion, leaping forward and sweeping his right hand back and out.

In the act of drawing his revolver, the Leather Knight was impaled in the throat. The horrifying shock of the knife in his neck stunned him. He opened his mouth to scream.

Rikki sprang, his legs arching upward in a graceful Yoko-tobi-geri, a side jump kick, his right foot, extended and rigid, slamming into the guard, catching his crooked nose dead center and smashing his head against the wall.

The guard grunted as his nostrils were crushed.

Rikki landed, his coiled frame in motion, spinning, executing a flawless Mawashi-geri, a roundhouse kick.

The guard was struck on his right cheek. He toppled

to the floor with a faint gasp.

Rikki looked at Lex. "Which room is it?" There were three doors on either side of the hallway.

Lex hastened to the closest door. She tried the knob. "It's not locked," she said, and shoved.

Rikki darted past her into the room.

It was empty.

"I don't get it," Lex stated. "I thought Terza was warm for Blade's form. Maybe she changed her mind about him. They might have decided to feed him to Grotto."

"Where?" Rikki asked.

"There's a special room downstairs hooked up to the sewers," Lex disclosed. "He might be there."

"Why the sewers?" Rikki inquired.

"That's where Grotto lives," Lex explained.

Rikki scanned the room. "We need weapons." He noticed a closet to the left of Terza's bed and walked to it.

"I'll keep watch," Lex offered, turning to the door, closing it.

Rikki opened the closet and found a dozen black-leather garments on wire hangers. Piled on the floor were sandals, black boots, and peculiar shoes with spiked heels. He closed the door and moved to rejoin Lex, but a pile of white clothing heaped on the floor by the bed attracted his attention.

"I hear voices!" Lex warned him.

Rikki knelt and touched the white clothing, a white-lace affair undoubtedly intended to expose more skin than it covered. About to stand, he detected a glimmer of silver from under the bed.

"They're coming this way!" Lex whispered urgently.

Rikki dropped to his knees and peeked under the bed. His pulse quickened at the discovery of the items he most wanted: Blade's Commando and Bowies and his own scabbard lying next to his katana. The Spirit was with them! He grabbed the scabbard and slid it through his black belt, then withdrew the katana from under the bed and with a practiced flourish returned the sword to its scabbard.

"They're almost here!" Lex said.

"Let them come," Rikki told her.

Lex turned from the doorway and glanced at him. "Why . . ." she began.

Rikki grinned and rose, the Commando and Bowies in his arms.

"Where did you . . ." Lex started to ask a question, then stopped as a loud shout filled the hallway.

Rikki ran to her side and handed over the Commando and the Bowies. "Hold these," he instructed her. He tiptoed to the door and pressed his left ear to the wood.

"—dead. Who the hell could have done it?" a man was demanding.

"The big guy is downstairs," mentioned another. "It has to be the runt or Lex."

"Let's check Terza's room," the first man said.

"I don't know," hedged the second. "She doesn't like anybody in her room without an invitation."

"She'll understand," declared the first man. "Come on."

Rikki motioned Lex away from the door. There were three lit lanterns in the room, and no time to extinguish them. He eased the katana from its scabbard and flattened behind the door.

Lex took cover behind the couch.

The door slowly opened, inch by inch. The barrel of a revolver materialized, jutting past the edge of the door.

"I don't see anyone," remarked the second man.

"We'd best check the whole room," said the first man.

Both studs entered, each with a revolver, and neither bothered to glance behind the open door.

"There ain't nobody here!" the second man groused.

Rikki rushed from concealment, his katana streaking up and in.

The first stud, a short man with a flowing mustache, never knew what hit him. The katana angled into his neck, severing half of his throat, causing large quantities of blood to gush from the cut vessels and pour over his chest and legs.

Rikki didn't wait for the first man to collapse. He took two lightning steps and aimed a slash at the second man.

The second stud crouched and whirled, pointing his revolver at the man in black. He was squeezing the trigger when the sword hacked his gunhand from his wrist.

Anyone could have heard his shriek a mile away.

Rikki finished him with a well-placed reverse thrust into the stud's heart.

The Knight gurgled, spitting up blood and bile, and tumbled to the carpet.

Lex emerged from hiding. She had seen the entire encounter by looking around the lower corner of the couch.

"We must hurry to Blade," Rikki said.

Lex nodded. "I hope you show me how to do that someday."

Rikki wiped his katana on the second stud's black vest. "Considerable practice is required."

"It'd be worth it," Lex said. "If I get half as good as you, no one would dare mess with me again."

"Take me to Grotto," Rikki directed her.

"What am I going to do about these knives?" Lex asked, referring to the Bowies. "I'm liable to poke myself before we get there."

Rikki debated a moment. Both Bowies and the Commando were quite an armful. When the Knights had stripped Blade's weapons, they'd merely

removed the Bowies from their sheaths. So Lex was
compelled to carry the Bowies with their keen blades
exposed.

"I'll take them," Rikki volunteered. He carefully
aligned each knife under his belt, insuring the belt
supported each knife by its guard, and slanted their
points away from his privates.

"That doesn't look too safe," Lex remarked,
worried by the proximity of the knives to his groin.

"Just hope I don't sneeze," Rikki joked. "Come
on."

They left Terza's room on the double, Rikki leading
until they had descended the stairs to the bottom
floor. Lex took over, cradling the Commando in her
arms, making for the pit room where Grotto was fed.
The hallways were a virtual maze, and Rikki chafed
at the delay.

"Isn't there a shortcut?" he asked at one point.

Lex stopped. "I'm sticking to the halls we don't use
too often. We might avoid the Knights this way."

Rikki glanced at the Commando. "Have you
checked it to see if it's loaded?"

"Damn! Never thought of it!" Lex admitted. She
fiddled with the magazine release until the magazine
popped free. She held it in her left hand and studied it
by the light of a nearby lantern. "The clip is full," she
announced, "but I don't have a spare."

"Blade usually carries those in his pockets," Rikki
informed her.

Lex replaced the magazine in the Commando.

"Will we be there soon?" Rikki asked.

"Pretty soon," Lex replied.

The sound of many voices in turmoil abruptly came
from behind them.

"What's that?" Lex whispered.

The turmoil was growing louder.

Lex motioned for Rikki to follow. They raced along
the passage until they reached a branch, and she took

a right.

The voices weren't far off.

Rikki drew Lex into the darkest shadows.

"—tell you I saw them!" a woman was bellowing angrily.

"Sure you did," another woman responded.

"But I did!" insisted the first. "About two hundred yards back. I saw them pass a junction."

"Then where the hell are they?" demanded yet a third woman.

"If we haven't seen them by now," chimed in a stud, "we'll never catch them."

"If they were ever there," griped one of the women.

"I saw them, damn you!" insisted the first woman.

There were eight of them, five sisters and three studs, and they reached the fork in the tunnels and stopped. None of them ventured into the branch concealing Rikki and Lex.

"So where do we go from here?" inquired one of the sisters.

"I'm tired of looking," said another. "Why don't we grab a bite to eat? I'm starving!"

"Will you listen to yourselves?" snapped the fifth woman. "They would hear us coming a mile off."

"So what do we do?" asked a stud.

"Let's try this way," suggested a sister, and entered the right branch.

A whirlwind in black, wielding a scintillating blade, pounced on them from the shadows. In the three seconds they required to react to the onslaught, four of them were dead. A stud whipped his pistol from its holster, but that streaking sword was lanced through his right eye and into his brain before he could fire. The sister responsible for initially glimpsing Rikki and Lex successfully pulled her revolver, but the katana bit into her forehead, slicing off the top of her head, hair and all, and she uttered an uncanny death cry as she fell.

Hidden in the shadows, Lex watched in dazed fascination, dazzled by Rikki's prowess with the katana. His sinewy body was a twisting, flowing dervish of destruction. To her untrained eye, it seemed as if he executed his movements without conscious deliberation, as if he and the sword were one.

Thirty seconds after they entered the right branch, the eight Leather Knights were dead.

Rikki cleaned his katana on a stud's pants and rejoined Lex.

Lex stared at him with unconcealed admiration. "I'm beginning to wonder if anyone can kill you," she said by way of a compliment.

"Anyone can kill me," Rikki stated. "We all die, sooner or later. It's the technique for translating our souls from this world to the next."

Lex wanted to reach out and touch him, to smother his lips with fiery kisses. Instead, she chuckled. "You're all right, you know that?"

"I do now," Rikki replied, smiling. Then he turned serious. "We must reach Blade as quickly as possible."

Lex nodded. "Come on."

They jogged along the tunnels, sometimes taking a right fork, sometimes a left.

"How far underground are we?" Rikki asked once.

"I don't know," Lex responded. "But Grotto's room is the last one we built."

"It would be," Rikki remarked.

After a series of winding hallways, Lex slowed and pointed to a wall ahead. "That's it."

"A dead end?" Rikki queried, perplexed.

"Not really," Lex said. "The door is hidden in the wall. It's one of our secret retreats in case the Reds ever invade St. Louis."

Rikki ran to the brick wall.

Lex checked to verify no one was in pursuit, then joined him.

"How do we get in?" Rikki whispered.

Lex groped over the wall, seeking the false brick, the one covering the latch for the door. "It should be here somewhere."

"I pray nothing has happened to Blade," Rikki said anxiously.

"I bet he's okay," Lex said optimistically.

A tremendous roar shook the wall, emanating from the other side.

"I can't find the latch!" Lex wailed.

18

Hickok crouched in the high grass bordering the former East Potomac Park and surveyed the airstrip. He knew this area had once been the East Potomac Park because he'd stumbled across a faded, weather-beaten sign at the side of Buckeye Drive, a sign replete with a miniature map of the Tidal Basin and the tract east of the Potomac River.

He'd been lucky so far.

Real lucky.

Hickok had been able to keep the helicopter in sight as it flew from the West Potomac Park, over the Jefferson Memorial, and landed at the airstrip. Traveling undetected from the West Potomac Park to the airstrip had been painstaking and arduous. Fortunately, the Jefferson Memorial had been leveled during World War III; all that remained were several shattered columns and the cracked and ruined dome lying on the ground. Hickok was glad the structure had been razed. Otherwise, he might have encountered large crowds similar to those near the Lincoln Memorial. He silently thanked the Spirit as he crept toward the airstrip, using every available cover.

Once, as he was nearing Buckeye Drive, a squad of soldiers had tramped past his position. They were marching toward the Washington Channel.

Hickok had crossed Buckeye and hidden in the grass, and now he was only 15 feet from the north-western perimeter of the strip. He parted the grass in front of him for a better look-see.

The airstrip was loaded with helicopters. Huge helicopters. Small helicopters like the one the SEAL had engaged. And medium-sized helicopters. Some had single rotors. Others, especially the immense ones, had twin rotors, one above each end of the whirlybird. Technicians and flight personnel crowded the airstrip. Several tanker trucks, evidently conveying fuel, arrived on departed at periodic intervals.

After he had observed the proceedings for a spell, Hickok's interest was aroused by one particular copter. It was one of the largest on the airstrip, and the hub of intense activity. Hickok deduced they were preparing the helicopter for takeoff. A red tanker truck had pulled up, and three men were involved in running a hose from the tanker to the copter. Other men were engrossed in loading supplies onto the helicopter. One of the items Hickok saw rang a mental bell.

What was it General Malenkov had said?

"Our helicopter will use a winch and a sling and fly it here."

Hickok was familiar with winches. The Family Tillers used small winches to store bales of hay and other perishables in F Block. So when he saw a gigantic winch mounted above the bay doors on the huge helicopter being serviced by the tanker truck, a surge of excitement pulsed through him.

What if it were the one they were planning to use to transport the SEAL to Washington?

Several minutes later, his hunch was confirmed. Two events took place. First, a steel, sling-like affair was placed aboard the copter. And secondly, Leiutenant Voroshilov drove up in a jeep.

Now what would General Malenkov's pet flunky be doing here?

Lieutenant Voroshilov carefully inspected the

tandem helicopter, apparently guaranteeing the ship was airworthy. To Hickok, it seemed as if the lieutenant spent an inordinate amount of time involved in the task. Voroshilov even climbed a ladder to examine the rotors. Wouldn't that task normally be a job for one of the noncommissioned types? the gunman asked himself. If so, why did Lieutenant Voroshilov devote so much energy to the work?

A troop transport approached the helicopter from the direction of a building situated along the Washington Channel. The brakes squealed as the truck stopped. Six soldiers emerged from the rear of the transport and formed a line.

Lieutenant Voroshilov walked up to the soldiers and returned the salute of a big man at the end of the line. They conversed for a moment, then the lieutenant walked back to the copter and the six men stood at ease.

Hickok thoughtfully gnawed on his lower lip. Those six must be the men Voroshilov was taking on the mission. He speculated on whether the copter would be departing soon, or if they would wait for nightfall. Considering the bustle of activity, they probably intended to take off soon.

Not so good.

If they waited for dark, he might easily slip aboard and hitch a ride to the SEAL. In a helicopter that tremendous, with so many crates and boxes being stacked in the cargo bay, it would be a cinch to hide out until they reached their destination.

But what if they didn't wait for night?

Hickok surveyed his surroundings. About 15 feet away was the edge of the airstrip. About 20 feet beyond rested an unattended small helicopter. About 40 feet past the small whirlybird was the tanker truck. And then came the jumbo copter.

How the blazes was he going to get from—

A portly military man was walking toward the small helicopter, a clipboard in his left hand. He whistled as he walked, and as he neared the copter he consulted his clipboard.

Hickok lowered his body until just his eyes were elevated. What was this hombre up to with the small copter?

The man peered inside the helicopter's bubble, studying the instrument panel. Then he slowly walked around the aircraft.

Hickok glanced in both directions.

None of the technicians or other personnel was nearby.

The gunman waited until the military man had his back to him, and then he charged, sprinting forward, his moccasins nearly soundless on the hard tarmac.

At the last second, the man with the clipboard sensed someone was behind him and started to turn.

Hickok rammed his right hand against the man's head, driving the soldier's skull into the helicopter bubble.

There was a resounding crack, and·the clipboard clattered to the blacktop. The man weaved back and forth, then slumped to the ground, a trail of crimson descending from the right side of his head.

Hickok knelt and scanned the airstrip.

No one had noticed.

Yet.

Hickok's vanquished antagonist was less than an inch shorter than the gunman, but his limbs were heftier and his stomach was downright paunchy.

Might do.

Hickok hastily removed the soldier's clothing, then his own gunbelt, and hurriedly donned the uniform, covering his buckskins. The shoulders and elbows felt a bit tight, but they adequately hid his buckskins and that was the important thing. Although the pants were too short, with the hem two inches above his ankles, Hickok decided to risk it anyway and hope the ill-fitting uniform was inconspicuous.

But what to do about the Pythons and the gunbelt?

Hickok frowned. There was no way he could wear the gunbelt in the open; the Reds would spot him right off. He could tuck the Colts under his belt, under the uniform shirt. And he could stuff the bullets from the gunbelt in his pockets. But where did that leave the gunbelt?

There was a sharp retort from the huge tandem helicopter, a mechanical coughing and sputtering, and suddenly the two rotors began to rotate.

They were getting set to leave!

Blast! Hickok reluctantly extracted his spare ammo from the gunbelt and filled his pants pockets. He dropped the gunbelt on the ground next to the unconscious soldier.

"Think of it as a trade for the duds," the gunman said.

The rotors were increasing their revolutions, and a distinct hum carried on the breeze.

Hickok scooped up the clipboard and jogged around the small copter.

It was now or never!

The hose had been secured on the red tanker, and the three men were standing near the truck watching the tandem helicopter.

Hickok raced for the copter.

Lieutenant Voroshilov was nowhere in sight. The six troopers had likewise disappeared.

The rotors were revolving at a fantastic clip.

Hickok passed the red tanker and darted toward the helicopter. The cargo bay doors were still open, and he angled for them, waving the clipboard over his head.

One of the troopers stepped into view, framed in the cargo doors. He was reaching for one of the doors, intending to close them, when he spotted the blond man with the clipboard.

Hickok plainly saw the confused expression on the
soldier's face. He smiled up at the trooper as he
neared the cargo doors.

The tandem helicopter started to rise.

No!

Hickok estimated there were ten feet to go. He took
three bounding steps and leaped, his arms extended,
his fingers outstretched, discarding the clipboard as
he clutched at the helicopter. He gripped the lower
edge of the cargo bay and held on for dear life.

The helicopter was ascending at a rapid speed.

Hickok could feel his body swaying in the wind as
his hands threatened to be torn from his wrists.

The tandem copter was 20 feet up and climbing.

Hickok grimaced as he attempted to clamber
aboard. He wanted to hook his elbows, then swing his
legs up, but the helicopter abruptly changed
direction, swinging from a southeasternly heading to
a westerly course. The motion caused the gunman to
slip and sag, and his left hand lost most of its hold. He
made a valiant effort to haul himself up, but his
tenuous grasp was unequal to the endeavor.

He was going to fall!

The copter was 60 feet up and still rising.

Hickok's left arm slipped free, and for a few
precarious seconds he dangled from his right arm,
envisioning what it would be like to be splattered all
over the landscape below.

Sturdy hands clasped the gunfighter's right wrist,
and he was unceremoniously lifted into the cargo bay,
scraping his shins as he was hauled onto his back.

Two soldiers straddled him. One of them, the one
he'd seen in the doorway earlier, was holding an
AK-47 pointed at the gunman's chest.

Hickok almost went for his Pythons. But they were
under the uniform shirt and their barrels were
wedged under his belt. He knew the trooper would

blast him before he could whip the Colts clear.

The one with the Ak-47 said some words to the Warrior in what Hickok assumed was Russian.

Hickok grinned.

The trooper repeated his sentence.

Hickok grinned wider.

The soldier leaned over and pressed the barrel of the AK-47 against the gunman's nose. "I will use English," the trooper stated. "I think I know who you are, and if you so much as twitch one of your little muscles, I will blow your nose off!"

19

Blade was beginning to think Grotto would never appear.

Hours had passed. Six more Leather Knights had joined the others already in the room. They took turns pounding the board against the side of the pit. Twice Blade had tried to initiate a conversation, but each time Terza had ordered him to shut his mouth. She became testier as the hours lengthened, pacing the lip of the pit, her hands entwined in the small of her back.

"Maybe Grotto ain't gonna show," Cardew said, voicing the thought most of the assembled Knights entertained.

"He'll show!" Terza barked.

"He's taken a long time before," Erika interjected. "Probably because he was far off in the sewers. But the damn thing has never taken this long."

"He'll show!" Terza repeated.

"What's the big deal?" Erika demanded. "So what if we don't feed this bastard to Grotto today? There's always tomorrow."

Terza ceased her nervous pacing and glared at Erika. "We're not leaving this room until Grotto shows."

"But why?" Erika insisted. "We're getting hungry. Why don't we call it quits for today?"

Terza's hands drifted to her Comanches. "Are you questioning my judgment?"

Erika retreated a step. "Now you hold on—"

"Are you telling me what to do?" Terza asked in a menacing tone.

Erika paled. "No. No! Of course I ain't! I didn't mean nothin' by it! Honest!"

Terza scanned the room. "Anybody else got anything they'd like to say?"

None of the Knights responded.

"Keep poundin'!" Terza shouted at the stud with the board, who had stopped while Erika and Terza were arguing.

"One big, happy hamily," Blade said.

Terza turned and faced him. "Another word out of you, asshole, and I won't wait for Grotto! I'll do the job myself!"

"Big talk when you're armed and I'm not," Blade boldly replied.

Terza took a step toward the Warrior, the right Comanche easing upward.

A sibilant hissing filled the room, the same hissing sound they had heard earlier in the day.

"I hope the damn thing shows up this time," Erika muttered.

The damn thing did.

Blade had seen many mutants over the years. Deformed and demented, they came in all shapes and sizes. Often they beggared description. There were the mutates themselves—former reptiles, amphibians, and mammals, transformed into ravenous, pus-covered horrors. There were the insects and their close kin, subject to rare strains of deviate giantism, thought to be a genetic imbalance caused by one of the chemical-warfare weapons employed during the Big Blast, or a combination of the chemicals and the massive radiation. There were numerous other . . . things . . . as well.

This was one of them.

A red snout appeared, visible in the subterranean

entrance to the pit.

"Grotto!" Erika said, sounding relieved.

Blade tensed, enthralled and repulsed simultaneously.

The red snout was at least four feet wide and two feet high. Slowly, the creature creeped into the pit. Its eyes and head seemed to fill the entrance, its eyes a luminous brown, wide and unblinking, while its head was a grotesque, bloated caricature of a beast vaguely reptilian or amphibious by nature. More of the mutant emerged. Its skin was a bright red, crisscrossed with black stripes. The stocky legs were short in relation to the rest of the body, and its clawed feet were webbed. The body was bulky, bulging with raw power. Its thick tail was equally as long as the head and body combined. Tiny holes just behind the eyes served as ears, and its mouth was a thin slit from ear to ear. The monstrosity entered the pit and stopped, hissing, while a putrid stench hovered in the air.

Blade estimated the creature was close to ten feet in height and about seven feet wide. The mouth was large enough to swallow him in two bites.

Terza, Erika, Cardew, and some of the other Leather Knights were poised at the edge of the pit, admiring their "pet." Every Knight in the room was gaping at it.

Blade was completely, momentarily, forgotten.

Blade saw his opening, and he took it. Warrior training encompassed years of intense instruction in the many facets of combat and war. One aspect was deliberately stressed by the Elders responsible for teaching the Warriors the tricks of their trade. As one Elder put it: "In a fight, in any life-or-death situation, victory is frequently predicted on recognizing the enemy's weaknesses, on using your foes mistakes against them. All they have to do is lower their guard for a split-second, and their defeat is assured if you take advantage of their mistake. Always remember: if

someone is trying to kill you or any other Family
member, your primary responsibility is to your
Family and yourself. Do whatever is necessary to
win. You won't get a second chance.''

So coordinated was Blade, so instantaneous his
reflexes, that he was in motion even as he perceived
his advantage. He took four steps and reached Terza
and Erika. The two Knights, concentrating on the
hideous Grotto, were unaware of his presence until a
steely hand pounded each of them on the back and
they were propelled over the edge of the pit, Erika
screaming in terror.

Blade whirled, his granite fist crashing into
Cardew's right cheek.

The stud tottered backward and collapsed.

Petrified shrieks were coming from the pit as Blade
spun and attacked a nearby sister.

The other Leather Knights began to react. Initially
stunned by the sight of Terza and Erika falling into
the pit, they recovered and attacked the giant
Warrior. One of the studs went to use his rifle, but
rejected the idea when he saw how close his target
was to several of his friends.

Blade slugged the sister in the abdomen, and kneed
her in the face when she doubled over.

Spouting blood from her pulverized nose, the sister
catapulted backward.

Blade was tackled by a stud. He felt arms encircle
his legs, and he was borne to the ground by the
impact. He desperately threw his body to the left to
avoid being knocked into the pit, and he succeeded in
digging his elbows and forearms into the very edge
before arresting his momentum. Hovering on the
brink of the hole, he glanced down.

A pair of slim legs protruded from the corners of
Grotto's gaping maw, and rivulets of blood poured
over its lower jaw.

Terza?

Blade couldn't waste time speculating on the
identity of the deceased. The stud holding his legs was
striving to push him over the edge. Blade glanced over
his right shoulder, noting his opponent's head was
just below his buttocks, and he twisted, rolling to the
left, throwing his entire weight into the movement.

The stud's grip slipped, and he lunged for the
Warrior's waist.

Blade reached back and down with his right hand,
his calloused fingers grasping the stud's long black
hair and yanking the Knight's head upward.

The stud cried out as his neck was wrenched. He
felt as if his neck were being torn from his shoulders.
Cursing, he pummeled the iron arm clutching his
hair, to no avail.

Blade heaved, drawing the stud higher until they
were eye to eye.

The Knight attempted to punch Blade in the face.

Blade sneered as he rose to his knees. He placed his
left hand under the stud's chin, braced his coiled
arms, and savagely snapped his hands to the right.

Several of the stud's vertebrae fractured with an
audible crack.

Two other Knights, both sisters, pounced on the
Warrior, one from the left, the other from the right,
clasping his wrists and trying to force him into the pit.

Blade flexed his arms and strained, throwing his
arms forward and tossing the sisters over the lip of the
pit. They screeched as they fell.

Pandemonium was rampant in the room. Some of
the Leather Knights were converging on their
prisoner. Others were bolting for the door. A few
were perched on the rim of the pit, guns at the ready,
watching Grotto. As Blade rose to his feet, the
pandemonium was compounded by three develop-
ments. Grotto clawed at the pit, scrambling to climb
to the top. The mutant raised its bloated head and
voiced a thunderous roar, shaking the walls and

causing dirt to crumble from the sides of the pit.
Three of the sisters reached the door and frantically
threw it open. Almost immediately, a diminutive
figure in black scooted into the room, a flashing
sword in his hands, and with three glimmering
strokes he dispatched the trio.

It was Rikki!

Blade started toward his fellow Warrior, but a stud
came at him, a knife in the Knight's right hand.

Grotto was in a frenzy, hissing and roaring as it
attempted to reach the pit rim. Its rear legs dug into
the side, spraying dirt in every direction. It gave a
stupendous heave and its front legs obtained a
purchase on the pit edge, not more than eight feet
from the Warrior.

Blade, concentrating on his adversary with the
knife, failed to see Grotto's achievement. He dodged a
wild swing of the knife and retreated a step, moving
three feet nearer to the creature's salivating jaws.

Near the door, a stud with a rifle sighted on the
swordsman in black, but a redheaded woman burst
into the room, her machine gun chattering, and the
stud's chest was stitched by a line of heavy slugs.

Lex had entered the fray.

Blade backed up another step as the stud with the
knife lunged again.

Grotto's head and shoulders were clear of the pit
and his body was still rising.

Rikki spotted Blade's danger, but before he could
race to his friend's aid he was confronted by two
sisters, both with drawn revolvers.

One of the sisters fired.

Rikki grimaced as his right side was creased, the
bullet tearing a furrow in his ribs. He doubled over,
feigning acute anguish, and when the sisters closed in
to finish him off, he suddenly straightened,
slashing the katana from right to left, hacking off the
first woman's left arm, her gun arm, and cleaving

open the second woman's stomach. The first woman
seemed petrified by the loss of her arm: her terrified
eyes frozen on the sight of her blood pumping from
the severed stump. She barely noticed when another
slash of the katana split her forehead, and she was
dead before her body struck the ground. The second
woman dropped her revolver and spread her hands
over her ruptured stomach, futilely endeavoring to
prevent her intestines and other organs from spilling
out. The sword strike through her heart was anti-
climatic.

Blade ducked yet another knife swipe, and caught
the stud's wrist in his powerful hands. He swept his
right knee up into the stud's elbow, and heard the pop
as it cracked.

The stud grunted and tried to jerk free.

Blade floored him with a right cross. He saw Rikki
heading his way and took a step toward him, but a
strident roar stopped him in his tracks. He whirled.

Grotto was almost on top of the pit. Except for its
pumping rear legs and tail, it was actually out of the
pit, squatting on the rim.

Damn!

Blade broke into a run, making for Rikki.

Lex downed two of the Knights with a burst from
the Commando. The sole Knight left in the room, a
tall blonde sister, was cowering against one wall.

Rikki darted toward Blade, but he was still 12 feet
away when Grotto surged over the rim of the pit and
went after the giant Warrior.

Rikki grabbed the hilt of one of the Bowies.
"Catch!" he shouted, and tossed the knife.

Blade deftly caught the Bowie on the fly with his
right hand.

Rikki threw the other Bowie.

Blade stopped, his keen eyes following the knife's
trajectory, and his left hand plucked it from the air
with deceptive ease. He spun, sensing the monster

was right behind him.

He was right.

Grotto was six feet from the Warrior, its mouth wide open, displaying upper and lower rows of small but pointed teeth. The motion of its ungainly legs and tail caused the creature to weave from side to side as it advanced. The first bite of its gruesome jaws closed on empty space.

Blade leaped to the right as the creature attacked, driving his left Bowie up and in, under the mutant's jawbone, into the fleshy area fringing the thick neck.

Grotto recoiled, feeling the pain, jerking his head away from the Bowie.

Knowing he would be too exposed if he tried to flee, Blade opted for the unexpected. He aggressively charged forward, under Grotto's neck, and buried both of his Bowies in the thing's vulnerable underbelly.

Grotto roared and scrambled to the right, not far from the pit, hissing as it swiveled and snapped at the puny human.

Blade felt the creature's foul breath on his face, like the rank stink of a decayed corpse, and flung himself backwards.

Grotto's teeth crunched together mere inches from its prey.

Blade stumbled, landing on his left knee. He saw Grotto rushing him, and he extended the Bowies to meet the assault.

A streak of masterfully crafted steel sliced the mutant from its neck to its shoulder as Rikki came to Blade's rescue. Green fluid sprayed from the wound, spattering the Warrior in black.

Grotto turned to face this new threat, enraged. Its jaw distended, it pounced.

Rikki rolled, avoiding the cavernous maw, and came up with the katana in a swirling motion, tearing open the side of Grotto's face. He backpedaled, scurrying to Blade's side.

"Glad you could make it," Blade quipped.

"Wouldn't have missed this for the world," Rikki rejoined.

Further conversation was precluded by Grotto; the mutant bellowed and charged the two Warriors.

Blade dived to the right, toward the pit, while Rikki sprinted to the left.

Grotto hesitated for a moment, uncertain of which victim to pursue. It snarled and went after Rikki.

The Family's consummate martial artist held his ground.

Grotto reached its quarry and hissed, spreading its jaws, its tongue flicking outward in spasmodic anticipation.

Rikki swung, slashing his katana up and around, the keen blade severing a third of the creature's tongue from its mouth.

Grotto recoiled and uttered a rumbling, shrill cry. It lashed its head from side to side, in misery, tormented by the loss of its tongue.

Blade found himself standing behind the monster, not four feet from its tail. He saw Rikki take another swipe with his sword, and Grotto try to take Rikki's head off. Rikki avoided the slavering jaws, but his left foot caught on the leg of a slain Leather Knight prone on the ground, and he lost his balance. He fell, landing on his left side.

Grotto roared and surged forward.

A desperate plan, a blaze of inspiration, pervaded Blade's consciousness, and with the idea came action. He ran toward Grotto, and when just three feet from the creature's tail he leaped, his coiled leg muscles carrying him over Grotto's tail onto its back, at the junction of the tail and the spinal column. His knees clamped on the tail, as he sank his Bowies to the hilt in the genetic deviate's back.

Grotto stiffened, then whipped its tail in an arc, striving to dislodge the man-thing.

Blade was clipped by the broad tail. He felt some-thing hard strike his left shoulder, and he was knocked forward, the Bowies wrenching clear of the mutant's rancid flesh. He rolled twice and came up on his knees, perched on Grotto's squat neck.

Grotto snapped its head up and down, shaking its whole body, attempting to toss the man off.

Rikki closed in and delivered a deep slash to Grotto's throat.

Blade, clinging to the pliant skin on Grotto's neck with all of his strength, racked his brain for a means of destroying the creature. There had to be a way! But how? It had sustained several severe injuries, it was pumping a sickly green fluid from its body by the gallon, and yet still it fought on, endowed with a fearless nature and a ravenous appetite. The Bowies and the katana seemed unable to deliver a death blow. Where would it be most vulnerable? In the heart? Where would the heart be located in a creature of this size? All these thoughts passed through his mind in the twinkling of an instant.

And then it hit him.

There was a way!

Blade lunged forward, wrapping his legs around the mutant's neck. He extended the Bowies as far as his arms could reach, one on each side of the creature's face, one next to each eye.

''Do it!'' he heard Lex scream.

Blade plunged the Bowies into Grotto's brown orbs, all the way in, and twisted.

Grotto reacted as if electrified by a bolt of lightning, its huge form convulsing and contorting, hissing all the while, its head shaking from right to left and up and down.

Blade could scarcely retain his grip. He felt the creature moving from side to side, and he could see Rikki yelling something to him, but he couldn't hear the words over Grotto's hissing.

Grotto's violent throes intensified.

"—pit! The pit!" Rikki yelled in alarm.

The pit?

The pit!

Blade jerked the Bowies free and rolled to the right, off of Grotto's neck. Something collided with his back, and he was sent flying, arms and legs flailing in the air, to crash onto the ground in a daze. He shook his head to clear his fuzzy mind, and rose to his hands and knees.

"Are you all right?" asked a concerned male voice.

Blade looked up.

Rikki smiled at him. "The Family will tell this tale for generations."

Blade glanced around, confused, disoriented. "Where . . ."

"The pit," Rikki answered before Blade could complete his question.

Blade stumbled to his feet. He tottered to the edge of the pit, his whole body aching like hell, and peered over the edge.

Grotto was lying in the center of the pit, on its side, its mouth open and slack, its eyes pools of green fluid, its legs curled up, its tail quivering.

Grotto was dead.

"I never saw anything like that!" Lex said as she joined them. "I wanted to shoot," she added, holding up the Commando, "but I was afraid I'd hit one of you."

Blade nodded absently, not yet fully recovered, staring at the creature on the pit floor.

"Are you all right?" Rikki repeated.

"Just a little dazed," Blade responded.

"Its head hit you as you were rolling off," Rikki disclosed.

Blade glanced at the black hole in the side of the pit, the hole providing access to the sewers. "Terza told me there are more of those things down there," he commented in a low voice.

"Yeah," Lex confirmed. "So?"

"So sooner or later those things are going to start coming out of the sewers to feed," Blade predicted.

"A few have already done it," Lex stated. "What's the big deal?"

Blade stared at her, sweat beading his brow. "Population growth is going to force more and more of them to take to the streets," he said wearily. "From what we've seen in our travels, many cities are like St. Louis. Living in them may become untenable."

Lex gazed at Grotto, frowning. "So what? I don't like living here anyway."

Rikki touched Blade on the left elbow. "We should be leaving."

Blade nodded. He realized he was still holding the Bowies, and he held them up. They were covered with the sticky green fluid. "Yuck," he said, and walked to a fallen sister.

Rikki scanned the room. "We are the only ones here," he observed.

Blade wiped his knives clean on the sister's black-leather vest. "You can bet reinforcements are on the way."

"You can have this," Lex offered, extending the Commando. "I'll take one of the rifles."

Blade sheathed his Bowies and took the Commando. "Thanks." He paused. "I appreciate all of the assistance you've rendered. And I know how you feel about living in St. Louis. How would you like to come and live with us?"

Lex grinned. "Rikki already made me the same offer."

"And?"

"And the sooner we get to this Home of yours," Lex said, "the better."

Blade smiled. "Lead the way."

Lex took a rifle from a dead stud, and found a handful of ammunition in his right front pocket. "Rikki told me you guys are called Warriors," she mentioned as she straightened.

"There are fifteen Warriors," Blade affirmed.

Lex swept the room with her right hand. "And you Warriors do this kind of thing all the time?"

"It does seem to happen a lot," Blade admitted. "Why?"

"Oh, nothing," Lex said. "But after seeing what you guys do for a living, I can't help but wonder what you do for kicks."

20

This was another blasted mess he'd gotten himself into!

The gunman was seated on a long bench on one side of the cargo bay. Across from him, on another wooden bench, sat five Red soldiers, each with an AK-47, each pointing their weapon in his general direction. Nearby, toward the rear of the aircraft, boxes and crates and miscellaneous equipment were stacked to the ceiling. In the opposite direction, a narrow alley between more crates and boxes led to a closed door. The sixth Red, the one he'd first seen in the cargo bay doorway and evidently a sergeant or of some equivalent rank, had disappeared through the door mere minutes before. After the sergeant and one other trooper had hoisted the gunfighter into the helicopter, they'd shoved him to the bench and ordered him to sit.

But the rascals had made a serious mistake.

Hickok wanted to laugh. The cowchips had neglected to search him for weapons. Consequently, the Pythons were safely tucked under his belt, hidden by the bulky uniform shirt over his buckskins.

"Any of you gents feel like shootin' the breeze?" Hickok amiably inquired.

None of them responded.

"I have a pard by the name of Joshua," Hickok genially told them. "He once told me a motto of his. You bozos could learn from it. If you ever want to make friends, old Josh once said, you've got to be friendly. You jokers sure ain't the friendly type.''

One of the Reds wagged his AK-47. "Shut your mouth. We are not your friends.''

"Why do we have to be enemies?" Hickok countered. "The war was a hundred years ago.''

"The war is not over until Communism has conquered the globe,'' the soldier said.

Hickok sighed. "You must be minus a few marbles. There ain't no way you turkeys will conquer the world.''

"In time we will,'' the trooper said confidently.

"You're breakin' wind.''

The soldier's eyebrows narrowed. "Breakin' wind?''

"Do you really expect the folks to just roll over and play dead while you run roughshod over 'em?" Hickok asked. "If you do, you must be eatin' loco-weed on a regular basis.''

The trooper was about to speak, but the door toward the front of the aircraft opened. The sergeant returned, followed by a familiar figure. They approached the gunman.

"Hello, Hickok," Lieutenant Voroshilov greeted the warrior. "This is a surprise.''

"Not as big of a surprise as I wanted," Hickok said.

"I just finished talking to General Malenkov on the radio,'' Lieutenant Voroshilov revealed. "He was equally surprised. It seems we underestimated you.''

"So how soon before we get back to Washington?" Hickok asked.

"We are not turning around,'' Lieutenant Voroshilov disclosed.

Hickok's own surprise registered on his features. "Why not? I reckon the general is a mite eager to get his paws on me.''

Lieutenant Voroshilov nodded. "He is most desirous of talking with you again,'' he said. "Only

the next time it will be different. Your escape angered
the general. He is going to have his . . . consultants
. . . question you next time. Perhaps you have heard
of them? They are the KGB."

Hickok shrugged. "Never heard of 'em."

"Why don't you relax," Lieutenant Voroshilov suggested. "We will be in the air several hours before we
refuel."

"Why aren't you takin' me back to Washington?"
Hickok inquired.

Lieutenant Voroshilov sat down on the bench alongside the gunman. His green eyes studied the warrior, as
if he were examining an inferior life-form. "Several reasons. Precious fuel would be wasted by the return flight,
and fuel is one resource we cannot afford to waste."

"Don't have a lot of it, huh?" Hickok interrupted.

"Not as much as we would like," Voroshilov said.
"We have two refineries in operation, but they can't
supply enough fuel for all our needs."

"Why don't you just get some more from Russia?"
Hickok queried.

Voroshilov's mouth tightened. "If only we could."

"Why can't you?" Hickok pressed him.

Voroshilov considered the question for a while. "I
see no reason why I can't tell you. The information
isn't classified, and you won't live to pass it on." He
thoughtfully stared at the closed cargo bay doors.
"We lost touch with our motherland thirty years ago."

"What? You're kiddin'," Hickok said.

"I do not jest," Voroshilov stated bitterly. "The war
took its toll on our country too. It depleted our natural
resources and restricted our industrial capability. The
non-Russian peoples in the U.S.S.R., the ones who
always resented our superiority and our control, saw
our weakness and decided the time was right to throw
off their yoke. The Balts and the Mordivians, the
Udmurts and the Mari, the Tartars and the Kirgiz, and
many others rose in rebellion." He stopped, his face

downcast.

"And what happened?" Hickok goaded him, stalling. The longer he could keep the lieutenant talking the further they would get from Washington and the more likely a chance would develop to make his play.

"We don't know," Voroshilov said sadly.

"You don't know?"

Voroshilov sighed. "During and right after the war, thousands of our troops were sent to America, to invade and conquer the capitalistic pigs. Our forces took over a large territory in the eastern U.S., but we did not have enough supplies and men to continue our push to the north and west of the Mississippi. Our drive through Alaska and Canada was stopped in British Columbia by the worst winter they had there in centuries. Over the decades, we have consolidated our domination of the American area we rule. Until thirty years ago, we maintained contact with the motherland. We knew the rebellion there had reached a critical stage. Then the shortwave broadcasts stopped. Cryptographic communications ceased. Every ship we sent to investigate failed to return. Our forces in America found themselves isolated, cut off from our motherland."

"Hold your horses," Hickok interjected. "You say you lost contact with Russia thirty years ago?"

"Yes."

Hickok pointed at the five soldiers on the opposite bench. "Then where the dickens did they come from? They sure don't look over thirty to me."

"They are not," Lieutenant Voroshilov replied. "Since we could not replenish our forces from the motherland, we've established a system of modified racial breeding."

"I don't follow," Hickok said.

"We impregnate selected American women," Lieutenant Voroshilov stated. "Their children are turned over to us for training and education. Our indoctrination is quite thorough. Russian history and values are stressed. Communism, of course, is exalted. The result you see before you. Soldiers every bit as Russian as if they had come from the U.S.S.R., and fluent in English and Russian.''

"Where do you get these American women?'' Hickok asked. "Do they volunteer?''

Voroshilov snickered. "They cooperate whether they want to or not.''

Hickok ruminated on the revelations he'd received. The information explained a lot. Like, why the Russians had not invaded the Civilized Zone, why the Reds hadn't taken over the whole country. Simply because they lacked the manpower and the resources to achieve it. "How much of the country do you have under your thumb?'' he ventured to ask.

Voroshilov reflected for a moment. "Let me see if I can remember the names of the states involved. New England we control,'' he said, "and southern New York, southern Pennsylvania, Maryland, New Jersey, southern Ohio, southern Indiana, portions of Illinois, Kentucky, Virginia, and West Virginia. We also have sections of North and South Carolina under our hegemony. We wanted to subjugate all of the Southeast, but the Southerners are a most hardy, independent lot. They resisted us every foot of the way and stopped our advance, leaving us the Northeast and a wide corridor in the middle of the East.''

Hickok stared at Voroshilov. "I can't get over you tellin' me all of this.''

Lieutenant Voroshilov grinned. "As I said before,'' he stated, "you won't live to pass it on. General Malenkov will not treat you so lightly the second time.''

Hickok idly gazed at the five troopers on the other wooden bench, and at the sergeant, standing to the right of Voroshilov. The five had relaxed their guard and lowered their weapons, but the sergeant still covered him with an AK-47. He needed to stall some more, and hope he had a chance to go for his Colts. "You said there were several reasons why you're not takin' me straight back to Washington," he reminded the lieutenant.

Voroshilov nodded. "Time is of the essence. We must reach your vehicle as quickly as possible, before your people can remove it."

"You still think you can tote the SEAL to Washington with this contraption?" Hickok smacked the metal side of the copter.

"Easily," Lieutenant Voroshilov bragged. "We will dig a small trench under your vehicle, and then slide our sling underneath. Once the sling is secured, our helicopter will lift the vehicle into the air and transport it to General Malenkov."

Hickok thoughtfully chewed on his lower lip. If the Reds could do what they claimed, it would be a piece of cake to lift the SEAL into the air, then lower it again on its wheels. Hmmmm.

Lieutenant Voroshilov stood. "I must rejoin our pilot. You will be removed at our first refueling stop and held there until our return trip. We will pick you up and carry you to Washington for your rendezvous with General Malenkov and the KGB."

"Do you mind if I take off this uniform?" Hickok asked. "I've got my buckskins on under it, and I'm sweatin' to beat the band."

"As you wish," Lieutenant Voroshilov graciously offered.

Hickok started to tug on the uniform shirt.

Lieutenant Voroshilov turned to the sergeant. "Did you find any weapons on him when you searched him?"

The sergeant blinked twice, then cleared his throat. "We did not search him," he confessed. "He did not appear to be armed—"

With a sinking feeling in his gut, Lieutenant Voroshilov spun, hoping his premonition was inaccurate. Instead, he saw his worst fear realized.

Hickok had pulled the uniform shirt from his pants, exposing his buckskins. And also exposing the Colt Python revolvers tucked in his belt. But even as the uniform shirt came clear, his hands streaked to the pearl-handled Magnums, his draw an invisible blur.

The sergeant awoke to the danger first, and aimed his AK-47 at the gunman's head.

Hickok was already on the move, rising and stepping to the left, putting a few extra feet between Voroshilov and himself. His right Python boomed, and the sergeant's face acquired a new hole directly between the eyes.

The sergeant was thrown backward into a pile of crates by the impact.

Lieutenant Voroshilov went for his pistol, his arms seemingly moving at a snail's pace compared to the gunfighter's.

Hickok crouched and whirled, the Colts held at waist level, his elbows against his waist, and they thundered simultaneously.

Two of the five soldiers on the opposite bench were slammed into the wall of the craft, their brains exploding from their heads in a spray of red and pink flesh.

The remaining three were bringing their AK-47's to bear.

Hickok's next three shots sounded as one, his aim unerring, going for the head as he invariably did.

One after the other, the three Red soldiers died, each shot in the forehead, each astonished by the speed of their adversary, each overcome by their own sluggishness.

Lieuteant Voroshilov, in the process of drawing his automatic, realized the futility of the attempt and darted forward instead, his arms outstretched.

Hickok pivoted to confront the lieutenant, and his

fingers were beginning to squeeze the Python triggers when he thought better of the notion. He allowed himself to be tackled, carried to the hard floor of the cargo bay by Voroshilov's rush, his arms pinned to his sides.

Lieutenant Voroshilov tried to knee the gunman in the groin, but missed.

Hickok grinned, then rammed his forehead into Voroshilov's mouth.

Lieutenant Voroshilov was jolted by the savage blow; his head rocked back and his teeth jammed together. For the briefest instant, his vision swam, his senses staggered. When they cleared, he discovered the gunman standing over him, the barrels of the Pythons centimeters from his face.

"Piece of cake," Hickok quipped. He cocked the Colts. "Don't move! Don't even blink!"

Lieutenant Voroshilov froze in place.

Hickok backed up a step and glanced toward the door. Had the pilot heard the gunfire? Maybe not. The twin rotors on the copter were making a heck of a lot of noise. On the other hand . . .

Hickok stared at Voroshilov. "On your feet! Real slow! Hands in the air!"

Lieutenant Voroshilov complied.

"We're gonna walk up to the pilot," Hickok directed him.

Voroshilov licked his dry lips. "He will see us coming and lock the cockpit."

"You'd best hope he doesn't," Hickok warned, "or you'll be gaining some weight right quick." He paused. "How much do you figure a couple of slugs would weigh?"

Lieutenant Voroshilov swallowed. Hard. "What do you propose to do?"

"I don't propose nothin'," Hickok retorted. "I'm plain doin' it! You're gonna fly me to the SEAL."

"You're crazy! We'll never make it. You will be

caught," Lieutenant Voroshilov said.

"No I won't," Hickok disagreed. "All I have to do is stay out of sight when you land to refuel. There's no need for any of you to be getting off the helicopter. You'll land, refuel, and take off again without letting anyone else on board."

"Ground control will become suspicious," Voroshilov stated. "There are papers to sign—"

"Tell 'em you're in a big hurry," Hickok instructed him. "Mention General Malenkov. That ought to make 'em listen."

"It won't work," Lieutenant Voroshilov declared.

Hickok's voice lowered to an angry growl. "You best pray it does work, or you'll be the first to go."

Lieutenant Voroshilov gazed at his fallen comrades. He thought of the disgrace he had suffered, the shame heaped on his name and career. If he lived, he would be demoted. Or worse, sentenced to hard labor in one of the concentration camps. Or even executed. The honorable course would be to compel the gunman to shoot him now, to end his life before his failure was discovered. If he died now, he would be hailed as a hero whose death was a tribute to the Party and the State. He looked at the gleaming barrels of the Pythons, and couldn't bring himself to make the necessary move, to try and jump the gunman. He wasn't a coward, but he didn't want to die.

"What's it gonna be?" Hickok demanded. "You either do as I say, or I'll ventilate your eyeballs."

Lieutenant Voroshilov took a deep breath. "I will do as you say."

"No tricks," Hickok warned.

"No tricks."

"And do all your talkin' in English," Hickok ordered him. "Now that I know your men can speak both languages, there's no risk involved and I'll understand everything you say."

Lieutenant Voroshilov frowned. Who would have

believed it? Looking at the blond gunman's inane, carefree grin and hearing his ridiculous Western slang, who would believe he was so competent a fighter?

"Let's mosey on up to the cockpit," Hickok said.

Voroshilov hesitated.

"Something wrong?" Hickok asked.

"Are there many like you?" Lieutenant Voroshilov asked. "Where you come from, I mean."

"A whole passel of 'em," Hickok said. "Why?"

"Oh, nothing," Lieuteant Voroshilov said as he headed forward, carefully passing the gunman. "But if there had been more like you a century ago, America would still be free."

Hickok laughed. "I ain't nothin' special."

"That's what you think," Lieutenant Voroshilov said, complimenting his enemy.

21

They emerged from the bowels of the library into the fresh air and bright light of day in an alley due west of the building.

"You know St. Louis better than we do," Blade said to Lex. "You've got to lead us out of the city. Stick to the alleys and back streets. We don't want to run into any more Leather Knights."

"I'll do my best," Lex promised. She led off, Rikki at her side.

Blade followed them, covering their flanks, constantly scanning to the rear. Amazingly, the expected counterattack hadn't materialized. They hadn't seen or heard a single Knight during their exit from the library.

Why not?

The rest of the Leather Knights undoubtedly were alerted to the debacle in the pit room. At least one of the Knights in the room at the time had survived and vanished.

So where the hell were they?

If the Leather Knights hadn't appeared, there must be a good reason. But what? Were the Knights afraid? It hardly seemed likely since they numbered in the hundreds. Perhaps many of the Knights were in other sections of the city, but there had to be enough in the immediate vicinity to overwhelm the two Warriors and the defector. Yet they hadn't attacked. Were the Knights wary of attempting to corner their former prisoners in the narrow confines of the underground hallways? Or, as sounded reasonable, were the Knights reluctant to pursue the trio through the labyrinth under the library for fear they would lose their captives in the maze? If that was the case, and if he were a Leather Knight, what would he do next?

The answer was so obvious, Blade stopped as if stunned by a physical blow.

There was only one possible recourse! To cover every exit from the library and wait for them to come forth.

Rikki and Lex had reached the mouth of the alley and moved into the street beyond.

Blade ran toward them. "Rikki!"

He was too late.

Hidden in the buildings on every side, over two dozen Leather Knights rose from concealment, some in windows, others in doorways, some hiding behind gutted cars on piles of trash.

"Now!" a sister shouted.

The Leather Knights opened fire.

Startled by the ambush, Lex still managed to raise her rifle and blast a stud in a nearby window. Then her left shoulder was jarred, and the rifle flew from her hands as she started to fall.

Rikki reached her side in the next instant, ignoring the hail of lead raining all around him. He placed his left arm around her waist and lifted, supporting her weight as he hurried to the alley, knowing he wouldn't reach its cover without aid.

Blade burst from the alley with the Commando leveled. He swept the surrounding buildings with a devastating spray of bullets.

Sisters and studs screamed as they were hit, or ducked from sight to escape the giant's onslaught.

Blade retreated into the alley.

Rikki was holding Lex in his arms. A bright red circle had formed on Lex's left shoulder and there was a hole in her vest.

"Lex?" Blade asked.

Lexine, although pale, was game. "I'm fine," she told Blade. "Tell this yoyo to stop worrying about me."

Rikki gently eased her onto the ground. "Stay put," he advised her. "We will attend to the Knights."

Blade leaned against the west wall and eased to the corner. There was a lot of commotion from every nearby building. The Knights were reorganizing.

Rikki joined him. "Any orders?" he asked.

"If they rush us," Blade said, "we'll never hold them."

"We could reenter the library," Rikki recommended.

Blade shook his head. "That could be what they want us to do. Once we're inside, they'll close off the alley and have us bottled up inside."

"Then what?" Rikki inquired. "Do you want me to take them one by one?"

"If it was dark you could do it," Blade said. "But they'd spot you in broad daylight."

"I'd get a few," Rikki vowed.

"True," Blade agreed. "But I need you here. Lex needs you here."

Rikki glanced at the redhead. "I've become quite . . . fond . . . of her," he said in a soft tone.

"I've noticed."

"I've never felt this way before," Rikki declared.

"I know."

Beyond the alley, there was the rattle of a tin can.

Blade looked behind him. There was an eight-foot wall at the far end of the alley. Piles of garbage and debris were scattered everywhere. The stench was awful. If the three of them could reach that wall—

There was a loud clanking outside the alley.

"What are they doing?" Rikki inquired.

Blade risked a hasty peek.

Leather Knights were advancing on the mouth of the alley from both directions. To his right, four studs

were pushing a wooden cart laden with metal trash
cans filled to the brim with trash. Two sisters were
carrying oddly shaped sticks or branches near the
cart.

No!

They weren't sticks or branches!

They were torches!

Blade glanced at Rikki. "They plan to smoke us out.
If we try to make a break for it, they'll cut us down in
a crossfire."

"We can't stay here," Rikki said.

"I know." Blade scrutinized the buildings lining the
street across from the alley. Knights weren't in
evidence, but that didn't mean a thing.

Lex moaned.

Blade placed his right hand on Rikki's shoulder.
"You'll have to hold them while I get Lex over the
wall." He nodded toward the far end of the alley.

"I will hold them," Rikki pledged.

"They'll try and rush us," Blade guessed. "Try and
shove a cart in here filled with burning trash, hoping
the flames will spread and force us from cover. If you
can hold them until I have Lex safe, I'll cover you
from the wall until you reach us. Fair enough?"

"Sounds okay to me," Rikki said. He looked at Lex,
clutching her shoulder in agony but not complaining.
"Take good care of her. If something should happen
to me . . . insure she reaches the Home safely."

"I will," Blade promised. "Here. Use the
Commando."

"And what will you cover me with? Your Bowies?"
Rikki grinned. "Get going."

Blade ran to Lex, slung the Commando over his
right shoulder, and knelt. "Hold on tight," he
cautioned her.

Lex opened her eyes. "Where are you taking me?"

"Out of here." Blade lifted her into his arms.

"I won't leave Rikki," Lex stated.

"You have no choice," Blade responded, and jogged toward the wall 40 yards away.

"Rikki!" Lex yelled.

Rikki smiled and waved, then flattened against the west wall. His sensitive nostrils detected the acrid scent of smoke.

It would be soon.

Blade and Lex were 20 yards off, Blade negotiating the trash and garbage as he threaded a route to the wall.

Rikki held his katana in front of him, calming his emotions. He had to shut Lex from his mind, to submerge his feelings for her and concentrate his total energy on the matter at hand.

Smoke drifted past the alley entrance.

It would be very soon.

Rikki emptied his mind of every distraction, focusing on the katana, wedding his instincts to the blade. He would buy Blade and Lex the precious time they needed, even at the expense of his own life.

"Do it!" a sister yelled from outside the alley.

There was a sudden clanking and rattling, and the Leather Knights swarmed toward the alley. The four studs pushing the cart were in the lead, the contents of the trash cans already ablaze, pouring whitish gray smoke into the air, obscuring the cart and the nearest Knights.

Rikki squatted, his eyes on the alley mouth.

The Leather Knights reached the alley, and for a moment they hesitated, their assault halted by a momentary confusion. Blinded by the dense smoke issuing from the cart, their confusion was confounded by all of them endeavoring to enter the alley at once. Unable to see their foes, they balked, and in so doing gave Rikki-Tikki-Tavi the advantage he needed.

Rikki plunged into their midst, holding his breath to minimize the effects of the odoriferous smoke. Wherever he saw a shape or shadow in the smoke, he struck. His katana cleaved to the left and the right, hacking limbs and tearing torsos.

Those Leather Knights at the forefront of the charge bore the brunt of the carnage. Prevented from firing by the density of their mad rush, they tried to retreat but were blocked by those behind them. The Knights in the rear, unaware of the clash because they couldn't see through the smoke, shoved those in front. Those in the lead, hearing the screams and shrieks of the wounded and dying and glimpsing a swirling figure in black, pushed against those in back.

Chaos reigned.

A lone stud with a Winchester appeared in the smoke, and Rikki slashed him across the neck.

The stud toppled backward from view.

Rikki saw a sister near the wooden cart, silhouetted by the red and orange flames, and he impaled her on the point of his sword. She gasped and grabbed the blade with her left hand, losing her fingers in the bargain.

"Damn you!" she defiantly cried as she expired.

Rikki crouched, his katana at the ready. Surely this was enough? Blade should have reached the wall by now! He picked his way over the bodies and through the smoke until he was in the alley. Gray tendrils drifted above the garbage and trash, obscuring the far wall. He hastened after Blade and Lex.

"Hold it, sucker!"

Rikki twirled, the katana extended.

It was the one called Erika, her portly features smeared with dirt, her leather garments begrimed a shade of brown. She held a shotgun in her hands, aimed at the man in black. Her eyes betrayed a maniacal quality, evidence of a personality on the brink of insanity. "You ain't going nowhere!" she barked.

Rikki stared at her fingers, waiting for the telltale flexing indicating she was going to pull the trigger.

"You thought you had me!" Erika cackled. "You and that big son of a bitch! Threw me into the pit! But I was too smart for the both of you! Grotto went after Terza, and I ducked into the hole connecting the pit to the sewers. I saw what it did to Terza!" Erika shuddered. "I stayed hid until after you left. Then some of the Knights showed up, and they tossed a rope to me." She laughed. "It was my idea to wait for you out here. I knew it'd take you a while to make it out." She tittered. "Pretty sharp, aren't I, lover boy?"

Rikki calculated five feet separated him from the crazed woman.

Erika raised the shotgun. "I'm going to enjoy this!" she declared, gloating, relishing her impending triumph. "Almost as much as I'll enjoy being the new leader of the Leather Knights!"

The street beyond the alley was quiet; the Knights apparently had retreated, abandoning their cart. Smoke continued to float into the alley.

"Any last words?" Erika baited Rikki.

A cloud of smoke drifted over Erika, enshrouding her head and shoulders in a mantle of gray. She coughed, recovered, and squeezed the trigger.

And missed.

Rikki threw his lean body to the left as the shotgun discharged. Her shot blew apart a pile of trash to the rear of where he had been standing just a moment earlier. Before she could fire again, his right arm swept back, then forward, holding the hilt of the katana, hurling the sword like he would a spear.

Erika, immersed in the suffocating smoke, experienced a burning sensation in her chest and glanced down. She released the shotgun and doubled over as the first waves of pain struck. "No!" she wailed. "No! No! No!" She dropped to the ground, her hands on the hilt, scowling in excruciating agony. A black foot appeared in her line of vision and she looked up, squinting.

The man in black was in a peculiar stance, his right hand rigid, the fingers firm and compact. "Yes," he said, and the right hand chopped downward.

22

"I don't believe it!" Blade exclaimed.

"I believe it," Rikki stated, grinning.

"I don't get it," Lex chimed in, gingerly adjusting the makeshift bandage on her left shoulder.

Directly ahead, parked in the center of the highway, upright, intact, was the SEAL. About 20 yards past the SEAL, also parked in the middle of the road, was an enormous Red helicopter. To the right of the SEAL, at the side of the highway, were two men in uniform, seated, propped against one another back-to-back, their wrists and ankles securely bound with rope.

"Is that your friend?" Lex asked Rikki.

"That's our friend," Rikki answered.

He was grinning from ear to ear, leaning on the SEAL's grill, his Colt Pythons tucked under his belt, his Henry cradled loosely in his buckskins clad arms. "Howdy!" Hickok greeted them as they approached.

Blade, stupefied, pointed at the pair in uniform and the helicopter. "Who? How? Where?"

Hickok winked at Rikki, then turned a somber expression to Blade. "You always did have a way with words, pard."

Blade found his voice. "How in the world did you manage this?"

"It was a piece of cake," Hickok replied.

Blade stared at the helicopter. "Where did that come from?"

"Washington," Hickok modestly responded.

"Washington? Washington, D.C.?" Blade and Rikki exchanged astonished glances.

"Yep."

"I want a full report," Blade told the gunman.

Hickok yawned and shrugged. "I figured we'd need some help gettin' our buggy on its tires again, so I moseyed to Washington and asked the Reds if they would lend us a hand. Well, sure enough, they obliged. And here I am. The SEAL checks out okay. We can leave whenever you're ready, pard, unless you reckon you'd rather fly to our Home in the copter."

Blade shook his head in bewilderment. "Knowing you, there has to be more to it than that. I want a detailed report on our trip back."

"You'll get it," Hickok promised. He gazed at Rikki. "Is the lady with you?"

"This is Lex," Rikki introduced her.

"I've heard a lot about you the past two days," Lex said.

Hickok stepped up to her and offered his right hand. "Any friend of Rikki's is a pard of mine. Pleased to meet you."

Lex shook. "Likewise. I can't wait to meet your wife. Rikki told me you're married to a lovely woman."

"I think so," Hickok said. "She has the looks and I've got the brains. We're quite a combo."

"You have the brains?" Rikki repeated skeptically.

Hickok ignored the barb. He looked at Blade. "So where the blazes have you been?"

"We ran into a spot of trouble," Blade replied. "Spent the last two days sneaking out of St. Louis." He paused, suddenly feeling extremely fatigued. "I'll fill you in on the way to the Home."

"We have a heap to talk about," Hickok admitted.

"I'm ready to leave now," Lex stated eagerly.

"What about them?" Rikki inquired, indicating the

two prisoners and the helicopter.

"I have an idea," Hickok mentioned. "We could use our rocket launcher on the helicopter," he suggested, "and those two vermin can fend for themselves. They can't tell us much I don't already know."

Blade reflected for a minute. "We don't want to leave the helicopter in enemy hands, so destroying it is our only option. As for the two soldiers," he said, then paused, studying them. "We don't have time to interrogate them here. The Leather Knights could show up in force at any moment. And I can't see lugging them back to the Home in the SEAL. It's too far, and we'd be too crowded. Hickok's right. We'll do as he suggests."

"Hickok is right?" Rikki asked in mock amazement. "Remind me to tell Geronimo about this when we reach the Home. He'll never believe you said that."

The gunman pretended to glare at the martial artist. "What did you do? Pick up a sense of humor in St. Louis?"

Lex took Rikki's right hand in hers. "He picked up more than a sense of humor," she said proudly.

"Oh, no." Hickok looked at Rikki. "Does this mean we're gonna have another wedding soon?"

Rikki shrugged. "If the Spirit so guides us."

Hickok frowned and shook his head.

"What's the matter with you?" Blade asked. "What's wrong with Rikki getting married? You and I are married, you know."

"It's just a mite sad to see another good man bite the dust," Hickok quipped. "Another Warrior who'll come down with a bad case of dishpan hands."

"Let's get out of here," Blade declared, "before the Leather Knights catch up with us."

"You three look tuckered out," Hickok said. "I'll drive."

Blade sighed. "Just when I thought I was safe . . ."

NEW YORK RUN

FOREWORD

It is 100 years after World War III. Give or take a year.
The good news? The planet is still here.
The bad news? The planet is still here.

The massive radiation and the staggering array of chemical-warfare weaponry unleashed on the globe precipitated an environmental disaster of incalculable proportions. In the U.S., much of the soil has been contaminated beyond reclamation, principally in the vicinity of nuclear strike zones, "hot spots." The climate has been altered; former fertile land might be withered dust, while former dry areas might receive an abundance of rainfall. The wildlife and human gene pool has been drastically affected by the radiation and the chemicals. Mutations are commonplace. Giantism increasingly frequent. The landscape is overrun by savage creatures of every conceivable shape and size.

Civilization is on the verge of complete collapse.
Chaos rules.
Almost.

Lingering outposts of humanity are resisting the rising tide of darkness, stubbornly clinging to the old ways or forging new paths of progressive development.

In the forefront of the strengthening forces of light, at the vanguard of the effort to reassert mankind as the dominant species on the planet, is the Freedom Federation. Comprised of a loose confederation of disparate groups, the Freedom Federation is valiantly striving to reestablish order in a world gone mad. Six factions constitute the Federation:

The Civilized Zone is the official title for a section in the Midwest embracing the former states of Kansas, Nebraska, Colorado, Wyoming, New Mexico, Oklahoma, portions of Arizona and the northern half of Texas. The government evacuated thousands of its citizens into this region during the war. Denver, Colorado, spared a direct hit during the conflict, became the new capital.

Montana has become the exclusive domain of the Flathead Indians, free at last from the white man's yoke.

The Dakota territory is the home of superb horsemen known as the Cavalry.

In northern Minnesota, deep underground, secure in their subterranean city, reside the people known as the Moles.

Also in northern Minnesota, in the former town of Halma, live the refugees from the Twin Cities called the Clan.

And finally, not far from Halma, on the outskirts of Lake Bronson State Park, in a survivalist compound constructed by a wealthy filmmaker named Kurt Carpenter immediately prior to the war, dwells the smallest faction in the Freedom Federation—but the one with the most influence. Carpenter's descendants are called the Family, and their 30-acre compound is known as the home. Like the Spartans of antiquity, they are renowned for two features: their wise leadership and their fearless fighters. The 15 Family members responsible for the defense of the Home and the preservation of the Family, collectively called the Warriors, have established a reputation for valor in combat matched by few others.

Several of the Warriors have ventured into uncharted realms east of the Civilized Zone. They've discovered that the city of St. Louis has become the turf of an outlaw motorcycle gang, the Leather Knights. And they've learned that the Russians have control of a corridor running through the center of the eastern half of the country.

They've also heard about other . . . things.

Evil things. Menacing things. Things better left alone. Things to be avoided at all costs.

Unless they come calling at your door . . .

1

The four members of Elite Squad-A7 could sense their impending doom in the dank air.

"Readings!" Captain Edwards barked, struggling to keep his voice under control.

The trooper with the pulse scanner strapped to his right wrist, Private Dougherty, was gaping down the dim passage to their right.

"Scan, damnit!" Captain Edwards ordered, slapping Dougherty on the left shoulder.

The youthful Dougherty, sweat beading his brow and coating his crewcut brown hair under his helmet, took a deep breath and glanced down at his scanner. "They're still after us!" he wailed. "Coming from every direction!"

"How many?" Captain Edwards demanded.

Dougherty shook his head. "I can't tell! There's too much interference!"

"We can't stay here!" Captain Edwards declared. "We're too exposed."

Elite Squad-A7 was silhouetted in the junction of two hallways, their shadows projected along the tiled walls by their helmet lamps.

"Stick together!" Captain Edwards commanded. "We can't afford to be separated!"

Private Dougherty and the two others, Geisz and Winkel, nodded their understanding, their helmet lamps bobbing up and down.

Captain Edwards took the passage to his left. His

palms felt sweaty on the Dakon II fragmentation rifle clutched in his hands.

"I've got a blip twenty yards behind us!" Private Dougherty yelled.

The four commandos spun, facing toward the junction they'd just vacated.

"On me!" Captain Edwards bellowed, leveling the Dakon II, his finger on the trigger.

Their combined lamp lights clearly illuminated the junction. A shadowy apparition appeared for an instant, and they caught a glimpse of a tall creature with grimy, gray flesh, gaping, reddish eyes, and a leering mouthful of yellow teeth. The monstrosity stopped and blinked in the bright light, starting to step backward, raising its left arm to shield its moldy face.

"Fire!" Captain Edwards shouted.

The passageway thundered as the four members of Elite Squad-A7 opened up, their fragmentation rifles chattering in unison.

The creature in the junction was struck in the chest and head, its body exploding in a violent spray of putrid flesh and a vile, greenish fluid. It shrieked as it died.

"Move!" Captain Edwards instructed his squad.

Geisz and Winkel took off, Geisz taking the point, her blue eyes alertly scanning the corridor ahead.

Private Dougherty followed them, studying the scanner.

Captain Edwards brought up the rear. "Readings!" he snapped.

"They've disappeared off the scope," Dougherty replied.

"That's impossible!" Captain Edwards responded.

"I'm telling you they're gone!" Private Dougherty said, disputing his superior.

"Let me see that!" Captain Edwards said.

Private Dougherty halted and swung his right arm around. "Here! See for yourself."

Captain Edwards leaned over the scanner, checking the grids for blips of white light.

Nothing.

"But that's impossible," Edwards repeated.

"Don't I know it!" Dougherty agreed.

"Let's go!" Captain Edwards kept his lamplight on the hallway behind them as he trailed Dougherty, his mind whirling. There was no way they could just vanish like that! So where the hell had they gone? Were there other passages or vents not marked on the blueprints the Technics possessed? Some way they could travel beyond scanner range in the space of a few seconds?

"Captain Edwards!" came a cry from further along the hall.

Edwards recognized the voice of Marion Geisz. "Hurry!" he prodded Dougherty, and the two of them hastened along the corridor.

Geisz and Winkel were waiting ahead, their helmet lamps pointed downward.

They'd found the stairwell. Again.

"It looks like there's no bottom," Geisz commented as Edwards and Dougherty reached her side.

"It gives me the creeps!" Winkel commented, his brown eyes wide from fright.

"Stow that crap, mister!" Captain Edwards stated. He stared down the stairwell, noting the dusty metal rails and the cobwebs covering the walls. "We know our objective, people! Let's get cracking! Geisz, the point!"

"What else?" Geisz quipped, and started down.

"I just hope the Minister was right about this place," Winkel said as he followed Geisz.

"Can the squawking!" Captain Edwards ordered. "You know better! You're the best of the best!" he reminded them. "Technic commandos! Act like it!"

The three troopers took the reprimand in resentful silence. Geisz, in particular, was irritated by Edwards' audacity. She'd seen far more combat than he had, and she knew what was expected of a professional storm trooper. Still, now was hardly the time to be distracted by petty animosities. She had to concentrate on the task at hand, or she might not live to see Chicago again. Moisture was trickling from under her helmet, plastering her crewcut blonde hair to her scalp, causing her skin to itch. She suppressed an impulse to scratch the itching, and focused on the stairs ahead.

Dust and spiderwebs.

And more dust and spiderwebs.

But nothing else.

Geisz saw the streaks of dust caking the metal railings, and suddenly realized there wasn't any dust on the stairs.

Someone . . . or something . . . must be using the stairs on a regular basis, but not bothering to use the railings.

Three guesses what they were.

Geisz reached up and cranked the volume control on her right ear amplifier. There was a crackling in her helmet, then a sustained hiss as the transistorized microphone strained for all its circuits were worth.

What was that?

Private Geisz slowed, listening intently. She thought she'd heard the muffled tread of a foot on the stairs below. She leaned over the railing and swept the lower levels with her lamp.

Nothing.

"Anything?" Captain Edwards asked from up above.

"I don't know," Geisz replied uncertainly.

"Stay alert!" Captain Edwards advised them.

Geisz almost laughed. As if they had to be told! She cautiously took another turn in the stairwell, walking to the right, her Dakon II at the ready.

Something scraped below her.

Geisz stopped, leaning against the wall to protect her back.

"What is it?" Captain Edwards demanded.

Geisz ignored him, striving to pinpoint the source of the noise.

"What is it?" Captain Edwards asked again. "Why the holdup?"

Geisz motioned for quiet. She could detect the faint sound of heavy breathing in her right ear.

"I'm getting something!" Dougherty suddenly yelled. "Lots of them! Above and below us! And . . ." he paused.

"And?" Captain Edwards angrily goaded him.

"And on both sides!" Dougherty said.

"Both sides?" Captain Edwards surveyed the stairwell. "There's nothing there but brick walls!"

"This damn thing must be broken," Dougherty muttered, adjusting the calibration control on his pulse scanner.

It wasn't.

The wall behind Private Dougherty abruptly collapsed, tumbling bricks and mortar onto the stairs and creating a swirling cloud of dust.

"What the . . .!" Captain Edwards began, and then he spotted the forms pouring from the gaping hole in the stairwell wall.

Dougherty saw them too, and he cut loose with his fragmentation rifle, the dumdum bullets ripping into the nightmarish creatures and blowing their grisly bodies apart. He downed two, three, four in swift succession, and then one of them reached him. Momentarily paralyzed with fear, he screamed as a cold, clammy, moist hand closed on his throat.

Captain Edwards saw the hulking figure towering over Dougherty, but he hesitated, unwilling to risk hitting the trooper. The cloud of dust reduced visibility to only a few feet, and he wanted to be sure before he pulled the trigger. He moved in closer, aiming his rifle, when strong hands clamped on his shoulders and lifted him bodily from the floor.

Private Geisz, enveloped in the dust, tried to catch a glimpse of her companions. She saw several struggling forms in the middle of the dust cloud, then felt her blood freeze as a terrifying screech reverberated in the confines of the gloomy stairwell.

There was a loud, crunching noise, like the sound of breaking bones.

"Captain Edwards!" Geisz shouted. "Doughboy! Wink! What's happening?"

No one answered.

A tall scarecrow shape loomed above her, its stick-like limbs clawing in her direction.

Something growled.

Private Geisz cowered against the wall, her

meticulous training overwhelmed by her instinctive loathing of the form on the step above. She could see one bony hand reaching for her neck, could see its wrinkled, gray flesh and its tapered, yellow nails, and could even see the brown dirt caked between its extended fingers. She wanted to bolt, to flee for her life, to get the hell out of there. But at the very second when those gruesome fingers touched her skin, instead of racing pell-mell down the stairs in reckless flight and abandoning her mates and friends, she reached deep within herself and discovered her innermost self, her true nature, her fundamental essence, the steel of her personality. Her bravery was tested to its limits, and she wasn't found lacking.

"Eat this, sucker!" Geisz stated defiantly, and angled the Dakon II toward the creature's midsection.

The creature hissed.

Geisz squeezed the trigger.

Her attacker was blown backward by the impact of the dumdum bullets, its body bursting apart across the chest and face.

Geisz didn't bother to check it; she knew the damn thing was dead. She punched the Dakon II onto full automatic and bounded up the stairs, into the dispersing dust cloud, searching for her companions.

Figures were all around her in the gloom.

"Captain!" Geisz yelled. As the last of the cloud dissipated, her helmet lamp revealed the hideous features of those nearest her. With a start, she realized she was completely surrounded by . . . them! There was no sign of her fellow commandos!

One of the creatures lunged at her, its red orbs glaring.

Geisz crouched against the railing and fired, swinging the Dakon II in an arc from right to left, taking out everything in her field of vision. She saw more monstrosities coming from the hole in the wall and fired into them, the fragmentation rifle functioning flawlessly, ripping them apart, literally blasting their shriveled flesh from their bones.

They fell in droves.

One of them was advancing down the stairs toward her.

Geisz spun to shoot them, but the Dakon II unexpectedly went empty.

Oh, no!

Geisz frantically released the spent magazine and heard it clatter on the stairs as she extracted a fresh magazine from her belt pouch and hurriedly inserted it into the rifle. She slapped her left hand on the bottom of the new clip, slamming it home, and she shot the creature in the face even as it sprang at her.

Suddenly, she was alone.

Geisz realized the creatures were gone. She scanned the hole, then up and down the stairwell. Bodies littered the steps, but none of them belonged to her friends or the captain.

What the hell had happened to them?

Geisz pondered her next move. If she were smart, she'd head for the surface and the jeep and take off for Chicago. But what if Doughboy and Wink and Edwards were still alive? Didn't she owe it to them to try and find them? She thoughtfully bit her lower lip. Yeah, she owed it to them. But how was she supposed to find them? The tunnels under the city were a virtual maze. Doughboy had carried their scanner, and without the pulse scanner she couldn't get a fix on their belt frequencies. She frowned, disgusted. Why the hell hadn't they issued scanners to everyone? She knew the answer to that one. The higher-ups wanted their arms free so they could carry more of the stuff up to the jeep.

And what about the stuff? The objective of their mission?

Geisz stared down the stairwell. It was down there, according to the Minister. About two floors below her present position. Canister after canister of it. Was the stuff worth so many lives? she wondered.

She had a choice to make.

Geisz shook her head in frustration. Either she could search for Edwards, Doughboy, and Wink, when she knew there wasn't a chance of locating them, or she

could retrieve one of the damned canisters for the
Minister.

Crap.

Private Geisz stood and moved down the stairwell,
treading softly, her right ear tuned to the amplifier in
her helmet. She descended two floors to the lowest level
without incident.

So where were the creatures?

She leaned against the wall at the bottom of the stair-
well and played her light over the passageway ahead.
What was it Doughboy had called the things? Zombies!
That was it.

So where were the Zombies?

Geisz detected a doorway about 30 feet away, in the
right-hand wall. On an impulse, she replaced the
partially spent magazine with a new one from her
pouch. There was no sense in being careless at this point
of the game! She insured the Dakon was set on full
automatic, then pressed the proper button to activate
the Laser Sighting Mode. Sure, it would be a drain on
the batteries, but she couldn't afford to waste precious
time sighting the rifle, especially now that she was
alone. The red dots could be a lifesaver when every
millisecond counted.

Here goes nothing!

Private Geisz sidled toward the doorway, keeping her
back against the right wall. Her head was constantly in
motion, sweeping her helmet light along the corridor.
Static crackled in her right ear. She glanced at the tiled
floor, then stopped, perplexed.

Dust covered the floor and the walls, a thick layer of
dust undisturbed by a solitary footprint.

Something was wrong here.

Geisz examined the floor for as far as her light
revealed, and it was all the same. Not a single print. But
why? she asked herself. The Zombies were all over the
place. They infested the ruins. Why didn't they use this
hallway? Why did they apparently avoid the lower
level? There was no evidence of anyone, or anything,
using this corridor in a long, long time.

Why?

Geisz grinned. What was the matter with her? Why was she looking a gift horse in the mouth? If the Zombies weren't down here, so much the better! It made her job that much easier! She walked to the doorway and paused before the closed wooden door.

What if they were waiting for her on the other side?

Geisz pressed the right side of her helmet against the door and listened, but the amplifier was silent.

Lady Luck was with her!

Geisz tried the knob, and wasn't surprised to find it locked. She took a step back, then spun, ramming her right leg into the door, her black boot slamming into the wood an inch from the knob. The door trembled, but it held. She kicked at it again, and again, and on her third attempt the aged wood splintered and cracked and the door swung open.

There was a rustling sound from inside the inky interior.

Geisz flattened against the wall and tensed.

Now what?

Geisz felt goosebumps erupt all over her flesh, and she resisted an urge to run. She wasn't about to quit when she was this close to their objective! Besides, all she needed was one lousy canister and the Minister would hail her as a hero. It might even mean a promotion, and she could use the extra pay.

She took a deep breath.

Geisz crouched and whirled into the doorway, the Dakon II pointed into the chamber, her helmet lamp illuminating the room and its contents.

The canister chamber was perhaps 20 feet square, and crammed with stack after stack of faded yellow canisters. The canisters, six inches in diameter and ten inches in height, were stacked in tidy rows from the cement floor to the ceiling.

All except in the center.

Geisz took a step forward. The middle of the chamber was covered with piles of fallen canisters, as if dozens of stacks had collapsed. All things considered, it was a minor miracle all of the stacks hadn't toppled over when the city was hit.

So what had made the rustling sound?

Geisz looked around the chamber, but nothing moved. She decided to grab a canister and scoot. Taking more than one was impossible. She would have her hands full fighting the Zombies en route to the surface. One would be burden enough. She hastened to the nearest stack, reached up, and took hold of one of the canisters. As she did, her helmet lamp focused on the ceiling, on the center of the ceiling directly above the collapsed stacks in the middle of the room.

It was perched in a huge hole in the ceiling, its legs bent, prepared to pounce.

Geisz gasped at the sight of it, stunned.

One of its four green eyes blinked.

Geisz backpedaled, elevating the Dakon II, a sinking sensation in the pit of her stomach.

The size of it!

She reached the doorway, and that's when the thing dropped toward her, roaring, its ten legs scrambling over the canisters and upending stack after stack as it surged after her.

Geisz crouched and squeezed the trigger, the Dakon II cradled in her right arm. The fragmentation bullets tore into the deviate, rocking it, chunks and bits of black flesh and shredded skin flying in every direction. The chamber shook as it reared up and bellowed in agony.

But it kept coming.

Geisz turned and ran, heading for the stairwell. She glanced over her left shoulder, knowing the thing couldn't possibly squeeze its gigantic bulk through the narrow doorway, confident she could escape before it breached the door. So she was all the more amazed when it flowed through the doorway without breaking its stride, its body seeming to contract as it passed through and expanding again once it was in the corridor.

No!

Geisz raced for her life, her heart pounding in her chest. She reached the stairwell and gripped the railing, risking one quick look down the hallway.

It was only a foot away, its cavernous maw wide, its fangs glistening in the light from her lamp.

Geisz swung the Dakon II up, the red dot clearly visible on the mutant's sloping forehead, and pulled the trigger.

The deviate roared and closed in.

Private Marion Geisz fired as the thing reached for her, fired as its claws clamped on her abdomen, and fired as it lifted her into the air and her stomach was crushed to a pulp. Her arms went limp, and blood poured from her mouth. She sagged and dropped the Dakon II, and the last sight she saw was the monster's teeth snapping at her face.

She thought she heard someone screaming.

2

The child was 18 months old, a stocky boy with full cheeks, impish blue eyes, and curly blond hair. He stared up at his father with an intensity belying his tender age.

"Now this is called a Colt Python," said the man, twirling the pearl-handled revolver in his right hand. "One day, these guns could be yours." He twirled the Colt in his left hand, then slid both Pythons into their respective holsters with a practiced flourish. To even a casual observer, the boy's lineage would have been obvious. The father was a tall, lean blond with long hair and a flowing moustache. His blue eyes seemed to twinkle with an inner light, reflecting a keen zest for life. The gunman wore buckskins and moccasins, as did the child. "Are you payin' attention to all of this, Ringo?" he asked the boy.

Ringo dutifully nodded, then grinned. "Ringo potty."

The gunman's mouth dropped. "What?"

"Ringo potty pease," the boy said.

"Blast!" The gunman grabbed his son and darted toward a nearby cabin. "Your mother's gonna kill me if I don't get you there on time." He jogged to the cabin, opened a door in the west wall, and dashed inside.

As the door was closing, another man appeared on the scene. He was huge, his powerful physique bulging with layers of muscles, his arms rippling as he moved. A black leather vest, green fatigue pants, and black boots

19

scarcely covered his awesome frame. Twin Bowie knives were strapped around his stout waist. His dark hair hung down over his gray eyes. Smiling, he strolled up to the cabin door and knocked.

"Who the blazes is it?" came a muffled response.

"Blade," the giant announced.

"I'm busy!"

"I'll bet you are," Blade said, chuckling. "I can wait."

"This might take a while, pard," yelled the gunman.

"I can wait," Blade reiterated. He leaned upon the rough wall and idly crossed his massive arms at chest height. This was the life! he told himself. Taking it easy. Enjoying his wife and son and discharging his responsibilities as head Warrior with a minimum of fuss. The fewer hassles, the better. A robin alighted in a maple tree at the west end of the cabin. A squirrel crisscrossed the ground 15 yards away. The scene was tranquil and soothing.

As life should be.

The cabin door was jerked open, the gunman framed in the doorway with a diaper clutched in his right hand. "Is this important?" he demanded. "I'm kind of tied up at the moment."

Blade grinned. "So I see. Did you reach the toilet in time?"

"You saw, huh?" the gunman asked sheepishly.

"I think I'm going to nominate you for daddy of the year," Blade joked.

Little Ringo waddled into view between the gunman's legs, his pants down around his ankles, his privates exposed to the world.

"Hi, Ringo," Blade cheerfully greeted him. "Is Hickok behaving himself?"

Ringo looked up at his father. "Ringo pee-pee," he said in his high voice.

"Now?" Hickok inquired.

Ringo nodded and proceeded to urinate all over the floor and Hickok's moccasins.

"Blast!" Hickok said, taking hold of his son and scrambling toward the bathroom.

Blade laughed. "You sure you know what you're doing?" he called out.

"Funny! Funny! Funny!" was the muttered reply from the bathroom.

"I don't know if Sherry should leave you alone with Ringo," Blade taunted his friend. "It could be hazardous to the boy's health."

"What about you, pard?" Hickok rejoined. "How come Jenny let you out of the house without your leash?"

"She's over at Geronimo's," Blade answered. "Where's your wife?"

"She went to see the Tillers about an extra allotment of veggies for Ringo," Hickok revealed. "He had the runs, and the Healers said he needs more greens in his diet."

"Gabriel had the runs last week," Blade said. "He's better now," he added, referring to his own son.

Hickok emerged from the bathroom a minute later with Ringo in tow. There was a distinct bulge on the left side of the boy's pants.

"Are you certain you put that diaper on correctly?" Blade asked.

Hickok glanced at his son. "Yeah. Why?"

"It doesn't look right," Blade said.

"You're just jealous 'cause you can't do it as good as me," Hickok retorted.

A slim, blonde woman, wearing a brown leather shirt and faded, patched jeans, walked around the east end of the cabin. A Smith and Wesson .357 Combat Magnum was belted around her narrow waist. "Hi, Blade," she greeted the towering Warrior.

"Hi, Sherry," Blade said to Hickok's wife.

Sherry's green eyes narrowed as they fell on Ringo. She shot an annoyed glare in the guman's direction. "What's wrong with his diaper?"

"He just went potty," Hickok stated proudly. "And I got him there in time. Well, almost in time."

"What did you do to his diaper?" Sherry reiterated.

"Nothin'. Why?"

Sherry knelt and tapped the bulge in Ringo's pants.

"What'd you put in there? A rock?"

"I just put on a new diaper," Hickok stated.

"What kind of knot did you use?" Sherry inquired.

"What does it matter?" Hickok said defensively.

"What kind of knot?" Sherry asked insistently.

"A timber hitch," Hickok mumbled.

"A what?"

"A timber hitch," Hickok declared. "I'm good at timber hitches."

Sherry glanced at Blade, rolled her eyes, and sighed. She picked up Ringo and stalked into the cabin. "How many times do I have to tell you," she said over her right shoulder, "you don't use timber hitches on a cloth diaper."

"So what's the big deal over a teensy-weensy knot?" Hickok wanted to know. "The diaper stays on, doesn't it?"

"Men!" Sherry exclaimed as she walked into the bathroom.

"Women!" Hickok muttered as he stepped outside and closed the cabin door. He looked at Blade. "So what's up?"

"Plato wants to see us," Blade said.

"How come?" Hickok asked as they strolled to the west.

"The Freedom Federation is going to have another conference," Blade disclosed. "The leaders are going to meet here in a couple of months, and Plato wants to go over our security arrangements."

Hickok snickered. "Just like the old-timer to get all frazzled about somethin' two months away!"

"Don't refer to Plato as an old-timer," Blade said testily.

"Why not?"

"You should treat Plato with more respect," Blade stated.

"I respect Plato," Hickok said sincerely. "But when a man is pushin' fifty, and he's got long, gray hair down to his shoulders, and more wrinkles on his face than there are cracks in the mud of a dry creek bed, then I reckon he qualifies for old-timer status."

"Plato is the Family Leader," Blade said archly. "He deserves our courtesy and consideration."

"But that doesn't mean I've gotta kiss his tootsies," the gunman remarked.

Blade sighed. "You're incorrigible, you know that?"

"Yep." Hickok nodded. "My missus tells me that at least once a day."

"She's right," Blade said.

The two Warriors were approaching the concrete block nearest the row of cabins, and Blade gazed at the compound ahead, marveling once again at how well the Founder had built the Home.

Kurt Carpenter had spent millions on the survivalist retreat. Square in shape, enclosed by brick walls 20 feet in height and topped with barbed wire, the Home was a model of efficiency and organization. The eastern half of the compound was preserved in its natural state and devoted to agricultural pursuits. In the middle of the Home, aligned from north to south in a straight line, were the cabins reserved for married Family members. The western section was the socializing area and the site of the large concrete bunkers—or blocks, as the Family called them. Arranged in a triangular formation, there were six in all. The first, A Block, was the Family armory and the southern tip of the triangle. B Block came 100 yards to the northwest of A Block, and it was the sleeping quarters for single Family members and the gathering place for community functions. C Block was 100 yards northwest of B Block, and it served as the infirmary for the Family Healers, members rigorously trained in herbal and holistic medicine. D Block, 100 yards east of C Block, was the Family workshop for everything from carpentry to metalworking. Next in line, 100 yards east of D Block, was E Block, the enormous Family library personally stocked with hundreds of thousands of books by Kurt Carpenter. Carpenter had foreseen the value knowledge would acquire in a world stripped of its educational institutions. Consequently, Carpenter had stocked books on every conceivable subject in the library. These precious volumes, frayed and faded after a century of use, were the Family's most cherished possessions. Finally, 100 yards southwest of the library was F Block, utilized for gardening, farming, and food-processing purposes.

The entire compound was surrounded by the brick walls and one additional line of defense: an interior moat, a rechanneled stream, entering the retreat under the northwestern corner and diverted in both directions along the base of the four walls, finally exiting the compound underneath the southeastern corner. Access to the Home was over a drawbridge positioned in the center of the west wall, a drawbridge designed to lower outward. Traversal of the moat was accomplished via a massive bridge between the drawbridge and the compound proper.

The cleared space between the six blocks was filled with Family members: families on picnics, children playing, lovers arm in arm, others chatting or singing or engaged in athletic activities.

"Who's on wall duty?" Hickok inquired.

"Beta Triad," Blade replied. The 15 Family Warriors were divided into 5 fighting units, or Triads, of 3 Warriors apiece. Designated as Alpha, Beta, Gamma, Omega, and Zulu, they rotated guard assignments and their other responsibilities during times of peace, but functioned collectively during any conflict and fought as a precision force during times of war.

Hickok, scanning the rampart on the west wall, nodded. "I can seek Rikki," he mentioned. Rikki-Tikki-Tavi was the head of Beta Triad. His Beta mates, Yama and Teucer, would be patrolling the other walls.

"I see Plato," Blade commented.

The wizened Family Leader was standing near the wooden bridge, his hands clasped behind his wiry frame, his gray hair whipping in the breeze of the August day.

"So what's the big deal about security arrangements for a conference two months from now?" Hickok absently asked.

"We'll find out in a minute," Blade said, and the pair made their way toward Plato.

A stocky Indian, dressed in green pants and a green shirt, with a genuine tomahawk tucked under his deer-hide belt and slanted across his right thigh, jogged in their direction.

Hickok beamed. "Looks like Geronimo's wife decided to let him get some fresh air."

Geronimo reached them and nodded. "I've been looking for you two."

"Why? Did you miss me?" Hickok asked playfully.

Geronimo, his brown eyes twinkling, feigned shock. "Miss you? Why would anyone in their right mind miss a monumental pain in the butt like you?" He ran his left hand through his short, black hair and, disguised by the motion of his left arm, winked at Blade.

Hickok touched his chest. "You've hurt me to the quick," he said in mock pain.

"To the quick?" Geronimo reiterated playfully. "If I didn't know better, I'd swear you've been reading some Shakespeare."

Hickok's nose crinkled distastefully. "Shakespeare? Are you joshing me or what? Give me Louis L'Amour any day of the week."

"*Aha*!" Geronimo exclaimed. "So you admit you can read!"

"I can read as good as you!" Hickok retorted. "I attended the same Family school you did, dummy!" He paused. "Why?"

"Because," Geronimo said, his full features radiating his impending triumph in their continual war of words, "anyone who talks like you do and acts like you do had to pick up their stupidity somewhere! And I know you don't come by it naturally, because I knew your parents and they were both normal."

Blade laughed. As his fellow Alpha Triad members and lifelong friends, Hickok and Geronimo were constantly at each other's throats. The lean gunman and his shorter partner were known to enjoy an abiding affection, the kind of friendship you only find once or twice in a lifetime. They were spiritual brothers, usually inseparable, and decidedly deadly when working in concert. Blade was grateful they were in his Triad.

The trio neared Plato.

"How's Ringo doing?" Geronimo asked Hickok.

"Fine," Hickok said, grinning. "He's a chip off the old block."

"Poor kid," Geronimo mumbled.

Plato turned as they reached him. His aged frame was clothed in an old, yellow shirt with a leather patch on both elbows and worn, brown pants. "Hello," he greeted them. "Thank you for coming."

"Blade's wife said you wanted to see all of us," Geronimo said.

Plato nodded. "We must discuss the Freedom Federation conference."

"But it's not for two months yet," Hickok stated.

"I don't believe in leaving important details until the very last minute," Plato said earnestly.

"We had a conference here about six months ago," Blade said. "We didn't have any problems then. All we had to do was post additional Warriors on the walls."

"True," Plato admitted. "But I've received a most disturbing communication from Wolfe."

Blade's piercing, gray eyes narrowed. Wolfe was the leader of the Moles, dwellers in a subterranean city located over 50 miles southeast of the Home. "When did you get word from Wolfe?"

"Late last night," Plato said. "His messenger arrived after you had retired, and I didn't see the need to awaken you."

"Where's this messenger now?" Geronimo asked.

"Sleeping in B Block," Plato said. "He was extremely fatigued from the journey. After he delivered his report, we fed him and told him to catch up on his sleep."

"So what was the message?" Blade asked the Family Leader.

Plato stretched and gazed at a group of children playing tag. "Evidently the Moles captured someone near their city. Wolfe suspected the man was spying and interrogated him. Unfortunately," Plato said, frowning, "this alleged spy did not survive the interrogation."

"Did he spill the beans before he kicked the bucket?" Hickok asked.

Plato glanced at the gunman. "Your colorful colloquialisms never cease to astound me."

"Can you lay that on me again?" Hickok responded. "In plain English this time?"

"Forget that!" Blade said, a bit impatiently. As head Warrior, his paramount concern was the safety of the Family. And if Wolfe was alarmed enough to send a messenger, the message must be critical. "What was the rest of the runner's report?"

"The man the Moles caught would not divulge any details concerning his origin or his reason for being near the Mole city," Plato said, "but he did make a few perplexing statements before he died."

"Like what?" Blade prompted.

"He gloated before he expired," Plato said. "He told Wolfe the Moles would all be dead before the year is done. He bragged that the Freedom Federation would be history, as he put it, before too long."

"How did he know about the Freedom Federation?" Blade asked.

"That's what bothered Wolfe," Plato stated. "That, and the equipment the man was carrying when apprehended."

"What equipment?" Geronimo interjected.

Plato scanned the compound. "I sent Bertha after it." He spotted a dusky-hued woman approaching from the armory, A Block. "When I first saw you coming."

Bertha was another of the Family's Warriors, a member of Gamma Triad. She was remarkably lovely in a striking sort of way. Her features conveyed an abundance of inner strength and a supreme self-confidence. Curly black hair cascaded over her ears and down to her shirt collar. She wore tight-fitting fatigues and black boots. Her brown eyes lit up at the sight of Hickok. "Hey there, White Meat!" she cried out. "What's happening?"

"Not much," Hickok replied uneasily.

"Relax, sucker!" Bertha said, laughing. "I ain't gonna jump your buns in public!"

Hickok hooked his thumbs in his gunbelt and glared at her. "How many times do I gotta tell you to stop talking to me like that? I'm married, remember?"

Bertha chuckled and nudged him with her left elbow. "I can't help it if I think you're the best-lookin' hunk in the Home!"

Geronimo couldn't resist the opening. "If you think Hickok is the best-looking man here," he chimed in, "then I'd suggest you have your eyes examined by the Healers!"

"Bertha!" Blade snapped with a tone of authority in his voice.

Bertha straightened and faced the giant Warrior, her chief. "Yes, sir," she said, all seriousness.

"Everybody knows you still have a crush on Hickok," Blade said, "but now's not the time to indulge it." He pointed at the items in her right hand. "Are these what Plato sent you to get?"

Bertha nodded and extended her right arm. "Yes, sir. Here you go."

Blade took the two pieces of equipment, a square, black box and a futuristic rifle. "Thank you. That's all for now."

Bertha wheeled, puckered her lips in Hickok's direction, smirked, and walked off.

"You were a mite hard on her, weren't you?" Hickok commented.

"We're Warriors," Blade stated testily. "We're supposed to be disciplined. There's a time and a place for everything." He saw the others studying him, silent accusations in their eyes, and he averted his gaze. Hickok was right. He had been hard on Bertha. And he knew the reason why. The prospect of another threat to the Freedom Federation, to the Family and the Home, agitated him greatly. The past several months had been peaceful. He'd been able to relax, to enjoy life for a change. The last thing he wanted was another damn threat to the Family's security! The very idea angered him, and he'd foolishly vented his budding frustration on Bertha.

Dumb. Dumb. Dumb.

"These are what the spy was carrying?" Blade needlessly asked to distract the others.

"Yes," Plato confirmed. "Wolfe was quite upset by them."

Blade could readily understand Wolfe's motives. Both the rifle and the mysterious black box were in superb condition. Indeed, both appeared to be relatively new. But where did they come from? Who had the industrial capability, the manufacturing know-how and resources, to produce items of such superior quality? The shiny black box was outfitted with a row of knobs and control buttons positioned along the bottom of the top panel. Above the knobs was a glass plate covering a meter of some sort. A small, vented grill occupied the upper right corner. "What is this thing?"

Plato shrugged his skinny shoulders. "We don't know. The Elders have examined it, but we're unable to ascertain its function."

"Can I see that, pard?" Hickok inquired, reaching for the rifle.

Blade handed the gun over.

Hickok whistled in admiration as he hefted the firearm. "This is a right dandy piece of hardware," he said in appreciation. The entire gun, including the 20-inch barrel and the folding stock, was black to minimize any reflection. The barrel was tipped with a short silencer, and an elaborate scope was mounted above the ejection chamber. A 30-shot magazine protruded from under the rifle near the trigger guard. There were four buttons on one side of the gun, close to the stock, and a small, plastic panel above the buttons. On top of the scope was a fifth button, and extending from the front of the scope, at the top, was a four-inch tube or miniature barrel. "I never saw a gun like this," Hickok said, marveling, "and I know our gun books in the library like the palm of my hand."

Plato stroked his pointed chin, running his fingers through his beard. "Can you imagine the threat if an army, outfitted with a rifle like that one, laid siege to the Home?"

"We've fought off attackers before," Hickok

boasted.

"Yes," Plato concurred, "but they were ill-equipped. The rifle you're holding is of recent vintage. What if the same people responsible for that automatic rifle can also fabricate larger weaponry on an extensive scale? What then?"

Hickok didn't answer.

"We must find out where these came from," Blade announced.

"How?" Geronimo asked. "Wolfe killed the spy."

"We'll think of something," Blade said optimistically.

"We must keep this information amongst ourselves," Plato said. "There's no need to instill unnecessary anxiety in the Family."

"We'll keep quiet," Blade promised. "And I'll have a word with Bertha. Who else knows?"

"Ares," Plato revealed. "He was on guard duty on the west wall last night when the messenger arrived."

"Ares ain't exactly a blabbermouth," Hickok noted.

Ares was the head of Omega Triad and a superlative Warrior.

"But how will we find out where the spy came from?" Geronimo reiterated.

Blade opened his mouth to respond.

The hot air was abruptly rent by the strident blast of a horn sounding from the west rampart, the horn the Warriors used to signal in times of danger!

3

The 15 Family Warriors were armed with their favorite weapons and on the brick walls within three minutes of the alarm. Alpha Triad, consisting of Blade, Hickok, and Geronimo, took its posts on the west wall. They were joined by Beta Triad: the diminutive Rikki-Tikki-Tavi, the Family's supreme martial artist; the silver-haired Yama, named after the Hindu King of Death; and Teucer, the bowman. Gamma Triad took the north wall: Spartacus, with his ever-present broadsword; the eighteen-year-old Shane, an aspiring gunfighter like his mentor, Hickok; and Bertha. The east wall was manned by the towering, Mohawk-cropped Ares, the head of Omega Triad, and his two subordinates: Helen, a raven-haired Warrior whose namesake was Helen of Troy; and Sundance, the pistol expert. On the south wall stood Zulu Triad, led by the powerhouse Samson, and including Sherry, Hickok's wife, and Marcus, the self-styled gladiator. Sherry, her M.A.C.-10 held in the crook of her right arm, surveyed the empty field and forest below the wall, thankful little Ringo was being watched by Jenny, Blade's wife, and worried about her husband on the west wall.

Rikki-Tikki-Tavi had been responsible for blowing the horn. Now he was stationed alongside Blade directly above the closed drawbridge, his five-foot frame clothed in black Oriental-style clothing constructed by the Family Weavers, his dark eyes scanning the forest to the west. His attire matched his lineage. Rikki was one of several Family members with an Oriental lineage.

31

"So what's the big deal?" Hickok demanded, standing on Rikki's right. "There's nothin' out there."

"Be patient," Rikki advised.

For 150 yards in every direction, the Family diligently kept the land cleared of trees, brush, boulders, and whatever else might be used for concealment by any enemy assaulting the Home. The flat, exposed field gave the Warriors an excellent line of fire. No one could reach the brick walls without sustaining heavy casualties.

Beyond the fields, dense forest prevailed. A crude road, little more than a flattened 15-foot-wide path, was maintained between the western edge of the field and Highway 59, approximately five miles to the west. A mile south from where the makeshift road met Highway 59 was Halma, dwelling place of the Family's allies, the Clan.

"You sure you didn't see a deer and mistake it for a mutate?" Hickok asked, joking with Rikki.

Rikki pointed to the west. "Does that look like a deer to you?"

Hickok took a look. "Nope," he admitted. "It sure don't, pard."

A jeep was visible, cresting the rise of a low hill, heading toward the Home.

"It's about half a mile away," Geronimo commented.

The jeep was joined by two military troop transports and yet another jeep.

"It's a small convoy," Blade observed.

"The only ones we know with vehicles like those are the folks in the Civilized Zone," Hickok declared.

Blade nodded. Why would the Civilized Zone be sending a convoy to the Home? Even in military vehicles, the trip was fraught with peril and not to be taken lightly.

Someone cleared his throat to Blade's left.

The giant Warrior turned and discovered Plato had ascended the rampart. "What are you doing up here?" he demanded. "You shouldn't be up here until we signal it's all clear."

Plato smiled. "I wanted to see for myself. I know it's against our rules."

Hickok grinned. "You're settin' a fine example for the munchkins, old-timer."

"I promise I will leave at the first hint of hostility," Plato said to Blade.

Blade frowned. "All right. You can stay. But keep your head down!"

The convoy was rapidly closing on the Home. The leading jeep reached the field west of the compound and angled toward the drawbridge.

"Hold your fire!" Blade commanded. He held a Commando Arms Carbine in his hands. Converted to full automatic by the Family Gunsmiths, and outfitted with a 90-shot magazine for its 45-caliber ammunition, it was a particularly lethal instrument of death.

"Darn!" Hickok stated. "I was hoping for some target practice." He hefted the Navy Arms Henry Carbine in his right hand.

The other Warriors were likewise armed and ready. Geronimo carried an FNC Auto Rifle and packed an Arminius .357 Magnum in a shoulder holster under his right arm. Rikki-Tikki-Tavi had his cherished katana angled under his black belt, and held a Heckler and Koch HK93 in his arms. Rikki's Beta Triad companions were equally prepared: Teucer, the bowman, bore a Panther Crossbow, armed with explosive tips instead of razor-edged hunting points, the camouflage shading of the bow with a pull of 175 pounds complementing his green Robin Hood-like wardrobe; while Yama, one of the few Family members who could claim a physique nearly as superbly developed as Blade's, carried a variety of weapons. Yama was unique among the Warriors. He'd taken his name on his 16th birthday from the Hindu King of Death, not because he leaned toward the Hindu religion spiritually, but because death was his profession and he was an expert at his craft. At Yama's insistence, the Family Weavers had made a one-piece dark blue garment with the silhouette of a black skull stitched into the fabric between his wide shoulders to serve as his uniform. He normally used a Wilkinson

Carbine with a 50-shot magazine, a Browning Hi-Power 9-millimeter Automatic Pistol under his right arm, a Smith and Wesson Model 586 Distinguished Combat Magnum under his left arm, a 15-inch survival knife strapped to his right hip, and a curved scimitar in a scabbard on his left.

All of the weapons came from the Family armory in A Block. Kurt Carpenter had meticulously stockpiled hundreds of diverse arms in the huge, concrete structure. Rifles, pistols, revolvers, shotguns, machine guns, and others of every conceivable make and description. He also included at least one of each and every type of weapon he could find, everything from Oriental weaponry such as nunchaku and sai and to American Indian artifacts such as Apache tomahawks. Thus, the Warriors were able to satisfy their personal predilections, whether it was Bowies for Blade, a katana for Rikki, a broadsword for Spartacus (because Ares already possessed the only shortsword), or a tomahawk for Geronimo—the only remaining Family member with an Indian heritage. Whatever their tastes, the armory supplied them. Carpenter had predicted the collapse of civilization after the war, and he knew his successors would require considerable firepower if they were to persevere in a world governed by the basic creed of survival of the fittest.

The convoy stopped, the jeep ten yards from the west wall, and a figure in uniform emerged and glanced up at the Warriors.

Blade felt his muscles relax. The man was an officer, about six feet in height with a lean build. His uniform was clean and pressed, with gold insignia on his shoulders. He had black hair, brown eyes, and rugged, honest features. He was General Reese, the foremost military commander in the Civilized Zone under President Toland.

General Reese waved. "Blade! We need to talk!"

Blade returned the wave. "Hold on! We'll lower the drawbridge."

Four Family members quickly lowered the massive mechanism, and moments later the convoy wheeled into the compound and parked near the moat.

"Raise the drawbridge," Blade instructed Rikki. "And keep your Triad here until we find out what's going on."

"Will do," Rikki said.

"After you," Blade said to Plato, motioning toward the stairs. He waited until Plato was descending, then turned. "You two stay close to me," he said to Hickok and Geronimo. "I trust Reese, but you never know. . . ." He let the sentence trail off.

"Don't fret, pard," Hickok stated. "You can count on us. We'll back your play all the way."

Blade hastened after Plato, Hickok and Geronimo in tow.

General Reese had climbed from his jeep. A dozen soldiers piled from each of the troop transports, and four more from the second jeep. The troopers formed into two rows, standing at attention.

Blade saw a man and a woman step from the general's vehicle. They wore green uniforms similar to those worn by the Civilized Zone soldiers, but theirs were a darker green and the new fabric clung to their bodies. Both the man and the woman were well-proportioned, conveying considerable strength in their posture, in the muscular contours of their physiques, and in the alertness of their eyes. Both wore their black hair in crewcuts, and both had pistols strapped to their right hips. Professional military types, obviously, but there was something about them, perhaps in the simple way they carried themselves, serving to set them apart and above the troopers from the Civilized Zone. Neither the man's square features nor the woman's angular facial lines reflected any warmth or humor.

"Hello, General Reese," Blade said as they reached the vehicles. "It's good to see you again."

"Blade!" General Reese advanced and extended his right hand. "The same here!" He shook hands warmly, then faced Plato. "And you, sir, must be the Family Leader I've heard so much about. It is a pleasure to meet you at last."

Plato shook hands. "And I have heard about you.

President Toland informed me at our last conclave how instrumental you've been in assisting in the reorganization of the Civilized Zone government."

"President Toland flatters me," General Reese said.

Blade indicated his two friends. "This is Hickok."

"The famous gunfighter?" General Reese asked.

Hickok's chest puffed up a good inch. "I reckon my name does get bandied about a mite." He offered his right hand.

"You Warriors are acquiring quite a reputation," General Reese remarked.

"And this is Geronimo," Blade said.

General Reese shook hands. "We met briefly when you were in Denver, remember?"

"You have a good memory," Geronimo said.

"Well, now that the amenities are over," Plato stated, "perhaps you will explain the reason for this extraordinary visit?"

General Reese nodded at the man and woman in the dark green uniforms. "First let me introduce you."

The man and woman moved closer.

General Reese swept the Warriors and Plato with his gaze. "Gentlemen, I'd like you to meet Captain Wargo and Lieutenant Farrow."

Captain Wargo nodded. "I've looked forward to this meeting for some time." His voice was deep, almost harsh.

"They're from Chicago," General Reese revealed.

Plato's surprise showed. Hickok and Geronimo exchanged glances. Only Blade remained immobile, a statue.

"When did the Civilized Zone send an expedition to Chicago?" Plato inquired. "I thought such missions must be approved by the entire Freedom Federation Council?"

"We didn't send one," General Reese responded. "They came to us."

Blade studied the pair. Chicago was east of the area presided over by the Freedom Federation, in hostile country. No one had ventured to the Windy City in over a century. But during the last run Alpha Triad had made, to the city of St. Louis—during which they'd battled the Reds—he'd been told about a group controlling Chicago. What was its name again?

"We're Technics," Captain Wargo said proudly.

"Technics?" Plato repeated, puzzled.

"I believe it started as a nickname decades ago," Captain Wargo explained. "You see, the scientists at the Chicago Institute of Advanced Technology refused to evacuate the city during the war. They dug in and used their knowledge to forge a new lifestyle. Eventually they came to rule the city."

"And now they're known as Technics," Plato deduced.

"Exactly," Captain Wargo confirmed.

"They even have several manufacturing facilities operational," General Reese interjected.

"Really?" Plato's eyebrows rose. "Quite remarkable. The war severely impaired the country's industrial capability. How were your people able to overcome the handicap of a shortage of raw materials and the requisite work force to produce your goods?"

Captain Wargo shrugged, downplaying the Technics' accomplishment. "Oh, we get a little bit here, a little bit there. You know how it is."

Blade saw Hickok's jaw muscles tighten.

Plato nodded. "We must have a great deal to discuss. Why don't we retire to my cabin? My wife, Nadine, can fix refreshments, and you can elucidate on why you've been looking forward to meeting us."

"Sounds great," Captain Wargo said.

"I'll dismiss my men," General Reese declared, walking off.

"I'll join you in your cabin," Blade told Plato. Then he looked at Wargo. "If you don't mind?" he added politely.

"To the contrary," Captain Wargo replied. "I was hoping you would join us. And bring Hickok and Geronimo too. Alpha Triad should be there."

"You know who we are?" Blade asked innocently.

Captain Wargo hesitated for a fraction of an instant. "Yes. General Reese told me all about you on the trip here.''

Hickok's right hand had drifted to the pearl grips on his right Python.

Blade smiled. "Plato, why don't you take Captain Wargo and Lieutenant Farrow to your cabin?" he suggested. "We'll join you in a bit."

"Fine," Plato said, and led the Technics to the east.

"I don't trust that hombre," Hickok snapped when they were beyond earshot.

"Neither do I," Geronimo affirmed.

"That makes it unanimous," Blade said.

"What do you reckon they're up to?" Hickok queried.

"We'll know shortly," Blade answered. He gazed up at the west rampart, at Rikki-Tikki-Tavi. "The alert is over!" he shouted. "Tell the Family they can come out of the Blocks! Post Gamma Triad around these vehicles!"

"That won't be necessary," interrupted General Reese, joining them.

"Just a precaution," Blade said. "Standard procedure."

"Yeah," Hickok quipped. "We wouldn't want one of our kids to steal a battery or a hubcap!"

"Have Omega Triad and Zulu Triad wait near the armory until they hear from me!" Blade yelled to Rikki.

"Consider it done!" Rikki acknowledged.

"Let's go," Blade said, and led them toward the row of cabins in the center of the Home. "What do you make of this Captain Wargo?" he inquired of the general.

Reese frowned. "He's a real tough nut to crack. Doesn't talk a lot, except when it suits his purposes. To be honest, I don't feel comfortable around him. Or her, for that matter. I receive the impression they're holding back on us, not telling us everything they should."

"You too, huh?" Hickok said.

"President Toland feels the same," General Reese disclosed. "He gave me a personal message for you, Blade."

"What is it?"

"He said to watch yourself," General Reese stated. "Use your best judgment, but watch yourself."

"We will," Blade vowed. "What are they doing here?"

"You'd better hear it from them," General Reese said.

"Did they just show up in Denver?" Geronimo asked.

"No," General Reese responded. "They showed up at a guard post on the eastern edge of Omaha, Nebraska. Demanded to see President Toland. Asked for him by name."

"How did they know Toland is the President of the Civilized Zone?" Blade asked the officer.

"Beats me," General Reese said. "The word has probably spread, though, even to the Outlands."

"The Outlands?" Blade reiterated.

"Oh. Sorry. Anything beyond the boundaries of the Freedom Federation, whether it's west of the Rockies or east of our borders, we call the Outlands," General Reese informed them.

"Appropriate name," Geronimo chipped in.

"Did you interrogate this Wargo?" Blade asked.

"No," General Reese answered, frowning. "I wanted to give him the works, but President Toland wouldn't hear of it."

"Why not?"

"Because, technically, Captain Wargo and Lieutenant Farrow are diplomatic envoys for the Technics. They initiated peaceful overtures and established contact with us." He sighed. "My hands are tied until and unless they commit a hostile act."

"I can't wait to hear what these bozos have to say," Hickok commented.

They walked in silence to Plato's cabin, the seventh from the north. Blade knocked on the west door, and a moment later Plato opened it and beckoned them inside.

"Come on in," Plato urged them. "Nadine is in the kitchen preparing food for our guests. Would you like some, General Reese?"

Reese patted his stomach. "Thanks, but no thanks. I'm on a diet. I've got to lose about ten pounds. It doesn't do to set a bad example for the ranks."

"I heartily agree," said Captain Wargo. He was seated at the living room table. Lieutenant Farrow stood behind his chair, her hands clasped behind her trim back.

Plato closed the door and took a seat across the oaken table from Captain Wargo. General Reese sat on his left. Hickok and Geronimo moved to the right and leaned against the log wall. Blade crossed to the table, but stayed standing next to Plato.

"Have a seat," Captain Wargo suggested.

"Thanks," Blade said, "but not right now."

Captain Wargo shrugged.

"You were about to tell me the reason you wanted to meet us," Plato prompted the Technic officer.

Captain Wargo leaned back in his chair and stared at each of them, smiling.

There was a phony quality about that smile. Blade shifted uncomfortably.

"First, allow me to congratulate you on the marvelous setup you have here," Captain Wargo said. "It's amazing, considering the barbaric conditions existing elsewhere."

"Our Founder deserves all the credit," Plato said. "We're merely perpetuating a system he started."

Captain Wargo glanced at Blade. "And what about the Warriors? Did your Founder start them as well?"

"Originally he had nine Warriors, but later they were expanded to twelve, and then, fairly recently, to fifteen," Plato divulged.

"I couldn't help but notice," Captain Wargo remarked. "You have a Warrior named Hickok, and one called Geronimo, and others named Yama and Samson, to mention just a few." He paused. "Where do you people get your names? We have a vast library in Chicago, and a mandatory educational regimen. It seems to me I've run across some of these names before." He looked at Plato. "Especially yours."

Plato nodded, grinning. "The Family also has a

sizable library," he told Wargo. "And many of us take our names from books in the library."

"You get your names from books?"

"Our Founder didn't want us to forget our historical roots. He was afraid we'd be tempted to ignore the lessons to be learned from a study of history. So he implemented a procedure, a ceremony we call our Naming. When all Family members turn sixteen, they are permitted to select any name from any book in the library as their very own. Years ago, we only used the history books. But now we adopt our names from practically any volume in the library. That's how I received mine," Plato elaborated. "Hickok, for instance, took his from a revered gunfighter of ancient times. Geronimo took his from an Indian he admires and respects."

Captain Wargo looked at the giant Warrior alongside Plato. "And you, Blade?"

Blade patted his twin Bowies. "I couldn't find a name I wanted in any of the books, so I picked a new one."

"One based on his preference in weapons," Plato added.

"I see." Captain Wargo glanced at Lieutenant Farrow, then resumed speaking. "I don't mind telling you, and I'm not attempting to flatter you by saying this, that your reputations have preceded you. As General Reese noted earlier, you've achieved some small measure of fame over the past few years."

Blade studied the Technic. "I can understand them talking about us in the Civilized Zone," he said. "After all, we fought a war with them some time back and won. But how is it you've heard of us clear in Chicago? Chicago is outside of the Civilized Zone. It's even outside of the Freedom Federation's territory. It must be hundreds of miles from here."

"About eight hundred," Captain Wargo offered.

"Are you telling me you've heard of us in Chicago?" Blade demanded.

Captain Wargo nodded. "Think about it for a moment. From what I was told, the Warriors have fought in the Twin Cities, in Montana, in the Dakota

Territory, and in the Civilized Zone. You were responsible for destroying Cheyenne, Wyoming, too, I believe. Did you really think all that would go unnoticed?''

Blade thoughtfully chewed on his lower lip. Verrrry interesting! First, Wargo said he'd heard about the Warriors from General Reese. Now he says he learned about them in Chicago.

"General Reese only confirmed the stories," Captain Wargo said, as if he could read Blade's mind. "Chicago isn't isolated from the rest of the world. We get travelers passing through every day. We were bound to hear about you sooner or later."

"I see," Blade said. Why was it he still felt as if Wargo were lying through his even white teeth?

"Actually," Captain Wargo said, "the Warriors are part of the reason I'm here."

"They are?" asked Plato.

"Yes," Captain Wargo confirmed. "The Warriors, and the SEAL."

Blade's steely eyes bored into the Technic. The SEAL was the Family's mechanical pride and joy, their main means of travel. The Founder, Kurt Carpenter, had spent millions of dollars developing it prior to World War III. His scientists had been instructed to construct an indestructible vehicle, and they'd nearly succeeded. Van-like in configuration, the SEAL was green in color and designed with a versatile array of special features. It had originally been called the Solar-Energized Amphibious or Land Recreational Vehicle. Carpenter had later hired mercenaries to incorporate devastating armaments into its body. Its sturdy structure was composed of a shatterproof, heat-resistant, super-plastic, deliberately tinted to prevent outsiders from viewing the interior but enabling the occupants to see in all directions. Four enormous tires provided a rugged means of locomotion. Two prototypical solar panels on the roof and a series of six revolutionary batteries positioned in a lead-lined case under the SEAL served as the key components in its power system. "You know about the SEAL too?"

Captain Wargo nodded. "A little. We knew you owned it, and our leader, the man we call our Minister, realized you might be able to assist us in a desperate enterprise. We knew the Family was connected with the Freedom Federation, but we didn't know exactly where to find you. So the Minister proposed sending us to President Toland and requesting his aid in contacting you." Wargo grinned. "It worked."

"One moment," Plato said. "What is this desperate enterprise you've mentioned?"

Captain Wargo's grin widened. "Our Minister would like your permission to send Alpha Triad and your SEAL on a mission."

"A mission? To where?" Plato inquired.

Captain Wargo scanned the room before responding. "Why, to New York City, of course."

Blade felt his abdominal muscles inadvertently tighten.

4

The four soldiers in the jeep, three men and a woman, were five miles from the Home, hidden in the woods to the east of Highway 59.

"So what's the scoop, Sarge?" asked the woman trooper.

"We sit tight until we receive the signal," the sergeant advised her.

"This is boring," commented one of the men, seated in the back beside the woman.

The sergeant turned in his seat next to the driver. "You're a Technic, Johnson. I don't want to hear that kind of shit again!"

"Yes, sir, Sergeant Darden, sir," Private Johnson said. "My apology, sir."

Sergeant Darden stared at his subordinate for a minute, trying to determine if Johnson was being his typically sarcastic self.

"What's the name of these dumb hicks?" inquired the driver.

"They're called the Family," Sergeant Darden informed him.

"The Family?" The driver snickered. "What a corn-ball name!"

"Don't underestimate them," Sergeant Darden warned.

"Give us a break!" Johnson said. "You don't expect us to get worked up about a bunch of dirt farmers, do you?"

44

"They're not dirt farmers," Sergeant Darden responded. "Only about a dozen or so actually till the soil. The rest perform other duties. Besides, the ones you need to worry about are the Warriors."

"The Warriors?" Private Johnson snorted derisively. "Give us a break! How bad can they be?"

"The baddest," Sergeant Darden said.

"Says who?" demanded Johnson.

"Says the Minister," Sergeant Johnson stated.

"So why are we wasting these hicks?" asked the woman.

"Because those are our orders, Rundle," Sergeant Darden remarked.

"But why?" Rundle pressed him.

Sergeant Darden shrugged. "What's it matter? We do as we're told, no questions asked. You know that."

"Just wondered, is all," Rundle commented absently.

"We were lucky we received that warning about Halma," mentioned the driver. "Another mile and we'd of blundered right on 'em."

"Who were those people in that town?" asked Rundle.

"Don't know," Darden told her. "But I'd imagine they're friends of the Family's if they live so close to their Home."

"Say, Sarge," Private Johnson said. "What's with the beeper?"

Sergeant Darden studied the black box in his lap. "It's still stationary. They haven't moved."

"Do you think this Family will get wise to us?" asked Private Rundle.

"No way," Sergeant Darden declared.

Private Johnson yawned. "Who cares if they do or not? One way or the other, this Family is history!"

"Fine by me," said Rundle. "I could use some action."

5

"New York City?" Plato repeated in astonishment. "You can't be serious!"

"I've never been more serious," Captain Wargo declared.

Hickok laughed. "Who does this ding-a-ling think he is? He waltzes in here and tells us to go to New York City, just like that?" He snapped his fingers.

"I'm *asking* you, not telling you," Captain Wargo said with a touch of annoyance. "Or, rather, our Minister is asking you on behalf of all humanity."

"You'd better explain," Plato told the Technic.

"Certainly." Captain Wargo leaned forward. "You know what it's like out there in the world. It's a real jungle. Mutants everywhere. Roving bands of looters and killers. The few outposts of civilization don't stand much of a chance, do they?"

Plato didn't answer.

"There's no need for me to tell you how bad it is," Captain Wargo went on. "You know. Even in the area under the jurisdiction of your Freedom Federation, even in the Civilized Zone, it's not safe to be out alone after dark. I'd be willing to bet it's not even completely safe here in your Home. Am I right? Have any of the mutants ever managed to scale the walls and attack you?"

"We've experienced a few incidents," Plato conceded.

"See? What did I tell you?" Captain Wargo pounded

the table. "Don't you think it's about time all of that changed? Wouldn't you like to see the world the way it was? Peaceful? Prosperity for all?"

"This world has never known true peace," Plato said. "And in the prewar societies, only the rich knew prosperity."

"True. True," Captain Wargo said. "But you must admit it was safer for the general populace before the war than it is now."

"Perhaps," Plato allowed.

"Anyway," Captain Wargo continued. "You know as well as I do that everyone is barely scraping by today. There's never enough food or ample clothing or medical supplies."

"Do the Technics intend to remedy the shortages?" Plato asked.

"With your help," Captain Wargo replied.

"How?"

"Follow me on this," Captain Wargo said. "Before World War III, there was an eastern branch of the Institute of Advanced Technology—"

"Located in New York City?" Plato guessed.

"Exactly. Shortly before the war they succeeded in perfecting a new strain of seeds. Fruit and vegetable and grain seeds, radically different from anything seen before. These new seeds could grow in barren soil and required absolutely minimal amounts of water. They were designated the Genesis Seeds. Can you imagine what those seeds could do today? They would be a godsend! Farmers everywhere would be able to grow crops again in abundance! Starvation would disappear! Once we've reestablished the food supply, we can devote our attention to meeting other essential needs. It would be fantastic!" Captain Wargo stopped, his face flushed with excitement.

"And I take it you want Alpha Triad to travel to New York City and retrieve these Genesis Seeds?" Plato deduced.

"Precisely!" Captain Wargo answered.

Hickok laughed. "You're out of your gourd!"

Plato held up his right hand for silence. "This is a

very grave matter, and some clarification is needed.
Let's consider your statements. You say these Genesis
Seeds would deliver us from our agricultural bondage to
a land contaminated and polluted by massive amounts
of radiation and chemical toxins. Let us suppose for a
moment these seeds really exist. Even if they are found,
and they can do all you claim, they won't necessarily
make the world a safer place in which to live."

"But it would be a start!" Captain Wargo said. "If
we don't have to devote so much time and energy to
food, we can channel them to our other problems like
the mutants and the degenerates."

Plato pursed his thin lips. "The scenario you paint
sounds encouraging. But look at the reality of your
request. Wasn't New York City hit during World War
III?"

"It was," Captain Wargo admitted. "We know the
Soviets used thermonuclear devices sparingly during the
war, apparently with the intent of conquering the U.S.
instead of wiping us off the face of the earth. They preferred to use neutron bombs and missiles on most of the
populated centers they struck. But New York and a few
others were exceptions. New York was hit by a
hydrogen-tipped ICBM."

"We understand the Soviets still control some of the
country," Plato mentioned.

"True. They occupy a belt in the eastern U.S., but
New York City is not included in the area they control,"
Captain Wargo said.

"So getting back to New York City," Plato stated,
"how do we justify sending our Warriors into a contaminated zone, into a potential hot spot?"

"New York isn't hot anymore," Captain Wargo said.

"You've verified that fact?" Plato demanded.

Captain Wargo nodded. "Let me explain." He
paused. "You said you're familiar with prewar
history?"

"Extensively," Plato affirmed.

"Good. Then you must know about the two Japanese
cities hit by nuclear weapons during World War II,

way, way back in the 1940s. I think their names were Hiroshima and Nagasaki.''

"They were," Plato declared.

"Like Hiroshima and Nagasaki, New York City was hit by an airburst of incredible magnitude. It obliterated a huge area and razed most of the buildings within a twenty-five-mile radius. But because it was an airburst, the fallout was minimal.''

"Why was that?" General Reese interrupted.

"Fallout," Captain Wargo elaborated, "is produced when a nuclear explosion takes place on the ground. The blast sucks up tons and tons of dirt and carries it into the atmosphere. All of this dirt then becomes radioactive, and when it falls back to the ground you get your fallout. But in an airburst, because the blast takes place up in the sky, no dirt is sucked up, and without the dirt there's nothing to fall back down. So no fallout." He cleared his throat. "Hiroshima and Nagasaki were hit, all right, but within thirty years of the strike you would have been hard-pressed to find any trace of the explosions. Both cities were densely populated. Both had lush landscaping and many flowering gardens. And if Hiroshima and Nagasaki were completely safe a few decades after the nuclear bombs were dropped, then New York City, from a radiation-contamination standpoint, is safe by now."

"Hmmmm," Plato said, reflecting.

"So you won't need to worry about your Warriors getting radiation poisoning," Captain Wargo told the Family Leader.

"Then let's tackle another issue," Plato said. "What makes you think the Genesis Seeds are still there?"

Captain Wargo smiled. "Because we know the building the seeds were stored in is still there."

"How do you know this?" Plato inquired.

The Technic frowned and gazed at the wooden floor. "We've already tried to retrieve the Genesis Seeds."

"You have?" Plato asked in surprise.

"Yes. We've sent in a few teams—"

"How many?" Plato broke in.

"I can't remember, offhand," Captain Wargo said. "A few."

"What happened to them?" Blade queried.

Captain Wargo sighed. "They failed. The first squad didn't even make it to the site of the building. The New York branch of the Institute of Advanced Technology was destroyed in the blast, all of it except for the lower levels. And the Genesis Seeds were placed in a vault deep underground. That's another reason we feel the Genesis Seeds are still there."

"What happened to your other teams?" Blade asked.

"The second squad reached the site and radioed they were going underground," Captain Wargo answered. "That's the last we heard from them."

"No idea what happened to 'em, huh?" Hickok chimed in.

Captain Wargo's thin lips twitched. "Oh, we have an idea. In fact, we know what probably got them. The Zombies."

Plato straightened in his chair. "The Zombies?"

Captain Wargo's eyes seemed to glaze slightly, and there was a hint of horror in his voice. "New York City is inhabited. We think a lot of the poor slobs stayed on after the war, not having anywhere else to go. They undoubtedly took to the sewers, the subways, and whatever other underground tunnels existed. Over the years the radiation took its toll on their bodies, on their genes—"

"But I thought you said there wasn't any fallout," Blade interjected.

"No radioactive fallout," Captain Wargo said. "But there still was some radioactivity, enough to produce the inevitable mutations. And those mutations now roam New York City at will, killing every living thing they encounter."

Blade felt a shiver run up his spine. He found himself fervently hoping Plato would decline the Technics' request.

"You call these mutations Zombies?" Plato asked.

Captain Wargo nodded. "Yes. Our last two teams

were able to penetrate the lower levels, but none of them came out alive. The Zombies ate them.''

''Ate them?'' This came from Geronimo, his tone shocked.

Captain Wargo looked up. ''Oh? Didn't I tell you? The Zombies are cannibals.''

There was a moment of strained silence.

''What makes you think our Warriors would fare any better than the teams you sent in?'' Plato demanded.

Captain Wargo brightened. ''Your SEAL. You see, we do have a manufacturing capability, and we can produce some rather sophisticated weapons, but nothing on a large scale. No tanks, nothing like that. And even if we could manufacture a tank, where would we obtain the fuel to operate it? And without a tank, or a similar vehicle, there's no way to guarantee our squads can reach the site in one piece. But with this SEAL I've heard tell about, we could get our people there intact. Then, all they'd need do is make it to the underground vault and retrieve the Seed canisters.''

''Is that all?'' Hickok chuckled.

Blade ran his right hand along the cool hilt of his right Bowie. Wargo was lying again. He was sure of it. His mind flashed to his run to St. Louis, and he remembered being told interesting information concerning the Technics: they ruled Chicago, they were technologically superior to anybody else, and they had formed a pact with the bikers running St. Louis. One provision of the pact called for the Technics to supply the bikers, known as the Leather Knights, with unlimited amounts of fuel for their bikes. And if the Technics could provide vast quantities of fuel to the bikers, then they also had enough to fuel a tank. Or a dozen tanks.

So what the hell was Captain Wargo up to?

''Our proposal is this,'' Capain Wargo said. ''Our Minister would like your Alpha Triad to transport a retrieval squad to New York City. In exchange, we will share the Genesis Seeds with you.''

''Share them?'' Plato repeated.

''Yes. Our Minister will give your Family half of all

the Seeds recovered. You can do with them whatever you like. Keep them for yourselves, or share them with your allies in the Freedom Federation."

"Your Minister is most . . . generous," Plato said.

"If the Genesis Seeds are recovered, we can afford to be," Captain Wargo remarked. "We won't need all of them. If you ask me, it's a pretty good deal."

"The Elders will discuss it," Plato told him.

"Fine by me." He rested his elbows on the table, then glanced behind him as if suddenly recalling something important.

Lieutenant Farrow was still behind his chair.

"I almost forgot," Captain Wargo said, facing Plato. "Our Minister wanted to prove his honorable intentions. He thought you might not trust us, or wouldn't believe our offer. So he authorized me to present a token of his sincerity."

"What sort of token?" Plato inquired.

"Lieutenant Farrow."

Plato's brow furrowed. "I don't understand."

Captain Wargo spread his hands on the table. "It's simple. Lieutenant Farrow will be our insurance."

Plato stared at the woman officer. "I don't see how—"

"Lieutenant Farrow will be your hostage," Captain Wargo detailed. "The proof of our performance, as it were."

"Our hostage?" Plato and Blade exchanged glances.

"Sure. She stays here until your Warriors return. We're putting her life in your hands as an example of our good intentions. If your Warriors don't return, kill her," Captain Wargo stated matter-of-factly.

"You can't be serious," Plato countered in amazement.

"Very serious," Captain Wargo said. "Our Minister is a man of his word, and this is his way of demonstrating the fact."

Plato opened his mouth to speak, then thought better of the idea. He glanced up at Blade, his face expressionless except for his eyes. Smoldering contempt flashed briefly, then vanished as he gazed at the Technics. "And how does Lieutenant Farrow feel about this hostage business?''

Captain Wargo looked at Farrow. "Tell him," he ordered.

"I am a Technic," Lieutenant Farrow dutifully intoned. "I do my duty."

"I see." Plato stared at the table for a minute. "This has been most interesting," he said at last. "I must discuss your offer with Alpha Triad and the Family Elders. In private."

"I understand," Captain Wargo said. "Would you mind if we took a tour of your Home in the meantime?"

"Be my guest," Plato said.

"We'll supply a guide for you," Blade quickly added.

Captain Wargo stood. "That won't be necessary."

"We don't mind," Blade informed him.

"But we don't want to impose—" Captain Wargo began.

"It's no imposition," Blade said, cutting him off. He glanced at General Reese. "Would you escort our guests to the west wall?"

"Certainly," General Reese replied.

"Relay a message to Rikki for me," Blade directed. "Tell him to have Yama conduct Captain Wargo and Lieutenant Farrow on a tour of the Home."

"Will do," General Reese said. He motioned toward the cabin door.

"I almost forgot!" Plato abruptly exclaimed. "What about your refreshments?"

"We can eat later," Captain Wargo said.

"As you wish," Plato commented.

General Reese, Captain Wargo, and Lieutenant Farrow departed the cabin.

"Your reactions?" Plato immediately asked.

"White man speak with forked tongue," Geronimo said somberly, then grinned. "But what else is new?"

"My nose was twitching the whole time he was yappin'," Hickok declared.

"Your nose was twitching?" Plato reiterated.

"Yep. That dude reeked of unadulterated manure!" Hickok stated.

"And if anyone knows about manure," Geronimo said, "it's Hickok." His face suddenly displayed deep shock, and he gaped at the gunman. "Did I hear you right? Unadulterated? Have you been reading the dictionary again?"

"And your assessment?" Plato asked Blade.

Blade shook his head. "I don't trust these Technics one bit. When we were in St. Louis I discovered a few facts concerning them."

"On the run the Chronicler refers to as the Capital Run?" Plato said.

"That one. Captain Wargo was lying to us. From what I learned, the Technics could easily fuel a whole squadron of tanks. And what about those other sophisticated weapons he mentioned? So why do they need the SEAL?"

"Mystery number one," Plato said.

"And do you really believe the Genesis Seeds exist? Even if they do, why should the Technics generously share them with us?" Blade inquired.

"Mystery number two," Plato said.

"And how do they know so much about us?" Blade went on. "Granted, they might have learned a lot while in the Civilized Zone. But they obviously knew about us before they showed up in Omaha. Did they really hear about us from passing travelers in Chicago?"

"Mystery number three," Plato said.

"And who is this Minister? How does he fit into the scheme of things?"

"Mystery number four," Plato said, waiting for Blade to continue. When the huge Warrior stayed quiet, he surveyed the three members of Alpha Triad. "You've each broached salient points," he said, "but you've failed to stress the most perplexing mystery of all."

"What's that?" Hickok queried.

"Specifically, what type of individual offers one of his own people as a hostage, as a token, as a sacrifice, treating her life as callously as you or I might regard a mere fly?" Plato asked them.

"He must not think too highly of her," Geronimo speculated.

"Or he thinks too highly of himself," Plato opined. "Either way, I received the distinct impression this Minister is a calculating, cold-blooded person. I don't trust their offer either."

Blade breathed a silent sigh of relief. "Then you'll recommend to the Elders we reject their proposal?"

"On the contrary," Plato responded. "I will recommend we accept the Technics' offer."

"But you just said you don't trust them," Blade exclaimed.

"I don't," Plato admitted. "Which is precisely the reason we should take them up on it." He saw the looks of confusion on the trio of Warriors. "My rationale is simple. If these Technics have concocted some sort of devious design, if they pose a threat to our Family and our Home, then it is up to us to ascertain the nature of their threat and eliminate it as speedily as possible. We could attempt to force the information from Wargo and Farrow, but they might not cooperate. Indeed, they might be unaware of the Minister's plans. So what does that leave us? Only one recourse. We must, as they say, play along with them until we can discover their true motives and, if necessary, thwart any hostile maneuvers." He paused. "You can see I'm right, can't you?"

"Sounds peachy to me," Hickok commented.

"I agree with you," Geronimo said.

Blade hesitated. He definitely didn't want to go on another run. Sooner or later, the odds would catch up with him and Jenny would find herself a widow. Still, as head Warrior, his primary responsibility was to the Family. If the Technics were a menace, then they must be eliminated. He sighed. "I agree too."

"Good." Plato smiled. "I will call a gathering of the Elders and we'll discuss the situation. I'm positive they will concur with my conclusions."

Hickok happened to glance in the direction of the kitchen doorway. He straightened and placed a finger over his lips.

Everyone turned.

Plato's wife, Nadine, was framed in the doorway, a tray of sizzling venison soup in her frail hands. Her hair was gray, her eyes a compassionate brown, her face wrinkled and conveying a sense of noble character. She wore a blue denim dress, sewn together from the remains of a dozen pair of jeans. Her eyes were watering. "Is there no end to the violence?" she asked her husband.

"How long were you standing there?" Plato inquired.

"Long enough," Nadine said. "Must you send Alpha Triad out again?"

"How else can we learn the Technics' true motives?" Plato responded.

"There must be another way."

"If you know of one," Plato told her, "I'm open to suggestions."

Nadine stared at the Warriors. "I feel so sorry for them. They are always going off somewhere or another, fighting for their lives. What about their families? What about their children? Don't they have the right to a peaceful life like the rest of us?"

"They're Warriors," Plato said gravely. "No one compelled them to take their oath of allegiance, and they can resign whenever they want." He twisted. "Do any of you want out?"

"Not me, old-timer," Hickok said. "I've always had a secret hankerin' to see the Rotten Apple."

"That's the Big Apple," Geronimo corrected him. "And where they go, I go. Someone has to babysit Hickok."

"And what about you?" Plato asked Blade.

There was only one possible answer. Blade knew it, although he balked at voicing the words. Plato had hit the nail on the head. No one had twisted his arm to become a Warrior. He'd chosen his profession because he firmly believed the Family's safety and survival were of paramount importance. If the Technics were a threat to the Family, then, as Plato had said, the threat must be removed. "Alpha Triad is a team," Blade said to Plato. "One for all, and all for one."

"Now where have we heard that before?" Geronimo inquired, grinning.

"Then it's settled," Plato announced. "I will convene a special meeting of the Elders. If all goes as expected, you should be able to leave by this time tomorrow."

"I can hardly wait!" Hickok said enthusiastically.

Blade balled his huge hands into massive fists. There was no escaping his destiny. As head Warrior, he *had* to go.

"Let's have a quick bowl of soup first," Plato proposed.

Hickok walked to the table and pulled out a chair. "Sounds good to me. I'm so hungry, I could eat a horse!"

"You're always hungry," Geronimo commented.

Nadine carefully placed the metal tray on the living room table. "Enjoy yourselves!" she advised them.

Hickok studied Blade. "Don't get uptight, pard," he said. "This will be a piece of cake!"

"You wish!" Geronimo rejoined. "We'll be fortunate if we come back alive."

Hickok leaned toward Blade. "Maybe we should leave Geronimo here this time," he suggested.

"Why's that?" Blade asked.

The gunman frowned. "I don't rightly know if I can take much more of his rosy disposition."

6

Lieutenant Alicia Farrow was impressed, and it took a lot to impress her. As a combat-tested veteran with seven years in the Technic Elite Service, the commando arm of the Technic Army, she'd seen countless soldiers over the years. She'd fought side by side with some of the toughest men and women around. So she wasn't about to be awed by other professional fighters, not unless they were exceptional.

The Warriors were exceptional.

She'd observed their training sessions: their marksmanship practice on the firing range in the southeast corner of the Home, their martial-arts tutelage under the direction of a stately Elder, and their individualized workouts with their favorite weapons. Over the past three days, she'd developed an abiding respect for the Warriors. She found herself, despite her better judgment, admiring their inherent integrity and devotion to the Family.

It was too bad they had to die.

But the Minister had been most explicit. The Warriors, even the entire Family, must be eradicated. If the Technics were to assume their rightful place as world rulers, then every potential rival must be destroyed. The Freedom Federation was too large to be overcome in one fell swoop. Accordingly, the Minister had decided to selectively smash the separate Freedom Federation members beginning with the Family. His reasoning was logical and sound. Although the Family was the smallest contingent in the Freedom Federation numerically

58

speaking, it exerted the controlling influence in the Federation's periodic Councils. The Family was becoming a symbol, a beacon of hope in a land ravaged by nuclear and chemical devastation. Wargo had told Plato the truth. Stories were spreading about the Family and the Warriors, and not just in the Freedom Federation but in the Outlands beyond. In an age when written and electronic communications and records were virtually nonexistent, fireside tales were the order of the day. Families would gather about their hearths at night, singles would congregate at crude "watering holes" where rotgut beverages were served, and in towns and settlements throughout the land everyone would exchange the latest information, the newest gossip they might have heard from a passing traveler. Serving as both a means of public dissemination of knowledge and a popular socializing entertainment, the stories grew as they were conveyed from mouth to mouth, from one inhabited outpost to the next. To some, the Home was becoming a sort of modern Utopia, while several of the Warriors had acquired mythical proportions. Ages prior, a Greek named Homer had regaled his listeners by extolling the herculean exploits of Achilles, Odysseus, Telamonian Aias, Diomedes and company. Now the cycle was being repeated, and the Minister did not like it one bit.

The Technics were determined to crush all potential opposition and assert their natural superiority. As long as the Family existed, the people had a source of inspiration and encouragement. If the Family fell, so would the hopes and aspirations of thousands, making the conquest of America easier. The Freedom Federation would become demoralized if the Family perished, and they might even disband without the Family's unifying persuasiveness to guide them.

As she stood near A Block, watching Rikki-Tikki-Tavi and Yama spar, Lieutenant Farrow reviewed the Minister's plan and marveled at his brilliance. The Family could be wiped out with a small force, the Minister had stated, his black eyes blazing at her from his elevated dais in the Technic throne room. The first step would be to gain their trust. The second to lure several of the Warriors and the SEAL away from the Home. And the final step would take place when the signal was given for the demolition team to level the Home, a demolition team of four commandos waiting in the forest outside the walls.

A signal Lieutenant Farrow had to give.

Farrow observed the flowing swirl of motion as Rikki and Yama engaged again, their arms and legs whirling, their martial-arts techniques honed to perfection.

Despite his diminutive stature, Rikki was more than holding his own. His black form pranced around the big man in blue, flicking hand and foot blows with precise control. For his part, Yama was hard-pressed to prevent any of Rikki's bone-shattering strikes from connecting. After several minutes of sustained mock combat, Rikki abruptly stepped back and bowed to his opponent, a grin creasing his face.

"You are improving," Rikki said.

Yama bowed and smiled. "Coming from you, that's a real compliment."

"Same time tomorrow?" Rikki asked, wiping his right palm across his perspiring brow.

"Fine by me," Yama replied.

Rikki glanced toward the Technic officer, ten yards away, his brown eyes narrowing. "She follows you everywhere, doesn't she?"

Yama nodded. "I've been appointed as her official Family liaison."

"I'm sure that's the reason she sticks by your side," Rikki remarked, his white teeth flashing.

"Are you trying to imply something?" Yama inquired. He ran his left hand through his fine, silver hair and stroked his drooping silver mustache.

"Not me," Rikki responded innocently. "But you should thank the Spirit Hickok isn't here."

"Why?"

"You know Hickok," Rikki said, still grinning. "He likes to tease everyone."

"But you don't?" Yama asked.

Rikki chuckled. "Of course not. A disciplined martial

artist does not demean himself by exhibiting crude humor.''

Yama laughed. "If you ask me, you've been hanging around Geronimo too much.''

"Why do you say that?''

"Because you're starting to sling as much bull as he does," Yama said, and the two Warriors laughed together.

Lieutenant Farrow moved toward them. "May I compliment both of you on your skill?''

Rikki bowed slightly. "Thank you.''

"Are all of the Warriors as proficient as you?'' Farrow inquired.

"All of the Warriors are skilled," Rikki answered.

"He's too modest," Yama interjected. "Rikki is the best martial artist in the Family.''

"From what I saw," Lieutenant Farrow said, "you're as good as he is.''

Rikki grinned at Yama. "I have duties to attend to. I'll see you later.'' His katana was leaning against a maple tree ten feet away to their right, next to Yama's usual arsenal. He walked over and reclaimed his sword, slid it through his belt, and headed toward B Block.

"Did I offend him?'' Lieutenant Farrow asked, her brown eyes probing Yama's blue.

"No," Yama told her. "He thought we might like to be alone.''

"Why in the world would he think that?'' Farrow demanded defensively.

Yama shrugged and walked to the maple tree. He replaced the Browning Hi-Power 9-millimeter Automatic Pistol under his right arm, and slid the Smith and Wesson Model 586 Distinguished Combat Magnum into his left shoulder holster. The 15-inch survival knife was returned to its sheath on his right hip, and the gleaming scimitar took its customary position on his left hip. Finally, he picked the Wilkinson Carbine up from the green grass, wiped the barrel, and slung the gun over his left shoulder.

"Do you always pack so much hardware?'' Farrow asked.

"Always," Yama replied.

"Why?" she wanted to know.

"The more diverse my arms, the more effective I can be," Yama explained.

"I get the impression you're very, very effective," Farrow said.

Yama was about to reply when a terrified scream rent the air.

"What was that?" Farrow questioned him, looking around.

Yama was already moving, heading in the direction of the drawbridge at a rapid clip.

Lieutenant Farrow hurried after him. "What is it?" she cried.

Yama didn't bother to respond. He ran faster as a second scream wafted over the compound, coming from the west, from the field beyond the west wall. The drawbridge was down, and he knew several Family members were in the field, working at removing a cluster of weeds growing about 40 yards from the wall. Normally a tedious routine, the clearing detail could be fraught with danger because of the proximity to the forest. Once a week three Tillers went outside the walls to attend to the clearing, guarded by the Warriors on the ramparts. Seldom did the Tillers encounter trouble so close to the Home, and never had the Warriors failed to protect them.

This day was different.

As Yama reached the bridge over the moat he glanced up and spotted Ares on the rampart directly above. At six feet, three inches in height, lean and all muscle, Ares was a formidable Warrior, but he accented his fierceness by shaving the hair on both sides of his head and leaving a trimmed, red crest from his forehead to his spine. He wore dark brown leather breeches, a matching shirt, and sandals, and carried a short sword on his left hip. Yama saw Ares furiously tugging on the magazine in his automatic rifle.

Ares saw Yama crossing the bridge. "The damn thing's jammed!" he yelled in frustration. "Hurry!"

Other Family members were hastening toward the

bridge.

Yama was the first across the drawbridge. He took in the tableau before him and darted toward the Tillers.

They desperately needed help.

Any help.

One of the Tillers, an elderly man, was already down, his chest torn to bloody ribbons. Two other Tillers, a youth and an attractive blonde woman, both wearing green overalls, were eight feet off, both seemingly riveted in place, frozen by the sight of their attackers.

Because there were two of them.

Once they might have been called gray wolves. Now they were deformed mutations, their very genes corrupted and transformed by the poisons in the environment. Born disfigured, these two had survived their infancy and struck off together to rear more mutations like themselves.

Accustomed as he was to the sight of mutations and the even worse mutates, Yama nevertheless repressed a shudder as he closed on the deviate duo.

Both wolves were over five feet at the shoulder. Both were covered with a coat of gray fur. But after that, any resemblance to a real wolf was strictly coincidental. Each had six legs instead of four, and each leg was tipped with tapering talons instead of paws. By a curious genetic quirk, both creatures had two tails and, incredibly, two heads. The second head extended from the front of each mutant's neck. It was somewhat smaller than the original head, but its mouth was equally filled with a glistening array of pointed teeth. Red, baleful eyes were fastened on the Tillers. Both were slavering and growling, standing side by side next to the dead man sprawled before them.

Yama never hesitated.

The wolves were 30 yards away when he unslung his Wilkinson and aimed into the air. The two Tillers still alive were between the wolves and him, and Yama didn't want to risk accidentally winging one of them. He elevated the Wilkinson barrel and fired a short burst into the air.

Neither wolf so much as flinched.

The mutants shifted their attention to the approaching man in blue. Four heads raised skyward, and four husky throats bayed their defiant challenge. They bounded forward, separating, one to the right and the other to the left, temporarily forgetting the two Tillers as they concentrated on the human in blue.

"Get down!" Yama shouted to the Tillers.

They didn't budge, gaping at their fallen companion.

Yama angled to the left, wanting a clear line of fire. He dropped to his right knee, raised the Wilkinson, and fired.

The mutant on the left was caught in mid-stride. It was knocked onto its side by the impact of the heavy slugs and lay still.

Yama shifted to cover the other wolf.

The first one sprang to its feet and resumed its charge.

Yama waited for the second wolf to get closer, his finger on the trigger of the Wilkinson. Focused on the second wolf, he mistakenly neglected to verify the first was dead.

The oversight cost him.

Yama was squeezing the trigger to fire at the second mutant, when someone behind him shrieked a warning.

"Yama! Look out!"

Yama swiveled, too late. He glimpsed a heavy body and a lot of fur, and then something slammed into his chest, sending the Wilkinson flying, and he landed on his broad back with the first wolf straddling his legs and snarling.

The second wolf was 15 yards distant and bounding toward its mate.

Yama tensed, his hands at his sides, waiting for the mutant to make a move. He knew if he so much as twitched, the wolf would be on him ripping and tearing with its strong teeth and talons. He didn't want to do anything to provoke it. He was tempted to grab his survival knife, but realized the consequences.

The mutant inched toward its prey's neck, puzzled by the human's inexplicable immobility.

A pistol cracked, four times in swift succession.

Yama saw the bullets hit the wolf straddling him. He

could see the thing jerk as the shots hit home.

Who was doing the shooting? Ares?

The wolf growled and leaped to the attack, vaulting over the prone Warrior after this new assailant.

Yama rolled to his feet, drawing his scimitar. His blue eyes widened when he found his benefactor. It wasn't Ares or one of the other Warriors.

It was Lieutenant Farrow.

The Technic officer was holding her automatic pistol in her right hand and using her left hand to brace her right wrist. Her legs spread wide, her left eye closed, she aimed and fired again.

The nearest mutant twisted, blood spurting from its ruptured throat, but it kept coming, saliva dripping from its lower jaws.

Lieutenant Farrow blasted the wolf two more times.

Yama raced after the mutants. They were almost upon Farrow, and her shots weren't having any apparent affect.

Farrow fired twice more, then her pistol clicked on empty.

Yama was too far away to lend her assistance.

The first mutant leaped for Farrow's jugular.

The Technic dodged to the right, narrowly evading the slashing talons of the genetic deviate. She turned, keeping her eyes on the first wolf, inadvertently exposing her back to the second.

Yama was ten feet off, still too far away to be of any use. Unless he could distract the mutants. "Try me!" he shouted savagely. "Me!"

The second wolf, bounding between Yama and the Technic, abruptly spun at the sound of the harsh voice to its rear. Its fiery eyes alighted on the Warrior in blue, and it charged.

Yama stopped, holding his scimitar at chest height, waiting, gathering his strength. If he missed, the mutant wouldn't give him a second chance.

The wolf was on him in a gray streak, its jaws snapping at his waist and legs, snarling ferociously.

Yama's bulging muscles powered the scimitar in a vicious arc, the curved sword gleaming in the bright sunlight as it whisked through the air and into the springing mutant, connecting, slicing into the creature's top head, into its forehead, neatly severing a section of the wolf's scalp in a spray of crimson, hair, and flesh.

The wolf went down in a disjointed heap.

Yama knew the thing was still alive, but he couldn't waste a precious second.

The first mutant had Farrow on the ground, its lower jaw locked on her left forearm, and was brutally wrenching her from side to side while its top head attempted to bite her neck.

Yama reached them in four strides. The scimitar drove up and down in a shining glitter of light, the razor edge entering the wolf behind its upper ears and penetrating six inches into its skull.

The mutant stiffened, released Farrow, and spasmodically tore to the right, away from the man in blue. The force of its momentum yanked the scimitar from Yama's hands. It staggered from the wound, its upper eyes glazing over but its lower orbs alert and enraged.

Yama reached down and hauled Farrow erect. Her left forearm was bleeding profusely, and her features were pale, although she tried to muster a reassuring grin.

Yama reached for his Browning, but even as he did Farrow pointed over his right shoulder and started to scream a warning. He turned, the Browning coming clear of its holster.

The second wolf, the one with the missing scalp, was nearly on them, eight feet distant and sweeping forward.

A small figure in black suddenly hurtled past Yama and Farrow, a katana gripped in both hands, darting toward the raging mutant. Without hesitating, without missing a beat, Rikki-Tikk-Tavi assumed the horse stance, squatted, and swung his katana with the blade close to the ground.

Surprised by the appearance of another foe, dazed from the blow Yama had inflicted, the second wolf was unable to react in time. It felt a searing pain in all six legs as its lower limbs were hacked from its body. It instantly collapsed, its means of locomotion gone, and landed on its stomach. The mutant endeavored to flip onto its left side, to evade the human in black.

It failed.

Rikki reared over the second wolf, the katana held aloft, and slashed once, twice, three times, each stroke splitting the mutant's body further, almost severing the twin heads from its bulky form.

Yama, fascinated by Rikki's skilled dispatching of the second wolf, suddenly remembered the first mutant and turned.

The scimitar imbedded in its top head, the first wolf lurched at the man in blue and the injured woman.

A lanky shape dressed in brown ran into view behind the first mutant, his red Mohawk bobbing as he jogged nearer, his face a study in primal fury. "Get out of the way!" he bellowed.

Yama looped his left arm around Farrow's trim waist and leaped, drawing her with him, dropping to the ground and flattening, glancing over his right shoulder and seeing Rikki performing a similar maneuver.

And then Ares was there. Perhaps it was his red hair, maybe his inherited temperament, but Ares was known as the most hotheaded Warrior. He had once escorted two Healers outside of the Home, protecting them while they searched for herbs. The Healers had stumbled across a large black bear, and the bear attacked. Ares came to their rescue. According to the Healers, the bear never stood a chance. Ares took it on with just his short sword and made mincemeat of the hapless predator. The Healers later stated Ares seemed to be enjoying himself as he fought. Too much. So whether justified or not, Ares was considered to be particularly bloodthirsty when his wrath was aroused.

And at the moment he was incensed beyond endurance.

Irritated by the jamming of his gun, inflamed by the death of the Tiller while under his guard, and racked by a tormenting sense of personal guilt, he had cleared his weapon and raced to aid Yama and Rikki. Now, his face contorted, his features livid, he raised his automatic rifle and fired at the first mutant, his slugs stitching across its heads and abdomen, and he fired as it stumbled and fell onto its knees, fired as it desperately tried to stand and lunge at him, and fired until both heads were a mass of shattered reddish pulp. Not content with the death of the first mutant, Ares advanced on the second. Although the wolf was limp, its eyes lifeless, its body flat on the ground, the Mohawk-topped Warrior slowly walked toward it, pumping round after round into the mutant, and only suspending his one-man barrage when the rifle lacked bullets to shoot.

Ares stood next to the decimated mutant, sweat coating his hawkish face, and kicked it.

"I think it's dead," Rikki remarked, standing.

Yama stood, helping Farrow to rise.

Ares gazed at the deceased Tiller. He turned to Rikki, his green eyes rimmed with moisture. "I killed him," he said in a subdued tone.

"You did not kill him," Rikki said, disputing Ares. "I was inside B Block when this began and I didn't hear the initial screams. One of the others told me about them, and I saw you working with your gun as I was running toward the drawbridge. Guns jam. It's a fact of life."

"I killed him," Ares asserted forlornly.

Rikki walked over to Ares and placed his right hand on Ares's left arm. "You did not kill him, my brother. Don't blame yourself."

Ares stared at the Tiller again. "Dear Spirit!" he said.

Other Warriors and Family members were emerging from the Home.

"We can talk about this later," Rikki offered.

Ares looked down at Rikki. "I want a Review."

"You what?" Rikki responded in surprise.

"I want an official Warrior Review Board to call a hearing and rule on my actions," Ares stated.

Rikki glanced at Yama, who frowned. "This isn't necessary," he told Ares.

"It is for me," Ares countered. "I demand a Review

Board, and as a Warrior it's my right to have one."

"But Blade is absent," Rikki said. "He usually heads the Review Boards."

"Don't stall," Ares responded. "Blade doesn't need to be here for a Review Board to be held. Besides, with Alpha Triad gone, you're in charge of the Warriors. You can call a Review Board. All you have to do is pick two other Warriors to sit on it with you."

Rikki sighed. "This really isn't necessary," he reiterated.

Ares gazed at the dead Tiller, his anguished eyes betraying his intense inner turmoil. He turned to Rikki. "Please, Rikki. For my own peace of mind."

Rikki was surprised by the distress Ares was suffering. Everyone had always considered Ares to be callous, to be impervious to any emotional affliction. They were certainly wrong. "I will call a Review Board for tomorrow," he said.

"Thank you," Ares stated, relieved. "I am in your debt."

Bertha, Spartacus, Teucer, and a score of Family members reached the scene of the tragedy and clustered around, everyone asking questions at once.

Yama took hold of Lieutenant Farrow's right hand. "We must get you to the Healers."

Farrow reluctantly allowed herself to be led toward the drawbridge. She examined the ragged tear in her left forearm. "It's no big deal," she said.

"Who are you kidding?" Yama retorted, weaving through the gathering crowd.

"You might be needed here," Farrow said.

"Rikki will handle it," Yama declared. He grinned at her. "What's the matter? Are you afraid of seeing the Healers?"

"I'm not too fond of having needles stuck into me," Farrow acknowledged.

"Our Healers don't use needles," Yama informed her.

"What kind of medicine do they use?" Farrow asked.

"Herbal remedies, primarily," Yama answered. "They employ a varied assortment of natural medicines."

"And they don't jab you with needles?" Farrow inquired.

"No."

"Then how do you take your medicine?" she queried.

"Orally," Yama responded. "Usually their remedies are incorporated into a tea. Otherwise, they make pills."

"And these remedies work?" Farrow asked.

"Every time," Yama said, "and without the adverse reactions people often suffered before the Big Blast to artificial chemicals and stimulants."

"Our scientists maintain herbal medicine is quackery," Farrow commented without real conviction.

"Let the Healers treat you," Yama proposed, "then you be the judge."

They reached the drawbridge and started across. More Family members were hastening to the field. Sherry, Hickok's wife, approached.

"What happened?" Sherry asked as she came abreast of Yama.

Yama nodded at Farrow's left arm. "See Rikki. We must reach the infirmary."

"I understand," Sherry said, and ran off.

"Your Family is really tight-knit," Farrow mentioned as they hastened in the direction of C Block.

"We're taught in childhood to love one another," Yama told her.

"Love? Isn't that strange talk coming from a Warrior?"

Yama shook his head. "Why should the quality of love be incompatible with being a Warrior?"

"Because your whole purpose in life is to kill," Farrow said. "You're like me. A trained fighter. Killing is all we know."

Yama paused and looked into her eyes. "If all you know is killing, I feel sorry for you."

"I don't need your sympathy!" Farrow snapped, withdrawing her hand from his.

Yama continued toward the infirmary.

"How do you do it?" Farrow asked, staying on his

heels.

"Do what?"

"Justifying killing, if you think so highly of love?" Farrow inquired.

"All of the Warriors learn to love before they learn to kill," Yama revealed. "Our early years with our parents and in the Family school are devoted to learning about love. What it is, how—"

"What is love?" Farrow interrupted.

"You don't know?" Yama rejoined.

"I'm serious. What is love? There are so many definitions," Farrow observed.

"We define love as doing good for others," Yama disclosed. "It's our golden rule. Do for others as you conceive your actions to be guided by the Spirit. Every child in the Family memorizes this teaching by the time they're seven."

"But if you're all taught so much about love," Farrow said, "how is it the Warriors become so adept at killing?"

"The Family exalts the ideal of spiritual love," Yama stated, recalling his philosophy classes under Plato's instruction. "Unfortunately, the rest of this crazy world doesn't see it our way. If the Family is to survive in an insane world where violence is supreme and hatred is rampant, then some members must be willing to do whatever is necessary to preserve our Home and our ideals. The Warriors are skilled killers, true, but we only kill because we love our Family and want to safeguard them from the degenerates out there." He waved toward the west wall.

"You kill because you love," Farrow said thoughtfully. "That's a new one." She clamped her right hand over the wound on her left arm to stem the flow of blood. The mutant had torn a six-inch gash in her forearm, and although she was still bleeding, the blood flowing down her arm and dripping from her elbow, there wasn't as much as before.

"We're almost there," Yama said, pointing at C Block.

"There's no hurry," Farrow said. "It's almost

stopped bleeding."

"Tell me," Yama stated. "Why do you kill?"

Farrow was taken unawares by the question. "I never gave it much consideration," she admitted. "I guess I kill because I'm a professional soldier. It's what I'm trained to do."

"Do you like to kill?"

"Not particularly," she confessed. "It's my job."

"Do you love the Technics?" Yama asked.

"Love the Technics? You mean the way you do the Family?" Farrow laughed. "Not hardly! They're all so damn selfish and self-centered! There's not much to love!"

They were nearly to the infirmary doorway. Yama stopped and stared at Farrow. "So you kill because it's what they trained you to do, but you don't really like killing and you don't much like the Technics you kill for?"

Farrow did a double take. "I never looked at it that way."

"What other way is there to look at it?" Yama retorted. "Frankly, I don't see how you live with your soul."

"What do you mean?"

"Look at yourself. Take a good, hard look. You're in a rut, stuck in a vocation you care little for, serving people you like even less. Where's your sense of self-worth? Where's your dignity as a cosmic daughter of our Maker?" He shook his head. "I don't see how you do it." He stepped to the doorway. "Come on."

"Yama . . ." Farrow said tentatively.

He hesitated, standing in the doorway to the giant cement Block. "Yes?"

"Thank you."

"For what?"

"For saving my life back there," Farrow said.

"You saved mine," he reminded her.

"And . . ." she began groping for the right words, "and for opening a window."

Now it was his turn to show bewilderment. "A window?"

"Yeah. A window to the soul I never knew I had."
Farrow smiled, genuine affection lighting her dark eyes.
"Thank you," she reiterated softly, gently.

Yama's blue eyes touched hers. "Any time."

7

"How much longer before we reach Chicago?" Blade
demanded, concentrating on steering the SEAL around
the multiple obstacles in the highway; there were ruts
and cracks, potholes and mini-trenches, and even whole
sections of former U.S. Highway 12 were buckled and
impassable or missing, necessitating constant detours to
avoid the problem spots.

"We should reach the outskirts of Technic City
soon," Captain Wargo replied.

The SEAL had been on the road for three days, three
relatively uneventful days of traveling while the sun
was up and pulling over to rest at night. They
deliberately skirted the larger cities in their path,
knowing from painful experience such urban centers
were invariably dominated by violent street gangs or
other hostile parties. The smaller towns and hamlets
they encountered were usually devoid of life and in
abject disrepair. Three towns did show signs of current
habitation, but the occupants had obviously fled at the
sight of the gargantuan green SEAL, its huge tires,
tinted body, sophisticated solar panels, and militaristic
contours all lending an ominous aspect to its appearance.

Blade was behind the steering wheel. Across from
him, on the other side of a console, Captain Wargo was
seated in the other bucket seat. Hickok and Geronimo
occupied a wide seat behind the bucket seats. The rear
of the SEAL was devoted to storage space for their
supplies.

"Technic City?" Hickok spoke up. "I thought we're headin' for Chicago?"

"Chicago was renamed long ago," Captain Wargo said, "although some people still refer to it by that antiquated name."

"You didn't tell us this earlier," Blade observed.

Wargo shrugged. "I didn't think it was important."

Blade repressed a frown. The more he came to know Wargo, the less he trusted the Technic. There was a sly, devious quality about the officer. So far, despite tactful probing by the three Warriors, Captain Wargo had stuck to his original story; the Technics wanted the Family's assistance in retrieving the Genesis Seeds. Blade didn't believe him for a moment, and had given orders for one of the Warriors to always be inside the SEAL even when they were parked for the night or taking "a nature break." If Wargo intended to steal the SEAL, Blade wanted to insure the Technic never got the chance. But during their three-day journey Wargo had behaved himself.

Blade was beginning to wonder if he was wrong about the man.

"Our Minister is looking forward to seeing you," Captain Wargo commented.

"Do tell," Hickok quipped.

"He will reward you richly for your services," Wargo said.

"We'll be satisfied with our share of the Genesis Seeds," Blade commented.

"Of course," Captain Wargo said, grinning.

Blade wanted to punch the smug so-and-so right in the mouth.

"Will we be staying in Chicago . . . Technic City . . . long?" Geronimo asked.

"No," Blade responded before Wargo could speak. "I want to reach New York City as quickly as possible."

"There's no rush," Captain Wargo said pleasantly.

"There is for us," Blade rejoined. "We want to get in, grab the Seeds, and get out. It'll take us five days, maybe more, to reach New York. Another day to find the Seeds. Then five more days to Technic City and three more to the Home. All tolled, we'll be gone from our Home about three weeks. I don't like being away from the Home so long. The sooner we get back, the better.''

"I can appreciate your feelings," Captain Wargo said, "but some things can't be rushed. It may take us more than one day to locate the Genesis Seeds in New York."

"You told us you know where they're located," Blade reminded him.

"We believe we know," Captain Wargo amended his statement. "We think our earlier teams did find the building they're in, but we really won't know for certain until we descend to the underground vault and examine it."

"Terrific!" Hickok muttered. "We come all this way, and it could all be a wild-goose chase!"

Captain Wargo twisted in his seat and glanced at each of them. "Don't you understand how important this is?"

Hickok chuckled. "How can we forget with you remindin' us every two seconds?"

Captain Wargo's jaw muscles tightened. "I'm sorry if I seem to dwell on the subject, but the future of mankind is at stake."

Geronimo suddenly leaned forward, pointing directly ahead. "Do you see what I see?"

Blade nodded. He'd seen it too. A giant metal fence across the highway ahead, its gleaming strands stretching into the distance on both sides of U.S. Highway 12.

"What the dickens is that?" Hickok queried.

As the SEAL drew nearer, Blade could ascertain more details. The fence was 15 feet high and tipped with four strands of barbed wire. Bright gray in color, the fence was a heavy-gauge mesh affair with peculiar metallic globes or balls imbedded in the mesh at ten yard intervals. Each of these globes was a yard in diameter.

"You'd better slow down," Captain Wargo advised. "They're expecting us, but they might not recognize the SEAL and open fire."

Blade could see a gate in the fence, and behind the gate, which was constructed of the same mesh as the fence, reared a huge guard tower. Over 30 feet in height and positioned on the left side of the road, it was manned with machine guns and several figures in uniform.

"You can stop now," Captain Wargo directed.

Blade applied the brakes, bringing the transport to a halt ten yards from the gate. "Do you have a fence blocking every road into the city?" he asked.

"We have a fence completely encircling the city," Captain Wargo answered.

"You mean this fence goes all the way around Chicago?" Hickok asked the Technic.

"Technic City is surrounded by this fence," Captain Wargo said. "It was built to keep unwanted intruders out. Do you see those regulators in the fence?"

"Those big metal balls?" Hickok stated.

"Yes. They're precision voltage regulators. Our fence is electrified with one million volts of electricity. If you were to so much as tap on the fence, you'd be fried to a crisp within seconds," Captain Wargo told them.

"One million volts?" Blade's mind was boggled by this revelation. The Family owned a functioning generator confiscated from soldiers in Thief River Falls, but fuel was scarce and they only used the generator on special occasions. Normally, they utilized candles and fires for their nightly illumination, and their plows and wagons ran on literal horsepower. The Civilized Zone produced electricity for its larger cities and towns, but their power plants were few and far between, their equipment outdated, and they suffered periodic outages on a regular basis.

"Perhaps you would like to visit one of our generating facilities?" Captain Wargo asked.

"How many do you have?" Blade inquired.

"Two. Between them, they produce more electricity than we can use. Most of it is diverted to our Atomospheric Control Stations."

"Incredible!" Blade acknowledged.

Captain Wargo reached for the door handle. "If you

don't mind, I will have the guards open the gate."

"Go ahead," Blade said.

Captain Wargo exited the SEAL and walked toward the gate.

"You reckon that varmint was tellin' the truth about one million volts in that fence?" Hickok asked.

"Why don't you touch the fence and find out?" Geronimo cracked.

Blade looked at the gunman. "I believe him," he said.

Hickok whistled. "If they can spare a million volts for a measly fence, what's it gonna be like in there?"

"We'll soon know," Blade commented, poking his head outside.

Captain Wargo approached the gate, his arms upraised until he stopped in front of it. He conversed with someone on the tower stairway, and within moments the gate was thrown open, clearing a wide path for the SEAL. Captain Wargo turned and waved, beckoning them forward.

"Stay alert," Blade cautioned his companions. He drove the SEAL to the gate and braked.

Captain Wargo climbed inside. "They've radioed the Minister. He'll be expecting us."

Hickok, studying the guard tower, suddenly gave a start and opened his mouth as if to speak. Instead, his eyes narrowed and he placed his right thumb on the hammer of his Henry, snuggled in his lap.

Blade accelerated, the transport cruising through the gate and into the unknown.

U.S. Highway 12 underwent a fantastic transformation, from a neglected roadway abused by over a century of abandonment to a perfectly preserved asphalt surface complete with white and yellow lines down the center of the highway.

Captain Wargo noticed the surprise flicker over the giant Warrior's features. "All of the roads in Technic City are maintained in excellent condition," he remarked.

Blade spotted a line of low buildings, perhaps 250 yards from the fence. Between the electrified fence and the buildings was a field of green grass, the grass interspersed with yellow, red, and blue flowers. Butterflies flitted in the air.

Captain Wargo indicated the field. "Looks peaceful, doesn't it?"

"Yes," Blade replied. "What is it, a park of some kind?"

Captain Wargo laughed. "No. It's a mine field."

"A mine field?" Blade repeated.

"It's our secondary line of defense," Captain Wargo explained. "Should any attackers get past the fence, they'd have to cross a field dotted with thousands of mines. The field, like the fence, surrounds the city."

Blade stared at a patch of flowers, pondering. If the mine field was intended to keep enemies out, then why wasn't it located outside the electrified fence? Why place it inside, where an unwary citizen, child, or pet could stumble into it and be blown to kingdom come? The mine field's position didn't make any sense—unless it was intended to keep people *in*.

The SEAL reached the line of buildings.

"These are individual residential structures," Captain Wargo detailed.

The buildings were unlike any Blade had ever seen, including those in the Civilized Zone. While the homes in the Civilized Zone were made of brick or wood or steel, these were composed of a synthetic compound similar to the SEAL's plastic body. Each building was only one-story high, and they were characterized by a diversity of colors and shapes with circles, squares, and triangles predominating. Windows were tinted in different shades. Yards were meticulously kept up, replete with cultivated gardens and lush green grass. The setting was tranquil, ideal for family life.

Only one thing was missing.

People.

"Guards," Hickok warned.

Blade saw four soldiers ahead and slowed.

"It's just a checkpoint," Captain Wargo declared. "You can keep going."

Blade drove past the quartet of troopers, who

snapped to attention and saluted as the transport passed.

"Flashing lights coming this way," Geronimo announced. "Three of them."

Vehicles of some sort were rapidly approaching from the east.

"Don't worry," Captain Wargo assured them. "It's just our escort."

"We need an escort?" Blade asked.

"Trust me," Captain Wargo said. "You'll understand better in a couple of minutes."

The vehicles turned out to be blue cycles. Blade had seen motorcycles before, but not like these. Instead of two wheels, each blue cycle had three. Their frames sat lower to the ground than the two-wheelers, and each one was outfitted with a miniature windshield. Riders in light blue uniforms with blue helmets were on each bike, and they guided their tri-wheelers with expert skill and precision, wheeling into a tight U-turn in front of the SEAL and assuming a line across the highway. The red and blue flashing lights were affixed to the front of the tri-wheelers, directly above the single front wheel.

"They're Technic police," Captain Wargo stated. "Just follow them and they'll clear the road."

"What the blazes are they drivin'?" Hickok asked.

"Trikes," Captain Wargo responded.

"Be careful you don't squish 'em," Hickok told Blade. "Our tires are bigger than them teensy contraptions."

"There's a reason for that," Captain Wargo said.

"I'd love to hear it," Hickok mentioned.

"You'll see in a bit," Captain Wargo said.

The Technic police gunned their trikes, and Blade fell in behind them. They traveled for over a mile, passing hundreds of seemingly vacant residential structures.

"You're about to see why we need your help," Captain Wargo commented.

"How do you mean?" Blade asked.

"While our technology is superior to anyone else's," Captain Wargo bragged, "we don't possess unlimited resources. Our vehicles reflect our dilemma. Ahhh.

Here. You'll see."

The Technic police had braked at an intersection.

Blade did likewise, scanning the area ahead, stunned by the sight before them.

Another quartet of soldiers was stationed at the intersection, two of them standing to the right, two to the left, idly watching the traffic. And traffic there was! Vehicle after vehicle. Red, brown, yellow, purple, green, black; every color in the rainbow and more. But they weren't the traditional vehicles Blade had observed elsewhere. The Warriors had appropriated a number of jeeps and trucks during the war against the Civilized Zone. Most of those had been returned after the two sides signed a peace treaty. President Toland had given two troop transports and two jeeps to Plato as a gesture of good will, but they were driven sparingly for two reasons. Plato didn't want the Family to develop a dependence on motorized transportation after more than a century without any, and, secondly, although the Civilized Zone operated a few refineries, their fuel output was minimal and barely served their own needs, restricting the scant amounts they could trade with the Family. So, while Blade was familiar with jeeps and trucks and cars, and knew traffic in large cities in the Civilized Zone was quite heavy, none of his prior experience had prepared him for *this!*

Trikes were the order of the day. Thousands upon thousands. Another vehicle, a cycle similar to a trike but with four wheels, was also in plentiful evidence. The four-wheelers had two seats, front and back, and could seat up to six occupants. The trikes and four-wheelers packed the highways. Each road appeared to handle traffic flowing in only one direction. The intersection would have been a madhouse, except for a yellow traffic light suspended above the middle of the junction, its red, yellow, and green lights apparently signaling directions to the drivers. When the traffic light facing one of the roads was red, Blade noticed, the vehicles on that road would stop. When the light was green, the trikes and four-wheelers would resume their travel.

"I don't believe it!" Geronimo said.

"Now you see what I meant," Captain Wargo stated. "We lack the resources to provide cars and trucks for our citizens, so we do the next best thing. Cycles don't require unlimited raw material, and they consume far less fuel than cars or trucks. We can manufacture enough cycles for everyone at a fraction of the cost a full-sized vehicle would demand."

"Does everyone own a cycle?" Blade asked, half in jest.

"Everyone of legal age, yes," Captain Wargo answered.

"Doesn't anybody around here know how to walk?" Hickok joked.

"Why walk when technology can provide a preferable alternative?" Captain Wargo responded. "Besides, vagrancy is illegal."

"Are you tellin' me it's against the law to walk?" Hickok inquired.

"Of course not!" Captain Wargo said, scoffing at the idea. "You can walk anywhere, anytime. Of course, you need to obtain the proper permit first."

"Of course," Hickok said.

Blade faced the Technic officer. "Why is there only traffic on the other three roads? Why are we the only ones on this one?"

"It should be obvious," Wargo said. "This road is an exit road. It leads to the fence. Why would anyone want to use this road?"

"What if they want to leave Technic City?" Blade queried.

"No one leaves the city," Captain Wargo said archly. "Why should they want to leave? You know how dangerous it is out there. We didn't have much trouble because even the wild animals and the mutants fled from the SEAL. But for someone on foot, it would be certain suicide."

"They could use a trike or four-wheeler," Blade suggested.

"Taking a vehicle outside of the city is strictly forbidden," Captain Wargo said, "unless you get a permit beforehand."

"Of course," Hickok interjected sarcastically.

For the briefest instant, a fleeting rage burned in Wargo's eyes. The look vanished as swiftly as it appeared.

The three Technic police abruptly pulled ahead, their lights flashing and their sirens sounding. All traffic ground to a halt, leaving the intersection free of vehicles. The Technic police headed due east, and it was as if a huge hand were parting a sea of cycles. The trikes and four-wheelers scooted to the sides of the highway, some to the left and some to the right, opening an aisle for the Technic police and the SEAL.

"Follow them," Captain Wargo directed.

Blade complied. He gazed at the vehicles lining the sides of the road and received a rude shock. Instead of staring at the SEAL, as any ordinary, curious person would do, the occupants of the trikes and four-wheelers averted their faces, deliberately turning away from the transport.

Or were they turning away from the police?

Blade was feeling distinctly uneasy. Something was definitely wrong here, but he couldn't put his finger on the exact cause. He doubted the Warriors were in any real danger; none of the troopers or vehicles they had seen so far could pose any threat to the SEAL. The transport's shatterproof structure could easily withstand small-arms fire. And the trikes and four-wheelers would be as fleas assaulting a grizzly if they endeavored to impede the SEAL. The Warriors were safe for the time being, but realizing the fact didn't dispel his nervousness.

The scenery shifted, the residential buildings being replaced by larger edifices, up to four stories high and covering several acres. They were either white, gray, or black.

"This is part of our manufacturing sector," Captain Wargo informed them.

Blade recalled seeing photographs in the Family library depicting prewar industry. "Where are the smokestacks?" he asked. "And how do you keep your factories so clean? I thought they were usually gritty and grimy, and made a lot of noise. Yours are so quiet."

Captain Wargo smiled. "You're comparing our modern, computerized, transistorized, and miniaturized factories to the obsolete monoliths prevalent before World War III. That's like comparing worms to shrimp. There just is no comparison," he stated with pride.

Worms to shrimp? What a strange analogy! Blade watched as the Technic police continued to part the traffic ahead. "This doesn't look like the Chicago I remember reading about when I was little," he commented.

"It isn't," Captain Wargo declared. "We rebuilt it from the ground up. The old ways were wasteful, inefficient. They deserved to be replaced." Wargo paused and looked at the passing factories. "Chicago wasn't hit during the war, but a lot of the city was damaged by the looters, the hordes of scavengers, the roving gangs, and the mutants after the war was over. When the Technics came to power, they knew they had to rebuild from scratch. Out with the old and in with the new."

"It must have taken an immense work force to accomplish all of this," Blade mentioned.

Wargo grinned and waved his right hand to the right and the left. "As you can see, our work force now numbers in the millions."

"All of these people?" Blade inquired, glancing at the ocean of humanity lining both sides of the highway.

"All of them. It's against the law for anyone not to work. Being unemployed is a major crime," Captain Wargo disclosed.

"What about your children?" Geronimo entered their conversation.

"What about them?" Wargo replied.

"Where are they?" Geronimo probed. "I didn't see any playing in the yards in the residential area. Where are they?"

"Depends on their age," Captain Wargo said. "Those over twelve hold down full-time jobs. Those under twelve are in school."

"What about the infants?" Geronimo asked.

"They're in school," Captain Wargo reiterated.

"Even those two years old?" Geronimo questioned.

"Compulsory day-care begins at six months," Captain Wargo said.

"Six months?" Geronimo exchanged astonished looks with Hickok. "How do the parents feel about that?"

"They don't have any say in the matter," Wargo replied.

"You mean the young'uns are stuck in day-care whether the parents like it or not?" Hickok demanded.

Wargo snorted. "Parents! What the hell do they know! The government knows what's best for the children, not the parents. We don't place the same emphasis on parenting your Family does."

"Do tell," Hickok retorted.

"In fact," Captain Wargo began, then hesitated, debating the wisdom of finishing his sentence. He shrugged and went on. "In fact, our children aren't raised by their natural parents."

"What?" Blade joined in.

"Biological bonding inhibits their effectiveness as productive citizens," Captain Wargo said. "The kids are brought up by appointed surrogate parents. This way, we avoid all that messy emotional garbage other societies are tainted with."

"I think they call that garbage love," Blade remarked icily.

"Don't take offense at our system," Captain Wargo stated. "Just because it's different than yours doesn't mean we can't live together in peace."

Blade's fingers tightened on the steering wheel. An intense revulsion swept over him. These Technics were worse than the government of the Civilized Zone had once been, and the Civilized Zone had been ruled by a dictator! How could they forcibly take innocent children away from their parents? How could they intentionally deprive the children of the caring and sharing during their formative years, qualities so essential to their later adult life? What kind of mon—

What in the world was *that*?!

The building was tremendous in size and magnificent in design. Ten stories in height, it reared skyward from its wide base and tapered to a point. The base was two acres in circumference, the structure progressively narrowing as it ascended. Its sides shone in the sunlight, resembling scintillating crystal. The doors lining the base were gold plated, as were the frames of all the windows. The sheer brilliance of the building dazzled the senses.

"Wow!" Hickok exclaimed.

"It's our Central Core," Captain Wargo revealed. "The seat of our government. Our Minister resides within."

"Are there any more of these?" Blade asked, dumfounded.

Captain Wargo laughed. "No. All administrative functions are handled from here."

"You say the Minister is waitin' for us in there?" Hickok inquired.

"A banquet will be held in your honor tonight," Captain Wargo answered. "We have quite a reception planned for you."

"Only two of us will be able to attend," Blade stated.

"Why can't all three of you come?" Wargo inquired politely.

"One of us must stay with the SEAL," Blade replied.

"The Minister will be very disappointed," Wargo commented.

"One of us must stay with the SEAL," Blade stressed.

Captain Wargo shrugged. "Whatever you want. But I don't see why you can't lock the doors and leave the SEAL unattended. It will be safe, I assure you."

"Thanks, but no," Blade said.

The Technic police reached a spacious parking lot surrounding the Central Core. Trikes and four-wheelers were parked in droves, and mixed among them were a few jeeps and trucks.

"What are those?" Hickok asked, leaning forward. "You said you didn't make them."

"I never said that," Captain Wargo answered. "We

don't produce them in quantity, but we do have a few. Trikes and four-wheelers can't serve all our needs."

Blade followed the police escort into the parking lot. The area was crawling with men and women in blue uniform. Civilians filled the sidewalks, hurrying to and fro, engaged in their daily activities.

"Pull in there," Captain Wargo instructed, pointing at a wide expanse of parking lot devoid of trikes. It was situated in front of the middle of the Central Core, not far from a pair of gold doors. "It's been reserved for you."

Blade drove to the spot indicated and braked, aligning the transport so the front end faced the Central Core.

The trio of Technic police positioned their trikes around the SEAL. They were joined by dozens of others, some coming from the parking lot, others from the Central Core. Within minutes, they had formed into a blue phalanx enclosing the SEAL on four sides.

"See?" Captain Wargo said. "No one will bother the SEAL."

"Not even if they get a permit first?" Hickok quipped.

Captain Wargo's right hand surreptitiously moved to his rear pocket. He slid his fingers inside and clasped a brown plastic ball with a solitary red button. Slowly, proceeding cautiously, he removed the object and eased his hand toward the floor.

Blade turned in his seat. "Geronimo, you stay here and keep an eye on the SEAL. Keep the doors locked. You know what to do," he said meaningfully.

Geronimo nodded. "The SEAL is in good hands. Don't worry."

Blade nodded. "Hickok, you're with me."

Hickok patted his Henry. "Like a shadow."

Captain Wargo opened his door. "Whenever you're ready?"

"My Commando," Blade said to the gunman.

Hickok twisted and reached over the back of his seat into the rear section. Blade's Commando was lying on top of the pile of food, ammunition, and spare clothing.

He grabbed it by the barrel and swung it around. "Here."

Blade took the gun. "Thanks. Let's go." He threw his door open and dropped to the ground.

Hickok followed suit.

"Last chance to change your mind," Captain Wargo said to Geronimo with a friendly smile, while his right hand crept under his bucket seat.

"I must stay here," Geronimo replied.

Captain Wargo nodded. "Suit yourself. You'll miss some great food, though." He pressed the red button on the plastic ball and gently placed it on the floor under the seat. "See you later." He clambered from the transport and closed the door.

Blade and Hickok walked to the front of the SEAL, next to the grill, their weapons at the ready, and waited for the Technic officer to reach them.

"You're in for a treat," Captain Wargo announced as he led the way toward the Central Core.

Blade glanced over his left shoulder and saw Geronimo locking the doors and rolling up the widows. Good. There was no way the Technics could break into the transport with the doors and windows secure, leaving Geronimo as snug as the proverbial bug.

The Technic police, all at attention, parted, allowing Captain Wargo and the two Warriors to cross the parking lot to the sidewalk and reach the gold doors.

"Is this real gold?" Hickok asked.

"We don't believe in imitations," Wargo cryptically responded. He extended his left arm and touched one of a series of buttons in a panel to the left of the doors. Immediately, the doors hissed open. "Pneumatically controlled," he said for their benefit, and entered.

Blade paused, examining the layout. Ahead was a huge foyer or lobby, lavishly adorned, but oddly empty. Across the room was a row of cubicles with lighted numerals projecting from the wall overhead.

The gunman also noted the cubicles. "I know what they are," Hickok said. "I've seen 'em before. They're called elevators."

Captain Wargo walked across the lobby toward the

elevators.

Blade and Hickok tentatively tagged after the officer.

"We'll take an elevator up to the reception room," Wargo said. He strode to the righthand elevator and stepped inside.

Blade and Hickok, constantly surveying the lobby, staying side by side, stepped up to the elevator.

"Can't we take some stairs?" Blade asked.

"Climb ten floors?" Captain Wargo replied. He snickered. "You can, if you want to. But I'm not about to climb ten flights when there's an elevator handy."

Blade hesitated, then entered the elevator.

Hickok strolled in, studying the overhead light, the bank of lit buttons on the right side, and the small grill in the center of the floor.

Captain Wargo smiled reassuringly. "There's nothing to be nervous about. Believe me, you'll never know this ride took place." His right hand stabbed one of the buttons.

The elevator door started to close. And that's when it happened.

Captain Wargo dived, his arms outstretched. His hurtling form narrowly missed the closing door.

Blade leveled the Commando, but the gunman was faster. The Henry boomed, but the closing door intervened, the slug hitting the edge of the door and careening outside.

The elevator door slammed shut.

"Blast!" Hickok fumed. "We're trapped!"

Blade pounded on the right wall, then the door. "They're too thick to break through," he commented methodically.

Hickok stared straight up. "What about the light?"

Blade inspected the overhead light. It was rectangular, about two feet in width. A man might be able to squeeze—

There was a loud thump from underneath the elevator.

"What the blazes was that?" Hickok asked.

"I don't know," Blade said.

Another distinct thump sounded.

"I don't like this, pard," Hickok remarked.

"We walked right into this one," Blade admitted, frowning. "I think they're after the SEAL, but they'll never get it. I left the keys inside with Geronimo."

"I hope you're right," Hickok stated, bending over to peer at the buttons. "Should I push one of these?"

"Go for it."

Hickok punched the button marked OPEN.

Nothing happened.

"Uh-oh," the gunman said.

Blade, scrutinizing the overhead light, felt a slight burning sensation in his nostrils.

"A bullet would ricochet off these walls," Hickok was saying. "Say, do you smell somethin'?"

Blade glanced down.

Curling, wispy white tendrils were emanating from the grill in the elevator floor. They rose toward the ceiling, spreading, congealing into a cloudy mass.

Damn! Blade crouched and laid his hands over the small grill, striving to cover the slits with his fingers and stifle the smoke. He was only partially successful. The smoke continued to seep out, filling the elevator.

"What a lousy way to go!" Hickok said, and coughed. His eyes were watering, his nose tingling, and his lungs gasping for fresh air.

Blade was feeling dizzy. He weaved unsteadily and put his left hand over his mouth and nose.

"Do . . . you . . . think it's . . . poisonous?" Hickok asked, doubling over and collapsing on his knees.

"Don't . . . know," Blade croaked, his throat parched and raspy.

The elevator was a muggy, misty white haze.

Blade's legs buckled and he fell to the floor. He wished he could apologize to Hickok. He'd stupidly led the gunman into a trap any amateur would have avoided. There was only one consolation. The bastards would never get the SEAL. Geronimo was locked inside safe and sound.

It served the bastards right!

Blade struggled to rise, but his limbs refused to obey, and he pitched onto his face with a protracted sigh.

8

Lieutenant Alicia Farrow was in a dire quandary.

What the hell was she supposed to do?

Farrow ran her right hand through her crewcut black hair, her dark eyes troubled.

What *was* she going to do?

Farrow was seated on the bank of the inner moat, 50 yards north of the drawbridge, her back leaning against the trunk of a tall maple tree. She stared at the slowly meandering water, dejected.

Her ass was grass!

She had deliberately violated her orders! The Minister would boil her in oil when he found out! Violating an order was an offense in the first degree, punishable by death.

Her death.

Farrow closed her eyes, deep in reflection. According to her instructions, she should have given the signal yesterday. Somewhere out there, lurking in the trees, waiting for her to activate her beeper, was the four-member demolition crew. What were their names? Sergeant Darden was one. And Private Rundle was another. There was a loudmouth named Johnson, and one other whose name eluded her. They would be wondering why she didn't signal. How long before they sent someone to check on her? How long before they discovered she was derelict in her duty?

But how could she do it?

How could she give the signal, knowing the

compound would be demolished by a series of devastating explosions?

How could she give the signal, knowing what it would mean to her newfound friends?

Dammit!

Why did she have to go and become attached to these people? She'd never acted this way before! She was allowing raw emotionalism to pervert her higher purpose.

But she couldn't help herself.

There was something intangible about the Family, some elusive quality supremely attractive in its simplicity. Maybe it was the way they all cared for one another. Really cared. Not the fake bullshit so common among the Technics, but authentic affection. She'd seen it. She'd experienced it. A peculiar sensation, new to her, alien in its profound impact on her mind and heart.

Was it—she balked at mentally framing the word—was it love? Real love? Not the artificial crap she'd known all her life. But sincere, unaffected, pure love?

Whatever it was, it scared the daylights out of her!

She felt it most when in Yama's presence. Incredibly, she couldn't get enough of him. She concocted excuses to be near him. Asked him questions to draw out their conversations, when she already knew the answers. She wanted to be near him every second of every day.

What the hell had happened to her?

Farrow opened her eyes and gazed at the moat. She had a decision to make, and she couldn't afford to wait any longer. Either she sent the signal, or she told Yama about the demolition team.

One or the other.

But which?

"Mind some company?" asked a deep voice.

Farrow glanced up, and there he was, the morning sun to his rear, adding a preternatural glow to the outline of his muscular physique, his dark blue garment bulging with power, his silver hair and mustache neatly combed, freshly washed.

Farrow couldn't force her mouth to function. She

swallowed, nodding.

Yama sat down next to her, laying his Wilkinson on the grass. "I was searching all over for you. Is everything all right?"

Farrow averted her eyes. "Fine," she responded huskily.

"Are you sure?" Yama insisted.

"I'm okay," Farrow asserted. "Why do you ask?"

"Just a feeling I have," Yama said. He scrutinized her features for a moment. "Are you homesick?"

"What?" Farrow replied in surprise.

"Are you homesick? Do you miss your fellow Technics? Is that why you're upset?" Yama inquired.

"I'm not upset," Farrow rejoined stiffly.

"Whatever you say," Yama said.

Farrow nervously bit her lower lip, then glanced at him. "I don't miss them," she confided. "Truth to tell, I don't even want to go back."

"Then don't."

Farrow laughed bitterly. "Oh, yeah! Just like that!"

"Why not?" Yama asked.

"They might not like it," Farrow said.

"So what? It's your life. You can do whatever you want," Yama declared.

"That's easy for you to say," Farrow stated. She decided to change the subject. "I'd like to hear some more about you."

"Me? You already know more than anyone else," Yama remarked.

"But I don't know everything, and I want to know all about you," Farrow blatantly told him. "For instance, how is it you Warriors are all so different? I mean, you all attended the same Family school. You all had the same teachers. Yet each of you is as different from the other as night from day."

"It's no great mystery," Yama said, his left arm propped on the ground, relaxed. "No two people are alike. We're as unique and individual as snowflakes. Different tastes, different likes and dislikes, different interests and talents. Some people have a talent for the soil and they become Tillers. Others are tuned to psychic circuits and become Empaths. A few, like Joshua, attain harmony with the cosmos and become spiritual sages, dispensing truth to troubled souls. Then there are the Warriors. Our talent lies in the skillful manipulation of violence. Not much of a talent, when you compare it to the others. But it serves to safeguard our Home and our Family.'' He paused, staring at the west wall. ''Even similar talents can be diverse in their expression. Take the Warriors as an example. We might be termed masters of death, but each of us has perfected the mastery of a different technique in the execution of our duties, all consistent with our talents and personal preferences. Hickok is a revolver specialist. Rikki is unbeatable with a katana. Blade has his Bowies. Teucer his bow. True, we were all raised in the same environment and instructed by the same Elders, but the environment and the instructions affected us differently because we are individuals. Each of us has formed our own philosophy of life. We live according to our highest concepts of truth, beauty, and goodness. We answer to the Spirit and ourselves and no one else.'' He stopped, bemused. ''Why is it, whenever I'm near you, I can't seem to stop talking?''

''Don't stop on my account,'' Farrow said.

''I've never had this happen,'' Yama commented.

''I don't mind if you don't,'' Farrow stated, grinning.

Yama stared into her eyes. ''I'll be honest with you, Alicia. I've come to care for you a great deal. I don't want you to leave. Not just yet anyway. I'd like to get to know you better.''

Alicia turned her face away.

''I'm sorry,'' Yama said. ''I didn't mean to upset you.''

''You don't understand,'' Farrow said huskily, refusing to let him see the torment twisting her features.

''Explain it to me,'' Yama said.

''I can't.''

''Why not?'' Yama pressed her.

''Please. Leave it alone,'' Farrow pleaded. She heard his clothes rustle as he rose.

''Whatever you want,'' Yama declared. ''But I'm

always ready to listen when you decide you can trust me.'' His footsteps receded to the southwest.

Farrow glanced over her right shoulder, her eyes misty.

Curse her stupidity!

Now she'd done it! Gone and driven him off! Maybe antagonized him!

There was no other choice! She *must* tell him about the Minister and the demolition crew! But how would he react? Despise her for being a part of the dastardly plot? Could she risk it?

Lieutenant Alicia Farrow drew her knees up to her chest and encircled her legs with her arms. She buried her face in the stiff fabric of her fatigue pants and silently weeped, torn to the core of her being.

To give the signal, and lose her new friends and probably Yama too, or to continue wavering and face execution?

To do her duty, or as her heart dictated?

That was the question.

But what the hell was the answer?

9

He became conscious of a dull ache in the back of his head, a palpable pounding at the base of his skull. There was a bitter taste in his mouth, lingering on his tongue and lips. For a minute, he was disoriented, striving to recall where he was and what had happened.

Suddenly, he remembered in a rush.

Blade's eyes snapped open and he tried to stand, mistakenly assuming he was still on the elevator floor.

But he was wrong.

The giant Warrior had been stripped naked. He was securely locked in steel manacles, one on each wrist and around each ankle, and was suspended several inches above a white, tiled floor, his limbs spreadeagled, on a smooth blue wall.

What the . . . !????

Blade found himself a prisoner in a rectangular room. Except for a brown easy chair eight feet away, the chamber was barren of furniture. The ceiling radiated a pale, pinkish light. From somewhere off in the distance came a muted rumbling.

Where was he?

Someone groaned to his left.

Blade turned his head in the direction of the sound and found Hickok four feet away, likewise manacled to the wall.

The gunman's eyelids fluttered, then slowly opened. "Oh! My achin' noggin! Did you get a description of the buffalo that hit me?"

"Afraid not," Blade replied, chuckling.

Hickok glanced downward. "What the blazes is this?" he exploded. "I'm in my birthday suit!"

"Join the club," Blade said.

Hickok's face became a vivid scarlet. He looked up, glaring around the room. "Some bozo is gonna pay for this!"

"We really walked into this one," Blade commented regretfully.

"Don't blame yourself, pard," Hickok stated. "These sleazy turkeys set us up real good. There was nothing else you could have done."

"I don't know—" Blade began, then paused as a door on the far side of the chamber opened.

In walked four people, three men and a woman.

Blade recognized only one of them, the bastard Wargo. He was bringing up the rear of the little group, possibly indicating an inferior social status. The leader was a scarecrow of a man with a peculiar magnetic quality about him. He wore light blue pants and a blue shirt, both trimmed in gold fabric, the shirt along the end of the sleeves and the pants along the hem at the bottom. Fastened to the lapels of his shirt were gold insignia: a large *T* enclosed in a ring of gold and slashed through the center by a lightning bolt. His hair and eyes were a striking black, his hair cropped close to his head and slicked with an oily substance. A regal, leonine expression lent a lofty aspect to his appearance, but his eyes dominated his countenance. With their large, unfathomable pupils, veritable pools of black, they gazed at their surroundings with an imperious, haughty air. Their owner crossed to the easy chair and sat down. He gazed at the two Warriors and smiled. "They don't seem so formidable without their apparel," he remarked in a gravely voice.

The three others laughed.

Hickok bristled. "Let me down from here, you cow chip, and I'll show you how formidable we are!"

The man in the easy chair locked a baleful stare on the gunman.

Captain Wargo walked around the chair and up to

Hickok. Without any warning, he slugged the gun-fighter in the abdomen.

Hickok gasped and tried to double over.

"You will address the Minister with respect," Captain Wargo instructed the gunman.

Hickok, resisting an impulse to gag, looked at the Technic captain. "Go slurp horse piss, you son of a bitch!"

Wargo drew back his right fist.

"That's enough!" the Minister ordered.

Captain Wargo stiffened, wheeled, bowed to the Minister, and took up a position behind the easy chair.

Blade studied the other two. The man wore a brown outfit similar to the Minister's blue one, but without the gold trim and the insignia. He was shorter, about five feet in height, and slightly hefty. His hair was gray, his eyes blue, his cheeks full and ruddy. He stood to the right of the easy chair.

On the left side was the woman, and a lovely woman she was. Dressed in a dainty yellow blouse and a short, short green skirt, she obviously intended to accent her ample physique. Her eyes were an alert green, her hip-length hair white with a black streak down the middle.

How did she fit into the scheme of things?

"As Captain Wargo has revealed," the man in the chair said, "I am the Minister."

"Should we kiss your feet now or later?" Hickok asked.

Captain Wargo started forward, but the Minister held up his right hand, halting the officer in his tracks.

The Minister frowned. "I had hoped we could conduct this on an intelligent basis."

"That's a mite hard to do when you're sittin' on your intelligence," Hickok cracked.

The Minister glanced at Blade. "Are you going to let this buffoon do all the talking?"

"Hickok's a grown man," Blade responded. "He can say whatever he likes."

The Minister grimaced distastefully. "That's democracy for you," he said.

The three others, as if on cue, laughed.

The Minister cleared his throat. "I placed you in this position to demonstrate my complete power over you. I could have you destroyed with a snap of my fingers."

"Then why don't you?" Hickok interrupted. "Anything would be better than hangin' up here with my dingus flappin' in the air."

"Your . . . dingus . . . is the least of my concerns," the Minister said acidly. "This is an object lesson, nothing more."

"Are we supposed to be impressed?" Hickok retorted.

The Minister ignored the gunman and turned to the head of the Warriors. "You agree I could have you killed on a moment's notice?"

Blade didn't reply.

"I'll construe your silence as agreement," the Minister said. "I trust I've made my point."

"What point?" Hickok rejoined. "That you're a pervert who gets his kicks ogling folks in the nude?"

The Minister turned to Captain Wargo. "Silence this moron!"

Captain Wargo nodded and walked to the center of the left-hand wall. He touched a circular indentation and a recessed panel opened. A metallic tray emerged from the wall bearing a syringe and a box of cotton balls. The syringe was tipped with a red plastic cap.

"Why is it some varmint is always tryin' to stick me with needles?" Hickok quipped, referring to an incident during their last run.

"You leave me no recourse," the Minister declared, smirking. "Nothing personal, you understand?"

'You've got it all wrong, jackass," Hickok said harshly. "I'm takin' this humiliation real personal-like. And you'll see just how personal when you let me down from here."

"I'm trembling in abject fear!" the Minister joked. His chorus laughed.

Captain Wargo had removed the red cap from the syringe. He walked over to the gunman and raised the syringe near his left arm.

Hickok's blue eyes narrowed. "The first thing I'm

gonna do if you let me go," he promised the Minister, "is kill you."

"Shut the fool up!" the Minister barked.

Captain Wargo plunged the syringe into the gunman's left arm, brutally, relishing the discomfort he caused.

Hickok winced, then glanced at Blade. "I'll be right here if you need me." He was about to say more, but the shot took immediate effect. His eyes drooped, then closed.

"Now that the imbecile is silenced," the Minister said, "perhaps we can proceed with a modicum of decorum?" He saw Blade examining the gunman with concern. "Don't worry about your friend. The tranquilizer Wargo administered will render Hickok unconscious for six to ten hours. He'll awaken refreshed and as obnoxious as ever."

Blade sighed in relief. He nodded at the shackle on his right wrist. "Why go to all this trouble? We were cooperating with you. We gave our word we would help find the Genesis Seeds. Why did you turn against us?"

The Minister hesitated. "Insurance," he answered at last.

"Insurance?"

"Of course. A man in my position, with so many relying on my every judgment, cannot afford to make mistakes. My people expect me to perform flawlessly, and I will not disappoint them." The Minister paused. "I know you promised to assist in retrieving the Genesis Seeds. But what's to stop you from confiscating the Seeds for yourselves after they're located?"

Blade leaned forward. "We gave you our *word*!"

"So you did. But your word means nothing to me. Actions, Blade—may I call you Blade?—speak louder than words. And there was nothing to preclude your taking action against us. I require insurance. I needed to compel your total cooperation. And I've achieved my goal."

"No you haven't," Blade said. "You can stuff your Seeds where the sun doesn't shine! We'll never cooperate now!"

The Minister smiled, displaying two rows of small, even teeth. He rolled up his left sleeve and stared at a watch. "I think you will."

"Why should we?" Blade countered. "You may have us, but Geronimo is still free. You'll never be able to stop him from leaving, from breaking through your fence and returning to the Home. The Freedom Federation will learn about your treachery. They'll put you out of business, Minister. You and this technological prison you call a city!"

The Minister grinned and shook his head. "My dear Blade! You are suffering from several delusions! First, Geronimo will not warn the Freedom Federation because he won't be leaving Technic City. Secondly, your bitterness is understandable but unwarranted. I don't intend to harm any of you. I could have done that while you were unconscious. As I already told you, this is merely a demonstration of my power. To show you what I could do if I wanted."

"What do you mean?" Blade demanded. "Why won't Geronimo be leaving Technic City?"

"You'll see shortly," the Minister stated. "Once you realize the futility of opposing me, you will assent to my wishes."

"Don't hold your breath!" Blade cracked.

The door on the other side of the room swung open, and in came three men. Two soldiers in green fatigues with a captive draped between them, sagging in their arms.

It was Geronimo.

Blade gawked at his friend, startled. "How—?"

"How did we do it?" the Minister finished the question. "Why, it was simplicity itself. Captain Wargo dropped a gas grenade in the SEAL before exiting. It was timed to release its knockout gas thirty minutes after being activated. Your poor Geronimo never knew what hit him."

Blade could readily envision the result A cloud of noxious gas filling the confines of the SEAL and overcoming Geronimo within seconds. "But the SEAL . . ."

"Ahhhh. Your vaunted vehicle!" The Minister cackled. "Presumably impenetrable."

"How did you break in?" Blade asked.

"We utilized a clothes hanger," the Minister replied.

"A what?"

"A clothes hanger. You know. Wires you hang clothes on," the Minister said gleefully.

"That's impossible!" Blade said.

"And an industrial diamond drill," the Minister added. "You see, we knew it would be useless to attempt any other method. We've heard stories about your vehicle. Bulletproof. Fireproof. But not clothes-hanger proof, eh?" He laughed uproariously, joined by his subservient trio.

Blade's mind was racing. They'd broken into the SEAL! No one had ever been able to do that! With the SEAL in enemy hands, the Warriors had lost their primary advantage. They were at the Minister's mercy!

"We drilled through the driver's window," the Minister was explaining, gloating, savoring his triumph. "I don't think you realize it, but you were unconscious six hours. In six hours an industrial diamond drill can penetrate any substance known to man, including the SEAL's unique plastic structure. Captain Wargo advised our driller on where to align his bit, and we drilled in adjacent to the door lock. Don't worry! The hole is a small one, not even noticeable unless you know where to look for it. Once the hole was drilled, we slid a straightened hanger through and unlatched the lock. An easy procedure, really. Prior to World War III, car thieves did it all the time." He chuckled. "The SEAL is now ours."

Blade, in a surge of frustration, strained against the manacles binding him. He'd failed! Failed the Family. Failed Plato. And, worst of all, failed Hickok and Geronimo. Why had he assumed the SEAL was invulnerable? He'd left it outside like a sitting duck! He'd acted like a grade-A chump! And look at what had happened!

"If you could only see the comical look on your face!" the Minister said, smiling broadly.

Fire flamed in Blade's gray eyes, and his powerful fists clenched and unclenched.

One of the troopers carrying Geronimo released his grip and marched to the easy chair. He saluted and held up a set of keys in his left hand.

The keys to the SEAL.

The Minister took the keys and waved the soldier away from his chair. "Do you see these?" He dangled the keys in the air. "I could get in the SEAL and drive it wherever I want. But I won't. Wouldn't you like to know the reason?"

"You'll tell me whether I want to know it or not."

"Be nice," the Minister cautioned. "I won't drive the SEAL off because I'm going to give the keys back to you."

"Why are you being so generous?" Blade asked sarcastically.

"Because I've proven my point. I have no need for your vehicle. You will resume your journey to New York City and retrieve the Genesis Seeds as originally planned." He paused, smirking. "Wouldn't you like to know the reason?"

Blade felt an intense rage welling within him. Had his arms been free, he would have throttled the Minister's neck. "Why?"

"Because that one," and the Minister pointed at Hickok, "will remain here. I told you I needed insurance. Well, the fool is my insurance. He will stay with us until you return. If you betray us, you will never see your friend again."

"Our relationship will be based on trust then," Blade commented dryly.

"Trust must be earned," the Minister said. "You must prove you are trustworthy, just as I have proven my reliability to you."

"You have?" Blade said skeptically.

"Certainly. I could have slain you, but didn't. I could have taken your vehicle, but I haven't. What more could I do to convince you I'm sincere?"

Blade almost laughed aloud. Sincere? The Minister was as sincere as the legendary serpent in the Garden of

Eden!

"Release him," the Minister said to Captain Wargo. "Take him next door and dress him. Then take Blade and Geronimo to the cafeteria and feed them. Have your squad report to you there. I will join you in an hour."

"As you command," Wargo said. His heels clicked together, and he moved to his left around the chair.

Blade tensed. He debated the wisdom of making a break for it, but discarded the idea. Hickok and Geronimo were both unconscious. He would be unable to carry them both to safety. Besides, there was little he could do while unarmed and naked. He would have to bide his time.

Captain Wargo produced a key and quickly unlocked the manacles securing Blade. "No hard feelings?" he asked.

Blade wanted to drive his fist into Wargo's smug face. Instead, he smiled. "No hard feelings," he lied.

"This way," Captain Wargo said, motioning for Blade to follow him.

The Minister nodded at them as they passed. He waited until Wargo, Blade, the two troopers and Geronimo were gone before he spoke again. "What did you think?" he inquired of the man in brown.

"An excellent performance," the man responded. "Blade appeared to be thoroughly confounded. He'll never suspect your true motives."

The woman raised her right hand and patted her hair into place. "I don't get it," she said in a squeaky voice.

The Minister faced her. "What don't you get?"

"Any of this," the woman said. "Why'd you hand the keys over to him? I thought you want the SEAL?"

The Minister sighed. He stood and moved next to the woman. "My one weakness," he said softly, gently placing his right hand under her chin, "and she has to be mentally deficient."

"Are you talking about me?" the woman asked in an annoyed tone.

The Minister smiled sweetly. "No, Loretta, darling," he said in a reserved manner, then abruptly thundered,

"I'm talking about the tooth fairy!"

The woman recoiled, but his hand gripped her chin, restraining her in place.

"How many times must I explain it to you?" the Minister angrily demanded.

Loretta wanted to speak, but her mouth was immobile, forced shut by the pressure on her chin.

"We have the capability of constructing a hundred SEALs," the Minister said, as if he were a teacher instructing a wayward pupil, his bearing condescending, his fingers digging into her skin. "With one exception. The SEAL is composed of a special plastic, an alloy unlike any other in existence, developed by Kurt Carpenter's scientists shortly before World War III. There isn't another vehicle like the SEAL on the face of the earth." He paused, his gaze hardening. "I want the secret of that alloy. I want to know how they made the SEAL's body. I want to duplicate their process, discover the formula they used. Once I have it in my hands, we will produce hundreds of war machines with the same plastic. We'll be unstoppable! The Freedom Federation will crumble before our armored might! And the Soviets will be next!" A fanatical gleam infested the Minister's black eyes. "We will assume our rightful place in the world! The Technics will subjugate the globe and establish a new world order! We will achieve a new and higher destiny!" He released his hold on Loretta's chin, lost in an inner rapture.

"So why don't you just take their SEAL and be done with it?" Loretta stupidly inquired.

The Minister's right hand swept up, ready to strike.

Loretta flinched, raising her right arm to protect her face. To her surprise, he lowered his hand and stepped back.

"Will you elaborate for this . . . this . . . *person*, Arthur," the Minister asked, stalking toward the door.

Arthur nodded. "We can't merely appropriate their vehicle because it might have a self-destruct mechanism."

Loretta's brow furrowed in confusion.

"The Warriors might have a way of blowing up the

SEAL if anyone attempts to steal it or drive it off,"
Arthur detailed. "Even drilling into the window
entailed a calculated risk. But it also accomplished
another purpose."

"What's that?" Loretta queried.

"Even as we speak," Arthur said, "our chemists are
analyzing the fragments we drilled from the window.
With any luck, they'll discover the secret of the SEAL's
adamantine plastic before Blade and the others return
from New York City. If not . . ." He shrugged. "We
will confiscate the SEAL."

Loretta grinned. "I get it! This way, you kill two
birds with one stone! The Warriors will get the canisters
you need, and you'll get the chemical formula you want.
With the canisters and the formula, our army will be
invincible!"

"Exactly," Arthur said.

"Are you two coming?" the Minister demanded. He
was standing in the doorway, holding the door open.

Loretta strolled toward him. "I'm impressed. How
do you keep coming up with such brilliant plans?"

The Minister grinned. "All it requires is an
exceptional intellect."

"Do you really think they can get the canisters?"
Loretta inquired.

"They'll have an excellent chance using the SEAL,"
the Minister said. "Once we have the canisters, we can
commence work on the projectiles. Our foes will be
putty in our hands."

"It's too bad you have to go to so much trouble,"
Loretta remarked. "Too bad you can't just take the
SEAL and be done with it."

"True," the Minister agreed. "But we can't risk
losing the SEAL before our scientists have unraveled its
secrets. Captain Wargo didn't detect any evidence of
any such device, but he couldn't be sure. And all Blade
would have to do is press a secret button while climbing
from the SEAL, and it might explode if we tampered
with it."

"So all that stuff you told Blade was to throw him off
the track?" Loretta said.

"Of course."

Loretta kissed the Minister on his right cheek. "I get all tingly when I think of how lucky I am to be your consort."

"Tingly? Really?" The Minister glanced at Arthur. "Tell Wargo I will join him in two hours instead of one."

"As you command."

10

Two more days had elapsed.

Two whole days! It was the morning of the third day!
And she hadn't done a damn thing!

Lieutenant Farrow was up early. She'd spent another
sleepless night, tossing and turning on her cot in B
Block. She rose before dawn, dressed in her uniform,
and slipped from the building unnoticed. Listless,
haunted by her dereliction of duty, she strolled to the
north and eventually reached the inner moat. Standing
on the bank, she idly watched the water flowing past
and contemplated her fate. In all her years as a professional soldier, she'd never exhibited any degree of
indecision. She'd always performed her duty as required.

Until now.

Starlings were chattering in a nearby pine tree.

Farrow gazed up at the northern rampart and spotted
one of the Warriors on guard duty. It wasn't Yama; he
was still sleeping in B Block. After a moment she
recognized the figure—the lean physique, brown shirt,
buckskin pants, and broadsword dangling from his
hip—as that of Spartacus, the head of Gamma Triad.

Spartacus, his right hand resting on the hilt of his
sword, saw her and waved.

Farrow returned the gesture. Why? she wondered.
Why did these people have to be so friendly? Her job
would have been much easier if they hadn't welcomed
her with open arms. She suspected Plato and the one

called Rikki were leery of her, but the rest of the Family treated her as one of their own.

The dummies!

Didn't they know it wasn't smart to trust strangers? To trust anyone, for that matter.

Farrow sighed and sat down on the bank. She thought of the moonlit stroll she'd taken with Yama the night before, and smiled. His affection for her was becoming more obvious every day. He'd escorted her to an open-air concert between the Blocks, an evening of musical entertainment presented by six Family members with outstanding talent. The Family owned eighteen instruments in all, from drums to a miniature grand piano, and they took great pains to maintain the instruments. The Family's best Musicians were an accomplished lot, and the six had played a diverse selection of masterful compositions, their own compositions. Seated under the twinkling stars, with Yama by her side, she had been in seventh heaven.

Despite her apprehensions, Yama hadn't pried into her unstable emotional state. He seemed to be waiting for her to make the first move, to tell him what was bothering her.

And she wanted to do it.

More than anything.

But each time she opened her mouth to reveal her part in the plot against the Family, she balked, concerned she would infuriate him and kill their budding romance.

The sky was much brighter, the sun beginning to clear the eastern horizon as the world awoke to a new day.

Farrow stood and hurried toward B Block. She'd finally made up her mind. She was going to ask Yama to join her for breakfast, then spill the beans. Tell him everything. And hang the consequences! She couldn't take another night of stifling anxiety.

The Family was coming to life. Over a dozen members were clustered near B Block, some exercising, some praying, others conversing.

Farrow hurried toward B Block, afraid she would chicken out before she found Yama. Not this time! she told herself. This time she would see it through.

A flash of dark blue to her right caught her attention.

Yama was 40 yards from B Block, talking to a young woman.

Farrow stopped, frowning.

Who the hell was she?

The woman was a brunette, petite, wearing green pants and a yellow blouse. She was laughing, her right hand resting on Yama's left forearm.

What were they talking about?

Farrow slowly advanced toward them. Yama had his back to her, and the brunette was concentrating on the Warrior, so neither would detect her approach if she was careful.

She *had* to know what they were talking about.

Farrow sidled to within 15 feet of the duo, staying to the rear of Yama, using his huge body to shield her from the brunette's line of vision.

"—delighted," Yama was saying.

The brunette squealed and clapped her hands together. "You will? Honest?"

"I said I would," Yama stated.

The brunette giggled and flung her arms around the Warrior's neck. "I can never thank you enough!"

Yama's reply was too low for Farrow to overhear.

The brunette giggled some more. "You've made me so happy!"

"I'd do anything for you. You know that," Yama said.

The brunette's expression became markedly serious. "You're my favorite. You always have been."

"I'll bet you say that to all the men," Yama commented.

"You know I don't," the brunette responded playfully. "The others can't hold a candle to you."

"You may change your mind when you mature," Yama said.

"Mature?" The brunette scowled in feigned annoyance. "In case you haven't noticed, I've matured quite nicely, thank you."

"You have filled out," Yama admitted.

Farrow edged a little closer. Her mind was in a daze.

What was this? Was the little bitch making time with Yama? Did Yama have another girlfriend, one he'd neglected to mention? Was he playing the field? Was that it?

"I've always loved you," the brunette said sincerely.

"And I've always loved you," Yama told her.

Farrow felt a lump forming in her throat as the brunette stretched on her toes and planted a kiss on Yama's lips. Her mouth dropped open in shock as her darkest forebodings flooded her mind.

That had to be it!

Yama had another woman!

Farrow started to back away before she was discovered.

Yama kissed the brunette on the forehead.

He loved her! He'd always loved her! The words seemed to reverberate in Farrow's brain. There was a sharp ache in her chest. She whirled and ran to the north, toward the moat. What else could it be? They must be lovers! Yama had been leading her on!

Farrow reached a solitary maple tree and leaned on the rough trunk for support, feeling dizzy. How could she have been so gullible? She'd fallen for the oldest ruse in the book! Yama was just like every other man! They all were after one thing, and they'd get it any way they could.

By hook or by crook.

She started forward, then hesitated. What if she were wrong? There might be a perfectly innocent explanation. She twisted, glancing over her left shoulder.

Yama and the brunette were hugging.

No!

No! No! No!

Farrow stumbled toward the moat, racked by despair. How could she give him the benefit of the doubt? What more proof did she need? She'd been played for a sucker. A dupe. A patsy. For all his idealistic talk, Yama wasn't any better than a typical Technic.

He'd used her!

And nobody, but nobody, used Alicia Farrow.

She reached the moat and halted, struggling to suppress her welling anguish. No way! She wasn't about to be weak a second time! Falling for Yama's line was bad enough. She wasn't about to cry over her gullibility.

She'd get even instead!

Farrow reached into her left rear pocket and extracted a small plastic object, square in shape, two inches by two inches, a powerful transistorized transmitter with a ten-mile signal radius. Without thinking of the consequences, motivated by her burning jealousy and shattering disappointment, she depressed a black button in the middle of the transmitter.

There!

It was done!

The demolition team, if they were constantly monitoring her frequency as ordered, had received her signal. They would await the cover of darkness, then enter the compound and set their charges. By tomorrow morning, the Home would be a pile of rubble and the majority of the Family would be dead.

It served them right!

Farrow crammed the transmitter into her rear pocket, then scanned the vicinity to see if she'd been observed. No one else was nearby, but she detected a motion out of the corner of her left eye. She swung around.

Spartacus was patrolling the rampart, headed from west to east. He was 20 yards from her, his posture loose, at ease.

Apparently, he hadn't seen her activate the transmitter.

Farrow forced a grin and waved at the Warrior.

Spartacus returned her wave, his blue eyes sweeping past the Technic officer to the compound beyond. He saw the Family members gathering in the area between the Blocks for their morning socializing. There was Plato and his wife Nadine, talking with Rikki. Ares was near A Block, working out with his shortsword. And there was Yama with his niece, Marian. She was the eldest daughter of Yama's older brother. Marian was walking with Yama toward B Block, their arms linked, beaming with joy.

Spartacus grinned. He could deduce the cause for her happiness. He knew she'd been after Yama to sponsor her boyfriend for Warrior status when another opening developed. Yama had wavered, and he'd confided to Spartacus he wasn't positive the boyfriend was Warrior material. Evidently, he'd changed his mind.

Marian suddenly released Yama and dashed toward her boyfriend, who was just emerging from B Block.

Spartacus nodded with satisfaction at the accuracy of his deduction. He glanced down and saw the Technic, Farrow, staring at Yama with a pained expression on her face.

Now what was that all about?

Spartacus shrugged. It was none of his business. He'd heard the rumor going around, linking Yama and Farrow. Perhaps they were having a lover's spat. If so, he definitely wasn't about to stick his big nose into it. He was a Warrior, not a Counselor.

Besides, Yama kept that scimitar of his *real* sharp.

11

"Why are you slowing down?" Captain Wargo demanded.

"I'm going to wait until they leave the roadway," Blade replied.

"No, you're not," Captain Wargo snapped. "You're going to drive right through them."

Blade's hands tightened on the steering wheel. They were three days out of Technic City, bearing east toward New York City. So far, the going had been frustratingly slow. Most of the major highways were in deplorable condition, ruined as much by the war as 100 years of neglect and abandonment. Lengthy sections, miles at a stretch, had buckled or collapsed or were in scattered bits and pieces, necessitating countless detours. In addition to the wrecked roads, they'd encountered a surprising number of inhabited outposts, some large towns. Wargo knew where each was located; they were marked on a map he carried, along with the approximate boundary of the corridor the Soviets controlled to the south. Wargo insured Blade stayed well north of the area under Soviet domination. But the innumerable detours, to bypass the demolished roads and avoid all occupied settlements as well as the Soviets, markedly delayed their progress. They had traveled for 12 hours both days, averaging approximately 45 miles an hour. Now, by Blade's reckoning, they were within 20 miles of New York City, to the northwest of the metropolis.

Or what was left of it.

Wargo was seated in the other front bucket seat. Behind Blade and Wargo sat Geronimo and two Technic troopers, Geronimo sandwiched between them to prevent him from causing trouble. And reclining on top of the pile of supplies in the rear third of the transport was a fourth soldier, his automatic rifle in his arms.

"Well, what the hell are you waiting for?" Wargo said. "Mow them down!"

Blade surveyed the road ahead.

About 70 yards from the SEAL, walking down the middle of the highway, were two dozen men and women. They were armed with rifles and handguns, none of which posed a threat to the SEAL. Their attire was scarcely more than crudely stitched rags.

It was obvious what they were.

Scavengers.

Looters.

A motley mob preying on anyone and anything. Such marauding bands were the scourge of the post-war age, raiding established settlements and robbing and killing hapless wayfarers, like a scourge of destructive locusts.

Blade paused, not out of any sympathy for the scavengers, but because he disliked taking lives without ample justification. If the scavengers were assaulting the Home, he'd mow them down without another thought. But this was different. This would amount to nothing more than cold-blooded murder.

"Do it!" Captain Wargo barked.

Blade was about to tramp on the accelerator when the issue was resolved for him.

A mutant abruptly appeared from the trees lining the right side of the road and plowed into the scavengers.

Blade applied the brakes.

Two forms of genetic deviations had resulted from World War III. One form, designated as mutants by the Family, was the product of genetic dysfunction and aberration caused by excessive amounts of radiation unleashed on the environment. Mutants were deformed progeny of normal parents, whether human or animal. The second form, on the other hand, was the result of chemical warfare compounds distrupting ordinary organic growth, creating the creatures the Family called the mutates. Mutates were former mammals, reptiles, or amphibians transformed into ravenous, pus-covered horrors by the synthetic toxins infesting their systems.

As Blade watched what might have once been a feral dog, but was now a slavering mutate, pounce on a female scavenger and tear her neck apart with a savage wrench of its yellow fangs, he thought of one more form of genetic deviation. The type intentionally developed by the scientists, the genetic engineers, in their quest to manufacture superior life forms. Gene-splicing had been quite common before the Big Blast, and the nefarious Doktor, the Family's one-time nemesis, had refined the technique into a precision procedure, breeding a personal army of deviate assassins.

But that was then, and this was now.

The mutated canine had dispatched four of the scavengers, and the rest had fled into the trees on the left side of the road without firing a shot. The mutate pursued them.

The road ahead was clear, except for the bloody bodies.

"Get going," Captain Wargo ordered.

Blade drove forward, weaving the transport around the forms on the highway. He saw one of them as he passed, an elderly bald man whose throat was ruptured, his blood pulsing onto the highway, his lifeless brown eyes open and gaping skyward.

"I suppose now is a bad time to mention I need to wee-wee?" Geronimo asked, grinning impishly.

Captain Wargo turned in his seat. "Are you serious?"

"When Mother Nature calls," Geronimo said, "there's not much you can do about it."

"Well, it's too bad, but you'll have to hold it for a while," Wargo told him. "We're not stopping just because you need to take a leak."

"I hope I can hold it," Geronimo said. "If not, then I hope these two clowns next to me don't mind yellow stains on their uniforms."

"Just for that," Captain Wargo retorted, "you can hold it until doomsday."

"I thought that was the date of World War III," Geronimo remarked.

Wargo turned toward Blade. "Sometimes I wonder if we would have been better off leaving Geronimo behind and bringing Hickok."

"They're two of a kind," Blade mentioned.

"A kind I can do without," Wargo said. He pointed at the windshield. "Watch out for more of those scum."

"Where exactly are we?" Blade inquired, steering the SEAL around a gaping hole in the highway.

"Almost to our destination," Captain Wargo revealed. "And it didn't take us the five days you estimated it would." He smiled. "The Minister will be pleased. We'll make it back to Technic City in record time."

"If we make it back," Geronimo interjected.

"You still haven't told us where we are," Blade declared.

"That last big town we bypassed was once known as Newburgh," Captain Wargo disclosed.

"Do we take this road all the way into the city?" Blade asked.

"No." Wargo shook his head for emphasis. "The previous squads we sent in ran into a ton of trouble by using the roads. The lousy Zombies are all over the place. No. We'll play it safe and use a new approach."

"What approach?" Blade wanted to learn.

"The Hudson River," Captain Wargo said.

"The Hudson River?" Blade repeated in surprise.

"Yes," Captain Wargo affirmed. "Why do you look so shocked? We know the SEAL possesses amphibious capability. By taking the Hudson south into the heart of New York City, we reduce the number of Zombies we'll have to face. Pretty clever, I think."

"Except for one small detail," Blade said.

"Oh? What's that?"

"We've never operated the SEAL in its amphibious mode," Blade told the Technic.

Wargo snickered in disbelief. "Yeah. Sure."

Blade stared at the officer.

Captain Wargo did a double take, examining Blade's features. "You're serious, aren't you?"

"Would I lie to you?" Blade stated in mock earnestness.

"You've never operated the SEAL in the amphibious mode!" Captain Wargo reiterated, upset by the news.

"Is there an echo in here?" Geronimo queried.

Captain Wargo unexpectedly pounded the dashboard in anger. "Damn it all! We've come so close! We're almost to our goal!" He glared at Blade. "Do you realize how much trouble we went to, how much time and manpower was expended to reach this point? Getting you and this vehicle to Technic City? Managing to reach this far? Did you know the Soviet line was only five miles south of us? Sometimes we were less than a mile from their northern perimeter. And we made it past the towns and the mutants and everything else!" His voice started to rise. "I don't care if you've never operated in the amphibious mode before! Because we are not, I repeat, *not* going to give up now! Not when we're so damn close! We will adhere to the Minister's schedule."

"Your plan sounds okay to me," Geronimo interjected.

Wargo glanced at the Warrior skeptically. "It does?"

"Sure." Geronimo smirked. "*I* can swim."

Captain Wargo made a hissing sound. He faced forward, then suddenly stabbed his right index finger straight ahead. "There! That's it!"

"What?" Blade asked.

"There! Turn left there!" Wargo cried.

"Where?" All Blade saw was a crumpled roadway, dense foliage to the right, and an embankment to the left.

"There! Damn it! Turn left *now*!" Wargo shouted.

Blade complied, wrenching on the steering wheel, sending the SEAL to the left, up and over the embankment, hurtling down a steep slope toward a . . . river! He slammed on the brakes and the transport lurched to a skidding stop on the grass-covered bank.

"I must be dreaming," Geronimo said in an awed tone.

Blade gazed at the vista beyond in sheer astonishment. It wasn't the bank or the blue river causing his stupefication; it was the eerie panorama on both sides of the river to the south.

"That's the Hudson River," Captain Wargo stated.

"And what is that?" Blade asked, indicating the wrecked landscape stretching to the far southern horizon.

"That," Captain Wargo said soberly, "is what's left of New York City."

Blade had never seen anything like it in all his journeys from the Home. He'd encountered ravaged towns and cities, dozens of them. But he'd never been this close to a city struck by a thermonuclear device, and the impression was instantly seared into his mind's eye. The material he'd read about World War III, the many stories he'd heard over the years, even knowing the mutants and the mutates were by-products of the conflict, none of it had prepared him for . . . this!

How could it?

Even here, even 20 miles from the heart of New York City, the devastation was awesome. Every building in sight, every former residence or office structure or retail establishment, had been destroyed. Most were mere piles of litter and debris. A few retained one wall, a small minority two walls. It looked as if a gigantic windstorm, a tremendous cyclone of inconceivable magnitude, had ripped into every building and literally blown them apart.

"It got to me the first time I saw it," Captain Wargo confided.

Blade tore his eyes from the desolation. "Got to you?" You never mentioned being here before."

"Once," Wargo confirmed. "Shortly before I entered the Civilized Zone to find your Family. I was here on a reconnaisance mission for the Minister."

"How far did you go?" Blade asked.

"This far," Wargo said. "But I was told it gets worse

the further we go.''

"How could it get worse?'' Geronimo wondered aloud.

"There's one way to find out,'' Blade said. He looked up at a control panel imbedded in the roof above his head. The SEAL's Operations Manual had been explicit in detailing the proper operation of the control panel. Unfortunately, he'd never had the occasion to test the instructions. Plato had been reluctant to operate the SEAL in the amphibious mode. What if it sank? he had speculated to the assembled Family. They could not afford to lose the transport, and their timid attitude had restrained them from verifying if the vehicle could function on water as well as land.

Now they had no choice.

Blade reached up and flicked a silver toggle switch. He waited a few seconds until he detected an audible "thunk" from underneath the carriage. With pain-staking care, his nerves on edge, he slowly eased the SEAL down the bank to the edge of the river, then braked.

"What are you waiting for?'' Captain Wargo demanded.

"We could all end up at the bottom of the Hudson,'' Blade commented.

Captain Wargo drew his pistol. "And where do you think you'll wind up if you don't keep going?''

Blade shifted his right foot to the accelerator, gently applying pressure.

The SEAL slid into the river.

Blade quickly raised his right hand and deftly punched two buttons. For a moment nothing happened, but then the SEAL bucked in the water and a loud clunking emanated from the rear of the transport.

"What's happening?'' Captain Wargo asked nervously.

"I closed the wheel ports before we entered the Hudson,'' Blade replied. "The tires have just retracted and been elevated above the water line. That clunk you heard was the outboard dropping from under the storage section.''

"What's next?" Wargo inquired.

"Just this," Blade said, and flicked a second toggle switch.

From behind and under the SEAL came a muted sputtering and metallic coughing, followed by a steady throbbing.

"Hey! The water back here is churning!" the soldier in the rear of the SEAL yelled.

"Is that the outboard motor?" Captain Wargo asked.

"What do you think?" Blade answered.

The SEAL was moving forward, plowing through the water, bearing due east.

Blade turned the steering wheel, gratified when the bulky transport angled to the south.

"We did it!" Captain Wargo said, elated. "The thing is working! Nothing will stop us now!"

"Aren't you forgetting the Zombies?" Geronimo remarked.

"The Zombies!" Wargo snorted. "We'll make mincemeat out of them. Here. Let me show you." He motioned at the trooper in the rear, and the soldier lifted an automatic rifle from the pile of supplies and passed it to the front.

Geronimo's eyes widened when he saw the gun.

Captain Wargo took the piece and hefted it in his hands. "Have you ever seen a beauty like this?"

Blade glanced to the right, getting his first good glimpse of the automatic rifle. He nearly betrayed his bewilderment. The gun was a carbon copy of the one taken from the man caught spying by the Moles. The same 20-inch barrel and folding stock, the same short silencer and elaborate scope, the same 30-shot magazine.

"Is something wrong?" Captain Wargo asked suspiciously.

"No. Why?" Blade responded.

"I don't know." Wargo shrugged. "Nothing, I guess." He stroked the rifle. "Isn't this a beauty?"

"Where did you get it?" Blade innocently inquired.

"We manufacture them, of course," Captain Wargo

said. "They are standard gear for every Technic soldier. They're state-of-the-art, as far as automatics go. Called the Dakon II. They fire four-hundred-five grain fragmentation bullets. They'll drop anything!" he boasted.

"Including Zombies, I hope?" Geronimo chimed in.

"Including Zombies," Captain Wargo declared. He tapped the small plastic panel on one side of the rifle, near the stock. "This is a digital readout. Lets you know exactly how many rounds you have left in the gun—"

"Is that because Technic soldiers can't count without using their fingers and toes?" Geronimo asked, interrupting.

Wargo ignored the taunt. "See these four buttons here? The first button activates the digital counter. The second is for full automatic, the third for semi-automatic. The fourth button ejects your spent magazines."

"What's the fifth button for?" Blade queried. "The one on top of the scope?"

Captain Wargo chuckled. "I told you this was the ultimate in killing power. The button on the scope activates the Laser Sighting Mode."

"It's a laser too?" Blade asked in amazement. He'd read a little about lasers in the Family science classes. Laser technology had been extensively employed prior to the Big Blast.

"Not in the way you mean," Captain Wargo said. "You see this four-inch tube projecting from the top of the scope? It generates a red light, a laser if you will, and this shows up on your targets as a red dot."

"Red dots?" Blade repeated questioningly.

"Yeah. When you see a red dot on your target, that's precisely where your gun is aimed. So to hit the spot you want, all you have to do is raise or lower the red dot to the point you want," Wargo explained.

"It must take the challenge out of aiming," Geronimo noted.

"You don't need to aim with these," Captain Wargo stated. "The Dakon II does everything for you."

"Does it wipe your derriere after you're done?" Geronimo cracked.

Captain Wargo was about to reply when he paused, gawking at the stark vista ahead.

Blade had seen it too. The SEAL was continuing on its course, staying well to the center of the Hudson River, cleaving the water smoothly as it sailed on a southerly bearing into the depths of New York City.

If "city" was the right word.

Any vestige of the former metropolis was gone. The demolished homes and other buildings had given way to a scene culled from a demented nightmare. The ground was parched, scorched, the earth a reddish tint. Vegetation was completely absent. Piles of twisted, molten slag were everywhere. Small piles. Huge piles. Isolated metal girders still stood here and there, like blackened steel trees amidst hills of melted structures.

Blade scanned both sides of the Hudson, astonished. From his schooling days at the Home, he knew New York City had once been inhabited by millions of people. Something like 15 or 20 million when the war broke out. He could scarcely conceive of every one of them, millions upon millions, being reduced to smoking ashes in a matter of seconds. Crisped to nothing in the space of a heartbeat. The very idea was mind-boggling.

"How could they do this to themselves?" Geronimo inquired absently.

"They were idiots," Captain Wargo said.

"Is that it? Is that the only answer?" Geronimo asked.

"What more do you need?" Captain Wargo encompassed both banks with a wave of his hand. "What else would you call someone who would do this? They were fools, because they possessed great power and they didn't know how to use it."

"What do you mean?" Geronimo queried.

"If the Americans had been smart," Wargo stated, "they would have thrown everything they had at the Soviets without warning."

"What?"

"I'm right and you know it," Captain Wargo said. "The Americans blew their chance by letting the Soviets catch up to them. The Americans developed a nuclear capability first. They should have used it before anyone else did the same and conquered the world.''

"You're putting me on," Geronimo declared.

"I am not," Captain Wargo responded. "You have a huge library at your Home. You must be familiar with American history."

"We studied it," Geronimo said.

"Right. Then you know what happened to the Americans. They let the Soviets produce their own nuclear arsenal, until it reached the point where neither side had a distinct advantage over the other. And look at what it got them! Mutual destruction. No, the Americans would have been wiser to launch a war before the Soviets built their first nuclear weapon. They could have conquered the globe in weeks and saved themselves a lot of trouble in later years." He paused. "Patton was right all along."

"Patton?" Geronimo reiterated.

"An American general during World War II," Wargo said. "He was all for putting the Russians in their place. He never trusted them. But the civilian leaders refused to subscribe to his opinions. They should have listened to him."

"I'm curious," Blade spoke up.

"About what?" Wargo replied.

Blade focused on the river, watching for floating logs or other obstacles. "I'm curious about the Technics. Do you consider yourselves Americans?"

"No."

"You don't?"

"Why should we?" Captain Wargo asked. "America is a thing of the past. They had their opportunity and they blew it. It's up to us, the Technics, to forge a new world from the rubble the Americans left as their legacy. And you can be certain we won't commit the same boneheaded blunders they did!"

"The Technics have it all planned out, huh?" Blade casually commented.

"You bet your ass we do," Captain Wargo stated proudly. "Why, by the time we're through everyone in North America will—" He abruptly paused, glancing at the giant Warrior in consternation. "Very clever," he said. "Very clever indeed."

"I don't know what you're talking about," Blade stated.

"Sure you don't," Wargo said, grinning. He gazed out at the expanse of river before them. "Let's change the subject. Why don't you give me a rundown on the SEAL's armaments."

"Again?" Blade asked.

"Humor me," Wargo directed. "I'll need to know what to do in case something happens to you." He smiled wickedly. "Not that we would want anything to happen to you, of course."

"Of course." Blade pointed at a row of silver toggle switches in the center of the dashboard. "Those switches engage our offensive weaponry. They're labeled from left to right with an M, S, F, and R. The M stands for the pair of fifty-caliber machine guns we have hidden in recessed compartments under each front headlight. When you flick the M switch, a metal plate slides upward and the guns automatically fire. The S is for Surface-to-Air Missile, a Stinger mounted on a rack in the roof above the driver's seat. A panel slides aside when the switch is pressed and the Stinger is launched. Our Stingers have an effective range of ten miles, and they're heat-seeking."

"And what about the F and R?" Captain Wargo prompted.

"The F is for the flamethrower positioned at the front of the SEAL, behind the front fender, in the center. Press the F and a portion of the fender lowers, the nozzle of the flamethrower extends six inches, and the flame spurts about twenty feet. The SEAL must not be moving when the flamethrower is used, or you run the risk of an explosion. Finally, we have the R switch. It's for the Rocket Launcher secreted in the middle of the front grill. There you have it."

Captain Wargo was grinning like a kid with a new toy. "Marvelous! Simply marvelous! There's no way the Zombies will stop us now!"

"Says you," Geronimo said.

"They won't be able to stop the SEAL like they did some of our jeeps and trucks," Captain Wargo predicted.

"Aren't you forgetting one little fact?" Geronimo queried.

"What fact?" Wargo responded, shifting in his seat.

"If memory serves," Geronimo reminded the Technic, "you told us some of your teams didn't reach the site of the underground vault. But some did, didn't they? And you said the last word you received was to the effect they were going underground. Am I right?"

"You're right," Wargo conceded grudgingly.

"So the real danger isn't in reaching the site of the New York branch of the Institute of Advanced Technology," Geronimo said. "The true threat comes when we leave the SEAL and descend to the underground vault. Correct?"

Captain Wargo looked worried. "That's true," he admitted.

"Typical white man," Geronimo said to Blade. "He gets all excited because we may reach the spot in one piece where raving cannibals are waiting to rip us apart and eat us for supper." He sighed. "How *did* your race ever defeat mine?"

"Beats me," Blade said, and laughed.

The SEAL was steadily continuing its southerly course. On both sides of the Hudson River utter desolation prevailed.

"There!" the Technic commando in the rear of the transport shouted. "I see something!"

Everyone glanced to the right, in the direction he indicated.

"I don't see anything," Captain Wargo said after a bit.

"I saw something," the soldier insisted.

"Are you sure, Kimper?" Wargo asked doubtfully.

"I'm positive, sir," Private Kimper stated. "I saw something moving."

Blade scanned the mounds of slag, dirt, dust, and rubble. The inhospitable, bleak land seemed to reek of death. "What would be moving out there?" he idly inquired.

"Only one thing," Captain Wargo said. "The Zombies."

"What do you know about these Zombies beside the fact they're cannibals?" Geronimo asked the officer.

"Not much," Wargo confessed. "We know there are thousands of them, and they eat anything they can get their grimy hands on. We also know they live in a maze of underground tunnels, old sewer and electrical conduit systems, not to mention the subway network."

"Thousands of them?" Geronimo stared at the wreckage. "How can they find enough to eat, enough to support so many?"

Captain Wargo shrugged. "They find a way." He thoughtfully chewed on his lower lip, then spoke. "And remember. We have reason to believe the Zombies aren't the only . . . things . . . down there. So when we descend to the vault, watch yourselves."

"I didn't know you cared," Geronimo joked.

"I couldn't care less about what happens to you," Wargo said. "But the Minister wants the SEAL returned to Technic City intact, and you two know more about it than I do. I know I could drive it, but I don't have the extensive experience Blade has accumulated. It would be better for our mission if one of you survives to drive the SEAL back."

"We'll do our best," Geronimo mentioned.

Blade cleared his throat. "How far down is this vault?"

"Far," Wargo said.

"How far, exactly?" Blade inquired.

"Fifteen stories underground," Wargo answered.

"Oh? Is that all?" Blade said facetiously.

"Fifteen floors, with Zombies dogging our heels every step of the way?" Geronimo chuckled. "Sounds like fun."

Captain Wargo picked up a map from the console between the bucket seats. He unfolded the map and consulted the coordinates, then looked up and pointed. "Do you see that?"

Spanning the Hudson ahead was the skeletal framework of an ancient bridge. The central section was gone, and the supports and ramp on the east bank were a mass of pulverized scrap, but the segment on the west bank, bent but intact, served to reveal the purpose of the construction.

"That, if my calculations are correct, was once called the Tappan Zee Bridge," Captain Wargo informed them. "We're getting close to our goal."

The SEAL puttered forward, its powerful outboard maintaining a sustained speed of fifteen knots.

Blade thought of his wife and child, Jenny and Gabriel, and wished he was with them instead of on this insane quest. He wondered how Hickok was faring in the hands of the Technics, and whether the gunman was even alive. If the Technics killed the gunfighter, he would personally insure they paid for the act. So far, in the constricted confines of the SEAL, he'd been unable to make a break for it. But, if Wargo supplied Geronimo and him with firearms, Blade was determined to dispatch the soldiers and head for Technic City. One opening was all it would take, one brief instant when the troopers were diverted by something else. Like a Zombie, perhaps. Blade almost hoped the cannibals would attack.

"Make for the east bank," Captain Wargo curtly ordered.

Blade turned the wheel, bearing toward the eastern bank.

"We should see a small hill," Captain Wargo said, his nose pressed to his window. "There! Do you see it?"

"I see it," Blade said. He surveyed the bank for any hint of movement. The SEAL bounced as it cruised toward the bank, a rhythmic up and down motion caused by the small waves on the Hudson and welling of the water the transport diplaced.

Captain Wargo looked at Private Kimper. "Pass out our helmets," he directed.

Kimper handed a helmet to each Technic soldier.

"Don't we get one?" Blade asked.

"When we reach the site," Wargo said.

"What about guns?" Blade inquired.

"What about them?"

"Do Geronimo and I get one?" Blade asked hopefully.

"Don't make me laugh!" Captain Wargo rejoined.

"But a while ago you said you want one of us to drive the SEAL to Technic City," Blade said.

"I do," Wargo confirmed. "Don't you worry. My men will look after you."

"I hope they do a better job than your other teams have done in dealing with the Zombies," Blade stated.

The SEAL was 20 yards from the bank.

Blade reached up and flicked the appropriate switch to shut down the outboard motor. The throbbing sound abated. Carried forward by its momentum and the flow of the river toward the bank, the transport kept going. Quickly, Blade ran his fingers over the control panel, securing the outboard and opening the wheel ports so the huge tires could assume their usual position.

The SEAL slowly approached the east bank. The tires crunched into the riverbed ten yards from shore.

Blade tramped on the accelerator and the transport wheeled from the Hudson River onto the bank.

"Go straight," Captain Wargo instructed the Warrior.

Blade cautiously drove into the ravaged remains of New York City. He checked his window to insure it was up and locked, then verified Wargo's was also secure. Being this close to the wretched ruins was strange, like driving on an alien planet. Oddly, a cloud of red dust hung suspended in the air, cloaking the city in a mysterious shadow. Some of the molten mounds were several stories high, others squat knolls on the ground. He couldn't determine where the streets and avenues had once been located. Everything was sort of welded together, fused by the intense heat of the thermonuclear blast.

"Keep going straight," Wargo said.

"I'm glad you know where we're going," Blade remarked.

Each of the Technic commandos was now armed with a Dakon II and wearing a camouflage helmet.

Blade noticed a clear plastic area on the front of the helmet, and small holes dotting the helmet area covering their ears. "It looks like your helmets are as elaborate as your guns," he commented.

"They are," Captain Wargo affirmed, keeping his eyes on the fantastic landscape. "Each one is outfitted with a lamp," and he tapped the clear plastic on the front of his helmet, "and sensitive microphones imbedded in the ear flaps. They amplify all sound, giving us superhuman hearing. Nothing can sneak up on us, catch us unawares.

"I trust the Zombies know that," Geronimo said.

"Speaking of the Zombies," Wargo mentioned, "where the hell are they? We should have seen them by now."

"Count your blessings," Geronimo declared.

The SEAL was going deeper and deeper into the ruins.

Blade fidgeted in his seat. He didn't like this one bit. Wargo had a point. Where were the blasted Zombies?

"That's it!" Captain Wargo yelled, leaning forward. "Stop there!"

Their destination was easy to spot. It was the only parking lot in the city. Three jeeps and four trucks were parked near a gaping hole in the ground.

"Those are the vehicles our other teams used," Captain Wargo detailed.

"Why didn't the Zombies drive them off?" Blade asked.

"The Zombies don't have brains enough to come in out of the rain," Wargo replied. "They wouldn't know what to do with those vehicles."

"What about the Soviets?" Geronimo inquired. "They'd drive them off if they found them."

"If they found them," Wargo agreed. "But our intelligence indicates the Russians never enter New York City. And why should they? Do you see anything here worth risking your life for? They're not stupid."

"What does that make us?" Blade wondered aloud. He eased the SEAL in a tight circle, drawing as near to the hole as he could. The closer, the better! The less ground to cover, the fewer Zombies they'd encounter. He braked the SEAL and stared at Wargo. "What next?"

"Stop the engine," Captain Wargo ordered.

"If you say so," Blade said, sighing, and turned the keys in the ignition.

After the sustained whine of the prototypical engine, the abrupt silence was oddly unsettling.

Captain Wargo stared at each of his men. "We've rehearsed this again and again. We'll make it in and out again if we play it by the numbers. Remember. You're the best of the best! Technic commandos! We never fail!"

Blade gazed at the three jeeps and four trucks, but kept his mouth closed.

Captain Wargo glanced at Private Kimper. "Hand me the extra helmets."

Two helmets were forwarded to the officer.

Wargo gave one of the helmets to Blade, the second to Geronimo.

"What am I supposed to do with this?" Geronimo asked. "Grow plants in it?"

"Wear it," Wargo said. "It could save your life. Each helmet contains a miniaturized communications circuit, what we call a Com-Link. We can keep in constant touch without having to shout. Everything you say will be picked up, overheard by the rest of us."

"I hope I don't burp," Geronimo quipped.

Captain Wargo turned to Blade. "What is this guy? The Official Family Comedian?"

"It's a tossup between Geronimo and Hickok," Blade replied.

"Well, I don't want anyone talking unless I give them an order," Captain Wargo instructed them.

"There is one thing I would like to bring up," Geronimo said.

"What is it?" Wargo impatiently snapped.

"I never did get a potty break," Geronimo reminded him. "If I don't go right now, I'll burst."

"Damn. I forgot," Captain Wargo said. "All right. Everyone will exit the SEAL and form at the front.

Blade, be sure the doors are locked and pocket the keys. I want you to stay close to me during this operation. Everyone ready?"

Wargo's men nodded.

"Okay. First, check your Com-Link. Do you see those two buttons under the helmet lamp?" Wargo said for the benefit of the two Warriors. "Press the one on the right for the Com-Link, and the one on the left for the lamp. But don't flash your lamp until we enter the hole. I don't want you draining your helmet batteries."

Blade and Geronimo each donned a camouflage helmet and pressed the Com-Link button.

"Can you hear me?" Captain Wargo asked.

Blade could hear Wargo's voice in his left ear. "I can hear you on the left," he responded.

"Me too," Geronimo added.

"Perfect. The right ear is your amplifier for detecting the tiniest noise. You'll find the control knob for it on your right ear flap. But wait until we're down below to use it. Got it?" Wargo questioned them.

"Got it," Blade said.

"Ditto," came from Geronimo.

"Okay." Captain Wargo clutched his Dakon II and took a deep breath. "Here we go."

The six men hurriedly bailed out of the SEAL. Blade verified the doors were locked. The three Technic soldiers under Wargo's command were professionals; they deployed in a skirmish line around the front of the SEAL, their Dakon IIs at the ready.

"Alright," Captain Wargo said. "Our first squad opened this passage leading to the underground vault. We go in one at a time, single file, Kimper on the point. Do you have the scanner?"

"Affirmative," Kimper replied, waving a device strapped to his right wrist.

"Then we're all set," Captain Wargo said.

"You're forgetting something again," Geronimo stated.

Captain Wargo, preoccupied with their impending descent to the exclusion of all else, stared at Geronimo in confusion.

Geronimo placed his right hand on his gonads and jiggled his pants up and down.

"All right!" Wargo snapped. "Go!"

Geronimo unzipped his green pants, then paused. "Well?"

"Well, what?" Captain Wargo demanded.

"Aren't you going to turn around?" Geronimo asked.

"Turn around? Turn around!" Captain Wargo cried in extreme annoyance. "What are you, bashful or something? We've all seen a pecker before, you dimwit!"

"Not my pecker," Geronimo said, and moved off to the left, near one of the abandoned trucks. He turned his back to the Technics and commenced relieving himself, grateful for the opportunity at long last. He'd had to go so bad his testicles had ached.

Blade grinned at the anger on Wargo's face. He shifted his attention to the large hole not ten feet away. A pile of metal, stones, bricks, and other rubble was stacked behind the hole. Evidently, the first Technic squad on the scene had spent hours uncovering the shaft.

"Activate your scanner," Captain Wargo directed Private Kimper.

Blade watched as Kimper pressed a button and turned several knobs on the black device attached to his right wrist. The scanner was rectangular, with a lot of dials and switches and a grid-laced plastic template.

"Calibrated, sir," Kimper announced.

"Anything?" Wargo queried anxiously.

"Just us," Private Kimper responded.

Blade glanced at his fellow Warrior. Geronimo was still saturating the dust at his feet with a steady stream of urine, a happy grin creasing his features.

"Hurry it up!" Wargo barked.

"Some things can't be rushed," Geronimo retorted.

Blade placed his hands on his hips, wishing he had his Bowies. But the Technics had refused to bring them. His prized knives and Commando and Geronimo's tomahawk, FNC, and Arminius were all in Technic City. The prospect of confronting carnivorous humanoid mutations without weapons was singularly distasteful. He could only pray the Technics knew what they were doing.

"All done," Geronimo said, zipping his pants. He examined the nearest slag mounds and ruins. Great Spirit, preserve them! He fervently craved a weapon, any weapon. The Zombies had to be lurking out there, somewhere. He contemplated the likelihood of being injured, or worse, and dreaded the idea. The last time he'd been hurt was in Catlow, Wyoming, when he'd been shot twice. Once in the head, a surface scratch, and once in the left shoulder. He'd mistakenly assumed his collarbone was broken, but it turned out the bullet had only penetrated the flesh near the collarbone. Still, the discomfort and pain had lingered for months, requiring consummate concentration on his part to prevent the injury from temporarily incapacitating him. All of the Warriors were required to take a course taught by a Family Elder entitled "The Mental and Spiritual Mastery of Pain." But even with such training, sometimes it was hard to—

What was that?

Geronimo tensed. He'd distinctly detected a faint scratching.

"Something!" Private Kimper suddenly shouted, focused on his pulse scanner.

"What is it?" Captain Wargo asked.

"Now it's gone!" Private Kimper said. He was young, inexperienced in combat, and scared out of his wits.

"Keep scanning," Captain Wargo commanded. He began to doubt the wisdom of bringing Kimper on the mission. But Kimper, amazingly, had friends in high places, and one of those "friends" was influential with the Minister. No less a personage than Arthur Ferguson had personally requested to have Kimper taken on the mission. Ferguson knew what success would mean to Kimper's career.

"There it is again!" Kimper exclaimed. "But I don't get it! The images keep fading in and out. How can they do that?"

Captain Wargo frowned. How could they indeed? They might, if the life-forms were continually passing between a solid object or objects containing steel and the scanner.

"The reading is getting stronger!" Kimper warned them.

"How many do you read?" Captain Wargo asked.

Private Kimper glanced at his superior, his skin pale. "It's off the scale!"

Geronimo, momentarily distracted by Wargo and Kimper, heard another scraping noise. He turned, perplexed, because all he could see was rubble and the abandoned jeeps and trucks.

The abandoned jeeps and trucks!

"They're here!" Geronimo yelled in alarm, even as a macabre form hurtled from the cab of the nearest truck directly toward him and a horde of repellant apparitions charged from the gloom of the benighted hole.

12

He almost had it!

Only an inch to go!

Hickok strained against the manacles binding his wrists, his sinewy muscles rippling, his shoulders corded knots, sweat coating his skin and blood dribbling down his wrists. It'd taken two days, two days of strenuous effort, secretly exerting himself to the maximum whenever the chamber was empty. Fortunately, a guard only checked on him four times a day, and he always announced his arrival by rattling his keys as he unlocked the door. Twice daily the guard would bring a tray of food and feed the prisoner.

And, by Hickok's reckoning, it was close to feeding time.

The gunman grunted and groaned as he wrenched his arms from side to side, twisting his wrists back and forth, torturously endeavoring to free his arms.

He could do it!

Hickok knew his escape was only a matter of time. Sooner or later, if he could maintain his frantic contortions, the combination of sweat and blood would provide the lubrication necessary for his wrists to slide from the manacles.

But could he do it before the guard arrived?

He must, the gunman told himself. Otherwise, the guard might notice the ring of crimson around his wrists.

He had to do it *Now!*

Hickok's hair was plastered to his head, drops of

sweat dripping from his chin, as he toiled at his task, his chest heaving from his laborious exertion. His eyes roamed about the room and settled on the white plastic bucket at his feet.

The bastards wouldn't even unlock the manacles and permit him to relieve himself!

They'd pay!

Dear Spirit, *how* they'd pay!

Hickok's mouth curved downward, exposing his grit teeth as he grimaced in agony.

It felt as if his arms were being torn from their sockets!

Hickok savagely jerked his right arm.

Come on!

With a pronounced squishing sound, the gunman's right wrist popped loose of the steel manacle restraining his arm. The momentum swung him around in a circle, tearing at the tendons in his left shoulder as his body sagged.

Bingo!

Hickok reached up and clasped the right manacle, still imbedded in the wall. Using the manacle for support, he pulled his left wrist free in moments.

Just as keys jangled at the door.

Perfect timing! Hickok gripped the left manacle, then drooped his body and lowered his chin, assuming his usual resigned position. A smile touched the corners of his mouth.

Now he was ready.

Let the son of a bitch come!

The guard entered the chamber, a tray of food in his right hand, his keys in his left. He wore a camouflage uniform, black boots, and an automatic pistol attached to his green web belt.

Hickok, feigning dejection, glanced up.

The guard, a solidly built soldier in his forties with brown hair and brown eyes, closed the door. "Well, how's our hick doing today?"

Hickok didn't respond. He was accustomed to being baited; the guards took perverted delight in amusing themselves at his expense.

The trooper advanced toward the gunman. "What's wrong with you? Antisocial or something?"

Hickok didn't answer.

The guard stopped in front of the gunman and stared at his weary face. "You look awful, stupid. Are you getting your beauty rest?" He cackled at his joke.

Hickok's blue eyes darted over the food tray. A glass of juice. A plate containing potatoes and a slice of meat. One fork and one knife, a dull butter knife from the looks of it. Not much, but it would have to do.

"You'd best enjoy this meal," the trooper was saying. "I've heard through the grapevine you don't have too many meals left."

Hickok's interest was piqued. "Why's that?" he asked.

"Ahhh! You are alive!" the guard cracked. "Do you really want to know?" he taunted the Warrior.

"You're the one who brought it up," Hickok said. "You probably didn't hear a thing."

"I did so!" the trooper said indignantly.

"Yeah. Sure."

"Think you know it all, don't you, smart-ass?" the Technic said.

"I know more than you."

"Is that so? Did you know the Minister plans to rack your ass after your buddies return from New York City?" the guard gloated.

"Nope," Hickok admitted. "I didn't know that."

The soldier smirked.

"But I know something *you* don't know," Hickok mentioned nonchalantly.

"Like what?" the guard demanded.

"I don't think you'd want to know," Hickok said.

"You tell me or I'll cram this food down your throat!" the soldier stated. His gaze fell on the white plastic bucket. "Better yet, I'll dump your shitpail on your head!"

"Are you sure you want to know?" Hickok asked, tensing.

"I want to know!" the Technic persisted.

Hickok shrugged. "If you insist." He lunged, his left

hand grasping the guard's shirt and yanking him off balance as his right streaked to the fork and grabbed the implement.

Completely startled, the Technic dropped the tray and the keys, the tray clattering as it struck the floor. He tried to pull away, but the gunman's left hand was locked on his shirt. The Warrior's upper torso, without the shackles securing the wrists to suspend it, pressed down on the guard, causing his knees to sag.

Hickok touched the fork tines to the guard's right eye. "Make one move and you're blinded for life!" he threatened harshly.

The guard gulped.

"Do exactly as I say or I'll ram this fork into your eye!" Hickok growled.

"What . . . what do you . . . want?" the trooper stammered.

"Reach down slowly, and I mean *slowly*, with your right hand and remove your pistol from your holster. Do it slow! One false move and you know what I'll do!"

"Yes," the guard stated in abject fright. He could feel the metal tines digging into his right eyelid.

"Use only your thumb and forefinger to draw the gun!" Hickok directed. "Lift it—slowly—up to me!"

The guard trembled as his right hand lowered to the holster flap and undid the snap. He carefully eased his thumb and forefinger under the leather flap and withdrew the pistol, holding it by the grips.

"Slowly!" Hickok said.

The Technic licked his dry lips as he moved in slow motion, raising the automatic to chest level, inches from Hickok's left hand.

"A little higher," Hickok instructed him.

The guard elevated the pistol to within an inch of the gunman's right hand.

Hickok glanced at the automatic, a 45 of indeterminate manufacture, probably produced by the Technics. He saw a safety button above the grips.

Blast!

The safety was on!

Hickok hesitated. He would need to drop the fork,

grab the pistol, and flick the safety all in one move, leaving himself vulnerable for the fraction of a second his right hand would be empty. Could he do it before the soldier reacted?

Was there any other option?

"You've been a good boy," Hickok said sarcastically. "But I still think I should put out your eye!"

"Please!" the trooper whined. "Don't!"

Hickok scraped the fork tines over the guard's right eyelid, and the soldier flinched, his eyes closing in instinctive defense as his face recoiled.

Which was just what the gunman wanted.

Hickok released the fork and snatched the automatic, his thumb flipping the safety off, and before the Technic quite knew what had transpired he found the fork replaced by the pistol. "Now we come to the easy part," Hickok said.

"Anything," the guard declared.

"Your momma sure raised a polite cuss," Hickok joked. "Oh. Sorry. I forgot. You Technic types don't know who your momma or pappa was, do you?"

"No," the trooper replied.

"Too bad. A little parental love might have changed you from a jackass to a thoroughbred." Hickok wagged the pistol barrel downward. "Now I want you to lower us down, real slow. I'll let you kow when to stop."

Struggling to support the gunman's weight, the soldier eased to his knees.

"I'm gonna let go of your shirt," Hickok said. "When I do, slide your butt backwards. Don't try anything stupid!"

The trooper nodded his understanding.

Hickok released his hold on the shirt, shoving the guard from him and dropping his left hand to the tiled floor to support his body. He wound up in the push-up position, his left arm bracing him, his ankles smarting like the dickens from the manacles above his feet.

The Technic was crouched not a foot away, staring at the pistol barrel.

"Pick up the keys," Hickok ordered.

The trooper immediately complied, stretching his left

arm to the keys and cautiously retrieving them.

"Now unlock my legs," Hickok said. "I'll have you covered all the way, and believe me when I say I can perforate your noggin if you so much as look at me crossways. Do it!"

The guard sidled to the left, still on his knees, toward the wall.

Hickok shifted his left arm, twisting his body, keeping the pistol in his right hand trained on the trooper.

The soldier reached the wall and quickly unfastened the first manacle.

Hickok felt a wave of relief as the agony in his left leg subsided.

The guard unlocked the last manacle.

Hickok rolled to his right, coming up on his knees, the automatic pointed at the Technic. "Thanks, pard. Now stand up and lock the manacles on yourself."

The soldier obeyed without complaining, securing his legs and left wrist.

"Now freeze!" Hickok said.

The Technic became a statue.

Hickok rose and walked up to the guard, placing the pistol barrel a centimeter from the soldier's nose. "Blink, and you'll wind up with a new nasal passage!"

The trooper's throat bobbed.

Hickok locked the right steel manacle on the guard's right wrist, then smiled. "Do you want to live?"

The Technic nodded.

"Then tell me where the blazes they've got my guns and clothes," Hickok directed.

"Right here," the guard responded.

"Here?" Hickok scanned the chamber. All he saw was the brown easy chair. He tapped the barrel on the Technic's nose. "You wouldn't be joshin' me, would you?"

"No!" the soldier assured the gunman. He nodded toward the right-hand wall. "There! You'll find them there!"

Hickok stared at the blue wall. "Where?"

"They're in a closet," the trooper said.

"A closet?"

"A compartment in the wall. Go to the center of the wall," the guard stated.

Hickok walked to the middle of the wall, the pistol trained on the trooper. If the wall was booby-trapped, he intended to blow the soldier away before he went.

"Look for a small button," the guard said. "A little circle on the wall."

Hickok recalled the incident with the syringe, and how Captain Wargo had touched a spot on the left wall, exposing the tray. He peered at the seemingly solid wall. "I don't see it."

"Keep looking!" the Technic said nervously. "It's there!" he assured the gunman.

Hickok saw a circular indentation to his right, about waist height. He pressed the indentation and it sank inward several inches. So that's how they did it!

With a whisk of air, a panel slid aside, a section of the wall simply disappearing as it slid into a recessed groove.

"Bingo!" Hickok said, smiling.

The compartment was six feet high by five feet wide. A metal bar was aligned across the space, six inches from the top. Dangling from silver metal hangers were the gunman's buckskin shirt and leggings. His moccasins had been deposited on the floor in a corner. Leaning against the back wall were Hickok's Henry, Blade's Commando, and Geronimo's FNC. Lying in a pile in the middle of the compartment were Blade's Bowies, Geronimo's tomahawk and Arminius, and one other item, the sight of which caused the gunman's eyes to light up and a wave of genuine joy to wash over him: his pearl-handled Colt Python revolvers in their holsters.

Praise the Spirit!

Hickok crouched and laid the Technic pistol on the floor. He drew one of the Pythons and checked the cylinder to insure it was loaded. Satisfied, he raised the revolver and stroked his right cheek with the cool barrel.

The guard was gawking at the gunman in amazement.

"What's the matter?" Hickok demanded gruffly.

"Ain't you ever seen anyone in love with a gun before?"

"You're crazy," the Technic mustered the courage to comment.

"You think so, huh?"

"What else would you call it?" the soldier countered. "I've never seen anybody act the way you do over a rotten gun."

"These Pythons have gotten me out of more tight scrapes than I care to remember," Hickok said. "I know they're just tools of my trade, but after all these years I've sort of developed a personal relationship with 'em. In a fix, they're the best friends I've got."

"Like I said," the guard reiterated, "you're crazy."

"And you talk too much," Hickok rejoined.

The guard clammed up.

Hickok hurriedly dressed, relieved to be clothed again. He strapped his gunbelt around his waist, then paused, considering the other weapons in the closet. What was he supposed to do about them? He couldn't leave them for the Technics. Besides, Blade was as fond of the Bowies and Geronimo as attached to his tomahawk as he was to the Pythons. Nope. He owed it to his pards to take the weapons with him, even if the extra weight slowed him down a mite. He picked up the tomahawk and slid it under his gunbelt in the small of his back. The Bowies, sheaths and all, he angled under the gunbelt, one on either side of the tomahawk. Bending over would pose a problem, but his hands had a clear path to the Pythons. Next, he slung his Henry over his right shoulder. The FNC went over his left. He was about to grab the Commando when he saw the Arminius still on the floor.

Blast!

The gunman unslung the FNC, then draped the Arminius's shoulder holster under his left arm. Finally, he slung the FNC over his left shoulder and took hold of the Commando.

He was ready.

Hickok walked over to the guard.

The Technic blanched. "I did everything you

wanted!" he said, his voice rising.

"And I appreciate it," Hickok remarked. "I surely do. But I'm afraid our friendship has reached the end of the line."

"Are you going to kill me?" the trooper timidly inquired. "I have a wife and son."

Hickok paused, thinking of Sherry and Ringo. "If you care so much for your missus and young'un, what are you doing in the Army?"

"I didn't have any choice," the guard replied.

"Everybody has a choice," Hickok said.

"We don't," the Tecnnic revealed. "We're given tests when we're teenagers, about sixteen. The jobs we're assigned are based on the test results."

"They tell you what kind of work you'll do?" Hickok asked.

The Technic nodded. "We don't have any say in it. They say our system is best because the service we perform for the community, for the common good of all, is based on our demonstrated ability, not on what we might like to do."

"But a person can have talent in more than one field," Hickok noted. "How do they know what'd make you happiest?"

"Make us happy?" The Technic snorted derisively. "Do you know what we're taught? Individual happiness is an illusion," he quoted from memory. "The good of all is the goal of the many. What is best for all brings real happiness."

"So they tested you and told you the Army was going to be your career, whether you liked it or not?" Hickok concluded.

"You got it."

"Pitiful. Just pitiful. Sort of makes me feel sorry for you. So I'll tell you what I'm gonna do. I'm not gonna whack you upside the head like I planned," Hickok said.

"Thanks," the Technic said, manifestly relieved.

"But on the other hand . . ." Hickok crouched and began unlacing the guard's right boot.

"What are you doing?" the Technic asked.

"Hold onto your hat," Hickok said. He removed the boot, then the black sock underneath.

The guard perceived the gunman's intent. "But that sock is dirty!" he protested.

Hickok rose. "Say Ahhhhhh."

"But—"

Hickok raised the Commando in his left hand. "Say Ahhhh."

The Technic opened his mouth wide. "Ahhhh—"

Hickok jammed the sock into the guard's mouth, all the way in. He hastily removed the lace from the black boot, lopped the lace around the guard's face, and tied it tight, the knot situated in the middle of his open mouth to prevent the sock from being spit out. "I reckon that ought to hold you for a spell. Adios."

The gunman crossed to the door. If all went well, he'd find a flight of stairs lickety-split and vacate the Central Core before they realized he was missing. If he could find an unattended jeep or truck in the parking lot, he'd swipe it and make for the western gate.

Yes, sir.

Things were finally going his way.

It was beginning to look like busting out of Technic City would be a piece of cake!

Hickok opened the door and peeked around the jamb. The corridor, white tiles on the floor and walls, yellow panels on the ceiling, was deserted.

Like he said.

A piece of cake.

Hickok stepped into the corridor and closed the door behind him, just as a squad of four Technic soldiers, each armed with an automatic rifle, rounded a corner to his right!

13

The Zombies were walking nightmares.

Each Zombie was naked, its gray flesh pitted and filthy, with peculiar patches of greenish blisters randomly distributed over the body. Their eyes were reddish and unfocused, their mouths gaping maws of yellow, tapered teeth. Although they stood well over six feet in height, they were emaciated, their arms and legs resembling broomsticks.

Geronimo nearly gagged as a putrid stench filled the air. He backpedaled as more Zombies poured from the abandoned vehicles.

Something collided with his back.

Geronimo whirled, and found Blade alongside him. "What do we do?" he asked.

The Technics opened up with their Dakon IIs, their fragmentation bullets tearing into the hissing Zombies and ripping them apart, blowing their chests and skulls to shreds or tearing limbs from their bodies. Greenish fluid sprayed everywhere.

The Zombies never broke stride. Their grisly arms extended, their yellow fingernails glinting in the sunlight, their thin lips quivering in anticipation of their next meal, saliva pouring from their mouths, they advanced on the Technics, row after ravenous row, undeterred even when an arm or leg was shattered by a dumdum bullet. Nothing short of their chest or head exploding into smithereens stopped them.

The thup-thup-thup of the Dakon IIs mixed with the sibilant hissing of the Zombies.

Blade and Geronimo found themselves pressed against the SEAL's grill, the Technics in a ring in front of them, the horde of Zombies beyond.

"What do we do?" Geronimo said in Blade's left ear.

Blade was about to reply when iron-like fingers clasped his legs and he was brutally wrenched to the ground.

One of the Zombies had crawled under the SEAL and grabbed him!

Blade, prone on his back, saw the hunched-over creature about to bite into his left calf. He drew his right foot up and drove it down, catching the Zombie on the chin.

The Zombie blinked once, shook its head, and hissed as it clutched at the Warrior's groin.

Blade reached up, gripped the fender, and tried to haul his body from under the transport.

The Zombie snatched his belt buckle and started pulling the Warrior down, its mouth inches from his thighs.

Private Kimper suddenly appeared, stooped over to the left of Blade, his Dakon II pointed at the Zombie. He pulled the trigger, the Dakon II recoiling as the heavy slugs tore into the Zombie's face.

Blade was spattered by shredded flesh and green mush as the Zombie's head burst apart. A pulpy substance landed on his right cheek. He swiped at the gore and wriggled his shoulders past the fender. Stout hands clasped his armpits and helped draw him to his feet.

"Are you all right?" Geronimo inquired apprehensively.

Blade nodded.

The Technics had dispatched the Zombies hidden in the trucks and jeeps, and were concentrating their fire on the monstrosities flowing from the hole.

"See?" Captain Wargo cried gleefully. "What did I tell you? We can handle these freaks!"

So it appeared. The Zombies disgorging from the hole were becoming fewer and fewer; stacks of their dead covered the ground between the Technics and the underground entrance.

Four more Zombies charged from the dark hole, and were promptly decimated by fragmentation bullets.

Captain Wargo turned to Blade, smirking triumphantly. "These Zombie's aren't so tough! I can't understand why the other squads had so much trouble."

Blade was concerned by Wargo's overconfidence. Overconfidence bred carelessness. "We're just getting started," he reminded the officer. He pointed at the hole. "Who knows what it will be like down there?"

"Let's find out," Captain Wargo said. "Kimper, watch that scanner! Stay near me! Gatti, take the point!"

The oldest trooper nodded and moved to the edge of the black hole.

"Stay close to me," Wargo said to Blade and Geronimo.

"Do we get a gun?" Blade asked.

"I told you before. No," Wargo replied.

"After what just happened?" Blade said.

"No gun," Captain Wargo stressed. "Let's move out! Check your Com-Links! Don't stray!"

Gatti flicked on his helmet lamp and vanished over the brink.

Captain Wargo led the rest to the rim, sidestepping gory Zombie remains all the way. He crouched, turned on his helmet lamp, and stared downward.

Blade and Geronimo joined the officer, activating their own lamps.

Private Gatti was one flight of stairs below them, sweeping the tunnel with his head lamp. "Nothing," he said softly, the word crisply audible to those perched above him, amplfied by their Com-Links.

"Wait for us," Captain Wargo ordered. He stood and started down the stairs.

Blade frowned, exchanged glances with Geronimo, and followed Wargo, Geronimo on his heels and Kimper behind Geronimo.

"Scanner's clean," Kimper said, his eyes glued to the grid.

"Keep me posted," Wargo directed.

They reached the first landing and paused.

Blade's helmet lamp illuminated dusty, cobweb-covered walls and railings. The light from the lamps penetrated 20 feet into the inky gloom; beyond loomed a curtain of ominous black.

"We take the stairs to the bottom," Captain Wargo said. "The vault is near the stairs, so we should be in and out before the Zombies can regroup."

"I hope you're right," Geronimo said. "Those Zombies give me the creeps!"

"No talking!" Wargo snapped. "Move out!"

Gatti headed downward.

"Still nothing," Kimper informed them.

Captain Wargo waved his right arm and resumed their descent.

As they passed landing after landing, six in succession without encountering more Zombies, Blade wondered if Wargo was right after all. Had the Zombies called it quits? The cannibals had taken quite a beating up above; the Dakon IIs had destroyed them in droves. Maybe the Zombies weren't as fierce as their reputation alleged. But if that was the case, then what had happened to the earlier Technic squads?

"Trouble," Private Gatti said from a flight below.

"What is it?" Captain Wargo demanded.

"I think you should see this for yourself, sir," Gatti replied.

The party hastened to the next level.

"See what I mean?" Gatti asked.

"Oh, no!" one of the other troopers complained.

Captain Wargo stared at the problem, dazed.

Blade looked at Geronimo.

"Now what do we do?" Geronimo inquired.

The stairs came to an abrupt termination; jutting struts and bars were suspended in midair, and pieces of debris lined the landing; a heavy steel girder protruded from the north wall, hanging in space; beyond was a stygian void.

"What could have caused this?" Captain Wargo questioned.

"Maybe a little thing like a nuclear war," Geronimo

remarked.

"Do we turn back?" Blade queried the Technic officer.

Captain Wargo shook his head. "No, we don't," he declared obstinately. "The stairs may still be intact farther down."

"And how do we reach them?" Blade asked.

Captain Wargo slowly pivoted, his helmet light playing over the stairs and the surrounding walls. "There must be . . ." He pointed at the west wall. "Look! A door! I knew there'd be one."

"Just our luck," Geronimo groused.

The door was ajar several inches. A faded sign read "STAIRWELL EXIT LEVEL #8."

"Gatti. Point," Captain Wargo directed.

Private Gatti hesitated for a moment, then cautiously pushed the door open. "There's a hallway here," he announced.

"Let's go!" Captain Wargo barked.

Blade detected a visible reluctance in the Technic soldiers. Their pensive features accurately reflected their growing apprehension. And who could blame them? The lower they descended, the more certain they were to encounter more Zombies. He followed Wargo through the doorway, stepping over a skeleton on the floor, a skeleton wearing a dust-covered camouflage helmet. "One of yours?" he asked Wargo.

"Must be," Captain Wargo answered. "I don't see his dog tags, but the helmet is definitely ours."

"The bones were picked clean," Geronimo observed.

"And if you let the Zombies catch you," Captain Wargo said, "the same fate will befall you."

"Do you always look at the cheery side of life?" Geronimo rejoined.

"Captain!" Private Gatti stated from up ahead.

"What is it?" Wargo asked.

"A junction," Gatti replied.

"On our way," Captain Wargo said.

They found Gatti 20 yards further ahead, shielded by the corner of a wall at the junction of two corridors.

"Scanner?" Captain Wargo declared.

Private Kimper studied his pulse scanner. "Faint readings, sir. Almost undetectable. Nothing close."

Wargo pondered for a minute. "Take that branch," he commanded Gatti, indicating the corridor to the left.

The point man took off.

"How do you know which one to take?" Blade inquired.

"I don't," Captain Wargo responded.

They slowly moved down the hallway, their helmets constantly becoming entangled in cobwebs, their feet kicking up puffs of dust with every step.

"May I make a comment?" Geronimo said.

"What is it?" Captain Wargo asked.

"Do you see all these cobwebs we keep bumping into?" Geronimo mentioned.

"Yeah. What about them?"

"So where are all the spiders?" Geronimo commented. "Hundreds of spiderwebs and not one spider. Doesn't that strike you as strange?"

"I never gave it much thought," Wargo admitted.

"Maybe the Zombies eat the spiders," Blade said.

"Yuck," Geronimo stated. "You could be right. The Zombies must have some sort of dietary staple if they're surviving in large numbers. Spiders would be as nutritious as anything else."

A disturbing speculation registered in Blade's mind. "Say, Wargo."

"What?"

"How many Zombies are there in New York City?" Blade inquired.

"I'm not sure," Captain Wargo replied. "Our experts estimate in the neighborhood of four or five thousand. Why?"

"Is that all?"

"Isn't that enough?" Wargo retorted.

"You're missing my point," Blade said. "Only four or five thousand. Why aren't there more of them?"

"How the hell should I know?" Wargo said stiffly. "Why don't you ask the next one you run into?"

"What is your point?" Geronimo wanted to know.

"The Zombies have been here since the Big Blast,

right?'' Blade answered. "They've had over a century in which to breed. So why aren't there more of them? Only four thousand in one hundred years doesn't seem like much."

"Maybe they have a hard time getting it up," Captain Wargo said.

"Or perhaps there is something else down here," Blade noted. "Something eating the Zombies and keeping their population down."

"Eating the Zombies?" Captain Wargo reiterated in disbelief. "What could possibly do that?"

"Let's hope we don't have to find out," Blade declared.

"Captain Wargo!" It was Gatti.

"What is it?" Captain Wargo answered.

"I've found a hole in the floor," Gatti informed his superior.

"Stay put," Wargo ordered.

They reached the point man within a minute, squatting at the rim of a jagged opening in the corridor floor.

"It leads to the floor below," Private Gatti told them.

Captain Wargo crouched and peered through the hole. The floor of another corridor was 12 feet below. "We go down one at a time," he instructed them. "Hang by the arms and drop. You won't have more than six feet or so to fall. Gatti, you first."

Private Gatti slung his Dakon II over his right shoulder and slid his legs over the edge of the hole.

Captain Wargo leaned down so he could see the hallway below. "Go ahead. I'll cover you."

Gatti eased from sight and released his grip. He landed unsteadily, but righted himself instantly, quickly unslinging his Dakon II.

"Cover us," Wargo told Gatti. He motioned for the rest to take their turn.

Private Kimper was the next to drop, then Blade and Geronimo. While the two Warriors waited for Wargo and the last soldier to reach the lower level, Blade tapped Geronimo's right shoulder and moved to one side.

Blade turned off his Com-Link, and Geronimo did the same. "We're going to make a break for it," Blade whispered. "The first chance we get."

"What about the Genesis Seeds?" Geronimo said softly.

"I doubt they even exist," Blade murmured. "This whole affair has been fishy from the start."

"Just give the signal," Geronimo stated.

"There will be no signal!" Captain Wargo said sharply, advancing on the Warriors with his Dakon II leveled. "How stupid can you be? Did you think by deactivating your Com-Links I couldn't hear your conversation? You forgot the amplifier on the right side of our helmet. I could hear you fart at one hundred yards!"

"I wish I had some beans," Geronimo quipped.

"If you attempt to escape," Captain Wargo warned them, "we will shoot to kill. We'd prefer to take you back to Technic City with us. But the bottom line, gentlemen, is this: you *are* expendable."

"Now you tell us," Blade said sarcastically.

"Let's move out!" Captain Wargo said.

Gatti moved along the inky corridor until his lamp was lost to view.

Captain Wargo shoved Blade with the barrel of his Dakon. "You two will stay in front of us. Move!"

Blade and Geronimo started forward.

"And switch on your damn Com-Links!" Captain Wargo ordered.

As Blade depressed the correct button, a shrill voice filled his helmet.

"Captain!" Private Kimper needlessly shouted. "Readings, sir!"

"How many?"

"Off the scale! Dozens!"

"At what range?"

"They're on the floor above us!" Kimper answered. "And they're heading for the hole we just came through!"

"On the double!" Wargo instructed them.

They began jogging after the point man.

Even as Gatti's terrified scream blasted their ears.

14

Hickok had seen those automatic rifles before: once at the Home when Plato had displayed the weapon appropriated from the spy slain by the Moles, and again at the fence bordering Technic City in the hands of the guards. He recognized a distinctly lethal armament when he saw one, and finding himself confronted by four troopers ten feet away, each with one of the rifles, he automatically reacted as his years of arduous training and experience dictated: he swept up the Commando and squeezed the trigger.

The corridor rocked to the booming of the Commando, the four soldiers taken unaware by the onslaught, their bodies jerking and writhing as they absorbed the large-caliber slugs. Only one of them uttered a sound, a gurgling screech, as he toppled to the tiled floor.

Time to make tracks!

Hickok whirled and ran, his speed impeded by the combined weight of the guns he was carrying. He saw an elevator ahead and paused, mentally debating. The elevator could be rigged, just like the one before. But it might take a minute or so for more troopers to arrive, and by then he could be far away. Besides, how would they know *he* was using the elevator? It could be any Technic.

Go for it!

The gunman sprinted to the elevator and pressed the down button. He didn't know exactly where he was in the Central Core, but odds were he was on one of the higher floors. How many did the Central Core have? Ten, wasn't it?

The elevator arrived with a loud ping and the doors hissed open.

Hickok ducked inside and examined the control panel. A circular button with an 8 imprinted on it was lit up. That must mean he was on the eighth floor! He stabbed another button, the down button, the one with an arrow pointing straight down, and the elevator doors closed.

So far, so good.

Hickok watched the lights flicker, apprehensive, praying he could reach ground level before the Technics realized he was making a bid for freedom.

The button for the sixth floor came on.

"Can't you go any faster?" Hickok asked aloud, and kicked the door. Why was the blamed contraption dropping so slowly? Was this typical of an elevator? A mare could deliver a foal in the time it was taking the blasted elevator to reach the ground!

The elevator had reached the fourth floor.

"Hurry it up!" Hickok said.

The third floor.

Somewhere in the distance a klaxon wailed.

They were on to him! Someone had sounded the alarm!

Second floor.

Hickok tensed, clutching the Commando. He must ignore the odds against him. So what if he was alone and outnumbered millions to one? So what if the entire Technic Army and Police Force would be after him? He was a Warrior, and Warriors never quit. Never. Ever.

The elevator reached the ground floor and the doors whisked open.

The lobby was crammed with people: soldiers, police in their blue uniforms, government officials, and civilians. Waiting outside the elevator was a Technic officer and one other, a man in a brown uniform with gray hair, blue eyes, and a hefty build. The gunman recognized him as the man from the interrogation room, the one who'd showed up with the Minister!

"Howdy! Guess who?" Hickok said.

The Technic officer was completely confounded, frozen, but the man in brown reacted; his blue eyes widened fearfully and his mouth sagged. "You!" he exclaimed.

"Bingo! You get the prize!" Hickok declared, and fired.

The Commando cut them in two, their chests exploding in a spray of crimson flesh.

Hickok burst from the elevator, heading for the gold doors visible on the other side of the spacious lobby.

A Technic policeman loomed ahead, blocking the gunman's path, clawing at an automatic pistol in the holster on his left hip.

Hickok cut loose, ripping the Technic from his crotch to his sternum.

A woman nearby was screaming her lungs out.

Another woman, with a young girl at her side, stood five yards in front of the racing Warrior, gaping.

Blasted bystanders!

Hickok skirted the pair, weaving and twisting as he ran, the crowd parting to allow his passage.

But not all of them.

Another Technic policeman was standing before the gold doors, pistol in his right hand.

Hickok leaped behind a potted fern as the policeman fired. A high-pitched shriek added to the general din. Hickok rolled to the left, and as he did he saw the little girl he'd bypassed falling to the floor with a hole in her forehead.

The rotten bastard!

Hickok came up on his knees, the Commando pressed to his right shoulder, and pulled the trigger.

The Technic in front of the gold doors was slammed backward by the impact, crunching into the doors and slipping to the floor, leaving a red swath in his wake.

Hickok sprinted to the doors. He paused, kicking the dead Technic in the face, crushing his nose. "I can't abide a lousy shot!" he growled, and pushed on the nearest door.

Nothing happened.

What the blazes! Hickok tried one more time with the same result. What the heck was going on? Why wouldn't the door open? He suddenly recalled Wargo using a button to the left of the doors when they entered the Central Core.

There!

Hickok was to the bank of buttons in an instant.

They weren't marked!

The gunman stabbed the first button on the right.

The doors remained closed.

Blast!

A bullet whined off the doors not six inches away.

Hickok punched the button on the far left.

The gold doors slid open.

Move it! his mind thundered, as he scurried outside. The doors slid closed again as he spun, the Commando bucking, the bullets striking the outside button bank and destroying it in a shower of plastic, metal, and fiery sparks.

Let 'em try and get those doors open now!

Hickok crouched and turned to face the parking lot, shocked by the sight he beheld.

Two dozen Technic police were lined up 15 yards away, at attention, their stunned faces focused on the Warrior. Between the formation of police and the gunman was a solitary jeep, and sitting in the rear of the topless vehicle, his features frozen in horrified shock, evidently paralyzed by the abrupt advent of the Warrior, was the Minister.

For the space of a heartbeat it was as if the tableau were in suspended animation. Hickok was hardly aware of a green truck parked alongside the yellow curb not ten feet to his right, or the squad of Technic commandos 40 yards off and approaching on the run. All he saw, the only object of his concentration, the sum total of his world, was the man responsible for subjecting him to the most acute humiliation he'd ever felt, the callous, egotistical tyrant who'd degraded him, who'd caused him to lose face, as Rikki would say, who'd made him eat crow and reveled in the gunman's debasement: the Minister.

For the space of a heartbeat no one moved.

And then the Minister opened his mouth to shout orders to his assembled men, his personal guard, and all hell broke loose.

Hickok fired, the Commando chattering, and the Minister's eyes and nose dissolved as his face was torn to gruesome shreds.

The Technic police went for their weapons.

The Technic commandos were now 30 yards distant.

Hickok raced toward the parked truck, bent over, presenting as difficult a target as possible, shooting as he ran.

Three of the Technic police hit the pavement, blood gushing from their riddled uniforms.

Hickok reached the truck with bullets chipping at the sidewalk and striking the Central Core. He passed a wide picture window and saw a female civilian on the other side, screaming in terror at the demise of the Minister. At least, he assumed she was screaming. Her mouth was open but no sound was audible.

How could this be?

The gunman could scarcely afford a moment's idle speculation. A trooper appeared around the tailgate of the truck, one of those fancy automatic rifles in his hands.

Hickok dived for the sidewalk as the soldier fired. His knees and elbows were lanced by excruciating agony, pain he ingored as he aimed the Commando and squeezed the trigger.

A distinct click greeted his efforts.

The Commando was empty!

There was no time to reload! Hickok rolled to his left, nearer the truck, his right hand flashing to his holster and the right Colt clearing leather even as the trooper sent a few rounds into the sidewalk to the gunman's right, concrete chips flying in every direction. The Warrior fired as the commando sighted for another shot, fired as the commando staggered backward with a hole where his left eye had been, and fired as the commando crashed to the ground with both eyes gone.

Hickok surged erect, his balance unsteady because of all the extra weapons he was carrying, and he lunged for the only available cover, the cab of the green truck.

A red dot appeared on the door of the truck, inches from his left hand.

A red dot?

The Commando clasped between his thumb and first finger, the gunman grasped at the truck handle as the door was hit, flying metal shards zinging every which way. A sharp piece burned a furrow in his left cheek. He instinctively ducked and whirled, cocking the Python.

A soldier was standing near the jammed gold doors, rifle to his shoulder.

Where the blazes had he come from?

Hickok snapped a shot as a red dot materialized on his chest, and the trooper toppled backwards.

Move!

Hickok wrenched the door open as a female member of the Technic police rounded the front fender with her pistol already out. He fired and she stumbled and crashed into the truck, her pistol clattering on the pavement.

This was no place for Momma Hickok's pride and joy!

The gunman scrambled into the truck, letting the Commando drop to the floor, his anxious gaze roving over the dashboard and locking on a set of keys, one of which was already inserted to the right of the steering column.

Eureka!

Hickok grabbed the keys as the windshield was splintered by a fusillade of gunfire.

The Technics were pouring everything they had at the cab.

Hunched over behind the steering wheel, the gunman turned the key and pumped the accelerator. He recollected the last time he'd driven a truck, from Wyoming to Minnesota, and he tried to remember the proper procedure. He recalled the ignition and the gas pedal, but overlooked one crucial component.

The clutch.

Hickok was taken unawares when the truck abruptly
jerked forward. Something thudded against the grill. A
bullet obliterated the rearview mirror. The truck lurched
ahead like a wobbly drunk, starting forward and
abruptly stopping, again and again, tossing him against
the steering wheel.

What the dickens was wrong?

A bullet penetrated the windshield and thudded into
the seat beside him.

Hickok glanced at the floor and spotted the third
pedal. The first was the gas pedal. And the one on the
left was the brake. But what was the other one?

A slug creased his right shoulder, breaking the skin.

The police and commandos were deploying in a
circle, enclosing the vehicle.

The clutch! That was it! Hickok tramped on the
clutch, grinding the gears as he shifted from first to
second and the truck roared across the parking lot. He
kept his head below the dash as round after round
ripped into the vehicle. The clamor was incredible:
metal whining and glass breaking and people shouting
and the windshield dissolving in a shower of glass.

There was another pronounced thud from the front
of the truck.

Hickok sat up to get his bearings. He was going due
south, the truck heading toward a row of parked trikes.

Not ten feet ahead was a solitary commando, a
woman, down on one knee, shooting at the truck engine
in an attempt to disable it.

Hickok floored the accelerator and the truck
lumbered forward. He saw the commando's mouth
open and her petrified eyes widen an instant before
there was a crushing thump and the truck bounced as if
the wheels had encountered a bump.

The passenger-side window blew apart.

Hickok frantically turned the steering wheel, but too
late. The vehicle slewed to the right, its rear end
smashing into the row of trikes and bowling them over.
He spun the wheel again, thundering down an aisle
between the trikes.

A jeep containing three Technic police was zooming

toward him.

Hickok wasn't about to stop. To stop was certain death. The Technics would be on him in a second. He intended to get as far as possible from the Central Core as quickly as possible, and no one or nothing was going to stand in his way.

Especially not one measly jeep!

Hickok's grip on the steering wheel tightened as the truck closed on the jeep. He could see a determined expression on the policeman driving. Obviously, the Technic wasn't about to surrender the right of way.

Thirty feet separated them.

Hickok hunched over the steering wheel and braced for the collision.

Twenty feet.

Would the truck survive the crash? It was a big vehicle, the green trailer it was hauling adding to its bulk, but a wreck at high speed would undoubtedly cripple the motor.

Ten feet.

Hickok held his breath as the two vehicles sped at one another. He flinched in expectation of the impact, and that's when the jeep unexpectedly altered course, swerving to the left and ramming into some trikes.

He'd done it!

Elated, Hickok didn't perceive the danger he posed to the mass of trikes occupying the avenue beyond the parking lot until the truck had jumped a curb and slammed into their midst. Chaos resulted. Screams and shrieks rent the air; battered bodies were flying everywhere; trikes and travelers alike were squashed beneath the huge truck tires, trikes crunching and their drivers and occupants being mashed to a flattened pulp; and random gunshots from the Technic police and the soldiers punctuated the general din.

Blast!

Hickok slammed on the brakes and the truck ground to a rocky halt, the motor idling. He saw dozens of trikes and four-wheelers crash as they wildly endeavored to avoid the melee.

Cries of torment and anguish were voiced by the

injured and dying.

Dear Spirit! What had he done? The gunman vaulted
from the cab, landing next to a demolished trike with an
elderly man prone over the handlebars. Hickok gaped at
the man's vacant brown eyes, appalled by the needless
deaths and misery he'd inadvertently caused. To his left
was a young boy, lying in a pool of blood. He was
shocked to his soul, and the gunman's senses swirled.

He'd killed innocent children!

Children!

A blast from a pistol brought Hickok back to reality.
He saw one of the Technic police sighting for a second
shot, and whipped his right Colt clear and fired.

The policeman pitched to the tarmac.

Hickok turned, seeking a way out. Six feet away was
a lone man seated in an idling four-wheeler, apparently
stunned by the destruction, gaping at the Warrior.

Just what he needed!

Hickok jogged to the four-wheeler and shoved the
Python barrel into the driver's chest. "Move out!" He
climbed into the four-wheeler beside the driver.
"Move!"

The driver, a man of 40 with a bald pate and jowly
jaws, his green eyes fearfully locked on the Colt,
nodded. "Yes, sir!"

"Go!" Hickok goaded him, glancing over his
shoulder. The police and soldiers in the parking lot were
prevented from reaching him by the gigantic traffic jam
blocking the avenue.

The driver of the four-wheeler pulled out, slowly
wending his way through the maze of trikes and other
vehicles. "Which way?" he asked.

Hickok alertly scanned the avenue for threatening
soldiers or Technic police, but the highway ahead was
filled with civilians. Very few of them had seen him
jump from the truck, but one or two glared at him as he
passed.

"Which way?" the driver nervously queried.

"Just keep going," Hickok told him.

"Yes, sir."

The four-wheeler reached an impasse, thwarted by a

veritable wall of vehicles halted by the wreckage and the truck.

"We can't go any further," the driver wailed.

"Yes we can," Hickok said, wagging the Python to the right. "Use the sidewalk. It's not as crowded."

"But that's illegal!" the driver objected.

Hickok rapped the driver on the temple with the Colt. "Take your pick. A spell in the calaboose or a bullet in the brain?"

"Calaboose?"

"The hoosegow," Hickok explained.

"Hoosegow?" the driver repeated, even more confused.

"The jail, dummy!" Hickok snapped.

The driver gingerly wheeled the four-wheeler onto the sidewalk. Shouts and oaths greeted this unprecedented action, but the civilians moved aside at the sight of the blond man in the strange buckskins carrying an arsenal.

Hickok glanced back at the carnage he'd caused. He remembered that little boy, dead, awash in crimson, and he shuddered. He thought of his precious Ringo, and he could vividly imagine the grief the parents of the boy would feel when—

Wait a minute!

That boy didn't have any parents! Not natural ones anyhow. Would his surrogate parents feel the same way a natural parent would?

"What's your name?" Hickok demanded of the driver.

Pale as the proverbial ghost, the heavyset man looked at the gunfighter. "Spencer."

"Do you love your parents?" Hickok asked.

If complete consternation was comical, then the driver was hilarious. But Hickok didn't feel much like laughing.

"My parents?" Spencer said. "You want to know about my parents?"

"Yeah. I know you folks in Technic City ain't raised by your true mom and dad," Hickok stated. "But what about the people who do rear you? Do you love them?"

"Of course not," Spencer responded while circumventing a squat blue box in the middle of the sidewalk marked with the word "MAIL." "You must not be from Technic City if you can ask a stupid question like that. . . ." Spencer's voice trailed off as the enormity of his own idiocy sank home. He'd called this crazy man stupid! What would the lunatic do?

Hickok disregarded the insult. "If you don't love 'em, how do you feel about them?"

"They raise us," Spencer replied. "That's it. Why should we feel anything? Emotion is for simpletons."

The lunatic, amazingly, grinned. "Thanks. I needed that."

Spencer, perplexed, shook his head. "I don't get it."

Hickok waved the Colt. "No. But you will if you don't quit flappin' your gums and pick up speed."

"I'm going as fast as I can," Spencer protested.

Hickok rammed the Python into Spencer's ribs.

The four-wheeler increased its speed.

15

The three soldiers and the pair of Warriors reached the end of the corridor and came to an abrupt stop.

The hallway was a dead end.

"The Zombies are on our level!" Private Kimper shouted, the pulse scanner held next to his face.

"We're trapped!" Captain Wargo exclaimed.

Blade surveyed the corridor. There was no sign of Gatti. Where was he?

"Where's Gatti?" Wargo demanded.

Blade ran, retracing their steps. He reached an open doorway on the right and peered inside, his helmet lamp revealing the interior. It was a room, perhaps 10 feet by 12, littered with the inevitable cobwebs, dust, and an antiquated wooden chair with two legs missing lying on the left side near the wall. Blade was about to pull away, when his lamp fell on the rear wall. Or what had once been the rear wall. Because now a large hole beckoned, providing access to an adjoining chamber. "This way!" Blade yelled, and took off, Geronimo dogging his heels.

The Warriors hastened through the opening and discovered another room exactly like the first. But instead of a dilapidated chair the chamber contained some newer additions: Private Gatti's blood-soaked helmet and Dakon II on the floor in the middle of the room.

Blade scooped up the weapon and checked the digital readout. A full magazine!

"I could use one of those," Geronimo mentioned as the trio of troopers entered the room.

"Where the hell did you get that?" Captain Wargo

barked, pointing his Dakon II at Blade.

Blade returned the compliment. "It was Gatti's. There's no sign of him."

"Hand it over!" Wargo commanded.

"No way."

Captain Wargo's features contorted into a furious mask. "When I give an order—"

"The Zombies!" Private Kimper interrupted. "Ten yards and closing fast!"

The five men spread out, facing the way they came, their rifles trained on the opening.

Blade looked over his left shoulder. There was a doorway five feet away, lacking a door. Good. They had a way to escape if the Zombies—

Two Zombies rushed into the room, hissing, their arms extended. A barrage of fragmentation bullets ruptured their chests and heads and they collapsed, spewing green fluid.

"Hold them!" Captain Wargo yelled.

Four more Zombies were framed in the opening, and a hail of bullets dropped them on the spot.

Blade frowned. This was easy. Too easy. Almost as if it was a trap. But that would mean the Zombies were behind them—

"Look out!" Geronimo shouted in warning.

Blade crouched and whirled, the Dakon II at hip level, and the movement saved his life. Zombies were pouring in the doorway, and one of them had clawed at the Warrior's neck even as he ducked. Blade let the mutation have it, blowing its face off.

The Technics were firing with total abandon, shooting as quickly as Zombies appeared at the opening or the doorway.

Geronimo, unarmed and feeling utterly helpless, stayed close to Blade.

The Warriors and Technics held their own for a while, downing Zombies until bodies were stacked on both sides of the room.

But then the tide turned.

Blade felt something strike his left shoulder, then his back, and he glanced up at the ceiling in time to see a slavering Zombie plummet through a narrow aperture. "They're above us!" he cried.

Private Kimper was standing three feet from Blade, and he turned to confront this new menace.

Too late.

The Zombie landed between the two men, and with an agility belied by its emaciated appearance, it coiled and pounced, hurtling at Private Kimper, brushing the Technic's Dakon II aside, and fastening its fingers in his throat.

Blade held his fire, concerned he would hit Kimper.

Kimper screamed as he was knocked to the floor, ineffectively flailing at the Zombie with his fists.

Blade closed in and hammered his stock onto the Zombie's head. Once. Twice. Three times, and the Zombie released Kimper and rose, its eyes gleaming savagely. Blade shot it at point-blank range, and his arms and face were pelted with more green gore.

Kimper, gagging, stumbled to his feet and grabbed for his Dakon II.

Three Zombies came through the doorway, and one of them reached Kimper in one mighty bound. The Technic was lifted from his feet and his head was brutally wrenched to the right.

Blade heard the snap of Kimper's vertebra even as he shot the Zombie in the forehead.

Geronimo saw his opportunity. He darted forward and grasped Kimper's Dakon II, then spun, firing, decimating the other two Zombies.

The attack unexpectedly ceased. Dust floated in the air. A preternatural quiet gripped the underground tunnels.

"Blade!" someone gasped.

Blade turned.

Captain Wargo was on his back, a dead Zombie straddling his legs. Four more of the mutations lay near his boots. The Technic was staring at the giant Warrior with a resigned expression, a fatalistic acceptance of his impending demise. "I blew it," he said softly.

Wargo's left arm was gone, missing, severed from his body, no doubt taken by a Zombie intent on consuming the limb as a tasty snack.

"Where's the last commando?" Geronimo asked Blade.

The two Warriors were the only ones standing.

Blade moved to Wargo and knelt next to the officer. He cradled Wargo's head in his left hand, watching the blood pump from the ragged stump where once the left arm had been.

"I've bought it," Wargo stated in a strained whisper.

"We'll get you out of here," Blade told him. "I'll carry you."

Wargo's brow furrowed. "You'd do that for me? After what I've done? After the way I've treated you?"

Blade glanced at the Zombie on Wargo's legs. "We can't let them have you."

Wargo moaned and closed his eyes. When he opened them again, they were rimmed with tears. "I want you to know I was only following orders."

Is that any excuse? Blade wanted to retort. Instead, he smiled and nodded. "I know."

Captain Wargo shuddered. "I'm so cold." He groaned. "I wish . . . I wish. . . ." His head sagged and his eyes shut again.

Geronimo was keeping them covered. "What are we going to do?" he inquired. "Get out of here, I hope."

"We're going after the Genesis Seeds," Blade said.

"But why?" Geronimo rejoined. "You said you doubted they even exist."

"But if they do," Blade explained, "we owe it to our Family, to the entire Civilized Zone, to do our best to retrieve them."

Captain Wargo trembled and coughed, blood appearing at the corners of his mouth. He opened his eyes, which looked haunted. "Don't," he croaked.

Blade leaned closer. "Don't what?"

"Don't go after the seeds." Wargo coughed some more. "They don't exist."

"Then why did your Minister go to so much trouble?" Blade asked. "Why lure us to Technic City and force us to come here? Why?"

"The mind-control gas," Captain Wargo disclosed as

a crimson streak gushed from his right nostril.

Blade and Geronimo exchanged astonished looks.

"The gas was developed by the Institute of Advanced Technology for the Defense Department at the outset of World War Three," Captain Wargo elaborated painfully, wheezing between words. "They planned to use it on the Soviets, but New York was hit before they could transfer the canisters of the gas from here to a military installation." He paused, gathering his breath. "The New York branch wired the Chicago branch of the shipment's readiness minutes before New York was hit. The canisters have been in the underground vault since."

"What does this gas do?" Blade probed.

"Makes a person susceptible to any command they're given," Captain Wargo said. "The Minister . . . intends to make more of it. Use it on the Freedom Federation and the Soviets."

"He wants to conquer the world," Blade observed.

"For the greater glory of the Technics," Wargo stated. "Needs samples to duplicate, like your SEAL."

Blade placed his right hand on Wargo's chest. "The SEAL? What does the SEAL have to do with it?"

Wargo was slipping fast. "Make . . . machines . . . tanks . . . from the same substance . . ."

"Why are you telling us this?" Geronimo asked.

Wargo's eyes fluttered. "Least I could do." His eyes widened, and for a moment he was mentally alert and in full possession of his faculties. He stared at Blade and, unbelievably, laughed, a hard, brittle tittering. "Besides . . . doesn't matter anymore . . . does it?" His body straightened and fluttered, he gasped once, and died.

"I can't say as I'll miss him," Geronimo remarked.

"Me neither," Blade confessed. "But we owe him for telling us about the mind-control gas."

"So what do we do now?" Geronimo questioned.

Blade stood. "We get out of here."

"*Now* you're talking!"

"Go through Kimper's clothes and gear," Blade directed. "We'll need all the spare magazines and ammunition for these Dakon IIs we can find."

"Got you."

The two Warriors searched Wargo and Kimper and found a total of six spare magazines and four boxes of ammunition.

"We'll each take three magazines and two boxes," Blade told Geronimo as he crammed one of the magazines into his right front pocket. He loaded his pockets, then crossed to Private Kimper and crouched next to his body.

"What are you doing?" Geronimo asked.

Blade unfastened the pulse scanner from Kimper's right wrist. "It looks like this gizmo is still on," he said. The screen contained a network of black lines.

"Do you know how to read it?" Geronimo queried hopefully.

"Not really," Blade admitted. "But . . ." He paused. Small, white blips had sprouted on the screen along its outer edge. They were swiftly converging toward the center. "I think company is coming."

"Zombies?"

"Who else?" Blade rose and hurried to the large hole in the wall.

Geronimo followed. "We don't want a canister as a keepsake?"

"The stairs may well be intact on the lower levels," Blade said, "but we're not going to bother finding out. We're going up. And fast."

"I like a man who knows his mind."

They reached the corridor and raced back the way they'd came. Blade saw additional white blips appear on the pulse scanner. If he was reading the thing right, the Zombies were moving toward the room they'd just vacated. And there didn't seem to be any blips corresponding to the hallway they were in. If he was correct, they'd reach the hole allowing access to the level above them without being attacked.

They did.

"How are we going to get up there?" Geronimo asked as his helmet lamp swept the opening 12 feet overhead.

"Easily," Blade said, slinging his Dakon II over his

right shoulder.

"Oh? Are we going to fly?" Geronimo quipped, studying the hole.

"One of us is," Blade responded. Before Geronimo quite knew what had happened, Blade stepped behind his companion, grabbing Geronimo by the back of his belt and the fabric of his green shirt at the nape of his neck.

"Hey! What are you doing?" Geronimo demanded.

"Relax and enjoy the trip," Blade told him. His bulging arms lifted Geronimo and swung his friend down and up, twice in fast succession, gathering speed with each swing. "Get set," he advised.

Geronimo, marveling at Blade's prodigious strength, clasped his Dakon II and grinned.

A third time Blade swung his fellow Warrior, and then he heaved and released his grip.

Geronimo was propelled through the opening, landing on his stomach with his legs suspended from the hole. He used his elbows to crawl to his feet, then looked down at Blade. "And how are you going to make it?"

Blade gauged the distance. "It's too high to jump."

"You'd best hurry," Geronimo cautioned him.

Blade glanced at the pulse scanner. "I agree." White blips were moving his way. He unslung the Dakon II.

"I've got an idea," Geronimo said.

"Make it fast," Blade stated. The blips were much closer.

Geronimo placed his Dakon II on the floor and removed his shirt. "Here!" He held onto one sleeve and dropped the shirt through the hole.

Blade scanned the corridor behind him, then looked at the shirt. The other sleeve was dangling about nine feet over his head. An easy jump for one of his enormous stature.

Footsteps pounded in the hallway to his rear.

Blade whirled, his helmet light illuminating four hissing Zombies closing in, four more of the detestable deviates with a craving for healthy human flesh. Blade blasted them with the Dakon.

The Zombies danced spasmodically as they were struck, then fell.

More blips filled the pulse scanner. Blade reslung the Dakon, crouched, and leaped, his arms stretched to their limit, his fingers clamping on the shirt and holding fast. "Pull!"

Geronimo was nearly upended. The weight was almost too much for his arms to bear. Crouched at the rim, he sagged, about to pitch forward, but caught himself in the nick of time. He gritted his teeth as his arms strained to raise Blade a couple of feet, hoping the shirt would hold. The Family Weavers had constructed his clothing, and their garments were renowned for their durability. But Blade felt as if he weighed a ton!

"Hurry!" Blade prompted him.

Every muscle on Geronimo's stocky body quivered as he rose an inch, then several more.

Swaying below the hole, Blade waited, his body taut. If Geronimo could get him close enough to the rim . . .

Something suddenly encircled the Warrior's legs.

Blade looked down, dumbfounded to see a Zombie clinging to his ankles. The creature's teeth were exposed as it snarled and snapped at his leg, tearing into his fatigue pants but missing the skin underneath.

Geronimo felt the shirt wrench to one side, and he glanced down.

Blade twisted, striving to extricate his legs, hoping the Zombie would not succeed in taking a chunk out of him. An insane idea occurred to him, a desperate maneuver to disentangle his legs and reach the level above. He balled his right fist and lashed downward, his left hand bearing the brunt of his massive weight, and crashed his fist into the Zombie's hairless skull.

Staggered by the blow, the Zombie released its grip and glared up at its dinner.

Which was exactly what Blade wanted.

The giant Warrior drew his legs up to his chest, then lashed his feet down, deliberately driving his boots onto the Zombie's slim shoulders. In the instant his soles made contact, Blade pushed upward, using the Zombie as a springboard, uncoiling and springing through the hole in the floor to sprawl beside Geronimo.

Geronimo tumbled backwards, landing on his posterior. He yanked on his shirt and smiled at Blade. "What? No full gainer?"

"Let's go!" Blade said, rising.

Geronimo hastily donned his shirt, and they fled, retracing their route, following the trail of their footprints in the dust. They arrived at the door leading to the stairs and paused, breathing heavily, leaning on the walls.

"Didn't we leave this door open?" Geronimo asked.

Blade couldn't recall. He shrugged and tugged on the door, grateful it flew open so readily.

Until he saw what lurked on the other side.

The landing was jammed with Zombies and the stairs were packed with more.

"They were waiting for us!" Geronimo cried.

Blade leveled the Dakon II as the front row started toward them. They were overwhelmingly outnumbered, and outrunning the monstrosities would be impossible at this close range. He could only hope to sell his life dearly, and he would have done so had not a very peculiar event transpired.

One of the Zombies uttered a weird, gurgling noise, and the effect on the assembled mutations was instantaneous and bewildering. They abruptly ran off, the majority heading up the stairs in a confused panic, while a dozen or so bolted past a startled pair of Warriors flattened against the corridor walls.

"What was that all about?" Geronimo nervously inquired after the last Zombie was lost to view.

"Beats me," Blade said. "But whatever it was, I like it! Let's get to the SEAL."

They walked through the doorway to the landing.

Geronimo bent his neck, craning skyward. "I can see the top!" he exclaimed. "And there isn't a Zombie in sight!"

"Good riddance," Blade commented. Now nothing would stop them.

Or so he thought.

There was a rumbling roar from directly below, and

the very tunnel shook, the stairs vibrating and the landing the Warriors occupied shimmying.

Blade, nearest the railing, leaned over the edge for an unobstructed view of the vertical shaft. The . . . thing . . . his helmet lamp revealed caused the short hairs on the back of his neck to rise, his skin tingling, and he unconsciously stepped away from the railing, staggered.

"What is it?" Geronimo asked, moving toward the railing.

Blade grabbed his friend by the shoulder and shoved, sending Geronimo in the direction of the steps. "Go!" he shouted, forgetting Geronimo could hear the slightest sound in his helmet earphone.

"But . . ." Geronimo protested, his left foot on the bottom step.

"*Go!*" Blade yelled.

Geronimo, disturbed and alarmed, took the stairs two at a bound. "Come on!" he urged Blade.

But Blade had other ideas. He would delay the . . . thing . . . until Geronimo reached safety. It was the only way one of them would get out alive. He stepped to the railing and gazed downward.

Just as the thing gave another deafening roar and rushed toward the landing.

16

"Turn in there," Hickok directed.

Spencer immediately complied, pulling the four-wheeler into a parking lot.

Hickok scanned the lot, noting a lot of civilians and trikes and other vehicles, but the Technic police weren't in evidence.

Good.

"Pull into that parking space," Hickok instructed the Technic.

Spencer parked between two other four-wheelers, one of them red, the other brown like his. "What now?"

"We sit here," Hickok said. He needed time to think. They were about three miles from the Central Core. Dozens of Technic police and military vehicles had passed them along the way, but the security forces were all headed toward the Core. Most likely, the Technics believed he was still in the vicinity of the Core. And they undoubtedly had their hands full cleaning up the mess he'd created with the truck. Not to mention the reaction the Minister's death would create, the turmoil it would stir up.

"How long?" Spencer inquired.

Hickok glared. "Until I say otherwise. Got it?"

"Yes, sir," Spencer said feebly.

"Turn the other way," Hickok instructed him. "Count the trikes for a spell."

Spencer twisted, his back to the gunfighter.

Hickok quickly reloaded the giant cartridges in his

175

right Python, keeping the revolver out of sight between
his knees. As he was slipping the last cartridge into the
cylinder, he suddenly realized something was missing.
He'd forgotten Blade's Commando! He'd left it on the
floor of the truck! "Damnit!" he declared in
annoyance.

Spencer turned in his seat. "What did I do?" he
asked in a fright.

"Nothin', idiot!" Hickok said. "Turn around or
else!"

Spencer obeyed.

Hickok sighed, pondering his next move. He had to
bust out of Technic City. The question was *how*? How
to get past a mine field and an electrified fence with
enough juice to fry him to a cinder? How to elude the
scores of Technic police and military types on his tail?
And how to reach the safety of the Home, alone and on
foot? This wasn't turning out to be a piece of cake after
all.

What to do?

Hickok idly surveyed the buildings surrounding the
parking lot on three sides. One of them, a two-story
structure with pastel walls, supported a billboard on the
side visible from the lot. A beautiful woman was seated
at an elegant restaurant, a bowl of soup on the table in
front of her, a heaping spoonful close to her red lips.

A siren wailed in the distance.

Hickok absently read the billboard as he deliberated.

"THE FINEST DINING IN TECHNIC CITY! AT A
PRICE YOU CAN AFFORD! KURTZ'S ON THE
MALL, AT 64TH AND THE DIAGONAL!
SHRIMP . . . $125. STEWED WORMS . . . $90.
WORMS A LA KING . . . $110. A DELECTABLE
TREAT FOR THE TASTE BUDS! RESERVATIONS
ARE—"

Worms?

Hickok's mind belatedly registered the menu
advertised. He read it again.

Worms?

"What's that mean?" Hickok demanded.

"What's what mean?" Spencer responded, watching

the traffic.

"That!" Hickok declared, pointing at the billboard.

"Can I turn around now?" Spencer wanted to know.

"Turn around!" Hickok stated, still pointing. "And tell me what that is all about."

Spencer shifted and gazed at the billboard. After a moment he looked at the gunman. "You've never seen a billboard before? Where are you from?"

"I'm talking about what's on the billboard," Hickok said, correcting the Technic.

Spencer seemed puzzled. "It's called an advertisement."

"I figured that out for myself," Hickok declared archly. "I want to know about the food."

"Oh," Spencer said, as if that explained everything. "Well, shrimp is a seafood. We get ours from the Androixians—"

"I know what the blazes seafood is!" Hickok cut Spencer short. "What about the worms?"

"Worms are these creepy-crawling things which live in the ground," Spencer explained. "They—"

Hickok's flinty blue eyes had narrowed. "Are you doin' this on purpose?"

"Doing what on purpose?"

"I know what worms are," Hickok said, peeved. "Why are they on the menu?"

"I'm not certain I follow you," Spencer said. "Worms are on the menu at every restaurant and diner in Technic City."

Hickok was shocked. "You mean to tell me you folks eat worms?"

"Do you mean to tell me you don't?" Spencer replied.

"But worms! How can you eat worms?" Hickok asked, nauseated by the mere idea.

"Worms are quite tasty," Spencer said. "You should try them sometime."

Hickok grimaced. "Not on your life."

"Everybody eats worms," Spencer detailed.

"Not where I come from," Hickok said. "I've never heard of anybody eatin' worms. What a bunch of cow chips!''

"What kind of food do you eat?" Spencer asked.

"Our Tillers grow a heap of vegetables," Hickok said, "and we have some fruit, but our meat is usually venison."

"What's venison?"

Hickok squinted at the Technic. "You're puttin' me on."

"We don't have venison," Spencer said. "What is it?"

"Deer meat."

"What's a deer?"

"You've never seen a deer?" Hickok queried incredulously.

"No. Is it some kind of animal? Animals are illegal in Technic City," Spencer disclosed.

"What about dogs and cats?"

"They're popular," Spencer commented, "but, personally, I don't like them as much as worms."

"You eat dogs and cats?" Hickok questioned him.

"You don't?"

Hickok studied the billboard, perplexed. He could understand eating dogs, because feral dogs were a rare Family fare. But worms! Revolting! He gazed around the parking lot, stared at the crowded avenue beyond, and perceived a spark of sanity in the notion. Technic City contained millions of people, all fenced in like cattle, herded into a limited area and forced to live out their manipulated lives subject to every whim of the totalitarian regime controlling them. With so many mouths to feed, and with scant dietary resources, the Technics had supplanted the typical prewar fare with the one food source capable of breeding faster than rabbits; with an abundant animal readily available at any time of year; with a creature easily cultivated and processed: worms. When you looked at it logically, Hickok grudgingly admitted, the idea sort of made sense.

Another siren sounded from afar.

Hickok dismissed the worms from his mind and concentrated on his escape. He glanced at Spencer. "I want

you to tell me everything you know about this buggy of
yours.''

"Everything?''

"Everything,'' Hickok affirmed. "How it runs, how
you stop it, what those things are on the ends of the
handlebars I saw you turning. Everything.''

Spencer commenced his instruction, and as the gunman listened, fascinated, a crafty scheme blossomed, a
devious ploy designed to achieve his deliverance from
the vile metropolis of worm-eaters.

17

The . . . thing . . . scrambled up the tunnel wall toward the landing, snarling viciously.

Blade had seen more than his share of genetically deformed mutations over the years. There had been mutates galore, and the Brutes in Thief River Falls, and Fant in the Twin Cities, and the Doktor's bizarre creatures such as Lynx, Gremlin, and Ferret. But never had he witnessed anything as horrendous as the mutant in the shaft.

The beast was an amalgam of insect-like traits. Its huge body resembled that of a centipede, with five over-sized segments and two legs on each segment. The body and legs were black, and the legs ended in tapered claws. Its head appeared fly-like, but it had four eyes, all bright green, instead of the usual two. Its elongated jaws were like those of a praying mantis, but glistening between the jaws were two rows of pointed, spiderish fangs.

Blade took all of this in as he rested the Dakon barrel on the metal railing and crouched, aiming for the creature's bloated cranium. He remembered the button on the scope and pressed it to activate the Laser Sighting Mode, and there it was, a bright red dot on the creature's sloping forehead.

The mutant was 15 feet below the landing, its claws clinging to the sheer walls, finding purchase where any other animal would slip to its doom.

Blade squeezed the trigger, the Dakon II recoiling

into his shoulder.

The creature rocked as its forehead exploded, spraying the wall with black flesh, a pale yellowish muck oozing from the cavity, but it kept coming, climbing higher.

The mutant was only ten feet from the landing now.

Blade frowned, perturbed. He'd gone for the head, for the brain, hoping to dispatch the thing with a minimum of fuss. His shots should have struck the brain, killing it.

If it had a brain.

He aimed again and fired.

The creature shrieked as its squat neck was hit, its jaws twitching.

But it kept coming.

Seven feet now.

Blade rose and pressed the trigger, sweeping the Dakon in an arc.

The fragmentation bullets stitched a straight line across the mutant's segmented body, geysers of flesh and pulpy gore raining on the wall.

But it kept coming.

And there wasn't time for another broadside.

Blade retreated toward the stairs, watching the landing edge for the first sign of the mutant. There was a loud scraping noise in his amplified right earphone, emanating from underneath the landing.

Directly underneath.

Blade paused. But that would mean the thing was crawling under the landing to the other side, using the landing as a shield from the Dakon.

That would mean he was being outflanked!

Blade spun, finding his deduction was accurate.

The mutant had passed under the landing and climbed up the railing behind its prey. It was perched on the railing, its head swaying as it examined its next meal.

Blade raised the Dakon.

Snarling, the creature flowed over the top rail, its head and first two segments reaching the landing in a blurred streak. It reared on its lower segments, then pounced like a bird taking a fish, its serrated jaws spearing down and in.

Blade was caught before he could react. He felt something strike both sides of the helmet, and the mutant's first pair of legs reached up, its claws digging into his broad shoulders.

It had him!

Blade rammed the Dakon barrel into the creature's exposed abdomen and blasted away.

The mutant wrenched its iron jaws upward, tearing the strapless helmet from the Warrior's head. It screeched as its jaws closed, crushing the helmet as effortlessly as a man would break an eggshell. Enraged by the agony in its belly, it flung its prey across the landing and into the opposite railing.

Blade's left side bore the brunt of the impact, and he doubled over as an excruciating spasm lanced his chest. The Dakon II dropped from his benumbed fingers, and he fell to his knees, gasping for air. He saw the creature climb the rest of the way over the railing.

The mutant's ghastly head and the first two segments of its hideous body rose from the floor, like a snake about to strike. It silently rocked from side to side, its jaws slowly opening and closing, opening and closing.

The squashed helmet was on the landing to its left.

If only he had his Bowies! He could dive under the monster and slash its guts out with a few swift swipes. But he didn't have them, and Blade sensed he might never see them again if he didn't come up with something fast. What he needed the most was a diversion, a distraction.

And he got it.

A loud war whoop from the stairs above caused the creature to bend its neck straight up as it searched for the source of the cry.

Geronimo was between landings, leaning over the railing. He aimed at the four green eyes and fired, sweeping the Dakon from side to side.

The mutant howled and thrashed, its head tilted, attempting to avoid the rain of lead. It suddenly bellowed and turned, its front sections climbing into the railing as it started up after this new pest.

Blade saw his chance. He rose, the Dakon II in his left hand, and ran toward the creature, grabbing the pulverized helmet as he did.

The monster's head and first section stretched toward Geronimo, momentarily suspended in midair.

Blade pointed the Dakon at the mutant's jaw below the head and squeezed the trigger.

The creature's throat erupted in a shower of black flesh and pale ooze, and it whipped its head down, jaws wide, primed to rip its quarry to shreds.

Blade swung the ruined helmet around and up, driving it into the thing's mouth, into its fangs, and as the mutant instinctively snapped its jaws shut, he released the helmet and stepped back, lowering the Dakon and firing at the mutant's body segments, at the top of its legs, at the joints, where the legs were attached to the individual segments, and the fragmentation bullets did as he wanted, rupturing the limbs, bursting the joints, blowing four of the creature's legs from its body.

With only four sets of claws still gripping the railing, the thing started to slip, loosing its balance, lurching precariously on the brink of the precipice.

Blade decided to help it along. He ran up to the mutant, reversing his hold on the Dakon II, gripping it by the barrel, and as the creature struggled to right itself, its grotesque head swinging down to the landing as its pair of front legs clawed for a purchase, he whipped the rifle like a club, slamming the stock into the monster's face.

The thing snarled and swiped its jaws at the Warrior's head.

Blade ducked and came up swinging, the butt end of the gun digging into the mutant's left eyes.

Furious, the creature lunged at its foe.

Blade dodged, then rammed the Dakon's barrel into the mutant's eyes, shifted his hands, and squeezed the trigger.

The thing was staggered. It reared up, in extreme torment, forgetting four of its legs were gone.

Blade closed in, firing, the fragmentation bullets exploding two more limbs from the hideous segments.

Incensed beyond measure, the mutant tried to turn and crush its adversary. The motion was more than its remaining legs could tolerate. It lost its footing and pitched over the railing, uttering a shrill scream as it plummeted into the inky gloom below.

Blade grasped the railing and leaned forward, listening, waiting for the creature to hit bottom. Or would it? Maybe the monster would arrest its fall by catching hold of a jutting pipe or beam. Maybe it would attack him again before he could reach the surface! He held his breath, tuned to his right ear amplifier.

The mutant's scream decreased in volume as it dropped, and its death cry was punctuated by a dull thud coming from the very bottom of the shaft. Then all was quiet.

Blade waited with baited breath, straining to detect a noise, to learn if the creature was going to renew its assault.

"Are you coming, or are you admiring the view?"

Blade glanced up at Geronimo. "On my way," he said, and ran up the stairs.

"Let's get out of here!" Geronimo stated as Blade rejoined him.

"You get no argument from me," Blade said.

Side by side, the Warriors hurriedly ascended the shaft to the tunnel entrance. They stopped on the rim and glanced down.

"What are we going to do about these canisters containing the mind-control gas?" Geronimo asked. "If we leave them there, the Technics will eventually find a way of retrieving them."

"I know," Blade said thoughtfully. "We can't let that happen."

"So what do we do?"

Blade studied the abandoned jeeps and trucks. "You check the jeeps. I'll check the trucks."

"What am I looking for?" Geronimo inquired.

"See if they have any gas left in them," Blade said.

"And look for spare gas cans or anything else we can use."

A quick search confirmed a minimum of half a tank of gas in each vehicle, and they discovered four spare gas cans in one of the trucks.

"This will do," Blade declared as he opened one of the cans.

"For what?" Geronimo queried.

"Find a hose we can use to siphon the gas from them," Blade directed.

Geronimo removed a hose from a jeep engine to serve as the siphon. "What now?"

Blade attended to the task of siphoning the gas, filling all four gas cans.

"I still don't get it," Geronimo said as Blade filled the last.

"Take two of these cans," Blade told him. "Pour the gas over the three jeeps. I'll do the same to the four trucks. Hurry, before the Zombies come after us."

Within minutes, all seven Technic vehicles were reeking from the pungent stench of the gasoline.

"Now what?" Geronimo asked.

"Refill the gas cans," Blade ordered. He covered Geronimo while more gas was siphoned from the jeeps and trucks.

"All done," Geronimo announced.

"Look in the trucks," Blade said. "I saw some rags in one of them. Find four rags we can use."

Geronimo, deducing Blade's plan, jogged to the trucks and collected the rags.

"Okay. Stick the rags into the top of the gas cans," Blade instructed. "Leave about six inches protruding from the can."

"Enough to light with a match," Geronimo commented.

"You got it." Blade ran to the SEAL, unlocked the driver's door, and climbed in. The transport purred to life as soon as he turned the key. He slowly drove toward the nearest jeep, aligning the SEAL's grill with the jeep's rear bumper. He'd never tried this before, and he wasn't positive it would work. Gingerly, he slowly accelerated, the SEAL's powerful engine surging as the transport pressed against the jeep. Blade increased his pressure on the accelerator, confident the immense transport could achieve his goal.

"Hold it!" Geronimo suddenly shouted. He ran up to the SEAL. "I just noticed! They left the key in the ignition! Probably wanted to be ready for a quick getaway! I'll put it in neutral!"

"Go for it!" Blade stated.

Geronimo slid into the jeep and twisted the key. The motor refused to kick over, but he found he could work the gearshift if he positioned the key halfway between Off and On. He shifted the jeep into neutral and jumped out.

Blade eased the SEAL forward, and this time the jeep was easily propelled forward, toward the shaft, up to the rim and over the rim, a rolling, metallic din echoing from the tunnel as the jeep tumbled and crashed to the bottom of the shaft.

Geronimo smiled and held his right thumb up.

Working rapidly, the two Warriors pushed one vehicle after the other into the tunnel. One of the trucks caught on the lip and had to be angled to the side before it plunged over the edge. Finally, the job was done.

Blade leaped to the ground and joined Geronimo at the shaft rim. "Here," he said, holding up the box of waterproof matches he'd taken from the SEAL's glove compartment, a new box recently received in trade from the Civilized Zone.

Geronimo lined up the four gas cans next to the tunnel.

Blade knelt and removed a match from the box. "Ready?"

"Ready as I'll ever be," Geronimo responded.

Blade quickly lit each rag, and only after all four were ablaze did he hand the matches to Geronimo. "This is for Hickok," he stated grimly, and with two swift flicks of his right foot he knocked all four cans into the shaft. "Move!"

They sprinted to the SEAL and clambered inside.

Blade gunned the engine and wheeled the transport in a right circle, heading for the Hudson, gaining speed. Ten. Twenty. Forty. And they were fifty yards from the tunnel when it blew, a fiery column of red and orange billowing skyward from the shaft, as an enormous explosion rocked the underground network.

Geronimo, looking over his right shoulder, whistled. "You should see it! The flames must be two hundred feet in the air!"

"So much for the mind-control gas," Blade said.

"What did you mean back there?" Geronimo probed. "About Hickok?"

"I doubt the Minister would keep him alive," Blade declared angrily.

"You don't think so? But what about the hostage we're holding at the Home? Farrow?"

"So what?" Blade retorted. "Do you really believe the Minister gives a damn about any of his people?"

"No," Geronimo admitted morosely.

"If the Minister hasn't killed Hickok yet," Blade said, "he will when we don't show up as expected. We can't go back there alone."

"What will we do?" Geronimo asked.

"We'll go back the same way we came," Blade stated. "We'll bypass Technic City." His fists clenched on the steering wheel. "And when we reach the Home, we'll call a Freedom Federation Council and urge them to declare war on the Technics."

"And what if they won't go along with us?"

"Then we'll do it alone," Blade vowed.

"The Family against the Technics? Won't we be a bit outnumbered?" Geronimo queried.

"We'll do it ourselves!" Blade promised vehemently. "We'll make them pay for their deceit! Their treachery must not go unpunished!" He glanced at Geronimo. "Besides, Hickok would want us to avenge him."

Geronimo shook his head. "I agree with you, but I can't accept the idea of Hickok being dead."

"Why not?"

"I don't know. It's hard to define. But Hickok has more dumb luck than any ten people I know. If there's a

way out of Technic City,'' Geronimo predicted,
''Hickok will find it.''
  ''I don't see how.''

18

The guard stationed at tower number four on the west side of Technic City turned to his three companions. "Who brought the cards?"

"We'd best hold off," one of the other soldiers said.

"Why?" the first one rejoined. "The captain made his rounds an hour ago. It's almost midnight. No one is going to bother us this late at night."

"I know," the other agreed. "But we're still on alert. They haven't found that Warrior yet, and they might conduct a surprise inspection."

"Yeah," chimed in a third trooper. "We'd better wait."

The first guard sighed. "Okay. Whatever you guys want. But I think you're making a mistake. You know how boring third shift can be."

"Better safe than sorry," opined the second soldier.

The first man shrugged and stared at the darkened city to the east. Curfew was at ten, and lights out in individual domiciles was set at eleven. Public buildings could stay lit until midnight. He could see the Central Core on the horizon, brilliantly illuminated by hundreds of lights, the heart of the city, a beacon in the night. He reflected on the day's news: the escape of the Warrior known as Hickok from the Core. He marveled at the Warrior's ingenuity. No one had ever busted out of the Central Core before. And he ruminated on the rumors spreading like wildfire through the city, rumors asserting the Minister and his First Secretary were dead.

189

The paper, radio, and tube hadn't mentioned the deaths, and the guard doubted they were true. He knew how readily gossip could circulate.

A sharp noise reached the tower, coming from the surrounding darkness, from the vicinity of the mine field.

"Did you hear something?" the first guard asked.

"Nothing," the second responded.

"You're hearing things," said the third.

"Probably," the first trooper grudgingly conceded. He gazed at the mine field, deliberately blackened to complicate escape attempts. Anyone would think twice before venturing across a mine field at night, never knowing when they might accidentally tread on a mine and be obliterated by a gigantic explosion.

Another sound became audible, the muted rumbling of a motor.

"Do you hear it now?" the first guard demanded. He was young and wanted to impress the others with his superior senses.

"Sounds like a trike," remarked one of the others.

"But who would be out with a trike at this time of night?" queried the young trooper. "The captain would be in his jeep."

They moved to the east side of the tower, listening. The trike motor abruptly revved louder.

"It must be the Warrior!" the second soldier exclaimed. "He's going to try and break through the gate!"

A beam of light abruptly appeared on the far side of the mine field.

"Here he comes!" cried the second soldier.

"No he's not!" disputed the third. "Look! He's going to try and make it across the mine field!"

Sure enough, the light zoomed toward the mine field, streaking for the far side.

"The fool will never make it," said the young trooper.

The trike was bobbing and bouncing as it raced across the field. It swerved from side to side in a weaving pattern.

"He'll never make it," reiterated the young guard, cradling his Dakon II in his arms.

A sparkling blast rent the air as the trike struck one of the mines. A ball of flame and smoke coalesced for several seconds, then dispersed.

"What a jerk," the young trooper said.

"You stay here," directed the second soldier. "We'll take the flashlights and the mine map and go have a look. Call HQ and tell them what happened."

"Right away," the youthful guard replied.

The young guard walked to the Communications Console while his three friends hastened down the tower steps. He picked up the headset and pressed the appropriate buttons. "Private Casey here," he said when the sergeant at the ComCenter in the Central Core answered. "Inform Captain Zorn we have a Priority Two. Repeat. Priority Two." He listened for a moment. "Yes, sir. On their way now." He glanced at his watch. "ETA five minutes? Yes, sir. Over and out." He replaced the headset and walked to the east side of the tower, watching through the window as his three companions moved across the field toward the smoldering wreckage of the trike. Their flashlights were proceeding very slowly, as they cautiously advanced while consulting the minefield map to insure they didn't step on a mine and wind up the way the driver of the trike had.

"Freeze!"

Private Casey tensed at the barked command. He started to turn his head.

"I said freeze!" the harsh voice warned. "One more twitch and you'll be feedin' the worms instead of vice versa!"

"Who are you? What do you want?" Casey asked.

"I'll do the talkin', pipsqueak! Set your piece on the floor, real easy like!"

Private Casey hesitated. He knew his duty. He should whirl and confront this stranger. But there was something about the man's deep voice, a steely vibrancy, a "Don't mess with me or else!" quality he found unnerving. He intuitively sensed he would die instantly if he disobeyed this man, and Casey didn't want to die. He laid the Dakon II on the floor.

"That's real sensible for a Technic," the stranger said.

Casey waited, expecting to hear the man cross the tower. Instead, something hard was jammed into his spine.

"Turn around!" the voice commanded.

Private Casey complied, discovering a lean blond man in buckskins with a rifle over each shoulder, a revolver under his left arm, and two more revolvers, both pearl-handled silver jobs, in his hands.

"Where's the key to the gate?" the blond man demanded.

"I can't give it to you," Casey mustered the courge to say.

The gunman sighed. "I'm tired, pipsqueak. Real tired. And I don't have the time to play games." He cocked the right revolver. "If you don't tell me where they keep the key to the gate, I'm gonna shoot you in the nuts."

Casey swallowed, and a prickly sensation erupted over his balls.

"I ain't got all night!" the gunman snapped.

Casey pointed at a desk in the northwest corner. "It's in the top drawer on the right."

"Thanks." The gunman sidled to the desk and opened the drawer.

"You're Hickok, aren't you?" Casey asked.

The gunman nodded as he withdrew a large key on a metal ring.

"I knew it!" Casey said. He didn't know what to do or say, and he was too excited to remain silent. "Did you really kill the Minister?" he blurted.

"Yep."

"I can't believe it!" Casey exclaimed, awed.

"How do I turn off the fence?" Hickok inquired.

"There's a circuit breaker in a box to the left of the gate," Casey revealed.

"What's a circuit breaker?" Hickok responded.

"Look for an orange lever," Casey said. "Pull it

down and you'll turn off the current.''

Hickok moved to the window and watched the trio of guards heading for the flaming debris in the mine field.

"Who was on the trike?" Casey asked.

"Nobody," Hickok answered.

"But trikes don't run by themselves," Casey stated.

"They do if you help 'em along a little," Hickok said. He motioned toward the stairs. "Let's go. You first."

Private Casey led off. "Are . . . are you going to kill me?"

"I'm not in the habit of gunnin' pipsqueaks," Hickok declared. "But don't push me or I might make an exception in your case."

They reached the steps to the ground. "How did you do it?" Casey queried as he descended.

"Wasn't too hard," Hickok said. "A bozo by the name of Spencer told me how the trikes run. To pick up speed, you have to turn a thingumajig on the handlebars. And to shift, your foot presses on a thingamabob. Hope I'm not bein' too technical for you."

"I know how to drive a trike," Casey told him.

"Then you'll appreciate how I did it," Hickok remarked. "I fired her up, with the shift in neutral, and turned the accelerator to where I wanted it. Then I tied it in place with Spencer's shoelaces. Those grips have deep ridges in 'em, so it was real easy to keep it from slippin' too much. After that, I kicked the buggy into gear and—presto!—the decoy I needed."

"Pretty clever," Private Casey admitted.

Hickok sighed. "Where's Geronimo when I need him?"

"Geronimo?" Casey said, puzzled.

"A pard of mine," Hickok stated. "Believe it or not, I don't get complimented on my smarts too much. I wish he'd been here to hear it."

"Wasn't one of the other Warriors captured with you named Geronimo?" Casey asked.

Hickok stopped. "Yeah. Have you heard anything about him or my other buddy, Blade?"

"You know they went to New York City?"

"So I was told."

Private Casey shifted uneasily. "I don't know how to tell you this." He stared at the pearl-handled revolvers.

"Give it to me straight," Hickok directed.

"It's not official," Casey said anxiously.

"Spill the beans!" Hickok ordered.

"We lost contact with them," Casey disclosed. "Now remember," he quickly added, "it's just some scuttle-butt I picked up. It hasn't been confirmed."

Hickok's features were obscured by the shadows. They were standing near the fence, the gate illumined by a spotlight on top of the guard tower. "Turn off the current," he said gruffly.

"I thought you were going to do it," Casey said.

"I can't. You see, I've got me this new motto I live by," the gunman declared.

"New motto?"

"Never, ever trust a lyin' skunk of a Technic!" Hickok stated harshly.

Private Casey gulped.

"Now kill the blasted fence!" Hickok commanded.

Casey immediately complied.

"Now the gate." Hickok tossed the key to the trooper.

Private Casey unlocked the gate and shoved it open.

Hickok strode up to the soldier and glared at him, nose to nose. "You've got two ways of playin' this, pipsqueak. You can run upstairs after I leave, and blab what happened to the bigwigs. Or you can play it safe and keep your mouth shut. It's up to you."

"If I report this, I'll be court-martialed," Casey predicted. "I'll wind up in prison or in front of a firing squad."

"So keep your big mouth closed," Hickok advised. "No one will ever know I was here except for us. They'll all reckon I was blown sky-high in the mine field. I left the varmint who owned the trike tied up back at a worm farm. He'll get loose soon and tell the authorities I stole it from him. They'll put two and two together."

"I really am going to live!" Private Casey exclaimed.

"I told you I wouldn't kill you."

"But they said you're a cold-blooded murderer," Casey remarked.

"A lot of folks think that way," Hickok conceded. He thought of the boy lying in the pool of blood. "But they don't know about my other new motto. Never, ever kill unless it's absolutely necessary."

"I like that motto," Casey remarked.

Hickok grinned. "You're all right, pipsqueak." He started through the gate, then paused. "Say, will they know you cut the juice to the fence?"

Private Casey nodded. "It'll register on the monitor in the Central Core."

"If they ask, tell 'em you don't know a thing," Hickok suggested.

"Lie?"

"Can you come up with a better way to save your hide?" Hickok asked.

Casey considered for a moment. "Nope."

"Then as soon as I skedaddle, close the gate and open the circuit. They might believe it was a temporary short."

"All of a sudden you're not as dumb as you act," Casey said.

"Thanks. I think." Hickok walked through the gate, holstered his left Python, and waved. "As a pard of mine might say, may the Great Spirit bless all your endeavors."

The night swallowed the gunman.

Private Casey blinked a few times, wondering if the incident might have been a dream. The killer of the Minister had spared his life! He hastily closed the gate, reset the circuit breaker, and ran up the stairs to the tower. The red light above the headset was blinking. He scooped it up and cleared his throat.

"Private Casey here . . . Sorry, sir, I was watching the mine field. . . . Yes, they're almost to the point. . . . No, the captain hasn't arrived yet. . . . Turned off the fence? No, sir. Why would I do that? . . . No, sir, I didn't notice. I was watching the mine field. . . . Yes, sir, those damn transformers can be a pain in the ass. . . . Of course, sir."

Casey replaced the headset, beaming. He'd done it!
Now there was just one thing he wanted to know: what
the hell was the Great Spirit?

19

Everything was proceeding according to the Minister's plan! The Home would soon be history!

Lieutenant Alicia Farrow smiled, her white teeth a sharp contrast to the inky night. Her luminous watch indicated the time was 15 minutes past midnight. In another 15 minutes the demolition team would come over the west wall, and she must be there to greet them. She had crept from B Block 10 minutes ago, and now was poised at the foot of the stairs leading from the inner bank of the moat to the rampart. The wooden stairs were located a few feet south of the closed drawbridge. She cautiously climbed the steps, scanning the rampart, searching for the Warrior on duty. She knew Omega Triad was scheduled, and she expected to find Ares manning the west wall as was his custom.

A dark form moved to her right, directly over the drawbridge.

Farrow squinted. It was a Warrior, patrolling the rampart. But something was wrong. The figure wasn't tall enough to be Ares. It was definitely a man, which ruled out Helen. And it lacked a hat, eliminating Sundance because he always wore a black sombrero.

So who the hell was it?

Farrow reached the top of the stairs and stopped, perplexed. The figure was gone! One instant it had been there, the next it had vanished! Had whoever it was seen her? Was he—

"Hello, Alicia."

Farrow gripped the rail to keep from plunging into the moat. Her senses were swimming. Not him! It couldn't be him!

But it was.

Yama materialized beside her, his Wilkinson in his right hand. "I'm surprised to see you here," he said softly. "You haven't spoken a word to me all day."

Farrow tried to speak but couldn't. Her mouth refused to respond.

"What did I do to upset you?" Yama asked.

"What are *you* doing here?" Farrow exclaimed.

"I have the night shift," Yama responded.

"But Ares is supposed to be here," Farrow asserted. "Omega Triad has wall duty tonight."

"I know," Yama said. "But Ares isn't feeling too well. The Review Board cleared him, but he's still upset. He's been moping around B Block since it happened. I offered to fill in for him tonight."

"Oh no!" Farrow said.

Yama moved closer. "What's wrong? Did you want to see Ares?"

"No," Farrow replied. "I expected him to be here, is all."

"I don't understand," Yama stated. "You didn't want to see Ares, but you expected him to be here?"

"Yeah," Farrow said nervously. "I wanted some fresh air, so I climbed up here. I knew Ares was on duty, but I didn't want to run into him. See?"

"Hmmmm," was all Yama said.

Now what was she going to do? Farrow knew the demolition team would arrive at any minute. And the first thing they would do after scaling the wall would be to snuff Yama. Yama! He was a lowlife, but she still felt affection for him. The prospect of his death was profoundly upsetting.

"If you'd rather be alone, I'll leave," Yama offered.

"No!" Farrow blurted out. She frantically racked her brain for a solution. If she could get him off the wall! "Care to walk along the moat with me?"

"You know I can't leave my post," Yama said.

Farrow saw him look from side to side, then stare at her. She squirmed uncomfortably, emotionally distraught.

"Stay here," Yama directed. He turned and moved to the middle of the rampart.

What was he doing?

"What are you doing?"

Yama didn't answer. She heard a scratching sound, and a lantern abruptly lit up the central section of the rampart. Yama was next to the lantern, blowing on a match.

Farrow hurried over to the Warrior. "Why'd you do that?"

The lantern was suspended from an iron hook imbedded in the lip of the rampart, just below the strands of barbed wire encircling the entire walled compound. Its flickering light played over his silver hair and mustache as he slowly turned to face her. His blue eyes bored into her. "I wanted to see you clearly," he said.

"But isn't it dangerous," she protested, "having the lantern on this way? Anyone out there," and she waved at the surrounding forest, "could see you."

Yama shrugged. "I doubt anyone is out there. Few people would be abroad in the woods at night. It's too hazardous."

Farrow fidgeted, repeatedly glancing at the tree line.

"Is something wrong?" Yama asked.

"I'm fine!" Farrow responded, her tone edgy.

"Come with me," Yama said. He took her by the left forearm and led her to the left, away from the lantern, to the stairs. He stopped on the upper step, both of them now shrouded in semi-darkness.

"What are you doing?" Farrow inquired.

"We're going to stand here for a while and enjoy the night sky," Yama told her.

Farrow tried to pull her arm free. "I'd like to go."

"I'd imagine you would," Yama said, his right hand a vise on her arm.

"You're hurting me!" Farrow objected.

Yama's right hand clamped tighter. "And how many innocent Family members did you intend to hurt?"

Farrow's breath caught in her throat. "I . . . I . . . don't know what you . . . mean," she stammered.

"I think you do," Yama stated. He released her arm and gazed at the area illuminated by the lantern. "How will they work it?"

"I don't know what you're talking about!" Farrow cried.

Yama looked at her. "Keep your voice down!" he warned.

Farrow was chilled by the iciness of his tone. She sensed her world was coming apart at the seams, and she was panic-stricken.

"Did you take me for a complete imbecile?" Yama demanded in a hard whisper.

"I never—" she started to say.

"I will admit," he said in a brittle, incriminating manner, "I was stupid enough to fall for your charade. I actually believed you cared for me! How dumb can I get!"

But I do! Farrow wanted to scream, but she couldn't bring herself to speak the words. She was overwhelmed by the stunning realization she'd been wrong all along. He did really and truly like her!'

"—but I couldn't understand why you were so tormented," Yama was telling her. "I tried to reason it out. I concocted a hundred and one excuses to justify your behavior." He made a contemptuous sound. "I allowed myself to think you were troubled because of your affection for me! You didn't want to commit yourself, knowing you would be returning to your own people! You already had someone special and didn't want me to know!"

"I don't have anyone—" Farrow mumbled, but he ignored her.

"And then today!" Yama said. "I see you at breakfast, and you won't even look at me, let alone converse! Why? I asked myself again and again. There was no rhyme or reason to the way you acted. I began to wonder if Plato and Rikki were right. They've been suspicious of you from the start, although Rikki gave you the benefit of the doubt. Before he left, Blade told us to keep an eye on you. Not to trust you.'' He paused, his voice lowering sadly. "Not to trust you! And I went and developed deep affection for you!''

"But—'' she began.

"And now you show up here! This late at night!'' Yama cut her off. "Why? I wondered. You were shocked to find me on duty. You wanted Ares to be here. Why? Because you knew I would suspect something was up. Ares doesn't know you as well as I do. He might accept your line about wanting fresh air. But I don't!''

Farrow fought back an impulse to burst into tears. "Yama . . .''

"Shhhhh!'' he cautioned her.

"Yama . . .''

Yama glanced at her, his face creased by lines of misery. "Don't talk!''

"They'll be using infrared goggles,'' Farrow informed him. "They can see in the dark.''

Yama studied her for a second, then took her hand and pulled her down to the third step. He crouched and tugged on her hand. "Get down!''

Farrow squatted beside him. Their heads were now below the rampart and invisible to anyone scaling the west wall. "I'm sorry,'' she said in his right ear. "I—''

He placed his right hand over her mouth. "Not now. Later.''

Farrow stifled a sob. She felt utterly helpless, a prisoner of her own emotions, unable to intervene, bound by her duty as a Technic soldier on one hand, and her love for Yama on the other. She couldn't violate her Technic oath, and she wouldn't betray Yama. There was nothing she could do but ride it out and hope for the best.

Yama looked at her. "Thanks for letting me know about the goggles,'' he whispered.

Farrow nodded, biting her lower lip. The demolition team would use a grappling hook and come over the northwest corner, where she was scheduled to meet them. What would Sergeant Darden do when they climbed the wall and discovered she wasn't there? Abandon the mission? Not very likely. Darden was dedicated. He would complete his assignment with or without her.

Yama had his left ear pressed to the top step, listening.

Farrow suddenly perceived the reason for the lantern. Yama was brilliant! Anyone coming over the wall would have a dilemma to resolve: what to do about the light? They could shoot out the lantern, but the Warriors would be alerted. They could circumvent the lighted portion of the rampart, but to do so would entail avoiding the stairs. And the stairs were the only means of reaching the inner bank, unless they dropped a line into the moat and swam across, a difficult proposition when carrying a backpack and field gear. No, the wisest recourse would be to leave the lantern alone, and attempt to reach the stairs undetected.

Only Yama was waiting for them at the top of the stairs.

Farrow tensed as a faint scuffing reached her ears. Was it Darden and the demolition team? She closed her eyes and performed an act she'd never done before; she prayed Darden would realize the lantern was a ruse and decide to abort the assignment.

Yama angled the Wilkinson barrel upward.

Her eyes now adjusted to the gloom, Farrow could distinguish Yama's features. She wanted to reach out and tenderly caress his cheek, to let him know she was sorry for her stupidity. The turmoil in his tone had convinced her of his sincerity. There must be a perfectly reasonable explanation for the incident with the petite brunette. She would ask him about it when this was over.

There was a muffled thump from the northwest corner of the rampart.

Sergeant Darden and the demolition team had arrived!

Farrow could scarcely breathe, dreading the impending conflict, waiting for Yama to make his move. She clenched her hands until her nails bit into her palms.

Yama raised his ear from the first step.

Farrow knew whatever was going to happen was going to happen soon. And she realized there was a chance Darden was aware someone was on the stairs. His ear amplifier might have detected Yama's breathing, or hers for that matter. If Darden had, his squad would have their Dakons trained on the steps. They would shoot at anything that moved. Yama would be cut to ribbons.

Something nearby clicked.

Farrow suddenly reached out and grabbed Yama's right arm. He glanced at her in surprise. "I love you," she whispered, then, before he could move to stop her, she unexpectedly rose, facing the rampart. Facing Darden and the three members of his demolition team.

Sergeant Darden was nearest the lantern, perhaps four feet to its right. Private Johnson, the loudmouth, was two feet from Darden. The one whose name she couldn't remember came next, not six feet from the steps. And Rundle, the plastics expert on the squad, was only two feet away, her Dakon II leveled, her finger on the trigger. She saw a shadowy form abruptly rise in front of her, and she instantly fired, the Dakon set on automatic.

Farrow was staggered by the impact. She felt an intense burning sensation in her chest, and she was flung across the stairs and against the opposite railing. Her left arm caught on the top rail, at the elbow, and she dangled limply with blood pouring from her wounds, her eyes riveted to the rampart, as Yama rose, his voice roaring a strangled *"No!"* as the Wilkinson chattered, and Private Rundle was smashed backward by the force of the slugs tearing into her body. Yama swiveled, and the unidentified trooper took several rounds in the face and was catapulted to the rampart. Sergeant Darden and Private Johnson opened up, but their target was already in motion, darting up the stairs and rolling across the rampart, coming erect near the lip, and the Wilkinson burped, slamming Private Johnson from his feet and hurling him over the edge and into the swirling moat below. Farrow saw Darden frantically pulling his Dakon's trigger, and she recognized the gun was jammed. He dropped the Dakon and went for his automatic pistol. Farrow was amazed by what transpired next. She gaped as Yama tossed his own gun aside and rushed toward Darden, darwing his scimitar in a streaking, fluid blur. She could see the terrified expression on Darden's face as he drew his automatic and tried to aim at the Warrior. But Yama was quicker, and he slashed the scimitar down, severing Darden's gunhand from his arm. Darden opened his mouth to scream, and Yama flashed the scimitar crosswise, splitting Darden's throat wide open, crimson gushing over the commando's neck, and then Yama sliced the scimitar into Darden's abdomen, once, twice, three times and tolled, and Darden's intestines spilled over his pants and legs as he futilely clutched at his stomach. He slowly sank to the rampart, gurgling and spitting blood.

Yama glared at the fallen Technic for a second, then whirled and raced to the stairs.

Farrow tried to grin as he dashed up to her. "Nice," she mumbled feebly. "Real . . . nice."

Yama dropped the scimitar and took her in his arms. "Don't talk!" he cautioned her. "Help is on the way! The Healers . . ."

"No," Farrow said weakly. "Too late . . ."

"Don't say that!" Yama said, his voice raspy.

"Need to know . . ." Farrow stated in a ragged whisper.

"What?" Yama asked, his face an inch from her.

"The girl . . . this morning . . ." Farrow managed to squeak.

"The girl? What girl?" Yama declared, perplexed, in anguish. "You mean Marian? My niece?"

"Niece?"

"My brother's daughter," Yama said. "What about her?"

Farrow eyes widened. "Your brother's daughter . . ."

"I don't see . . ." Yama began, then paused as an

intuitive insight flooded his mind. "You didn't think she and I . . . ?"

Farrow mustered a smile. "Never . . . was too bright." She coughed, blood smearing her lips and chin. "Kiss me. Please."

Yama bent down and touched her lips with his own. He could taste the salty tang of her blood on his lips and tongue, and then she stiffened and gasped, expelling her dying breath into his mouth.

Yama felt his eyes moisten, and he buried his face against her left shoulder.

It was another minute before footsteps pounded on the stairs, and Rikki-Tikki-Tavi appeared, gleaming katana in his right hand. He reached the third step and paused, then proceeded to the rampart. Shouts and yells were mingling in the compound below. He scanned the bodies, then moved down to Yama's side. "Yama?"

"Go away." The voice was muffled by the fabric of Farrow's shirt.

"Are you all right?"

Yama's response, when he finally answered, was tinged by an immeasurable melancholy. "No. I'll never be all right again."

20

The day was marked by a bright sun and a clear blue sky. The drawbridge was down as a party of Hunters prepared to leave the Home. Although the Family included four Hunters in its ranks, the Warriors frequently assisted in hunting the venison so necessary for their continued survival. The four Hunters were hard pressed to find the quantity of game the Family required, and they gladly welcomed any help the Warriors offered.

Rikki-Tikki-Tavi was on duty on the west wall, watching the Hunters preparing to depart. The Hunters and one other. Yama had volunteered to go along. Rikki suspected Yama needed the activity, needed to do anything to take his mind off Lieutenant Alicia Farrow. They had buried her four days ago with full honors.

A muted whine arose from the west.

Rikki looked up, elated to see the SEAL traveling toward the Home at breakneck speed. "Alpha Triad is coming!" he called out. "The SEAL is coming!"

The word spread like wildfire. Family members were running toward the drawbridge. Rikki could see Plato in the vanguard. And there was Sherry, Hickok's wife, carrying little Ringo. And Jenny and Cynthia, Blade's and Geronimo's spouses, toting their children. And all of the other Warriors except Teucer, who was on the north wall, and Ares, who had agreed to fill in for Yama on the east wall.

The SEAL rolled from the trees and across the field,

up to the lowered drawbridge. It braked and the engine
was shut off.

Blade vaulted from the transport, a beaming smile on
his face. He surveyed the assembled crowd and spotted
his wife. "Jenny!" He ran forward and clasped his wife
and son in his arms.

Geronimo was next to emerge. He jogged the ten feet
separating the transport from the gathered welcomers,
and took his wife in a tender embrace.

Rikki saw Sherry staring apprehensively at the SEAL.
He glanced at it, suddenly worried, wondering why
Hickok hadn't appeared. He cupped his hands around
his mouth. "Hey! Where's Hickok?"

Geronimo released the raven-haired Cynthia and
crossed to the transport. He leaned in the passenger-side
door. "Wake up! We're being attacked by mutants!"
he yelled, and stepped back.

A sleepy Hickok stumbled from the SEAL, his
Pythons in his hands, swinging the revolvers from left to
right, seeking the mutants. It took a moment for the
reality of the situation to dawn on his fatigued senses.
When the Family began laughing at his stupefied
reaction, his face turned a livid scarlet and he glared at
Geronimo, holstering the Colts. "I should of known!
You never can trust an Injun!"

Geronimo, chuckling, draped his right arm around
Hickok's shoulders. "I wish you could have seen your
face!"

"I know what I'd like to do to yours!" Hickok
groused.

Sherry and Ringo hurried toward the gunman.

"I want you to know," Geronimo said as she neared
them, "we had our chance and we blew it."

Sherry, too relieved at finding her husband returned
and unharmed, paid scant attention to Geronimo.
"Oh?" she replied absently.

"Yeah," Geronimo said as Hickok hugged his
family. "We could have left him back on Highway 94,
but Blade insisted we had to pick him up. Personally, I
think the walk back might have done him some good.

Get rid of that flab . . .'' He stopped, realizing his barbs were being wasted.

Hickok and Sherry were kissing passionately.

Rikki grinned, delighted at the arrival of his three companions. Now Blade could assume command of the Warriors, and things would go back to normal, the way they should be. His eyes happened to alight on Yama.

Not everything would be the way it was.

Rikki thought of Alicia Farrow, and of his own beloved Lexine, and he thanked the Spirit she was safe, ever eager to share her love and laughter with him. He saw the Family milling about Alpha Triad, happy, engaged in lively banter.

All except one. Yama was walking toward the forest, Wilkinson in hand, going hunting.

Rikki sighed. He knew, given time, Yama would recover. Time, so the cliche went, healed all wounds. Which was true. But Time couldn't erase human memory, couldn't deliver a person from periodically experiencing pangs of heartfelt grief. What was it that religious book in the library had taught? "The supreme affliction is never to have been afflicted. You only learn wisdom by knowing affliction.'' Which must make Yama, temporarily at least, the wisest man in the universe.

Enough!

Rikki dismissed such somber reflections from his mind, and watched a cardinal winging on the wind. Affliction might be inevitable, but life went on. Life invariably went on.

And such was the way it would always be.